H. E. Bates was born in 1905 at Rushton in Northamptonshire and was educated at Kettering Grammar School. He worked as a journalist and clerk on a local newspaper before publishing his first book, *The Two Sisters*, when he was twenty. In the next fifteen years he acquired a distinguished reputation for his stories about English country life. During the Second World War, he was a Squadron Leader in the R.A.F. and some of his stories of service life, *The Greatest People in the World* (1942), *How Sleep the Brave* (1943) and *The Face of England* (1953) were written under the pseudonym of 'Flying Officer X'. His subsequent novels of Burma, *The Purple Plain* and *The Jacaranda Tree*, and of India, *The Scarlet Sword*, stemmed directly or indirectly from his war experience in the East.

In 1958 his writing took a new direction with the appearance of *The Darling Buds of May*, the first of the popular Larkin family novels, which was followed by *A Breath of French Air*, *When the Green Woods Laugh* and *Oh! To Be in England* (1963). His autobiography appeared in three volumes, *The Vanished World* (1969), *The Blossoming World* (1971) and *The World in Ripeness* (1972). His last works included the novel, *The Triple Echo* (1971), and a collection of short stories, *The Song of the Wren* (1972). Perhaps one of his most famous works of fiction is the best-selling novel *Fair Stood the Wind for France* (1944). H. E. Bates also wrote miscellaneous works on gardening, essays on country life, several plays including *The Day of Glory* (1945); *The Modern Short Story* (1941) and a story for children, *The White Admiral* (1968). His works have been translated into 16 languages and a posthumous collection of his stories, *The Yellow Meads of Asphodel*, appeared in 1976.

H. E. Bates was awarded the C.B.E. in 1973 and died in January 1974. He was married in 1931 and had four children.

H. E. Bates

The Grapes of Paradise

Eight Novellas

Penguin Books
in association with Michael Joseph

Penguin Books Ltd, Harmondsworth,
Middlesex, England
Penguin Books, 625 Madison Avenue,
New York, New York 10022, U.S.A.
Penguin Books Australia Ltd, Ringwood,
Victoria, Australia
Penguin Books Canada Ltd, 2801 John Street,
Markham, Ontario, Canada L3R 1B4
Penguin Books (N.Z.) Ltd, 182–190 Wairau Road,
Auckland 10, New Zealand

These eight novellas were first published in
Penguin Books in two volumes entitled
Death of a Huntsman and *An Aspidistra in
Babylon*, 1964.
This collection first published in Penguin Books 1974
Reprinted 1974, 1976, 1977, 1979

Copyright © Evensford Productions, 1957, 1960
All rights reserved

Made and printed in Great Britain by
Hazell Watson & Viney Ltd,
Aylesbury, Bucks
Set in Monotype Times

Except in the United States of America,
this book is sold subject to the condition that
it shall not, by way of trade or otherwise, be lent,
re-sold, hired out, or otherwise circulated without
the publisher's prior consent in any form of
binding or cover other than that in which it is
published and without a similar condition
including this condition being imposed on the
subsequent purchaser

Contents

Death of a Huntsman

Every week-day evening, watches ready, black umbrellas neatly rolled and put away with neat black homburgs on carriage racks, attaché cases laid aside, newspapers poised, the fellow-travellers of Harry Barnfield, the city gentlemen, waited for him to catch – or rather miss – the five-ten train.

As the last minutes jerked away on the big station clock above wreaths of smoke and steam the city gentlemen sat with jocular expectation on the edges of carriage seats or actually craning necks from carriage windows, as if ready to check with stop watches the end of Harry Barnfield's race with time.

'Running it pretty fine tonight.'

'Doomed. Never make it.'

'Oh! trust Harry.'

'Absolutely doomed. Never make it.'

'Oh! Harry'll make it. Trust Harry. Never fluked it yet. Trust Harry.'

All Harry Barnfield's friends, like himself, lived in the country, kept farms at a heavy loss and came to London for business every day. J. B. (Punch) Warburton, who was in shipping and every other day or so brought up from his farm little perforated boxes of fresh eggs for less fortunate friends in the city, would get ready, in mockery, to hold open the carriage door.

'Action stations.' J. B. Warburton, a wit, was not called Punch for nothing. 'Grappling hooks at ready!'

'This is a bit of bad. Dammit, I believe –' George Reed Thompson also had a farm. Its chief object, apart from losing money, was to enable him to stock a large deep-freeze every summer, with excellent asparagus, strawberries, raspberries, spring chickens, pheasant, partridges, and vegetables, all home-raised. 'Harry's going to let us down – !'

'Nine-ten, nine-fifteen.' Craning from the window, Freddie Jekyll, who was a stockbroker and rode, every spring, with great success at local point-to-points, would actually begin to check off the seconds. 'Nine-twenty –'

'Officer of the watch, keep a sharp look-out there!'

'Aye, aye, sir.'

'All ashore who are going ashore.'

'Aye, aye, sir.'

'A firm hold on those grappling hooks!'

'Dammit, he's missed it. I make it eleven past already.'

Sometimes a whistle would blow; sometimes a final door would slam with doom along the far hissing reaches of the waiting express. But always, at last, without fail, the city gentlemen would be able to raise, at first severally and then collectively, a joyful, bantering cheer.

'Here, Harry, here! Here, old boy!'

Cheering, signalling frantically from windows, thrusting out of it malacca handles of umbrellas as if they were really grappling hooks, they would drag Harry Barnfield finally aboard.

'Five-nine point twelve,' they would tell him. 'New world record.'

Panting, smiling modestly from behind sweat-clouded spectacles, Harry Barnfield would lean shyly on the handle of his umbrella, struggling to recover breath. Laughing, the city gentlemen would begin to unfold their papers, offering congratulations.

'Well run, Harry. Damn near thing though, old boy. Thought you were doomed.'

But that, they always told themselves, was the great thing about Harry. You could always rely on Harry. You could always be sure of Harry. Harry would never let you down.

What a good sport he was, they all said, Harry Barnfield. There were no two ways, no possible arguments about that. There was no shadow of harm in Harry Barnfield.

2

All his life Harry Barnfield, who looked ten years more middle-aged than forty-three, had been fond of horses without ever being a good rider of them.

His body was short and chunky. It had the odd appearance, especially when he rode a horse, of having had a middle cut of six or seven inches removed from between ribs and groin, leaving the trunk too short between legs and shoulders. It was also rather soft, almost pulpy, as if his bones had never matured. This pulpiness was still more noticeable in the eyes, which behind their spectacles were shy, grey, protuberant and rather jellified, looking altogether too large for his balding head.

All this gave him, in the saddle, a floppy, over-eager air and, as the black tails of his coat flew out behind, the look of a fat little bird trying hard to fly from the ground and never quite succeeding. Riding, he would tell you, was awful fun, and his voice was high and squeaky.

Every evening, ten minutes before the arrival of the train that brought him back to the country with his friends the city gentlemen, he started to give a final polish to his spectacles, the lenses of which were rather thick. For five minutes or so he polished them with scrupulous short-sightedness on a square of cream silk that he kept in his breast pocket, huffing on them with brief panting little breaths, showing a pink, lapping tongue.

The effect of this scrupulous preparation of the spectacles was to make his face seem quite absurdly alight. Smiling from behind the glittering lenses, calling good night to his friends, he came out of the station with wonderful eagerness, head well in front of the chunky body, black umbrella prodding him forward, attaché case paddling the air from the other hand, bowler hat tilted slightly backward and sitting on the loose crimson ears.

Once out of the station he sucked in a long deep breath – as if to say: ah, at last, the country! The short little body seemed transformed with eager exhilaration. Fields came down almost to within reach of the fences surrounding the station coal-yards and on late spring evenings the greening hedges were brilliant and thick as banks of parsley. Primroses and sprays of pale mauve lady-smocks sprang lushly from damp dykes below the hedgerows and along the roads beyond these were black-boughed cherry orchards in white thick bloom. A few weeks later apple orchards and great snow mounds of hawthorn came into blossom and in the scent of them he could taste the first milkiness of summer just as surely as he tasted winter in the first sweet-acid tang of the big-toothed Spanish chestnut leaves as they began to swim

9

down from the trees in November, haunting the dark staves of baring copses.

Then, as he drove home in his car, much of his eagerness vanished. He gradually took on the air of being calm and free: free of the dusty odours of city offices, city termini, free of his friends the city gentlemen in the smoky train. His body relapsed completely into quietness. His big eyes stopped their agitation and became, behind the bulging lenses of the spectacles, perfectly, blissfully at rest.

It took him twenty minutes to drive out to the big double-gabled house of old red brick that had, behind it, a row of excellent stables with a long hay-loft above. He had been awfully lucky, he would tell you, to get the house. It was absolutely what he wanted. The stables themselves were perfect and at the front were four good meadows, all flat, bordered by a pleasant alder-shaded stream.

The fields were about twenty acres in all, and from three of them, in June, he gathered all the hay he would need. Then in early autumn he took down part of the fences and put up a run of four brushwood jumps and over these, on Saturdays and Sundays, he started practising jumping. Sometimes, too, in the same inelastic way that never improved during the entire hunting season, he practised jumping the brook. Then by late November the alders lost the last of their leaves; the hazels, the willows and the sweet chestnuts became naked too and presently he could feel the sting of frost in his nostrils as he brought his horse in through the blue-grey twilights across which the sound of croaking pheasants settling to roost clattered like wintry frightened laughter.

'That you, Harry? I hope to God you didn't forget the gin?'

'Yes, it's me, Katey.'

If it had not been that he was almost always blinking very slightly, with a sort of mechanical twitch, behind the glasses, it might have seemed that he had never lost the habit of surprise as his wife called to him, her voice somewhere between a croak and a cough, from the kitchen.

It might also have seemed, from the snap in her voice, that she was not very tolerant of forgetfulness. But fortunately neither surprise nor forgetfulness were habits of his. He was never surprised and he never forgot the gin.

'On the hall table, Katey,' he would tell her. 'Any message from Lewis? I'm just hopping across the yard.'

His inquiry about Lewis, his groom, was never answered, except by another cough, and this never surprised him either. His only real thought was for his horses. In summer he had only to whistle and they came to him from across the meadows. In winter he walked quietly across the courtyard to the stables, let himself in, touched for a moment the warm flanks of the two animals, said good night to them exactly as if they were children and then, almost on tip-toe, let himself out again. Outside, if there were stars, he generally stopped to look up at them, breathing over again the good country air. Then he stiffened, braced his short pulpy body and went back into the house again.

'Where the hell did you say the gin was? Every bloody evening you slink off like a badger and I'm left wondering where you dump the stuff.'

'I told you where it was, Katey.' From the hall table he would quietly pick up the gin-bottle and take it to the kitchen. 'Here. Here it is.'

'Then why the hell couldn't you say so?'

'I did say so.'

'You talk like a squeak-mouse all the time. How do you expect me to hear if you talk like a damn squeak-mouse?'

His wife was tallish, fair and very blowsy. She looked, he always thought, remarkably like some caged and battered lioness. Her hair, which she wore down on her shoulders, had passed through several stages of blondeness. Sometimes it was almost white, bleached to lifelessness; sometimes it was the yellow of a ferret and he would not have been surprised, then, to see that her eyes were pink; sometimes it was like coarse rope, with a cord of darker hair twisting through the centre. But the most common effect was that of the lioness, restless, caged and needing a comb.

'Any news, Katey?' he would say. 'Anything been happening?'

'Where, what and to whom?' she would ask him. 'To bloody whom? Tell me.' The fingers of both hands were stained yellow

11

with much smoking. Her lips were rather thick. She had also mastered the art of getting a cigarette to stick to the lower, thicker one without letting it fall into whatever she was cooking. She was very fond of cooking. The air, every evening, was full of odours of herbs, garlic, wine vinegars and frying onions. The smell of frying onions invariably made him ravenously hungry but it was always nine o'clock, sometimes ten, occasionally still later, before she would yell across the hall to where he sat sipping sherry in the drawing-room:

'Come and get it if you want it. And if you don't want it – ' the rest of the sentence asphyxiated in coughing.

Sometimes, so late at night, he did not want it. Excellent though the food often was, he found himself not hungry any more. He sat inelastically at table, ate with his fork and sipped a glass of claret, perhaps two. She, on the other hand, more than ever like the lioness, ravenous far beyond feeding time, ate eyelessly, no longer seeing the food, the table or himself through mists of gin.

'Forgot to tell you – Lewis saw that kid riding through the place again today. Rode clean through the courtyard, by the cucumber house and out the other side.'

'Good Heavens, didn't Lewis choke her off?'

'Gave her hell he says.'

'And what happened? What did she say?'

'Said she'd been told it was perfectly all right. You'd never mind.'

'But good grief,' he said, 'we can't have that. We can't have strangers riding through the place as if it's their own. That won't do. That simply won't do – '

'All right,' she said. 'All right. You tell her. I've told her. Lewis has told her. Now you tell her. It's your turn.'

She lit a cigarette, pushed more food into her mouth and began laughing. A little stream of bright crimson tomato sauce ran down her chin. A shred or two of tobacco clung to her front teeth and there was actually a touch of pink, the first bloodshot vein or two, in the whites of her eyes.

'But who *is* she?'

'Search me. *You* find out. It's *your* turn – '

Open-mouthed, she laughed again across the table, the cigarette dangling this time from the lower lip as she mockingly pointed her glass at his face.

He knew that this gesture of fresh derision meant that she no longer saw him very well. Already the eyes had begun their swimming unfocused dilations.

'All right,' he said. 'I'll speak to her.'

'Good,' she said. 'That's the brave Harry. Brave old Harry.'

As she threw back her head, laughing openly now, letting the cigarette fall into her plate of half-eaten food, revealing relics of her last mouthful smeared across her lips and her tongue, he did not ask himself why he had ever married her. It was too late for asking that kind of question.

'When does she appear?' he said.

'Oh! off and on. Any time. On and off –'

'I'll try to catch her on Saturday,' he said. 'Or Sunday.'

Derisively and deliberately she raised her hand, not laughing now, in a sort of mock benediction.

'Now don't be rash, Harry dear. Brave old Harry,' she said. 'Don't be rash. She might catch you.'

3

On the following Sunday morning, as he walked up past the cucumber house to where a path led through two wicket gates to the meadows beyond, a light breeze was coming off the little river, bringing with it the scent of a few late swathes of hay. The glass of the cucumber house, with its dark green under-tracery of leaves, flashed white in the sun. The summer had been more stormy than fine, with weeks of August rain, and now, in mid-September, the fields were flush with grasses.

He stopped to look inside the cucumber house. Under the glass the temperature had already risen to ninety-five. Thick green vines dripped with steamy moisture. Columns of cucumbers, dark and straight, hung down from dense masses of leaves that shut out the strong morning sun.

The cucumbers were his wife's idea. She was very imaginative, he had to admit, about cucumbers. Whereas the average person merely sliced up cucumbers, made them into sandwiches or simply ate them with fresh salmon for lunch in summer, his wife was acquainted with numerous recipes in which cucumbers were cooked, stuffed like aubergines or served with piquant sauces or high flavours such as Provençale. Harry Barnfield did not care much for cucumbers. More often than not, cooked or uncooked, they gave him wind, heartburn or chronic indigestion. But over the years of his married life he had learned to eat them because he was too good-natured to deny his wife the chance of surprising guests with dishes they had never heard of before. He well understood her cucumbers and her little gastronomic triumphs with them.

That Sunday morning, as he stood under the steaming shadowy vines, he thought he saw, suddenly, a bright yellow break of sunlight travel the entire length of the glasshouse outside. The leaves of the cucumbers were so thick that it was some moments before he grasped that this was, in fact, a person riding past him on a horse.

Even then, as he discovered when he rushed out of the cucumber house, he was partly mistaken. The horse was merely a pony, blackish brown in colour, with a loose black tail.

With impatience he started to shout after it: 'Hi! you there! Where do you think you're going? Don't you know –?' and then stopped, seeing in fact that its rider was nothing more than a young girl in a yellow sweater, jodhpurs, black velvet cap and pigtails. The pigtails too were black and they hung long and straight down the yellow shoulders, tied at the ends not with ribbon but with short lengths of crimson cord.

The girl did not stop. He started to shout again and then, quite without thinking, began to run after her.

'Young lady!' he called. 'Young lady! – one moment, young lady, one moment please –'

It was thirty or forty yards farther on before he caught up with her. By that time she had stopped, bent down and was already lifting the catch of the first of the wicket gates with the handle of her riding-crop.

'Just a moment, young lady, just one moment –'

As he stopped he found himself short of breath and panting slightly. She turned very slightly in the saddle to look at him. Her eyes were brown, motionless and unusually round and large. They seemed, like his own, rather too big for her face.

'Aren't you aware,' he said, 'that this is private property? – this path? It's private property!'

She did not move. She looked, he thought, fifteen, perhaps sixteen, not more than that, though rather well developed for her age. The sleeves of the yellow jumper were half-rolled up, showing firm brown forearms that glistened with downy golden hairs. Her face was the same golden brown colour, the lips without make-up, so that they too had a touch of brown.

'You really can't ride through here like this,' he said. 'You've been told before. You really can't, you know.'

Again she did not move. He did not know if the large motionless eyes were utterly insolent or merely transfixed in frightened innocence and he was still trying to make up his mind about it when he noticed how straight but relaxed she sat on the pony. He had to admit, even in vexation, that she sat very well; very well indeed, he thought.

'It's very tiresome,' he said, 'all this. You simply can't ride rough-shod over other people's property like this.'

'Rough-shod?'

Her voice surprised him very much by its deepness. It almost seemed, he thought, like the voice of a woman twice her age.

'Do you really think,' she said, 'I'm riding rough-shod?'

The eyes, still holding him in enormous circles of inquiring innocence, disarmed him with sheer brightness.

'That's neither here nor there,' he said. 'The simple fact is that you cannot ride when and how you please over other people's property.'

'I was told I could.'

'Told? By whom?'

'My mother.'

At this moment his spectacles began to mist over. For the next second or two she seemed to melt away and become lost to him.

Uneasily he thought to himself that he ought to take his spectacles off, polish them and put them back again. He began to feel inexplicably nervous about this and his hands groped about his face. Then when he realized that if he took off his spectacles he

15

would, with his weak, short-sighted eyes, be able to see her even less well he made the unfortunate compromise of trying to look over the top of them.

She smiled.

'Your mother?' he said. 'What has your mother to do with it? Do you mean I know your mother?'

'You *knew* her.'

'Oh! and when pray would that be?'

He hadn't the slightest idea why he should ask that question and in fact she ignored it completely.

'My name is Valerie Whittington.'

'Oh! yes. I see. Oh! yes,' he said slowly. 'Oh! yes.' He was so intensely surprised that, without thinking, he at once took off his spectacles and rubbed the lenses on his coat sleeve.

'Is the colonel – ?'

'He died last year.'

Again he polished the lenses of the spectacles quickly on the coat sleeve.

'We've taken the gamekeeper's cottage at Fir Top. I don't suppose you know it,' she said.

'Oh! yes.'

Something made him keep the spectacles in his hand a little longer.

'I can ride down through the park and along by the river and then back through the woods across the hill,' the girl said. 'It's a complete circle if I take the path through here. If not I have to go back the same way again and you know how it is. It's never so nice going back the same way.'

He murmured something about no, it was never so nice and then put on his spectacles. Clear, fresh and with that remarkable blend of insolence and innocent charm, she stared down at him, making him feel a baffled, fumbling idiot.

'So it was your mother told you about the path?'

'She just said she was sure you wouldn't mind.'

Why, he wondered, did she say that?

'She said you were the sort of man who never did mind.'

Again he felt baffled and stupid.

Then, for the first time, the pony moved. Up to that moment

she had kept remarkably still and it was in fact so quiet, standing erect in the hot September sun, that he had been almost unaware that it was there until now, suddenly, it reared its head and shuddered.

Instinctively he put one hand on its flank to calm it down. It quietened almost immediately and she said:

'I'm afraid he's really not big enough for me. But he's the best we can afford for the time.'

She ran her hand down the pony's neck, leaning forward as she did so. He saw the muscles of the neck light up like watered silk. At the same time he saw the flanks of the girl tauten, smooth out and then relax again.

'Does your mother ride now?' he said.

'No,' she said. 'Not now.'

'She used to ride very well.'

'Yes. She said you'd remember.'

Again he felt baffled; again he groped towards his spectacles.

'Well,' she said. 'I suppose I must go back.'

She started to turn the pony round. He found all his many uncertainties stiffen into astonishment.

'I thought you wanted to go on?' he said – 'over the hill?'

'You said you didn't want me to.'

'Oh! yes I know, but that was – I admit – Oh! no – well I mean – ' He found himself incapable of forming a coherent sentence. 'By all means – it was simply that I didn't want – well, you know, strangers – '

'I ought to have come and asked you,' she said. 'I know now. But you were never at home.'

'Oh! no, no, no,' he said. 'Oh! no.'

The pony was still facing the cucumber house, uneasy now. Sunlight was catching the angle of the roof panes, flashing white glare into the animal's eyes in spite of the blinkers, and Harry Barnfield put his hand on its nose, steadying it down.

'I'll be putting up jumps next week,' he said. 'In the meadows there.' The touch of the animal brought back a little, but only a little, of his assurance. 'You could – well, I mean if you cared – you could use them. I'm never here week-days.'

She smiled as if to begin to thank him but a flash of light from

17

the cucumber house once again caught the pony's eye, making it rear.

'You'd better turn him round,' he said, 'and take him along. It's the sun on the cucumber house.'

'I will,' she said.

He moved forward to unlatch the gate for her. The pony also moved forward. A new wave of uncertainty ran through Harry Barnfield and he said:

'Remember me to your mother, will you? If she would care – Oh! I don't suppose she would like a cucumber? We have masses. We have too many cucumbers by far.'

'We neither of us care for them,' she said, 'but I'll tell her all the same.'

She rode through the gate. He shut the gate after her, leaned on it and watched her ride, at a walk, up the path. After forty or fifty yards the path began to go uphill to where, against the sky-line, clumps of pine grew from browning bracken hillocks before the true woods began. The morning was so clear that he could see on the tips of these pines the stiff fresh crusts of the light olive summer cones. He could see also the brown arms of the girl below the rolled sleeves of the yellow sweater, the flecks of white on the short legs of the pony and the knots of red on the pigtails.

He was suddenly aware that there was something disturbing about her without being able to say what it was. In that insolent innocent way of hers she rode very well, he thought, but the pony was quite ridiculous. Her body and the pony simply did not fit each other, any more than her body and her voice seemed part of the same person.

'Edna should get her a horse,' he said aloud and then, with sweat breaking out again from under his misty spectacles, began to walk back to the cucumber house.

There he was overcome by embarrassment at remembering how he had been stupid enough to offer the girl a cucumber; and in remembering it forgot completely that he had called her mother by name.

Soon after that he began to come
ings to a recurrence of mild gin-dr
really mind being quipped; the c
that sort of thing.

'Your girl-friend was jumpir
morning and back again befor
five. I'd have offered her a bed but ɪ

'I wish you wouldn't call her my girl-frienu.

'Best I can think of, Harry. You put her up to this gan.

Presently she began to use his jumps not only on week-days but on Saturdays and Sundays too. Sometimes he would wake as early as eight o'clock, look out across the meadows and see the yellow sweater dipping between the barriers of brushwood.

He saw it also as it faded in the twilights. And always he was baffled by the ridiculous nature of the pony, the pigtails and the long impossibly dangling legs of the girl as she rode.

'Your girl-friend certainly works at it. Lewis tells me she was here at six the other morning. He was mad. The animal kicked up his mushrooms.'

'I do wish you wouldn't call her my girl-friend. She's fifteen. Sixteen if she's that.'

'From the day they're born,' Katey said, 'they're women. Never mind their age.'

At first he found it an embarrassment, slight but uneasy, to join her at the jumps. He supposed it arose from the fact that in his inelastic way he often fell off the horse. That did not matter very much when he jumped alone but it was awkward, even painful when people were watching.

In this way he began to ride more cautiously, more dumpily, more stiffly than before. For two week-ends he did not jump at all. At the third he heard a clatter of pony hooves on the stable yard, looked up to see her long legs astride the pony and heard her deep voice say:

'I thought you must be ill, Mr Barnfield, because you weren't jumping. Mother sent me to inquire.'

er than ever, he thought, startled and disturbed
mbled for words.

Oh! no. Perfectly all right, thank you. Oh! no. It's
e countryside has been looking so lovely that I've been
e jumps a miss and riding up on the hill instead. In fact
st going up there now.'

Do you mind if I ride that way with you?' she said.

Some minutes later they were riding together up the hillside,
under clumps of pines, along paths by which huge bracken fronds
were already tipped with fox-brown. Late blackberries shone
pulpy and dark with bloom in the morning sunlight and where the
bracken cleared there ran rose-bright stains of heather, with
snow-tufts of cotton-grass in seed.

'You can smell that wonderful, wonderful scent of pines,' she
said.

He lifted his face instinctively to breathe the scent of pines and
instead was distracted, for it might have been the fiftieth time, by
her incongruous legs scratching the lowest tips of bracken fronds
as she rode.

'My wife and I were having a slight argument as to how old
you were,' he said. 'Of course it's rude to guess a lady's age
but –'

'Oh! I'm ancient,' she said, 'Positively and absolutely ancient.'
He started to smile.

'And how old,' she said, 'did you say?'

'Oh! fifteen,' he said at once, not really thinking at all. 'Perhaps I'll give you sixteen.'

'Give me sixteen,' she said. 'And then seventeen. And then
eighteen. And then if you like –'

She stopped. Looking up from the pony she turned on him the
enormous circular eyes that appeared so often to be full of naïve
insolence and then waited for him, as it were, to recover his
breath.

'And then nineteen. And then if you like, next month, you can
come to my twentieth birthday.'

He was too staggered to bring to this situation anything but
absolute silence as they rode to the hill-top.

'I think you're surprised,' she said.

'Oh! no. Oh! no,' he said. 'Well, yes and no, in a way –'

'Don't you think I look twenty?'

'Well, it's not always absolutely easy –'

'How do you demonstrate age?' she said and he rode to the crest of the hill-top without an answer, his head sweating under his close tweed cap, his spectacles misting and turning to a premature fog-bound landscape the entire valley of morning brilliance below.

He was temporarily saved from making a complete and disastrous fool of himself by hearing the pony breathing hard, in partial distress.

'I think you should give him a blow,' he said. 'It's a pretty long drag up here.'

She thought so too and they both began dismounting. Then, as she swung to the ground, he had a second surprise.

This, he suddenly realized, was the first time he had actually seen her when not on the pony. Standing there, at his own level, she seemed to enlarge and straighten up. He was aware of a pair of splendid yellow shoulders. Riding had made her straight in the back, throwing her breasts well forward, keeping her head erect and high. She was also, he now discovered with fresh uneasiness, slightly taller than he was.

He turned away to tie his horse to a pine. When he had finished he looked round to see her walking, with surprisingly delicate strides for so tall a girl, towards the ridge of the hillside.

Finally she stopped, turned and waved to him. For a single moment he thought she had in her hand a flower of some kind and it looked, he thought, like a scarlet poppy. Then he saw that it was one of the cords she had snatched from her pigtails.

'Come over and look at the view,' she called.

By the time he joined her she was sitting down in a patch of bracken. He sat down too: looking, not at the view below him, the map of copse and pasture and hedgerow flecked already with the occasional pure bright chrome of elm and hornbeam, the dense oaks and grass still green as summer, but at the sight of the girl now unplaiting and combing out the mass of bright brown hair into a single tail.

'You look surprised,' she said, 'but then I notice you always do.'

She started to let her hair fall loosely over her shoulders, until it half-enclosed her face. Then she put her hand in the pocket of her jodhpurs and pulled out a powder compact, a lipstick and lastly a small oval mirror with a blue enamel back.

'Do you mind holding that?' she said.

He held the mirror in front of her face. Once or twice she stretched forward, touching his hand and moved the mirror to one side or the other.

In silence, for perhaps the next five minutes or so, he watched her make up her face. He saw the lips, freed of their dull brown-ness, thicken, becoming very full, almost over-full, in redness. He saw her smooth with the powder-pad the skin of her face, giving it a tone of milky brown.

Finally she threw back her hair from her shoulders and he had time to notice that the enlargement of the lips, so bright now and almost pouting, had the effect of bringing into proportion the large brown eyes.

'How do I look?' she said.

His immediate impression was that the make-up, the loosened hair and the fuller, brighter lips had softened her completely. It was very like the effect on parched grass of warm and heavy rain.

At the same time he could not help feeling desperately, awk-wardly and embarrassingly sorry for her.

'Now do I look twenty?' she said.

It was on the tip of his tongue to say 'More – older' and after-wards he knew that it would have pleased her very much if he had, but he said instead:

'What made you do that just now? – just here?'

'Oh! God!' she said and the sepulchral wretched cry of her deep voice shocked him so much that his mouth fell open, 'I'm so miserable – Oh! God! I can't tell you how miserable I am.'

She turned suddenly and, not actually sobbing but with a harsh choke or two, lay face downwards in the bracken, beating her hands on the ground.

Pained and discomforted, he started to move towards her. She seemed to sense the movement and half-leapt up.

'Don't touch me!' she howled.

It was the furthest thing from his mind. He stood for a moment

22

with his mouth open and then started blunderingly to walk away.

'Where are you going?' she moaned.

At that second sepulchral cry he stopped.

'I thought you'd rather have it out by yourself.'

'I don't want to have it out! 'she said. 'I don't want to have it out! I don't want to have it out!'

It was beyond him to understand and he wished unhappily that he were back home, jumping or talking to Lewis or having a glass of sherry with Bill Chalmers, his neighbour, or with Punch Warburton, who sometimes came over and talked horses and weather and general gossip before Sunday lunchtime.

'Then what do you want?' he said.

'God only knows,' she said quietly. 'God knows. God only knows.'

By that time she was really crying and he was sensible enough to let her go on with it for another ten minutes or so. During that time he sat on the ground beside her, mostly staring uneasily across the bracken in fear that somebody he knew would come past and see him there.

That would be a miserable situation to be caught in, but as it happened, nobody came. There was in fact hardly a sound on the hill-top and hardly a movement except an occasional late butterfly hovering about the blackberries or a rook or two passing above the pines.

When she had finished crying she sat up. The first thing she did was to begin to wipe off the lipstick. She wiped it off quite savagely, positively scrubbing at it with a handkerchief, until her lips again had that dry brownish undressed look about them.

Then she started to plait her hair. When she had finished one plait she held the end of it in her mouth while she tied it with the cord. Then she did the same with the other. Finally she tossed the two plaits back over her shoulders and, with a rough hand sweep, straightened the rest of her hair flat with her hands.

'There,' she said bitterly, 'how will that do?'

The bitterness in her voice profoundly shocked him.

'It can't be as bad as all that,' he said, 'can it?'

Her eyes stared at him, blank and sour.

'As bad as all what?'

'Well, whatever – can't you tell me?'

'I've never told anybody,' she said. 'I wouldn't know how to begin.'

He started to say something about how much better it was if you could get these things off your chest when he saw her standing up. Once again, for the second time that morning, he was aware of the splendid yellow shoulders, her tallness and the contradiction of the ridiculous scarlet-fastened pigtails with the rest of her body.

'I'd better get back,' she said, 'before she starts creating hell at me.'

'She?'

'Mother,' she said. 'Oh! and by the way. I almost forgot. She sent a message for you.'

'For me?'

'She says will you be sure to come along on Tuesday evening for a drink? She's having a few friends in. About seven o'clock.'

He began to say something about his train not always getting in on time, but she cut him short:

'I think you'd better try and make it if you can. She said to tell you she positively won't take no for an answer.'

'Well, I shall have to see –'

'You won't,' she said. 'You know mother, don't you?'

'I did know her. Years ago –'

'If you knew her then,' she said, 'you know her now.'

He started to feel uneasy again at that remark and said something about he would do his best and did it include his wife, the invitation?

'Nothing was said about Mrs Barnfield.'

A few minutes later, at the crest of the hill, he was holding her foot in the stirrup while she mounted the pony. There was really no need for that piece of help of his, since she could almost have mounted the animal directly from the ground, but she seemed touched by it and turned and gave him, without a word, a short thankful smile.

This touched him too more than words could possibly have done and he mounted his horse in silence. After that they rode, also in silence, for two hundred yards along the hill-top to where the path forked and she said:

'This is my way back. Thank you for everything. Don't forget Tuesday. I'll get it in the neck if you do.'

This again was beyond him and he said simply, raising his cap:

'I'll do what I can. Good-bye.'

Then, turning to ride away, she gave him an odd miserable little smile and once again he found himself appalled by the ridiculous sight of her sitting on the pony. Somehow the picture was not only fatuous. It struck him as being infinitely lonely too.

'And no more crying now,' he said. 'No more of that.'

She turned, rested one hand on the rump of the pony and stared, not at him but completely and far past him, with empty eyes.

'If you listen carefully,' she said, 'you'll probably hear me howling across the hill in the night-time.'

5

It was past half past seven and already dark, the following Tuesday evening, when he drove up to the old keeper's cottage on the opposite side of the hill. There were lights in the narrow mullioned windows of the little house but, much to his surprise, no other cars.

Edna Whittington herself came to the door to answer his ring, holding in her left hand a half-empty glass and a cigarette in a bright yellow amber holder.

'Sweet of you, Henry. Absolutely and typically sweet.'

As she leaned forward so that he could kiss her first on one cheek and then the other he caught an overpowering fragrance, sickly in the night air. He did not fail to notice too how she called him Henry.

'But come in, Henry, come in, come in, you sweet man. Let's look at you.'

He went in and, inside, discovered that the house was empty.

'I'm sorry I'm so late,' he said.

With magenta-nailed fingers she took his black homburg hat and umbrella and laid them on a window sill. 'The train lost time.'

25

He looked round the room to make perfectly sure, for a second time, about its emptiness. 'Has everybody gone?'

'Everybody gone?'

'I thought it was a party.'

'Party?' she said. 'Whoever said it was a party?'

'Valerie.'

'Oh! my little girl,' she said. 'That little girl of mine. My silly little girl.'

He started to say that he thought the girl had been pretty emphatic about the party but Edna Whittington laughed, cutting him short, and said:

'She never gets it right, Henry. Never gets anything right, the silly child, just never gets it right.'

'Isn't she here either?'

'Out to a little birthday party,' she said. 'Just a teeny-weeny affair.'

She poured him a glass of sherry. Her voice was husky. It was nearly twenty-five years since he had seen her before and he remembered, in time, that the voice had always been husky.

'Well, cheers, Henry,' she said. 'Resounding numbers of cheers. Lots of luck.'

She raised her glass, looking at him with chilled, squinting, remarkably white-blue eyes. Her hair was bluish too and there were shadows of blue, almost violet, in the powder on her face. Her chest, flattish, was steely and bare, except for a double row of pearls, to the beginnings of the creased pouches of her breasts, and her face had a strange bony prettiness except in the mouth, which twisted upward at one side.

'Come and sit here on the sofa and tell me all about yourself. Tell me about life. Here, dear man – not there. Just the old Henry – afraid something will bite you.'

He did not think, he said, as he sat beside her on the settee, that he had anything very much of himself to tell; or of life for that matter.

'Well, I have,' she said. 'Here we've been in the neighbourhood six months and not a bleat from you.'

'I honestly didn't know you were here.'

'Then you honestly should have done. It was in all the

papers. I mean about the colonel. Didn't you read about that?'

He had to confess, with growing wretchedness, that he hadn't even read in the papers about the colonel, who had dropped down of thrombosis a year before. Nevertheless he was, he said, very sorry. It was a sad thing, that.

'He'd got awfully fat,' she said. 'And of course marrying late and so on. He was a man of forty-five before Valerie was born.'

He knew that it was not only the colonel but she too who had married very late. He sat thinking of this, sipping his sherry, watching a meagre fire of birch logs smouldering in the round black grate, and she said:

'Yes, I call it pretty stodgy, Henry. Two miles away and not a single lamb's peep out of you. The trouble is you live in a stew-pot.'

'Now here, I say –'

'Well, don't you? Up to town with *The Times* in the morning. Down from town with the *Standard* in the evening. If that isn't stew-potism tell me what is. Doesn't anything else go on in these parts?'

'Oh! blow it,' he said. 'It isn't as bad as that.'

'Isn't it?' she said. 'I think it's absolutely fungoid.'

He suddenly felt very slightly incensed at this and went on to explain, as calmly as he could, how you sometimes held parties, had people to dinner, went in spring to the point-to-points and, damn it, in winter, hunted quite a lot. He didn't think you could call that stew-potism, could you?

'There's the hunt ball in a month's time too,' he reminded her finally. 'You can chalk that up for a whale of a time.'

'I would,' she said, 'if anybody had invited me.'

Before he realized what he was saying, he said:

'I'll invite you. Both of you. Delighted.'

'Oh! the child could never come.'

'No?'

He could not think why on earth the girl could never come.

'She's a mere infant, Henry. Hardly out of the shell. She never does these things. Besides, I'd never let her.'

'Why?'

'Oh! Henry, she isn't fledged. She's only half-grown. She isn't fit for that sort of thing. You know what these hunt affairs are too. Wolf-packs. Those gangs are not hunts for nothing.'

In his direct, harmless, simple way, the way in which, as everybody always said, there was never any malice, he said:

'But you'd come, wouldn't you?'

'Like a lamplighter, Henry. Absolutely adore to.'

He began to murmur something in polite satisfaction about this when she added:

'That's if Katey wouldn't explode.'

'I don't think Katey would mind.'

That, he always thought, was one nice thing about Katey. She was a good sport, Katey: never jealous in that way.

'And how,' she said, 'is Katey?'

He shrugged his shoulders: as if there were nothing of very great moment to tell of Katey.

'Tell me about her, Henry,' she said. 'You can tell me.'

There was nothing, he thought, that he possibly wanted to tell.

'I'm sorry,' she said, 'have I boobed? I simply thought – well, people talk and you know how it is. Somehow I got the impresh – well, you know the impresh one gets – that you and Katey weren't pulling all that steamingly well in harness.'

He was roused by the increasing absurdity of her language. She was like a piece of iced-cake that one finds in a silvered box, in a forgotten drawer, among silver leaves, thirty years after the voices at the wedding have faded away. The brittle archaisms of the language were like the hard tarnished silver balls left on the cake. They had seemed so magnificently bright in his youth but now – Good God, had he and Edna and the rest of them really talked like that? If it hadn't been for that absurd, husky clipping voice of hers he would never have believed they had.

As if her thoughts were running in the same direction she said:

'We had some great times, Henry. You and I and Vicky Burton and Freddie Anstruther and Peggy Forbes and Carol Chalmers and Floaty Dean – he was a bright moonbeam, Floaty – do you ever hear anything of any of the crowd?'

'I'm afraid I've lost touch with all of them.'

'Well, not all, Henry. Don't say that. You haven't lost touch with me.'

Here, as so often in the conversation, she smiled, played with the pearls above the thin steely bosom or extended, to its full length, the arm holding the dying cigarette in its yellow holder.

'Do you remember a day on the river at Pangbourne?'

He pretended not to remember it while, in reality, remembering it very well. That day she had worn her pale yellow hair in a bob and a hat like a round pink saucepan. Her white dress had been short and waistless, revealing round and pretty knees below the skirt.

There was no doubt in his mind that she too had been very pretty and she said:

'But you remember coming home, through the woods? You wanted to go with Carol but I wanted you to come with me. All the rhododendrons were out, big white and pale pink ones so that you could see them in the dark, and I made an honest man of you.'

She laughed distastefully.

'You *surely* don't forget, Henry, do you?' she said. 'After all, it was the first time with you and me, even if it wasn't the last, and you know how –'

'Look, Edna, we were all a bit crazy at that time and I don't think we have to drag it all –'

He was relieved to hear the sound of car-brakes in the road outside. Then he heard a car door slam and the sound of feet running up the path outside.

A moment later Valerie Whittington came in. She was wearing a blue gabardine school mackintosh and a plain grey felt hat and white ankle socks above her plain flat shoes. The mackintosh was too long for her by several inches and when she started to take it off he saw that underneath it she was wearing a plain dark blue dress that was full and bushy in the skirt. It too was too long for her.

'Well, there you are at last, child. Say good evening to Mr Barnfield before you go up. I know you know him because he was kind enough to let you use the path.'

'Good evening, Mr Barnfield.'

He said good evening too and knew, as he did so, that she had the greatest difficulty in looking at him. He tried in vain to catch the big, brown, too-circular eyes.

'Well, up you go now, child. It's late. It's past your time. Say good night to Mr Barnfield.'

'Good night, Mr Barnfield.'

He nodded. He thought she made a sort of timid, half-urgent effort to protest but she turned away too quickly, leaving him unsure. The last visible sign of what she might be thinking was a shudder of her lower lip, hard and quite convulsive, just before she turned, opened the door and went out without a word.

'I must go too,' he said.

'Oh! not yet, Henry. Have another sherry –'

'No, no,' he said. 'Really, no, no. Katey will have dinner –'

'Give her a ping on the blower and say you'll be another half hour. We've hardly exchanged the sliver of a word –'

'No, honestly, Edna,' he said. 'Honestly I must go.'

She came with him, at last, to the door. In the light from the door she stood for a moment gauntly, thinly framed, a piece of silver cardboard, and he thought again of the wedding cake. Then she half closed the door behind her. The October air was mild and windless but as she stretched out long fleshless arms to say good-bye he said hastily:

'Don't come out. Don't get cold. I'm perfectly capable –'

'Good night, Henry,' she said. 'Sweet of you to come. And that's a date, then, isn't it? – the ball?'

'That's if you'd care –'

'Oh! Henry.' She laughed huskily. 'Care?'

She offered her face to be kissed. He made as if to inflict on it, somewhere between cheek and ear, a swift dab of farewell. The next moment he felt her thin fingers grasp him about the elbows. Then they moved up to his shoulders and suddenly she was offering her mouth instead.

'You can do better than that, Henry, can't you?' she said. She laughed with what he supposed she thought was tenderness. Her voice crackled on its rising note with a brittle snap. 'I know you can. From what I remember of the rhododendrons. And not only the rhododendrons.'

'Look, Edna, I've already told you. That's all over long since,' he said, and escaped, leaving her mouth in air.

6

He was surprised, the following Sunday morning, to see no sign of the yellow sweater among the brushwood jumps in the meadows.

'Your girl-friend has passed you up,' Katey said. 'She hasn't been near all week, so Lewis says.'

After breakfast he rode out to the meadow and jumped for half an hour in cool exhilarating air, across grass still white-wet from frost. In the hedgerows leaves of maple and hornbeam were growing every day more and more like clear light candle-flame and up on the hill the beeches were burning deeper and deeper, fox-fiery beyond the pines, against ice-blue autumn sky.

The hill was irresistible and finally he rode up, slowly, in bright sunshine, about eleven o'clock, through acres of dying bracken and birches that were shedding, in pure silence, after the night frost, the gentlest yellow fall of leaves.

One or two people were walking on the crest of the hill but no one except himself was riding and he was half in mind to turn the horse, ride down the opposite hillside as far as *The Black Boy* and treat himself to a whisky there at twelve o'clock, when he suddenly saw walking across the bracken a tall figure in a black skirt and a puce-pink blouse.

It was a pigtail-less, hatless, horseless Valerie Whittington, waving her hand.

'I thought it must be you,' she said and even he was not too stupid to know that she must have been waiting for him there.

'Where's your pony?' he said.

'I've stopped riding.'

'Oh?'

It was all he could think of to say as he raised his cap, dismounted and stood beside her.

He saw at once that she was wearing lipstick. She had also managed to bunch up her hair into thick brown curls and to make an effort to match the colour on her face to the puce pink of the blouse. Except for the evening at the cottage he had not seen her in skirts before and now he saw that her legs were long, well-shaped and slender.

'Given up riding?' he said. 'How is that?'

'I've just given up riding,' she said.

Even from the tone of this remark he saw that she had changed a great deal. Like her voice, her face was grave, almost solemn. Her eyes seemed queer and distant.

'Have you time to walk a little way?' she said.

He said yes, he had time, and they walked slowly, in cool sunshine, he leading the horse, to where he could see once again the entire valley of oak-woods and pasture below. In a few weeks he would be hunting across it, drinking the first sharp draughts of winter.

'I'm afraid I behaved like a fool up here the other day,' she said, 'and I'm sorry about the other night.'

He said he couldn't think why.

'Well, it's all over now,' she said, 'but I just wanted to say.'

Exactly what, he asked, was all over now?

'Me,' she said. 'I'm leaving home. I'm going away.'

It was instantly typical of him to ask her if she thought that was wise.

'Wise or not,' she said, 'I'm going.'

Everybody wanted to run away when they were young, he said, but it was like measles. You got over it in time and you were probably all the better for having been through the wretched thing.

'Yes, I'm better,' she said. 'Because I know where I'm going now. Thanks to you.'

He couldn't think what he possibly had to do with it and she said:

'I like being with you. I grow up when I'm with you. Somehow you never take me away from myself.'

This odd, solemn little pronouncement of hers affected him far more than her tears had ever done and he glanced quickly at her face. It was full of another, different kind of tearfulness, dry and barren, with a pinched sadness that started dragging at his heart.

'You know what I've been doing since last Sunday?' she said.

'No.'

'Coming up here.'

'Yes?'

'Every day,' she said. 'Walking. Not with the pony – I haven't ridden the pony since that day. Just walking. I think I know every path here now. There's a wonderful one goes down past the holly trees. You come to a little lake at the bottom with quince trees on an island – at least I think they're quince trees.'

If he had time, she went on, she wanted him to walk down there. Would he? Did he mind?

He tethered his horse to a fence and they started to walk along a path that wound down, steeply in places, through crackling curtains of bracken, old holly trees thick with pink-brown knots of berry and more clumps of birch trees sowing in absolute silence little yellow pennies of leaves.

At the bottom there was, as she had said, a small perfectly circular lake enclosed by rings of alder, willow and hazel trees. In the still air its surface was thick with floating shoals of leaves. In absolute silence two quince trees, half-bare branches full of ungathered golden lamps of fruit, shone with apparent permanent candescence on a little island in the glow of noon.

'This is it,' she said.

Neither then, nor later, nor in fact at any other time, did they say a word about her mother. They stood for a long time without a word about anything, simply watching the little lake soundlessly embalmed in October sunlight, the quince-lamps setting the little island half on fire.

'I don't think you should go away,' he said.

'Why not?'

He answered her in the quiet, uncomplex way that, as everyone so often remarked, was so much part of him, so much the typical Harry Barnfield.

'I don't want you to,' he said.

She started to say something and then stopped. He looked at her face. He thought suddenly that it had lost the dry, barren tearfulness. Now it looked uncomplicated, alight and free. The big glowing brown eyes seemed to embrace him with a wonderful look of gratitude.

'What were you going to say?' he said.

33

'Nothing.'

'You were.'

'I was,' she said, 'but now it doesn't matter.'

All at once she laid her hands on his shoulders, drawing them slowly down until, quite nervously, she plucked at the lapels of his jacket. In shyness she could not look at him. She could only stare at her own fingers as she drew them slowly up and down.

Suddenly she let them fly up to his uncertain, spectacled, honest face with a breaking cry.

'Oh! my God, hold me,' she said. 'Hold me – just hold me, will you? – for God's sake please just hold me –'

In a stupid daze Harry Barnfield held her; and from across the lake the sound of a duck's wing flapping somewhere about the island of quinces reached him, long afterwards, like the echo of a stone dropping far away at the bottom of a well.

7

Soon, as the autumn went on, his friends the city gentlemen began to notice a strange, unforetold change in his habits. No longer was it possible, several days a week, to wait with expectation and cheers to put the grappling hooks on Harry Barnfield as he ran, spectacled and panting, to catch the evening train.

The reason for this was a simple one: Harry Barnfield was, on these evenings, not there to be grappled.

By the time the train departed he was already away in the country, saying good-bye to the girl on the hillside or, in bad weather, as they sat in his car by the road. A train at two-thirty gave him an hour or more before, at six o'clock, he watched her, with a dry twist in his heart, walk away into twilights filled more and more with storms of blowing leaves.

Earlier in the afternoon they walked by the little lake. As late as the first week in November the lamps of the quinces hung miraculously suspended from the grey central islands of boughs and then gradually, one by one, dropped into the frosted reeds below.

By the middle of November there remained, on the south side of the island, where the sun caught it full in the early afternoons, one quince, the last of the autumn lanterns, and as Harry Barn-field and the girl came down the path through thinning alder trees she got into the way of running on ahead of him to the edge of the lake, always giving the same little cry:

'Look, Harry, our quince is still there!'

For about a week longer they watched, as if it were some mar-vellously suspended planet glowing above the wintry stretches of water where thin ice sometimes lingered white all day in the thickest shadow of reeds, the last remaining quince, suspended bare and yellow on frost-stripped boughs.

'When it falls I shall feel the summer has gone completely,' the girl said.

Soon Harry Barnfield felt as she did: that this was the last of summer poured into a single phial of honey. When it fell and split at last he knew he would hear, dark and snapping, the breath of winter.

By the fifteenth day of the month the quince, looking bigger and more golden than ever in an afternoon of pure, almost shrill blue sky already touched on the horizon by the coppery threat of frost, still remained.

'Look, Harry!' the girl said, 'our quince is still there!'

For some time they walked slowly by the lake. In the breathless blue afternoon the one remaining globe of fruit glowed more than ever like the distillation of all the summer.

'It's nearly two months now,' the girl said, 'since we first came down here. Have you been happy?'

He started to say that he had never been so happy in his life but she cut him short and said:

'What made you happy?'

He could not think what had made him happy except, perhaps, that he had been freed, at last, from the shackles of his daily ride in the train, the banterings of the city gentlemen and above all from the evening crackle of Katey's voice calling that she hoped to God he hadn't forgotten the gin. But before he had time to reply the girl said:

'I'll tell you why it is. It's because you've made someone else happy. Me, in fact.'

'I'm glad about that.'

35

'You see,' she said, 'it's like shining a light. You shine it and it reflects back at you.'

'But supposing,' he said in his simple, straightforward way, 'there's nothing to reflect back from?'

'Oh! but there is,' she said, 'there's me.'

He smiled at this and a moment later she stopped, touched his arm and said:

'I wonder if you feel about it the same way as I do? I feel in a wonderful way that you and I have been growing up together.'

He hadn't a second in which to answer this odd remark before, across the lake, the quince fell with a thud, almost a punch, into the reeds below. The sound startled the girl so much that she gave a sudden dismaying gasp:

'Oh! Harry, it's gone! Our quince has gone – oh! Harry, look, it's empty without it!'

He stared across to the island and saw that it was, as she said, quite empty.

'Now,' she said, 'it's winter.'

He thought he caught for the briefest possible moment a colder breath of air rising from the lake, but it was in fact her shadow crossing his face, shutting out the sun, as she turned and looked at him.

'The quince has gone and it's winter,' she said. 'The week has gone and tomorrow it's Friday. Have you forgotten?'

'Friday?' he said. 'Forgotten?'

'Friday,' she said, 'is the Hunt Ball.'

'Good God, I'd forgotten,' he said.

Now it was her turn to smile and she said:

'Whatever you do you mustn't forget. You simply mustn't. You're coming to fetch us. Will you dance with me?'

'If – ' He was about to say 'If your mother will let you,' but he checked himself in time and said, 'If you don't mind being trodden on. It's some time since I danced, especially to modern things.'

'I've a new dress,' she said.

There crossed his mind the picture of her coming home, as he vividly remembered it, from the birthday party: the dress long, straight and blue under the blue school mackintosh; and he felt his heart once again start to ache for her, afraid of what she would wear.

'Nobody has seen it,' she said.

It was on the tip of his tongue to say 'Not even – ' when he checked himself again and she said:

'I hope you'll like me in it. Nobody knows about it. I bought it alone, by myself. It's the colour of – No, I won't tell you after all. You'll see it tomorrow and then you can tell me if it reminds you of something.'

Suddenly she stretched up her arms in a short delightful gesture.

'You will dance with me?' she said, 'won't you? A lot?'

'I warn you – ' he said, and then: 'I'm pretty awful.'

'I don't believe it,' she said. 'Show me. Dance with me now.'

For the second time she held up her arms. She put her left arm lightly on his shoulder and he took her other hand.

'I'll hum the tune,' she said. 'Listen carefully.'

She started humming something but although he listened carefully he could not recognize at all what tune it was.

'You'll have to guide me,' she said. 'My eyes are shut. I always dance with my eyes shut. And by the way next week I'm twenty. Ancient. Had you forgotten?'

He had forgotten about that too.

'You dance nicely – very nicely – we go together – nicely – very nicely together – '

She started to sing the words to the tune she was humming, the tune he did not recognize, and as he danced to it, steering her about the frost-bared path along the lake, he remembered the sound of the quince dropping into the reeds, the last vanishing phial of the summer's honey, filling his mind like a golden ominous echo.

8

When he called alone at the keeper's cottage next evening about half past eight he saw at once that all his fears were justified. It was she who opened the door; and already, as he saw, she was wearing the blue school mackintosh. He even thought he caught,

37

as she turned her head, a glimpse of two pigtails tucked inside the half-turned-up collar at the back.

Nervously picking first at his silk evening scarf and then his black homburg hat he stood in the little sitting room and wished, for once, that Edna was there.

'Mother will be a few minutes yet,' the girl said. 'She always takes an awful time. She said I was to give you sherry. Or is there something else you'd rather have?'

He was about to say that sherry would suit him perfectly when she smiled, leaned close to him and said:

'This, for instance?'

She kissed him lightly. Her lips, not made up, with that curious undressed brownish look about them, rested on his mouth for no more than a second or two and then drew away.

'How many dances,' she said, 'are you going to dance with me?'

'Well –'

'Dance with me all evening.'

'I shall have to dance with your mother –'

'Dance one dance with mother and then all the rest with me.' Again she kissed him lightly on the lips. 'All night. For ever. Dance with me for ever.'

Miserably, a few moments later, he took the glass of sherry she poured out for him.

'I'm not allowed to drink,' she said. 'But I'm going to. Mother will be ages.'

With increasing wretchedness he saw her pour another glass of sherry, hold it up to him and say:

'Do you know what I used to say when I was a child and wanted to describe something that was very, very good?'

'No.'

'I used to call it the bestest good one.' She laughed with large shining eyes and drank half the sherry in a gulp. 'Here's to our evening. May it be the bestest good one in the world.'

All this time she kept the blue gabardine school mackintosh closely buttoned at the neck. He would not have been surprised to see that her stockings were black, though in fact they were flesh-coloured, and once he found himself looking down at her black flat-heeled shoes.

'Oh! that reminds me,' she said. 'Would you hide these in the car for me? They're my dancing shoes.'

He took the brown paper parcel she gave him and went out to the car and put the parcel on the back seat. The night was starry and crisp, with a half moon in the west.

Immediately, as he got back to the house, he heard the husky voice of Edna Whittington asking where he was.

In the sitting room she greeted him with outstretched thin bare arms, fingers crooked.

'Henry. I thought you were leaving us, trotting out there in the cold. I thought my little girl wasn't looking after you.'

She was wearing a skin-tight dress that looked, he thought, as if it were made of silver mail. It made her look more than ever like a sere cardboard leaf left over from a wedding cake. Her long finger nails and her lips were a sharp magenta and the skin of her chest and face was powdered to a rosy-violet shade.

'No Katey?'

Her voice was full of petulant mock regret.

He apologized and said that Katey was, on the whole, not a great one for dancing.

'Poor Katey. Well, anyway, all the more luck for me.'

In the intervals of talking and, he thought, smiling too much, she poured herself a glass of sherry and then filled up his own. All this time the girl stood apart, schoolgirlish, meek, hands in pockets of her mackintosh, not speaking.

'Henry,' Edna Whittington said, 'it's terribly sweet of you to take us to this thing and it's mean of me to ask another favour. But would you?'

'Of course.'

'What time does this affair break up?'

'Oh! hard to say,' he said. 'Three or four. I've known it to be five.'

'Shambles?'

'Quite often,' he said. 'Well, it's the Hunt Ball and you know how people are.'

'I know how people are and that's why I wanted to ask you. Would you,' she said, 'be an absolute lamb and bring Valerie

39

back by one o'clock? I've promised her she can come on that one condition.'

'If you think –'

'I do think and you're an absolute lamb. She doesn't mind being alone in the house and then you can come back for me and we'll stay on to the end.'

The girl did not speak or move. Her large brown eyes were simply fixed straight ahead of her, as if she actually hadn't heard.

Ten minutes later the three of them drove off, Edna Whittington sitting beside him at the wheel, wearing only a white long silk shawl as a wrap, the girl at the back, motionless and obliterated in the darkness, without a word.

'Oh! look! they've floodlit the mansion! The whole place looks like a wedding cake!'

As he turned the car into tall high park gates Edna Whittington's voice ripped at the night with a husky tear. At the end of a long avenue of bare regiments of chestnuts a great house seemed to stare with a single candescent eye, pure, white, across black spaces of winter parkland. And as the car drew nearer he thought that it looked, as she said, like a wedding cake, just as she herself, thin, shining and silver, looked more than ever like a leaf of it that had been long since torn away.

Less than ten minutes later he was inside the long central hall of the mansion, bright with chandeliers and crowded already with dancers, many of them his acquaintances of the hunting field, some his friends the city gentlemen, hearing Edna Whittington say with a smile of her bony once pretty magenta mouth:

'It's over twenty years since I danced with you, Henry, and I can't wait to have a quick one. What are they playing? What are you looking at?'

'I was wondering,' he said, 'where Valerie had –'

A moment later, before he could complete the sentence or she could answer it, he felt himself pressed to the thin sheer front of her body and borne away.

9

It might have been half an hour, perhaps only twenty minutes, when he turned in the middle of the second of his dances with Edna Whittington and became the victim of exactly the same kind of momentary illusion that he had suffered one brilliant Sunday morning in the cucumber house.

For a second or two, out of the corner of his eye, he thought he saw a strange but remotely recognizable fragment of yellow light cross a far corner of the room and disappear behind a triangular tier of pink chrysanthemums.

He was suddenly stunned to realize that this was Valerie Whittington, wearing a remarkably long pale yellow dress and long black gloves that showed her pale bare upper arms and her completely naked back and shoulders. He was so numbed by this appearance that only one thought raced through his head, in reality the rapid recollection of something she had said by the lake on the previous afternoon:

'Nobody knows about it. It's the colour of – No, I won't tell you. You'll see it tomorrow and then you can tell me if it reminds you of anything.'

Instantly he recalled the quinces and how the lamp of summer had gone out.

Somehow he got through the rest of the dance without betraying that he was in a turmoil of fright and indecision. He had broken out already into a cold and sickening sweat but as the dance ended he had presence of mind enough to mop his forehead with his handkerchief and say:

'It's awfully hot in here, Edna. My glasses are getting misty. Do you mind if I go and clean them? And wouldn't you like a drink? Can I bring you something – gin and something? – would you? – by all means, yes –'

He escaped, spent five minutes in an empty back corridor breathing on his spectacles, polishing them and then in sheer fright breathing on them again. After that he worked his way to the corner of the bar and restored himself with a whisky, saying desperately at the last moment:

'No, a large one, large one please.'

Then he took the drink back into the corridor. He had hardly leaned against the wall and had actually not lifted the glass to his lips when he looked up and saw Valerie Whittington suddenly appear at the far end of the corridor as if she had in some miraculous way come up through a trap door.

She started to walk towards him. She walked quite slowly, upright, shoulders square and splendid, the motion of her legs just breaking the front of the dress with ripples. And across the vision of her walking slowly down towards him he caught for the flash of a second the former vision of her in the gabardine mackintosh, schoolgirlish, tense and obliterated, the pigtails tucked into the collar at the back.

A moment later she was saying:

'I know what you're thinking. You're thinking did I have it on under the mackintosh, aren't you?'

'Partly that –'

'I hadn't,' she said. 'It was easy. I got the shop to send it here. I'd hardly a thing on under the mackintosh.'

She started to smile. Her lips were made up, a pale red, and she had managed once again to pile her hair into a mass of curls. She did not speak again for a moment or two. She continued to smile at him with the large circular brown eyes that so often seemed to embrace him with tenderness and then at last she said:

'Does it remind you of anything?'

'Of course,' he said.

To his surprise the two words seemed to move her very deeply and he saw that there were sudden tears in her eyes.

'You're the bestest good one in the world,' she said and she pressed her face against his own.

He too found himself very moved by that. He wished he had nothing to do but take her by one of the long black gloves and into the dark spaces of parkland outside the house, but he remembered Edna Whittington.

Some of his anxiety about this must have crossed his face because almost immediately she said:

'I'll tell you something else you're thinking too, shall I?'

Harry Barnfield, only too well aware of what he was thinking, could not answer.

'You're thinking you've got to dance with me.'

'Well –'

He inclined his head a fraction down and away from her. When he looked up at her again he was struck by a wonderful air of composure about her face, the wide bare shoulders and especially the hands, black in their gloves, clasped lightly before the waist-line of the yellow dress. She could not have looked more composed if she had been wearing the dress for the fiftieth instead of the first time but he knew, somehow, in spite of it all, that she was frightened.

'It's got to be done,' she said, 'and I can't do it without you.'

He tried not to look into her eyes. They were no longer wet with even the suspicion of tears. They gazed back at him, instead, with an almost luminous composure and now, at last, she stretched out her hands.

'Come along,' she said. 'Take me.'

If there had been no other person on the dance floor as he led her on to it some moments later he could hardly have felt more pained and conspicuous. It was like dancing in some sort of competition, naked, in the middle of an empty field, before a thousand spectators.

The amazing thing was that whenever he looked at the face of the girl it was still alight with that astonishing luminous composure.

'Look at me,' she said once. 'Keep looking at me.'

Whether she was thinking of her mother, as he was the whole time, he did not know. He could not see Edna Whittington. But as he danced he became more and more obsessed with the haunting impression that she was watching him from somewhere, evilly and microscopically, waiting for the dance to end.

When it did end he turned helplessly on the floor, arms still outstretched, very much like a child learning to walk and suddenly deprived of a pair of helping hands. The girl, composed as ever, started to move away, the skin of her back shining golden in the light of the chandeliers. The dress itself looked, as she had

43

meant it to do, more than ever the colour of quinces and he saw on her bare arms a bloom of soft down like that on the skin of the fruit.

Then as she turned, smiled at him with an amazing triumphant serenity, holding out her arm for him to take, he saw Edna Whittington.

She was standing not far from the tier of pink chrysanthemums. She did not look, now, like a piece of silver cardboard. She looked exactly like the perfectly straight double-edged blade of a dagger rammed point downwards into the floor: arms perfectly crossed, feet close together, thin body perfectly motionless under the tight silver dress, small microscopic eyes staring straight forward out of a carved white face, fixed on himself and the girl as they crossed the dance floor.

Suddenly he was no longer uneasy, self-conscious, or even disturbed. He began to feel strangely confident, almost antagonistic. And in this sudden change of mood he felt himself guide the arm of the girl, changing her course across the dance floor, steering her straight to Edna Whittington.

Suddenly the band started playing again. The girl gave a quick little cry of delight, turned to him and put her hands on his shoulders. A moment later they were dancing.

Then, for what was to be the last time, she spoke of her mother.

'Is she looking?'

'Yes.'

'Tell me how she looks,' she said. 'You know I dance with my eyes closed.'

'There's no need to think of her.'

Whether it was because of this simple remark of his he never knew, but suddenly she rested her face against his and spoke to him in a whisper.

'You don't know how happy I am,' she said. 'Oh! don't wake me, will you? Please don't wake me.'

She spoke once more as they danced and it was also in a whisper.

'If I told you I loved you here in the middle of this dance floor would you think it ridiculous?'

'That's the last thing I would ever think.'

'I love you,' she said.

At the end of the dance a frigid, pale, supernaturally polite Edna Whittington, holding a glittering yellow cigarette holder in full stretched magenta fingers, met them as they came from the floor. Rigidly and antagonistically he held himself ready to do some sort of brave and impossible battle with her and was surprised to hear her say:

'You did book our table for supper, didn't you, Henry?'

'Of course.'

'You should have told me where it was,' she said. 'Then I could have sat down.'

Throughout the rest of the evening, until one o'clock, this was as sharp as the tone of her reproach and resentment ever grew. She regarded himself, the girl, the dancing, and even the dress, with the same unmitigated calm. When he danced with her, as he did several times, she talked with a kind of repressed propriety, saying such things as:

'It's a most pleasant evening, Henry. And not noisy. Not a brawl. Not half as crowded as I thought it would be.'

'The Hunt's going through a difficult patch,' he said. 'Rather going down, I'm afraid. There isn't the interest. There aren't the chaps.'

'You seem to know a lot of people, even so.'

The more polite and calm she grew the more unreal, he thought, the night became. Alternately he danced with herself and the girl. Friendly and bantering from across the floor came exchanges of manly pleasantry with friends like Punch Warburton, Freddie Jekyll, and George Reed Thompson, the city gentlemen, from odd acquaintances like Dr Frobisher, Justice Smythe, and Colonel Charnly-Rose: stalwart chaps, the solid backbone of the Hunt.

Away somewhere in the distance lay the even greater unreality of Katey: Katey drowned throughout the years of his marriage in mists of gin, Katey the tawdry lioness, Katey with her garlic-raw, smoke-stained fingers, calling him a squeak-mouse.

He felt himself left, over and over again, with the one reality of his life that had ever meant anything. All the rest had shrivelled behind him like black burnt paper. Nothing made any sense in any sort of way any more, except the voice of the girl imploring him with the tenderest, most luminous happiness:

'Oh! Don't wake me, will you? Please don't wake me.'

It would be the best possible thing now, he thought, to get it over quickly: to go straight to Katey, in the morning, and tell her what had happened and how, because of it, he could not go on with the old, damnable, dreary business any longer.

He had arrived at this, the simplest of decisions, by midnight, when Edna Whittington, the girl, and himself sat down to supper. To his relief and surprise it was a remarkably pleasant supper. He poured champagne and the girl, unreproached, was allowed to drink it. He fetched, with his own hands, as she and her mother expressed their fancy, plates of cold chicken or salmon, frozen strawberries and ice-cream, mousse and mayonnaise.

'Did I see someone with pineapple gateau, Henry?' Edna Whittington said and he went dutifully to search for it, pursued by a voice of unbelievably husky-sweet encouragement: 'And be a lamb and find cream, Henry, if you can. Dancing makes me hungry.'

In the next hour the wine, the food and the utter absence of malignity in all that Edna Whittington said or did had lured him into a state where he was no longer apprehensive or uncertain or even ready to go into brave and antagonistic battle against her.

In consequence he was as unprepared as a rabbit sitting before a stoat when, at one o'clock, Edna Whittington looked at her watch, then at the girl, then at himself and said:

'Child, it's time for you to go home. Henry, are you ready to take her?'

10

The girl did not move. He felt the ease of the evening shatter with an ugly crack. His nerves upheld his skin with minute pin-pricks of actual pain.

'I said it was time to go home, child. Get your things. Put your coat on. Mr Barnfield will take you.'

The girl still did not move or speak. Looking at her, he was reminded of the first morning he had ever met her. The innocent insolence had come back to her face again and he understood it now.

'Valerie.'

Edna Whittington waited. He lifted his glass, drank some champagne and waited too. The girl still did not move. She sat with black gloves composed and crossed on the table in front of her. Her eyes, not so wide and circular as they often were, looked half down at her hands, half at the dance floor. Just above the cut of the yellow dress her breasts started to rise and fall rather quickly but otherwise she did not stir.

'I am not in the habit of telling you twice,' Edna Whittington said. The voice was icy. 'Get your things at once and go home.'

The band had begun playing. He clenched the stem of his glass, then relaxed his fingers and looked straight at the ice-grey microscopic eyes of Edna Whittington.

'She's not going home,' he said.

'Will you please mind your own business?'

He found himself drawing on remarkable reserves of calm, backed by the echo of a voice which kept saying 'I feel in a wonderful way that we've been growing up together'.

'Child –'

'I have told you, Edna, that she is not going home.'

'Will you kindly mind your own business!'

He lifted his face, pushed his glass aside and looked straight into the eyes of the girl.

'Shall we dance?' he said.

She hesitated for a fraction of a second. He thought he saw at the same time an indecipherable shadow run across her face, as if she were actually in a turmoil of indecision. And for a moment he was in horror that she would fail, break down, and go home.

Instead she smiled and got up. As the skirt of the yellow dress moved into full view from below the table he remembered the shining lamp of the solitary remaining quince burning in the blue November glassiness above the lake on cooling crystal afternoons, the last phial of the summer's honey, and he knew that now, at last, there was no need to doubt her.

A moment later they were dancing. They danced perhaps twice round the room before she even looked or spoke to him. Then slowly she lifted her face, staring at him as if she could not see him distinctly.

'You're the bestest good one,' she said. 'The most bestest good one in the world.'

And as she spoke he found, suddenly, that he could not bear to look at her. Her huge brown eyes were drowned in tears of happiness.

11

It was nearly three o'clock when Edna Whittington said to him in a husky discordant voice that betrayed, at last, the first snap of anger:

'If you feel you've enjoyed yourself enough I should like to go home.'

'I'm ready whenever you are,' he said. 'Shall I take you alone or shall we all go together?'

She paused before answering; and he thought for a moment that she was going to laugh, as she sometimes did, distastefully. Instead she picked the minutest shred of tobacco from her mouth, looked at it and then flicked it away.

'We'll all go together,' she said. 'I want to talk to you.'

'As far as I'm concerned there's nothing to talk about.'

'She's my daugher,' she said, 'and I want to talk to you.'

'Very well, Edna,' he said. 'Talk to me.'

'I'll talk to you,' she said, 'at home.'

They drove home in frosty darkness, under a starry sky from which the moon had gone down. The girl sat in the back of the car, as before, and no one spoke a word.

When he pulled up before the cottage no one, for nearly half a minute, moved either.

'Will you come in?' Edna Whittington said at last.

'No thank you.'

'Then I'll talk to you here.' She turned to the girl.

'Go inside, Valerie. Here's the key.'

The girl did not move or answer. Harry Barnfield turned, saw her sitting there motionless, mackintoshless, cool in the yellow dress, and said:

'Better go.' He took the key of the cottage from Edna Whittington and handed it to the girl. 'I think it's better.'

'I'm going,' she said very quietly. 'Good night. See you tomorrow.'

Then, and he could only guess what it cost her to do it, the girl leaned over, turned his head with her hand and kissed him on the lips, saying:

'Thank you for everything. Good night.'

Before he could move to open the door for her she was out of the car, running. He heard the key scrape in the lock of the cottage door. Then the door opened and shut and he was alone, in silence, with Edna Whittington.

He said at once: 'I don't know what you have to say, Edna, but it's very late and I'd like to get home.'

'How long has this been going on?' she said.

'About twenty years.'

'If you're going to be flippant I shall probably lose my temper and –'

'I'm not going into explanations,' he said, 'if that's what you want, and the sooner you get it into your head the better.'

She gave the distasteful beginning of a laugh.

'All right. I'll just ask you one question. If that isn't too much?'

'Ask.'

'I suppose you're going to tell me you love this child?'

'Very much.'

'Setting aside the word infatuation,' she said, 'do you suppose she loves you?'

'I do, and she does,' he said.

This time she did laugh. It was husky, unpleasant and briefly sinister.

'I honestly think you're serious about this.'

'I'm not only serious,' he said. 'It's my whole life. And hers.'

She started to light a cigarette. He disliked very much the idea of smoking in cars and he was annoyed as he saw the thin masked face, so drawn that it was almost skeletonized, in the light of the match and then in the burning glow of the cigarette held between the drooping magenta lips.

'You know, Henry,' she said. She blew smoke with what

49

appeared to be unconstricted ease. 'Somebody will have to be told.'

He instantly thought of Katey: Katey the shabby lioness, passing through her blonde phases, her gin-mists; Katey yelling at him, calling him a squeak-mouse; messy, lost, groping, scrofulous Katey.

'Oh! Katey will be told,' he said. 'I'll tell Katey. Tomorrow.'

Edna Whittington blew smoke in a thin excruciated line.

'I wasn't thinking of Katey.'

He couldn't think who else could possibly be told and for a moment he didn't care.

'I daresay my friends have put two and two together,' he said, 'if that's what you mean.'

'I wasn't thinking of your friends.'

'Who then?'

She drew smoke and released it. The smoke had a strange repugnant scent about it. He saw her eyes narrowed in the narrow face, the mouth drawn down, almost cadaverous, and he grasped that this was a smile.

'Valerie,' she said. 'Valerie will have to be told.'

'Told?' he said. The car was half full of smoke, tainted with the scent of it. He felt his annoyance with her rising to temper. 'Told what, for God's sake?'

'About us,' she said. 'You and me.'

'Us? And what about us?'

He suddenly felt uneasy and on edge, nerves probing, the smoke sickening him.

'I think she has to be told,' she said, 'that you and I were lovers. Of course it was some time ago. But wouldn't you think that that was only fair?'

He could not speak. He simply made one of his habitual groping gestures with his hands, up towards his face, as if his spectacles had suddenly become completely opaque with the white sickening smoke of her cigarette and he could not see.

'Not once,' she said, 'but many times. Oh! yes, I think she has to be told. I think so.'

She did not know quite what happened after that. He seemed suddenly to lose control of himself and started yelling. She had never known a Harry Barnfield who could yell, show anger, make foul noises or use violence and now he struck her in the face. The blow partially blinded her, knocking the cigarette from her lips, and in the confusion she heard him yelling blackly as he turned the key of the car.

When she recovered herself the car was travelling down the road, very fast. As it turned under dark trees by a bend, she realized that the headlights were not on. He was bent forward over the wheel, glaring wildly through the thickish spectacles into a half-darkness from which trees rushed up like gaunt shadows.

'I'll kill you, I'll kill you,' he kept saying. 'I'll kill you first.'

She started screaming. Out of the darkness sprang a remembered figure of a Harry Barnfield in a white straw hat, white flannel trousers and a college blazer, a rather soft Harry Barnfield, simple, easy-going, good-time-loving, defenceless, and laughing; one of the vacuous poor fish of her youth, in the days when she had kept a tabulation of conquests in a little book, heading it *In Memoriam: to those who fell*, her prettiness enamelled and calculated and as smart as the strip-poker or the midnight swimming parties she went to, with other, even younger lovers, at long week-ends.

Almost the last thing she remembered was struggling with the door of the car. When at first she could not open it she struck out at Harry Barnfield with her hands. At the second blow she hit him full in the spectacles. She heard them crunch as they broke against the bone of his forehead and then the car door was opening, swinging wide, and she was out of it, half-jumping, half-falling on to the soft frosted grass of the verge.

The car, driven by a blinded Harry Barnfield, swerved on wildly down the hill. She was conscious enough to hear a double scream of brakes as it skimmed the bends and then the crash of glass as it struck, far down, a final telegraph pole.

12

On the afternoon of Harry Barnfield's funeral the wind rose greyly, mild in sudden rainless squalls, across a landscape bare of leaves. The heads of many of the mourners were very bald and as they followed the coffin, in a long slow line, they gave the appearance of so many shaven monks solemnly crossing the churchyard.

At the house, afterwards, there were tea and coffee, with whisky and gin for those who preferred something stronger. The Hunt was well represented. The city gentlemen, J. B. (Punch) Warburton, Freddie Jekyll, and George Reed Thompson, were there. The Sheriff of the County was represented. The Masters of several other Hunts, two from a neighbouring county, together with three local magistrates and two doctors from the local hospital were there. Colonel and Mrs Charnly-Rose, Justice Smythe and his two daughters, both excellent horsewomen, and several clergymen, farmers, horse-dealers, and corn-merchants were there. It was impossible to say how many people, from all sections of society, from villagers to men of title had come to pay tribute to Harry Barnfield, who as everyone knew was a good huntsman, a good sort, a great horse-lover, and a man in whom there was no harm at all.

In addition to the tea and coffee, whisky and gin there were also cucumber sandwiches and many people said how excellent they were. Several people, as they ate them, walked out of the crowded house into the garden, for a breath of fresh air. Others strolled as far as the edges of the meadows, where Harry Barnfield's horses were grazing and his run of brushwood jumps stood dark and deserted beneath a squally sky.

As they walked they wondered, as people do at funerals, about the future: what would happen, who would get what and above all what Katey would do. Across the fields and the hillside the wind blew into separated threads the wintry blades of grass, over the parched fox-like ruffles of dead bracken and, rising, rattled the grey bones of leafless boughs. 'We'll miss him on the five o'clock,' the city gentlemen said and confessed that they had no idea what would happen, who would get what or above all what Katey would do.

Nor could anyone possibly hear, in the rising winter wind, in the falling winter darkness, any sound of voices weeping across the hillside in the night-time.

Night Run to the West

He first met her on an early spring evening when he was doing the night run from London to the West, a journey that he could do in six and a half hours, if things went well, with a full load on the truck. That night he was about halfway, somewhere on the long chalk switchbacks about Salisbury, when he blew a gasket. An almost full moon was shining starkly on the slopes of white hill-sides, where leafing bushes of hawthorn looked very much like shadowy herds of cattle crouched and sleeping. It was almost eleven o'clock by that time and he pulled up at the first house he saw.

He was glad to see a light in one window and still more glad to see the twin white cups of a telephone on the side of the house and the wires running across the garden, above a neglected mass of old lilac and apple trees, in the clear moon. At first sight it did not seem to be a very large house; he was deceived by the flat brick front, by what was really a large hooded doorway that through long years had become dwarfed to a mere hole under a drab arch of dusty ivy. It was only later that he discovered that its frontal narrowness concealed a house that seemed to stretch back without ending; as if successive owners had been shamed by that flat funereal front into adding piece after piece behind, until the final glassy crown had been achieved by putting on a large hexagonal conservatory at the back.

She came to the door with a book in her hand and wearing a dressing gown. At least, that first time, he had the idea that it was a dressing gown. Afterwards he saw her once more in the same garment, in better light, and he realized then that it was a dark blue woollen dress, old-fashioned, waistless, tied about the middle with a cord. She continually played with this cord, making motions of tying and untying it, without achieving any change in it at all.

He apologized and raised his cap to her and asked if he might use the telephone.

'What is the matter?' she said.

'My truck,' he said. 'I blew a gasket. I want to get a garage –'

'There's no telephone here,' she said.

He said something about the wires going across the garden but she said:

'I had it cut off. There wasn't much use for it. Nobody called much.' And then: 'There's a box half a mile down the road.'

He said thank you and how sorry he was for disturbing her at that time of night and asked which way the box was.

'It's on the corner of the little road. The one on the left you passed a little way back.' Up to that moment she had been framed with an almost faceless obscurity under the canopy of ivy, against a background of a single electric bulb of meagre wattage that seemed to bathe the hall and staircase behind her in a kind of smoky orange varnish. Now she came out into the moonlight and said:

'I'll just show you. Where's your truck? Where are you from?'

'London,' he said and he found she was looking with a sort of microscopic, eager curiosity, almost queerly, up into his face.

'London,' she said. 'You drive all that way? This time of night?'

'Three nights a week,' he said.

'Where do you sleep?'

'Sleep before I start,' he said. 'I get five minutes doss sometimes in the cab –'

He could not see her face very clearly in the moonlight and now he discovered it was for two reasons. She had a habit of walking with her head down, as if she was fascinated by her hands playing with such restless indetermination with the cord of her dress. Her face too was three parts obscured by a frame of thick black hair. Afterwards he saw her hair in that particular fashion, like the dress, only once more, but that first night it gave him an impression of untidy, uneasy strength, so that he found himself suddenly glad that the telephone box was down the road.

Then she said: 'Does it mean your truck is stranded? Can't you go any farther? How much farther have you to go?'

'About a hundred and fifty,' he said.

She seemed to consider this and once again he found her looking at him with microscopic inquisitiveness, from eyes that were simply two dark holes under the drawn-down frame of hair. Then suddenly she said:

'You can use the telephone if you like. That wasn't true what I said about being cut off. But I didn't know who you were – you've got to be careful, haven't you? But I can see you're all right now – you're a nice fellow. I can see that.'

'Thanks all the same. I won't bother you. I'll hop down the road.'

'No, no,' she said. 'Oh! no. Don't do that. It's a long way. Don't do that. Come in now. You can use the telephone. I've got some tea going. I always have tea going at this time. I drink tea all night.'

He thought for a moment that she was going to pull him by the hand. Her own hand seemed to snatch at the moonlight in a hungry sort of gesture, almost a pounce, not unlike the grab that a child might make, too late, at a butterfly'.

'You could ring up the Acme Service,' she said. 'They'll come out. They're four miles down the road. Then you can have some tea while you're waiting.'

He thanked her and said all right, he would, and he followed her into the house. The telephone, an old-fashioned fixed wall model, was in the hall, under the single small electric bulb, and while he was telephoning he could smell the fumes of a spirit kettle coming from a room somewhere beyond.

The garage would be an hour, they said; they had only one night-service breakdown truck and that was out. When he heard this he remembered he still had his supper in a haversack in the cab.

'Where are you going?' she said.

'I've got a bit of food in the truck,' he said. 'I'll just get it –'

'Oh! No. Don't bother with that. I've got food. If you're hungry I have food.'

So he followed her into the first of what he knew later were many rooms beyond it. It was a large room, furnished in a sort of suburban Jacobean, with a heavy beamed ceiling, encrusted white wallpaper, a big panelled oak fireplace and a bulb-legged dining table in the centre. In one corner was a divan covered by a blue and purple paisley shawl. She sat untidily, almost sloppily, on this divan, in the light of a small brass table-lamp and the mauve flames of the spirit kettle, and told him that this was where she slept.

'That's when I do sleep,' she said. 'I don't sleep much. I'm like you – awake most of the night. I have tea and read and then drop off when it's day.'

He saw that the spirit kettle was silver, like the big teapot she presently filled with water. The cups were of thin china, fancily flowered, with high handles.

'I hear the trucks go by all night,' she said. 'It's funny – I expect I've heard you go by many a time. What's your name? Mine's Broderick. Mrs Broderick.'

'Charlie,' he said. 'Charlie Williams.'

'Like the prince, eh?' she said.

Now, in the double light of the lamp and the spirit kettle, he could see her face more clearly. It was a very white face, the kind of face moulded by sleepless nights and airless days into a mask of paste that made it difficult for him to tell how old she was. He noticed she did not smile. Once or twice it occurred to him that she was a woman of fifty or so, and then suddenly her head would turn sideways in the mauve and yellow glow of light. The profile, no longer depressed by the huge black bunch of hair, became delicate, the line of the pale lips unexpectedly much younger.

All this time she was lighting one cigarette after another: lighting it, putting it down, forgetting it, lighting a second from the first and then forgetting again. In this distracted fashion it was some time before she remembered she had promised him some food.

'I'm sorry. What would you like? Meat or something? Some cheese?'

'Cheese,' he said, 'thank you.'

She went away and came back after some moments with the bone of a leg of lamb and a loaf of bread and a big bone-handled carving knife. She held the bone in one hand and sliced off chunks of meat with the other and laid them between pieces of bread.

'You remind me of somebody,' she said. 'I've got an idea I've seen you before.'

'Perhaps going by in the truck,' he said.

'No,' she said, 'it couldn't be that.'

She seemed to lapse into a momentary coma of thought, disturbed, stubbing her cigarette absently into a saucer, her head down.

'Tell me about yourself,' she said. 'I know you live in London and you come by three nights a week. What else? Where do you live?'

'Paddington.'

'Married?'

'No,' he said. 'Not me.'

'Not you?' she said. 'A young fellow like you?'

'Pick 'em up and lay 'em down,' he said, 'that's me for the moment. I don't want to get tied up. Who wants a night driver anyway? They want you home and in bed.'

She laughed for the first time. Her voice had been pitched rather low, much as if she had become fixed in the habit of talking to herself, but the laugh was several notes higher, lifting, rather delicate, a pleasant singing spring of relief.

'You make me laugh,' she said.

She turned up the flame of the spirit kettle and then poured more water on the tea. She filled his cup and her own again and said:

'When will you be going back?'

'Ought to be going back tomorrow,' he said. 'Depends on the gasket.'

'It's funny about people,' she said. 'You coming by here hundreds of times and then you suddenly have trouble and come in and here we are talking.'

It was after midnight when the breakdown truck arrived. As he walked out into the road with the driver he had an impression that she was coming too, but when he turned she had gone from the doorway and back into the house.

It was while he and the driver were still fixing the tow-chain that he heard her coming across the road. She was running with light, almost palpitating steps and she had a vacuum flask and a paper parcel in her hands.

'I almost thought I wouldn't catch you,' she said. 'It's just a flask of tea and the lamb-bone. You can have it at the garage while you wait. I saw how you tucked into the lamb –'

'That's kind of you,' he said.

'Not a bit. You can bring the flask back when you come by again. I'd be glad of it back.'

She stood in the road, huddled, thoughtful, watching the two of them hitching the tow-chain, for about ten minutes longer. Her face was dead white in the moon. When the chain was fixed and just before he got up into the cab he thanked her again and said good night. She lifted a thin arm in farewell and at the same moment he heard from the direction of the house a man's voice calling, in a snapped, thin screech, what he afterwards knew was her Christian name:

'Francie! Francie! For heaven's sake where are you? – Francie!'

And as if it had nothing to do with her or she had not heard it or did not care if she heard it she stood impassively by the trucks and said to him up in the cab:

'Don't forget the flask, will you? I shall be here.'

Before he could speak the voice screeched for her again but she still stood there, unmoved, in impassive indifference, waiting for the trucks to go. He called down that he would not forget the flask. In that moment he saw her smile again and that was how he came to see her for the second time.

She must have thought that he was coming back by night. But the garage was small, the size he wanted in gaskets was not in stock, and it was well past breakfast time before he was on the road again. In that way, instead of coming back by night, he was driving through the long switchbacks of low chalk hillsides soon after noon the following day.

Stopping the truck by the house, getting down with the flask in his hand, looking at the ugly deceptive brick front half-lost in its scabby broken apple tree, he did not attach much importance to it all. He had had kindness on the road from women before and he had often given kindnesses, in the way truck drivers do, to people in trouble or cars that had broken down, and sometimes women had slipped a note in his hand. There had been a time, once, in Wiltshire, on a late summer evening, when he had helped an old woman get back a charging sow into a sty. The old woman was weeping; she kept saying that her old man would knock her brains out when he came back from the pub and found she had let the pig loose; but he comforted her and she too, like the others, gave him tea. She even promised him a cut of bacon when the pig was killed and cured, but he had never bothered to go back and claim it. When you travelled about so much, especially at night, you came up against some odd capers.

It had been rather warm for April that afternoon and with the sun full on the glass of the cab he had been glad to drive in his shirt sleeves. He felt cheerful in the sun; already he was beginning to feel that he could look forward to the warmer, easier nights of summer-time.

The bell on the front door was one of those old-fashioned iron pulls that connect far back into the house, and he pulled at it several times before he realized that it was no longer working. He tried the front door gently but it was locked and he was thinking of leaving the vacuum flask in the porch when he thought he heard sounds from the back of the house.

That was how he first discovered how far back the house extended. Bit by bit, bay by bay, its owners had grotesquely enlarged it, trying to cover, and at the same time always increasing, its original hideousness. On one side a tower, a red-brick pepper box with terra-cotta sills and facings, had been built, and above it was a flag-pole. Beyond it was a wing that seemed insecure in its attachment to the rest of the house and that someone had fortified with four stout stone buttresses.

And then, at the extreme back, behind another shrubbery of lilac and rose and flowering currant, all deep in the witherings of last summer's grasses, he came upon the conservatory. It was hexagonal in shape and its upper windows were panes of coloured glass, deep blue, green, yellow, bright blood red. And to his astonishment it was full of flowers.

He did not know much about flowers but as he pushed open the door the scent of them from the steamy interior poured out at him with powerful intoxication. That afternoon the inside temperature of the house must have been a hundred degrees; he could actually see steam rising from rows of pipes under the banks of staged flowers. He did not know the name of a single one of these flowers; he was simply stupefied, for the next few seconds, by the mass of exotic blossom rising from banks of dripping fern.

That was only the beginning of his astonishment. Some seconds later he was aware of being looked at. What seemed to be a face, sprinkled, flower-fashion, with splashes and blobs of blue and crimson and yellow and green, was staring at him from under the rim of a pale straw hat.

This small figure resolved itself presently into that of a man in a biscuit-coloured alpaca jacket, a narrow starched collar and black pin-stripe trousers. The fact that he wore no neck-tie gave a semi-naked, half-finished appearance to what was otherwise a dapper little body that sat with a kind of doll-like erectness in a wicker chair. The face would have been deep yellow under the sparse white hair if it had not been blobbed with scraps of reflection from the coloured panes in the roof above. It was these blotches of mingled blue and crimson and yellow and green that gave it an unhealthy appearance, the total unreality of a curious, bright disease.

For some seconds the figure did not move. It seemed torpid in the hot and steamy air. The lids of the eyes were exactly like those of a frog flabbily sunk in stupor.

Then Williams saw them shoot into squinty wakefulness, and the voice that screeched at him was the voice he had already heard, once before, calling the woman Francie.

'Get out,' it said.

'O.K.,' Williams said, 'no harm. I was just looking for Mrs Broderick to give her the tea-flask back.'

'Mrs Broderick is not here. Get out.'

'All right, guvnor, all right.'

'And to bring what back?'

'The tea-flask. That's all. It doesn't matter though. I can leave it here –'

'Where did you get that thing?'

'She lent it to me. The other night. I busted a gasket and she give me some tea.'

'Get out!' he screeched. 'I don't like people roaming about here. I don't like louts in here.'

'Louts?'

Up to that moment Williams had been patient, unruffled, a little amused. Now he felt the personal affront, the whip of the word louts, go ripping him with anger. The small figure in the chair suddenly looked to him like a dressed-up maggot. It reminded him powerfully of one of those advertisements for pest-killers in which grub and caterpillar sit up on their hind legs with expressions of sinister greed among the flowers they live to destroy. He felt his big arms twitch as he looked at it. He felt that with one single twist of them he could have rubbed it out. There would have been a little mess on the wet, steaming bricks between stagings of bright flowers and then it would all have been over.

Then he calmed; his sense of humour came back.

'Look here, grandad, don't you call me lout. I don't like it, see? See that, grandad? I don't like it.'

In a moment his impression of looking at a dressed-up maggot was gone. His vision cleared. He saw before him once again nothing but the bloodless torpid little figure, pathetic and somehow spurious in the straw hat.

'You want to git out in the fresh air, grandad,' he said. 'It ain't healthy in here. You git hot under the collar –'

'Get out!' The screech, this time, was several times louder than before. It set the mouth blubbering with a series of foaming convulsions. 'You cheap lout! – get out of here!'

A moment later Williams caught himself in the act of throwing the vacuum flask. He actually had it poised above his head. At the word cheap all his rage came rushing back.

'You call me cheap just once more, grandad, and I'll lay you among the daisies –'

He did not know quite what he was ready to do at that moment. Once more he could see the maggot in the chair; once more he was aware of the ease with which he could rub it out.

It was her voice which stopped all this:

'Good afternoon,' she said. He turned to see her standing behind him, in the blue old-fashioned dress: grey-eyed, pale. calm, almost phlegmatic, her appearance, as he thought, somewhere between a governess and a housekeeper who had come in time to stop a bout of rowdiness between two boys.

'I beg pardon, Mrs Broderick,' Williams said. 'I just came to return the tea-flask. Only I don't think grandad likes me.' His humour, dry and sprightly, was already back. 'Don't like my face or something, do you, grandad?'

He turned as he said this and he saw that the chair was empty. And all at once he felt himself tricked by an illusion that it had never been occupied. The maggot was a myth; the straw hat, the torpid-eyed creature sitting among the sweltering forest of fern and flower had never been.

'Where's grandad?' He was laughing wryly. 'Must have slipped down a hole or something –'

'I'm sorry he annoyed you.'

She paused and was looking at him again with grey, microscopic curiosity. 'Don't let him do it again. Just stop him. Be hard with him. It's the only way. It's just his childishness.'

It had been too dark to notice the colour of her eyes before. Now he saw how brilliant and startling their greyness was. He saw also that his impression of a woman of fifty or so was quite ridiculous. In the bright afternoon light she was clearly not more than forty. And if the thick black hair had drooped less about her face and the blue woollen dress less about her figure he might even have given her, he thought, the benefit of thirty-five.

'I thought you would come last night,' she said.

He explained how he had not been able to make it earlier.

'I had the tea made. I waited. I suppose a hundred trucks must have gone by.'

'Well, thank you for the flask,' he said. 'I got to push on.'

'Oh! no,' she said. 'I've got some tea made. Just a cup. And there's something I want to ask you. Oh! it won't take a moment – you can spare a moment, can't you?'

She smiled; the grey eyes were steeped in a brilliant mist of persuasion, not very obvious or insistent, but so positive that it did not enter his head to do anything else but follow her into the house.

The tea, as she said, was already made, but this time in a big brown homely sort of pot. 'I know you like it strong,' she said. 'You drivers always do.' She carved him from a large square block a slice of heavy fruit cake. 'And you like that too, I know.'

He did not know quite what to say to this easy and friendly attention and he started talking, as people mostly do, of the weather.

'It's turned out a nice day,' he said. 'Like summer in the cab.'

'Oh! has it?' she said. 'I hadn't noticed. I'm always asleep in the daytime. Or half-asleep. Besides it always rains here, across the hills. This is where the cloud breaks.'

For the next few minutes, as he drank a second cup of tea and ate a second piece of cake, he kept thinking of the little man in the conservatory. He was puzzled about the torpid grub-like figure crowned by the straw hat. He was mystified by its sudden disappearance out of the forest of flowers. He wanted to ask about it and did not know how to frame his question. Instead he said:

'You were going to ask me something, weren't you?'

'When you've finished your tea,' she said. 'Another cup? Another piece of cake?'

He thanked her and said no, it was really time he got on. The grey eyes were fixed on his forearms, where the light brown hairs were almost sandy against the muscular flesh still white from winter.

He suddenly felt slightly self-conscious about this gaze and got up. What was she going to ask him? he said.

'You won't think I'm imposing on you, will you?' she said. Now she too was standing up. She was fairly tall, so that her face was level with his own. 'You won't, will you?' She was smiling; the grey eyes were pleasantly pellucid, mercurial, with soft light. 'I feel it's awful cheek, I know it is – but would you do a little errand in London?'

'Well, sure if I can.'

'It's just a note about a dress,' she said.

She had an envelope in her hands.

'If you would just take this note to this address, they will give you the dress and then perhaps you could bring it back next time you come down? Could you?' She smiled again and gave a relieved sort of sigh. 'I feel so ashamed about asking you.'

It crossed his mind that it was odd she could not post her envelope, but she seemed ready for that:

'The last time they sent a dress down the box broke open and there was a fruit stain on it. I could never wear it. I could never get it out.'

She saw him looking at the address on the envelope and said:

'Oh! yes, it's off Wigmore Street. It isn't a stone's throw from you. I've told them who you are in the note and it will be all right. Are you sure you don't mind?'

'Not a bit.'

'I'm so glad. When will you be back?'

'Day after tomorrow.'

'At night?'

'At night,' he said. 'About eleven.'

She came out with him as far as the truck. The sun was hot on the white chalk road. Sprigs of apple-blossom were breaking on the old scabby trees; the crest of every hedgerow was sprinkled with the bright lace of new leaves.

'Good-bye,' she said. She waited for him to climb up into the cab. 'It's most awfully kind of you to do that for me.'

Something, at the last moment, made him feel that he was entitled to a gesture in return.

'By the way,' he said, 'who was grandad? He didn't seem to like me.'

Obliquely she looked past him, as if troubled by the sun.

'That's Calvin,' she said. 'That's my husband.'

The motor was running; he let in the clutch smoothly. She stood in the road, watching him with a face that was negative, with grey eyes that were still so unstirred and so incalculable that they were almost without identity.

'At least what's left of him,' she said. 'But take no notice of that.'

After that he began to stop at the house every time he went down and every time he came back again. At first she provided the excuses to stop. And they seemed, he thought, like casual excuses. There was a dress to be brought down from London, another to be taken back. She was short of tea once and he bought a small chest for her in Yeovil as he came up from the West. Through the nights when she did not sleep she did a great deal of reading and now and then he would collect a parcel of books for

her in London. Once or twice there was change from the money
she gave him for these things and each time she said:

'No, you keep that. That's for you. Buy yourself a drink with
that.'

Then, after a week or two, there was no need for the invention
of excuses. It became a simple and congenial habit to stop by the
craggy, blossoming apple trees, whose scent he could smell in the
warm wet May darkness. It became something to look forward
to: tea, a meat sandwich, a hunk of fruit cake, a rest in the dark
subdued house, in the mauve light of the spirit flames, perhaps
a wash after the oily hot drive down.

And perhaps because it was now always night when he saw her
he did not, for a week or two, notice any change in her. But
presently the days were almost fully lengthened; the evenings
began to be white with mid-summer. And on an evening in early
June, after a long bright day, the light had still not faded when he
parked the truck.

That evening the front door of the house was open but she was
not lying down, as she nearly always was, on the paisley-shawled
divan in the big front room. The spirit lamp was not burning. The
room was still quite full of light.

While he waited he walked about the room, looking at many
photographs of her that stood on tables and shelves and the big
oak mantelpiece. There were perhaps a dozen or fifteen of these
pictures of her and he had never really noticed them before.

He was still looking at them when she came in. She said something about Calvin being naughty, Calvin playing up, and how
tiresome it all was. 'He is getting so that he has a taste for the
barbitone,' she said. 'Just a craving. Like people do for whisky.
He used to sleep well with one or two. Now it's three or four or
five.'

She had been quick to notice that he had been looking at the
photographs and now she said:

'Oh! don't look at those awful pictures of me. They're deadly.
I ought to hide them up.'

'I thought they were very nice,' he said.

'Oh! you did? Which one did you like best?'

More at random than anything else he picked on one in which

65

she was wearing a white blouse and rather tight-fitting black skirt; the blouse had a square neck, rather low, across which there was a strip of lace insertion. Her dark hair was piled rather lightly and her figure, under the smooth white blouse, was thrown rather high up, so that she looked full-fleshed and assertive and strikingly young.

'Why that one?' she said. 'Why do you like that one?'

'I don't know,' he said. 'I just do –'

'I'm glad you like that one. Do you know why?'

He said no, he couldn't think why.

'Because it's the last one taken before I was married,' she said. 'Ten years ago. Seems like a life-time.'

The room was still quite light and perhaps he turned instinctively to see if the woman he had known for only four or five weeks could possibly be the same person as the girl in the picture. He was at once arrested by some odd quality of change in her; she seemed to have become, for some reason, uncannily like the younger girl. There was an air of something fresher about her face and his apparent difficulty about accounting for this seemed to amuse her.

'You can see something different in me?' She was smiling, showing her teeth.

'I think there is something different,' he said.

'Don't you know what it is?'

No: in his obtuse, clumsy, masculine way he did not know what it was.

She gave her body a full turn, suddenly, and then said:

'It's my hair. Didn't you notice? I'm doing it in the old way.'

His surprise at his own stupidity at not noticing how her hair was now piled high again, achieving an effect of lightness and freshness in her entire face, must have been responsible for him giving a gasp of pleasure.

'You like it, do you?' she said.

'Yes.'

'I hoped you would. I went down today and had it done. You know why today?'

He had not the slightest idea about that either. The circumstances had the effect, altogether, of bewitching him a little and he could only stare.

'Because it's my birthday,' she said. 'At least it will be at twelve o'clock. Did you bring the dress?'

'Yes, I got it.'

'That's for my birthday too. I treated myself.'

The dress was in its box on a chair. She untied the string and parted the tissue wrappings and said, 'Emerald. Do you think emerald will suit me? You don't think green is unlucky, do you?'

She took out the dress and held it in front of her, pinning it to her shoulders with the points of her fingers. The light was fading by that time and the colour of the dress was a sharp strong green.

'Well, say if you like it.'

Yes, he liked it, he said. He was still feeling the effects of a sense of slight bewitchment and he hardly heard her say:

'Shall I put it on? I was going to put it on for the party anyway.' He could not conceive what she meant by a party but she went on: 'A party for me. Tonight – just you and me. That's if you'll stay. You don't mind if I slip it on here, do you? It's nearly dark now –'

She began to slip off the dress she was wearing, the old blue woollen dress that he had seen several times before, and then she put the new dress quickly over her head and shoulders. In her haste she forgot to undo the clips at the neck, so that she had to take it off and begin again. Something about this repeated upward stretch of her white arms in the darkening room turned his sense of bewitchment into a final moment of distraction. In another moment he was holding her by the soft upper part of her arms. His blood was beating heavily through him and she was reaching up to him with her mouth.

She found it hungrily; and then, when he had kissed her for that first time, she had only one thing to say.

'I began to think,' she said, 'that you'd never notice me.'

He had not intended to go as far as that; he had never had any thought that it would be more than a casual episode. The situation took him by surprise. It was another pick 'em up and lay 'em down affair and he could not resist its distraction.

The Grapes of Paradise

But that night, after what she called her party, he was not so much aware of the pleasant nature of her body as the insistence of her voice, suddenly freed, emotionally charged, talking on into the morning, disjointedly, telling him about herself, about Calvin, her marriage and how she had come there and what a dreary bore it was.

The party had consisted of a bottle of gin, a pile of thick ham sandwiches which she had tried in vain, in a bungling way, to make elegant by removing the crusts, and a large white sugary cake, her birthday cake, made by herself and inscribed with her own best wishes:

'Lisa: A Happy Birthday.'

He was puzzled by this inscription.

'I thought your name was Francie,' he said.

'So it is,' she said. 'But Lisa – that's my pet name. It's a name somebody used to call me.'

'Old flame?'

'In a way,' she said, 'yes. We went to a play together once and there was a girl in it named Lisa. You know how people are. Perhaps he saw something in her that was like me.'

Anyway, she said, she didn't want to talk about that. Her hands groped for him in the semi-darkness. Where was he? she said. He seemed so far away. Then her mouth found his face again and she said:

'That's better than any talking, isn't it? Don't you like that better?'

Then, some time later, he was saying:

'That fellow. The one you went to the play with. Was he the one you thought I was like?'

'Partly,' she said. 'But you're bigger. You're a bigger man altogether –'

'What made you marry this one?' he said.

'Calvin?' Her voice, he remembered long afterwards, was surprisingly casual. It seemed, he thought, almost off-hand. 'Oh! the usual – sort of rebound.'

'From the other one?'

'He was killed,' she said. Emotionlessly she spoke of the war, a raid somewhere, a bomb that with impersonal lack of drama had wiped a man out. 'He went into a cinema somewhere and never came out again. There was nothing left. We were going to be married. I was going to have someone all to myself, and then – '

She laughed with a sort of dry stutter, almost a cough.

'And now here I am. Stuck,' she said. 'At first I came as house-keeper. Then he wanted to marry me.' Her voice was flat. 'Like that it was cheaper. He didn't have to pay me.'

He said it occurred to him, not for the first time, that a simple solution would be to pack her bags and walk out.

Again she gave the short laugh that was between a cough and a stutter.

'Walk out? On about four hundred thousand?'

Before he had time to do anything about expressing his astonishment she asked him if he had ever heard of the Fresco Patent Clip Spring? She hadn't more than a vague idea what it was herself. It had something to do with time-fuses, she thought.

'I think it's fuses,' she said. 'Something to do with the way a bomb goes off or a gun fires. I've never even seen one. But Calvin invented it. He draws a royalty on it until the end of time.'

Thoughtfully he considered his picture of the little figure in the straw hat, the torpid angry maggot among the flowers.

'It wouldn't be bad, would it, four hundred thousand?' she said.

Her way of saying this too was casual. He could not even determine whether she was really addressing him or not. They were lying together on the shawl-covered divan. He could feel her body pressing against him in the darkness, and himself the centre core of a quietness that was as unreal as her voice going on to frame her thoughts:

'What would you do with that much money if you had it? With even half of it? You know what I'd do? What I'm going to do? I'll have a house on an island somewhere where the sea's warm, where I can swim all day and lie in the sun. How's that, do you think? After years in a dump like this.'

'How do you know you'll get this money?'

'I've seen the will,' she said. 'I know. It's in my favour. There isn't anyone else except me. And besides, he's fond of me. He likes me.'

Walk out, his mind began saying, walk out. Before it's too late.

Before you're in any deeper. Don't be a fool. And all the time he knew that he was a fool to be lying there with her, a woman of that particular sort of temperament, with a husband somewhere upstairs, and he turned involuntarily at the sound of a bough scratching the wall of the house outside.

'Lie still,' she said. 'There's nothing to be worried about.'

Worried? he thought. Why should he be worried by the wizened maggoty little figure of grandad? Worried by grandad? That made him laugh.

'What are you laughing at?' she said.

Something made him say: 'Me on an island. I was thinking of that. Nothing to do but lie in the sun all day. Swim and lie in the sun. What a caper.'

He laughed again, amused by the sheer fantasy of it.

'What's funny about it?' she said.

'I'm a night driver. I drive a two-ton truck.'

'You're twenty-five,' she said. 'Is that what you want to do all your life? Drive a truck? Slog up and down here?'

Was it what he wanted? No, he supposed it wasn't. He hadn't thought about it. He must always have supposed it was what he wanted. He'd got used to it. It wasn't bad.

Before he could speak she stirred in the darkness. She raised herself on one elbow and leaned over him, brushing her mouth against his face with a surprising, delicate tenderness and the curve of her body against his own.

'It's nearly daylight,' she said. 'You must love me and leave me. You're hours behind.'

'I'll make it up.'

He lay still on the divan, resting the back of his head on his hands.

'Don't you want to go?' she said. 'Do you like it with me? Do I make it so nice for you?'

'I wouldn't call it bad.'

She laughed quietly, kissing him again.

'I wish I was coming with you. A free day and a long ride – just you and me in the truck. That would be nice wouldn't it. But perhaps some day I will ride with you – what do you think? When I get out of this?'

'But not in a truck.'

'No, not in a truck,' she said.

When she came out to see him drive away she had her birthday cake wrapped up for him in a box.

'It seems funny, doesn't it?' she said. 'Having to make your own birthday cake and put your name on it and give it to yourself? If it hadn't been for you I wouldn't have known I had a birthday.'

For the first time she seemed to speak with bitterness; she seemed to gasp in suppression of a sob. He felt all at once affectionately sorry for her. He thought how touching and nice she looked standing there, in the growing daylight, below his driving-cab, in the new emerald dress.

'That's how I live,' she said. 'I might as well be a widow on a shoe-string.'

In a sudden effort to cheer her up he winked.

'See you tomorrow, Lisa.'

The grey eyes seemed to draw slightly together as they smiled, like two bright steel points closing together to hold him there.

'I love you for saying that,' she said.

It was three weeks later when he drove up, late one night, in a raging thunderstorm. The August air was heavy with the stifling vapour of nearly a day of hot and steaming rain. In the big numerous flashes of lightning he could see whole fields of wheat and barley lying flattened as white straw mats under a dripping sky. And as the weight of his truck hit the floods of water the road in front of him kept exploding in white waterspouts, like the echoes of thunder.

He had never been so glad of the thought of her as he was that night. His clothes were drenched with sweat and most of the time his thought was of a dry room, tea, something to eat, a chance to lie down in quietness with her, out of the harsh dazzle of his headlights on the streaming windscreen in the humid darkness and rain.

But the moment he saw her he knew that there was no chance of quietness. Instead of the usual lamp by the divan, together with the blue flame of the spirit kettle, he saw that the big heavy

Jacobean chandelier was full on. She was walking up and down underneath it, smoking a cigarette, pulling hard at it in agitation. On the table was a full ash-tray of cigarette stubs. The front of her dress was dusty with ash and for the first time since he had seen her, on the night he had blown the gasket, he thought she looked untidy and old and tired.

She was so agitated that she made no attempt to kiss him. In fact in a queer way he had an idea that she resented his presence there.

'I didn't think you'd turn up in this,' she said.

He said something about having to try to make it whatever the weather was, but he had an impression that she neither heard nor cared what he said. Some of the time he had been thinking of her idea of an island in the sunshine. 'Somewhere out of this blasted rain. Out of this God-forsaken climate,' he had been thinking. 'Anything to get out of this.'

And now, almost as if she knew he had been thinking exactly that, she said:

'I think Calvin is on his way out. I think he might even be dead. I daren't go up to him.'

He said 'God,' very quietly, under his breath. Through his mind went a reminder, jolting, preposterous, a little sickening, of the four hundred thousand she had spoken about and he said unsteadily:

'What makes you think that? What's the matter with him?'

'It's the dud heart,' she said. 'And the thundery weather. He can't get his breath in this weather.'

'I better push on,' he said.

'No, don't go,' she said. 'We've got to find out if he's all right before you go.'

We? he thought and a first sensation of wild uneasiness shot through him like a palpitation.

'He always has a glass of whisky about nine and then two or three tablets. That puts him off generally,' she said.

'Has he had them yet?'

'Not yet,' she said. 'I went up at six and he was lying there like a stone. I haven't been up since. I daren't go up. He was lying there like a stone.'

'Must have been asleep.'

'It didn't look like sleep. It looked queer. Different from sleep,' she said.

He did not know quite how he walked up the wide carpetless oak stairs. His shoes were so noisy that he felt a horrible and compelling notion that he ought to take them off in deference to the possible dead lying there somewhere in the rooms above him. At the last moment she had reminded him to take the whisky bottle and a glass, but he had even forgotten to ask her which room, and then suddenly she called up to him from below:

'You'll see it. The room at the end of the corridor. There's a light. There's always a light there.'

He felt he ceased, in that moment, to be himself. It was exactly as if he had taken his shoes off and was walking under the compulsion of a series of muffled reflexes. And before he really knew it he was in the bedroom.

It was a big bedroom and in the centre of it, not pushed back against the wall, was a cheap brass bed. The floor was covered with linoleum and a single night-light in a saucer was burning on a table beside the bed. On the west wall of the room a high sash window had been left open and rain was pouring in on the linoleum, which shone like grey wet skin in the flashes of lightning.

'Mr Broderick,' he said quietly, 'Mr Broderick.'

There was to be one more occasion after that when he was to stand there before the little bloodless figure and say the same words and wait with breathless, still more terribly anxious tension for an answer. This first time there was no answer. All his own breathing seemed to have stopped by that time and all he could hear in return for his third mention of Broderick's name was the stiff croak of a throat slowly gasping, like the dry gyrations of some old unoiled machine, for breath.

Then he saw Broderick sitting up, dummy-wise, hands stiff and outstretched, in the bed. He did not know whether it was pure relief or vexation or fright about something that made him stride across the room and shut the window. The edges of its frame were so wet that his hands slipped as he grasped it and it came down with a crack on the flooded sill. Rain was still coming down

73

heavily but the storm was veering away now and the flashes of lightning were simply like far-off stabbing light-echoes on the hills.

'Mrs Broderick sent me up to shut the window,' he said.

That seemed as good an excuse as any, he thought, to offer to the figure that had not moved an inch in the bed since he had opened the door. Now he went a few paces nearer the bed and said:

'All right, grandad? Why don't you go to sleep now?'

He rubbed the sweaty palms of his hands down the sides of his trouser-legs and began to feel better as he saw, in the glow of the night-light, the little eyes responding with dumb delicacy to his stare.

'You remember me, don't you, grandad?' Again there was no answer. 'Why don't you be a good boy, grandad, and have your whisky and drop off for a while?'

He was quite near the bed now. The sound of Broderick gasping for breath reminded him of the croak of the sheep he sometimes heard when he stopped his truck in some remote still place in the dead of night-time.

And suddenly, inexplicably, again perhaps out of pure relief, he felt sorry for him. There was something appalling and touching about the little erect dummy sitting there in half-darkness, in mute paralysis, in the sound of thunder and driving rain, like a child frightened by a storm.

Something made him put out his hands and touch the hands that lay outstretched on the bed. The contact of their scabby frigid flesh was something he never forgot. He felt he was touching death in living flesh and only once again, afterwards, was he so repulsed and so frightened.

'Come on, grandad,' he said. He took the unresisting, terribly light shell of bone and skin in his hands and tried to make it, very gently, lie back on the pillow.

'Where is Francie?' it said.

'She's tired. She's having a lay-down. She's tired out worrying about you.'

'She's a good girl, Francie,' he said. 'It's not much fun for her here.'

74

That too, Williams found, was surprisingly touching. He had always suspected something in the nature of a feud between them: one of those dreary drawn-out feuds that each side knows only death can extirpate. Now his surprise was all the greater, not only because there was affection there, on the part of the old man at any rate, but because Broderick suddenly said:

'You're the truck driver, aren't you? She told me how kind you'd been to her.'

'Ah! that's all right,' he said. 'Like to help people if I can.'

'Do you? She's been very kind to me. Very kind. For a long time. She deserves a little herself.'

'What about having your tablets now, grandad, and dropping off for a bit?'

'I can't sleep with this weather,' Broderick said. 'I can't get my breath.'

'You have your tablets and a drop of whisky and you'll sleep like a cat,' he said.

'Whisky?'

'Whisky – yes. I brought it up,' Williams said. 'It's over on the chest of drawers here.'

'Who said I could have whisky? I'm not supposed to have whisky. For several years I've not had whisky. I used to be very fond of it –'

'Ah! come on, you can have whisky. You know you can have whisky. Mrs Broderick says you can.'

'I used to have it – a year or two back, but –'

'You have a tot, grandad,' he said. 'It'll do you good.'

He poured a fair measure of whisky into a glass and one of his clearest images of Broderick that night was of the little quivering figure sitting up in bed with a strange grin on its face in the glow of the night-light. It was the sunny, bright-eyed grin of a boy who had been bribed by sweetness or promises to lie down and be good and go to sleep at last. With loud relish the old dry mouth sucked and lapped at the whisky as Williams said:

'How many tablets?'

'I've been taking three or four.'

'All right. Say four.'

Just before they said good night Williams picked up the whisky bottle and said: 'All right now, grandad? Think you can get off now?' and he saw the old eyes, already woken from their torpor by the excitement of liquor, regarding him and the bottle with keen, bright greed.

'Now, grandad, don't tell me you want a refill already. You on the wagon all this time too.'

'Just a thimbleful.'

As Williams filled up the glass the hands quivered with a start of greedy joy.

'What about you?' Broderick said. 'A drop for you?'

He said something about it being late and there not being another glass, but Broderick pointed to the bottle. There was actually the crease of a smile on his face as he did so. Williams picked up the bottle and took a deep steady gulp of whisky and Broderick said:

'At one time the doctors used to say it would kill me. Why don't you sit down a minute with me?'

'Better not, grandad. Got to push on.'

'Where are you going? You're the night driver, aren't you? She told me about you.'

'Other side of Exeter. Get there by breakfast time.'

'I see. It's very nice of you to stop with me. How do you find the whisky? I prefer it neat, don't you?'

All this was said slowly, with croaking difficulty, between crackling gasps for breath. In spite of it all, the crease of a smile actually reappeared once or twice again. Finally he made another gesture or two towards the whisky bottle and one more towards his glass.

'No more, grandad. Got to drive, y'know. You'll get me for the high jump, smelling like a four-ale bar.'

'Well: all right. But you'll come in again, won't you?'

'Some time. Don't have much time, most nights.'

'Please come in,' Broderick said, and the crease of a smile, yellowish, more than ever like the crinkle in the neck of a pale maggot slowly turning its head, came back again. 'I like to talk to you. Don't get much chance of talking.'

As he went out of the room with its dim night-light embalming and enshrining Broderick with its upward glow Williams felt the absence of death so keenly that he could do nothing but joke about it as a man jokes about an escape from it.

'Perky as a chicken,' he said. Downstairs, in the hall, she was waiting for him exactly as he had left her, almost as if she might have been listening all that time. 'Probably live to be a hundred.'

'Don't talk like that,' she said. Her face was an extraordinary sight in the poorish light of the one electric light bulb shining through its stained glass bowl above her. It seemed twisted with tension. The muscles of the neck and cheeks were sucked in, darkly, making her fiercely alert and cadaverous. 'You mustn't talk like that. If you'd seen him this afternoon – '

And then suddenly:

'What about the whisky? Did you give him his whisky?'

'Whisky?' Williams laughed softly. 'You should have seen us. Totting it out. The two of us. Having a good old buddies' party.'

'I can't understand why you joke about it,' she said.

And long afterwards, when it was all over, that was one of the things he could not understand himself. Only the blindest kind of a fool could have joked about it. But that night, in his relief that he had not had to deal with death, he was glad of it as something of a distraction to seize on. It was not really that he was joking about it; perhaps the whisky had pepped him up a bit, he thought. He was just relieved that death had not complicated things. He did not want to be mixed up with death. If there was anything he loathed and hated it was dying and the dead. He had once seen the body of a man on the roadside, just out of London, lying on the grass, after a smash, the face covered with a sheet of newspaper, and the sight of it leered backwards and forwards across his mind, grotesque and haunting, for nights and days.

'You'd better go now,' she said.

When he took hold of her shoulders to say good night he found that she was shivering. The tendons of her neck were drawn and cold. If it had not been for the intense pressure of light burning in the eyes it might have been, in fact, that she was the person who had died.

'Here, come on. Come on,' he said. 'You got to pull yourself together. You got to snap out of this.'

He heard her teeth crack against themselves, like a key snapping in a lock.

'I don't want to be alone when it happens,' she said. 'That's all. I can't bear to be alone here with that.'

'Don't get jittery,' he said. 'I'll be back tomorrow.'

'All right,' she said. She seemed to make a great effort to calm herself. She drew in a deep rasping breath. 'You'll know by the blinds if anything has happened.'

He supposed he must have called again five or six times, for perhaps ten days or so, perhaps two weeks, before two things occurred. Like so many other things that had happened, both were casual. Each time he repeated the habit of going upstairs and saying good night to Broderick – 'coming to tuck you up, grandad, and give you your night-cap' – seeing that the old crinkled neck swallowed its tablets, talking a little, sharing a glass of whisky with him, and it was after about the fourth or fifth of these visits that she said:

'You know, he's quite taken to you. He likes you. He told me so today. He quite looks forward to your coming.'

And then, as if in an afterthought, more casually still:

'He told me something else about you.'

'Bad, I'll bet.'

'No. He's probably going to alter his will and leave you a little money, that's all.'

'Stone the crows,' he said.

'There,' she said, 'wouldn't that be nice?'

'Well, knock me down.'

'Now you'll be able to have your own island, won't you?'

'Now why would he want to do that?' Williams said. 'I'm nobody. He hardly knows me.'

'He says you help him to go on living,' she said. 'You give him confidence, he says.' She smiled. 'Of course I may have helped a bit. Just a bit – for you.'

Later, on the divan, before he left, she again drew out of the half-darkness, for only the second time for several weeks, the old, insidious dream of the island: the sun, the sea, the leisure, the way they could live together. 'Like this,' she said. 'All the time.

No more of this awful country. Where you can't get warm. Where it's always raining. And these awful winters.'

'That's me,' he said. 'I can go for plenty of that.'

'Perhaps it won't be long now.'

'Oh! I can wait – I can wait till Doomsday for stuff like that.'

'And how long do you think I've been waiting?' She was almost yelling at him now, in a curious forced undertone, hoarse in the darkness with anger and frustration. 'I've been waiting ten years and it seems like ten thousand – how long would you like to wait like that? No, fun, no bed, no nothing. When I married him they said he wouldn't live a year – not six months. A cardiac complaint like that, they said – it can't live. One bit of over-exertion and he'll drop down and it's all over.'

Her voice was rasping now with a tearless, suppressed rage. 'But you see it's never the sick that die, is it? It's the healthy that drop down dead. The sick just go dragging on for ever.'

For a moment it seemed that she was going to break into uncontrolled weeping. He heard her mouth sucking air in an enormous sob. Then it stopped suddenly and she said:

'I'm sorry. I didn't mean to get worked up like that. I don't know what I'd have done without you.'

He did not know quite what to say. He was distracted, not for the first time, by the emotional change of her voice. It almost mesmerized him and then she said:

'It was bad enough when there wasn't you. But now it's awful. I can't wait like that any more – I can't wait much longer.'

Before he went that night he thought he heard Broderick calling from his bedroom. 'Yes, perhaps it's him,' she said. 'He's terribly restless. Would you go up? You could give him another tablet or two if he's still awake. And just a sip to calm him down.'

Two days later it happened that a mate of his, a day driver named Davies, broke his wrist at the depot when a starting handle kicked. He had been going to drive a load of plaster-board to Bristol. And that was how Williams found himself driving out of London at eight o'clock in the morning instead of eight o'clock at night, in misty September rain that sprayed back on his windscreen in a greasy film that never wiped away.

Twenty miles out he decided to stop and wash his windscreen and have a plate of eggs and bacon and some tea at a shack where he sometimes breakfasted coming back to London from the West. Whilst the eggs were cooking the woman who kept the shack lent him the morning paper and he sat for some moments with elbows on the counter, reading it, casually wondering whether he should do a horse named Snow Flurry at 40–1 at Hurst Park that afternoon or be sensible and have something each way on the favourite at Worcester, Lorelei.

Then while he was still reading the woman leaned over from behind the tea-urn and said:

'There's a thing there that give me a turn when I got down this morning. Here, where is it, I was reading it when you come in. I'll see I never take another, if I lay awake a week. You see that?' she said. She turned the pages over for him. 'My blessed fingers are all thumbs this morning. There – there it is.'

Dully, not fully grasping it for a moment, he found himself reading the piece the woman had found for him. It was the account of the inquest on an actress who had died. Her death, the coroner said, was the third of its kind in a month: an alarming situation that should serve as a warning to people who took sleeping tablets and a night-cap of neat brandy or whisky on top. It could not be stated too strongly that the combination of these things was likely to be fatal.

'I done it,' the woman said. 'Two or three times last winter. And once last week. Two tablets and a tot of Johnny Walker. And neat at that. I hadn't slept right for a week. I felt I'd got to have something –'

The smell of eggs and bacon was suddenly an insufferable sickness, searing in his throat. A few moments later he was walking out of the shack, slopping through big black puddles of rain that lay all across the cinder surface of the pull-in.

For some time he did not know whether it was raining or not. It was perhaps ten or fifteen miles farther on that the clap-clack of windscreen wipers on dry glass really woke him. His hands were smeary with sweat and there was a dry acid crust on the walls of his throat. Most of the time he was not really seeing the road before him, drying in the September sun, but only the recurrent entangled, haunting picture of the big ugly house that no one had ever seemed to stop building. It was a picture with something evil and luminous about it. He saw it in the purplish glow of the spirit kettle, then in the feeble aura of the night-light and the broad stabbing flashes of lightning on the night he had first gone up to Broderick. He tried to remember how many times he had been up to that room and how many tablets and glasses he could have given Broderick and above all he kept thinking what a fool he had been ever to go there and stay there and listen to her.

The sun was hot in a clear noon sky by the time he came to within sight of the house. He decided to park the truck half a mile away, on the top of a hill, and walk the rest of the way to the back of the place. The air was humid and thick after rain and when he got out of his cab he felt his knees buckle and sag underneath him with a complete absence of feeling that was more sickening than sudden pain.

He walked through a field at the back of the house and came into the garden through a fence that had fallen down under the weight of blackberry and bindweed. Instinctively he looked at the windows, but the blinds were not down. Up to that time he did not know quite what he was looking for. He was aware simply of groping in a scared cold way through sensations of nausea, through horror at being caught in a trap, through revulsion at the dead.

Then he remembered the conservatory. He remembered that that was where Broderick sat during most of the afternoon. He had heard her speak of a gardener named Smithson who came in for two hours in the morning to work among the flowers and then left at noon.

He did not know how long he stood in front of the conservatory door in exactly the way he had stood in the bedroom, in the storm, calling Broderick's name.

'Mr Broderick,' he said, 'Mr Broderick.'

The little figure in the straw hat was sitting among the flowers. It seemed to be transfixed in the same torpid coma as when Williams had first seen it there. The skin of the face was blotched, as it had been then, with blobs of coloured light streaming down, diffused, from the roof above, giving it the appearance of a marbled, artificial flower.

For a moment he could not make up his mind whether in fact he was not, after all, looking at the dead. All his sickness and revulsion came rushing back. Then he turned the handle of the door and through the steamy unreal heat of the conservatory he saw Broderick stir, raising his eyes from their torpor.

'Williams,' Broderick said, 'what are you doing here?'

Under the torrid glass, brilliant in the September afternoon sun, the bloodless face was actually bathed in sweat.

'Are you all right, Mr Broderick?' Williams said. 'I dropped in to see how you were.'

'Perfectly all right.' The face tottered in the over-heated air like a petal about to fall. 'This isn't your time, is it?'

'Got a change of job,' Williams said. 'I'm on day shift now. Are you sure you're all right, Mr Broderick? Don't you want some air in here?'

'Perfectly all right,' Broderick said. 'Thanks to you.'

Incredulously Williams listened. In stupefaction he heard Broderick mumble on: 'The whisky seems to have given me a new lease of life. Done me a power of good. Gives just enough stimulus to the heart without affecting it.'

In the stifling heat, among the scent of flowers, Williams felt his own sweat prickling harshly through every pore.

'I got to go now, Mr Broderick,' he said. 'Got to push on. Got to get down as far as Bristol before tea-time.'

'Haven't you seen Mrs Broderick?'

'No.'

'Don't you want to see her? I fancy she's asleep in the house somewhere.'

'Not today,' Williams said. 'I got to push on today.'

By that time he was standing by the door of the conservatory, holding it open, ready to go. Behind him the free cool air was blowing in.

'Shall I give her a message?' Broderick said. 'Is there some message I can give?'

Message? For some moments he stood thinking that there was no message. He had nothing to say that made sense about an island, the sea, the sun, or about Mrs Broderick, who could not sleep at night-time.

Then he decided, after all, that there was a message.

'Tell Mrs Broderick,' he said, 'that I shan't be coming this way again.' He was outside now; he was breathing at last the cool, sweet, free air. 'Tell her that from now on I'll be working in the day-time.'

Summer in Salandar

Manson lifted one corner of the green gauze window blind of the shipping office and watched, for an indifferent moment or two, the swift cortège of a late funeral racing up the hill. It flashed along the water-front like a train of cellulose beetles, black and glittering, each of the thirty cars a reflection of the glare of sun on sea. He wondered, as the cars leapt away up the avenue of jade and carmine villas, eyeless in the bright evening under closed white shades, why funerals in Salandar were always such races, unpompous and frenzied, as if they were really chasing the dead. He wondered too why he never saw them coming back again. They dashed in black undignified weeping haste to somewhere along the sea-coast, where blue and yellow fishing boats beat with high moon-like prows under rocks ashen with burnt seaweed, and then vanished for ever.

He let the blind fall into place again, leaning spare brown elbows on the mahogany lid of his desk. He was thinking that that evening a ship would be in. It could not matter which ship – he was pretty sure it was the *Alacantara* – since nobody in their senses ever came to Salandar in the summer. There would in any case be no English passengers and he would meet it out of pure routine. After that he would go home to his small hotel and eat flabby oil-soaked *esparda* that had as much taste in it as a bath sponge and drink export beer and read the English papers of a week last Wednesday. In the street outside men would sit on dark door-steps and spit golden melon seeds into gutters, coughing with tubercular mournfulness. The flash of an open-air cinema down the street would drench the plum-black air above the sur- rounding courtyards with continuous gentle fountains of light, above little explosions of applause and laughter. In one of the old houses behind the hotel a woman would lull her baby to sleep with a prolonged soft song that was probably as old as the moon- curve of the fishing boats that lined the shore. Under the infinite stars the red beacons on the radio masts would flame like big impossible planets above the mass of the fortress that obscured, with its vast and receding walls, nearly half the sky. And that would be his evening: a lonely and not surprising conclusion to a tiring day when nothing had happened, simply because nothing ever happened in summer in Salandar.

From across the quayside, out on the landing pier, he suddenly heard the sound of more voices than he thought was customary. He got up and parted the slats of the window shade. The pier was massed with emigrants, emigrant baggage, emigrant noises, the messy struggle of emigrant farewells. He remembered then that the *Alacantara* was not coming in. It was the *Santa Maria*, coming from precisely the opposite way.

That sort of trick of memory always overtook him at the height of summer, two months after the tourist season had died. It was the delayed shock of seasonal weariness. He was as unprepared for it as he was unprepared for the sight of the *Santa Maria* herself, a ship of pale green hulls with funnels of darker green, suddenly coming round the westerly red-black cliffs of the bay. It made him less annoyed to think that he had to meet her. He did not like to hurry. There was no need to hurry. There was nothing to hurry for. He was not going anywhere. He was not meeting anyone. The point of his meeting a ship on which he had no passenger was purely one of duty. Like most of the rest of his life on Salandar it was a bore.

Was there a passenger? With the precision of habit he turned up a black ledger of passengers' names that gave him nothing in answer. It was nice to be assured, anyway, that he was not mistaken.

A moment later he called to the only clerk to tell the porter that he wanted the launch in five minutes. His voice was dry from the summer catarrh that came from living low down, at sea-level, in the rainless months, in the sandy dust of the port. He cleared his throat several times as he went out into the street and the sun struck him below the eyebrows with pain. On the corner of the pavement he stood and closed his eyes briefly before he crossed to the water-front and as he opened them again the last black beetle of the funeral cortège flashed past him, expensively glittering, lurching dangerously, chasing the dead: a car filled with weeping men.

2

On the ship the air seemed absorbent. It sucked up the life of the fanless purser's cabin on the middle deck.

'She got on at Lisbon, Mr Manson,' the purser said. 'She said she cabled you from there.'

A small quantity of pearl-grey luggage, splashed with varnished scarlet labels, among them the letter V, stood by the purser's door. Staring down at it, Manson tried to remember back through a long drowsy day to some point where a cable might have blown in, rushed past him and, like the cortège of racing mourners, have disappeared. He could not recall any cable and the purser said:

'I had better take her luggage up. I promised to look after her.' He began to pick up suitcases, tucking the smallest under his arms. 'She seems to like being looked after. Perhaps you will bring the last one, Mr Manson? – thank you.'

No one else had come aboard except a harbour policeman in flabby grey ducks, so thin that he seemed impossibly weighed down by black bayonet and revolver, and a customs officer in crumpled washed-out sienna gabardine. These two stood sweating at the head of the companionway, the policeman with thumbs in his drooping belt. There was not even the usual collection of hotel porters' caps on the ship simply because every hotel was closed.

'Where is she staying?' Manson called. 'There isn't a single hotel open.'

'I told her that. She said she did not mind. I told her you would see all about it.'

'She's nothing to do with me.'

'She's English. I told her you would do it –'

'Do what? I'm not a sight-seeing guide for anybody who comes and dumps themselves down here in the middle of summer.'

He felt his hands grow sweaty on the high-polished fabric of the suitcase handle. He knew, he thought, all that English women could be. Ill-clad in worsted, horribly surpliced in porridge-coloured shantung, they arrived sometimes as if expecting the island to yield the horse-drawn charm of 1890, where everything could be had or done by the clapping of hands.

'Anyway I had no warning,' he said. 'What warning had I?'

He thought he saw the customs officer grin at this, and it annoyed him still further.

'She said she cabled you herself, Mr Manson,' the purser said.

'I've seen no sign of a cable,' he said. 'And anyway cable or no cable –'

'It was awfully good of you to meet me,' a voice said.

When he turned, abruptly, at the same time as the sweat-bright faces of the policeman, the customs officer, and the purser, he saw her standing behind him: a tall black-haired girl, with an amazing combination of large pure blue eyes and black lashes, her hair striped across the front with a leonine streak of tawny blonde.

He found himself at once resenting and resisting this paler streak of hair.

'It was really very good of you,' she said. 'My name is Vane.'

He checked an impulse to say 'Spelt in which way?' and she held out a hand covered with a long cream glove. This glove, reaching to her elbow, matched a sleeveless dress of light cool linen.

'I know you think I've come at the wrong time of year,' she said.

'Not at all.'

'No?' she said. 'I thought I heard you say so.'

He was so irritated that he was not really conscious of helping her down the gangway. He felt instead that the gangway had begun to float on air. It was nothing but a shaky ladder of cotton-reels swaying above the calm sea. It seemed almost perpendicular, pitching him forward as he went down first and waited to help her into the launch below.

The red triangular pennant of the company drooped above the burnished deck house and she said, staring beyond it:

'Everyone told me it was so brilliant. So much flashing colour. But the rocks are black. It looks burnt out, somehow.'

'That's just the summer,' he said.

Out of politeness he stared with her at the shore. He thought there was a great deal of colour. It was simply that it was split into a fractional mosaic of blacks and browns, of bleached pinks and the dull ruby reds of house-tops, half-smothered by green. A tower of pale yellow, the new school, was raised like a fresh sugar stick above the black sand of the shore, at the end of which an astonishing summer residence of blue tiles, polished as a kitchen stove, was wedged into the cliff. Two or three rowing-boats, piled with white baskets, with curtains of island embroideries in scarlet and green, were motionless on the oily bay, where in the high season a hundred of them clamoured about liners like fighting junks, manned by brown shivering men diving for coins. Lines of high-prowed fishing boats, up-curved like horns, striped in green and blue and ochre, were pulled up along the water-front, and far away and high above them he could see the water splash of a spouting *levada*, poised like gathered spittle in a fissure of rock and eucalyptus forest, pure white in the blinding sun.

He suddenly felt himself defending all he saw. He wanted to say that there was plenty of colour. Only the sun, burning ferociously, created an illusion of something cindery, melting dully away.

'It's just a question of – '

'Oh! my bag,' she said.

She stood on the lowest rung of the gangway, lifting helpless arms, imploring with a smile.

'In my cabin – so sorry – twenty-three – you'll see it. Probably on the bed.'

As he mounted the ladder quickly, more insecure than when he had come down, he remembered that cabin twenty-three was one of four on the boat deck and he walked straight for it, before the purser could speak or stop him.

He found her handbag on the bed. Unstripped, the bed was disorderly and the bag, which was why she had forgotten it, was partly covered by her pillow. Its clasp sprang open as he picked it up. Its white jaws spilled lipstick and handkerchief, a few letters, a mirror, a little diary in black morocco.

He felt intensely curious and wanted to open the diary. The bag gave out a perfume that floated about him for a moment, arousing in him a startling sensation of intimacy.

Then he felt nervous and shut the bag quickly and rushed out of the cabin, only to find the purser coming to meet him on the deck, saying:

'What was it, Mr Manson? Was it something you could not find?'

He went on without answering, slipping hastily once again on the insecure mahogany cotton-reels of the gangway, down to a sea on which the launch's scarlet pennant and the yellow dress were the only things that did not melt and sway.

'You were very quick,' she said. 'It was very kind of you.'

The sea was so calm that it was possible for himself and the girl to stand motionless on the launch all the way from ship to shore. She stood erectly looking about her, searching the bay, the shore, and the abrupt hills above the town for colour.

'It surprises me,' she said. 'I'd expected something more exotic.'

'It's exotic in winter,' he said. 'It's all colour then. You should have come in the winter. That's when everybody comes.'

It suddenly struck him that, after all, she was really not looking at the approaching shore. Something about her eyes made them seem glazed with preoccupation.

'I'm afraid it was my fault about the cable,' she said. 'It should have been sent. But I was in a dreadful hurry. I made up my mind all of a sudden and then somehow – '

'I don't know what you had in mind about hotels.'

'I suppose they're all shut,' she said.

'All the recognized ones.'

'Where do you live? In one not recognized?'

'I wouldn't recommend it,' he said.

Forgetfulness about the cable, forgetfulness about the bag – he stood pondering uncertainly, staring at the approaching harbour pier, wondering where to take her.

'I do apologize about the cable,' she said. 'I'm afraid you're peeved.'

'I was trying to think of a possible solution to the hotel problem.'

'It's no problem,' she said. 'I'm not particular. I shall find something. I always do.'

'Had you any idea of how long you were staying?'

'As long as I like it.'

'It isn't always possible to leave when you think you will,' he said. 'Ships are very irregular here. They don't just happen when you think they're going to.'

'Does anything?' she said.

The launch began to make its curve to the landing pier, the change of course uplifting the scarlet pennant very slightly. Above steps of baked white concrete a line of idle taxis stretched out, with a few ox-carts, in the shade of flowerless jacarandas. A smell of oil and hot bullock dung and rotting sea-weed seethed in the air and he said:

'I'm afraid you'll find anything down here in the port very hot.'

As the launch came into the jetty he leapt out. On the steps he held out his hand to her and she lifted the long cream glove.

'The man will bring the bags up to the top,' he said.

At the top of the jetty he realized with concern that she was hatless. Heat struck down on concrete and then back again as if pitilessly forced down through a tube, dangerously compressed under the high enclosure of hills.

'I hope you're all right?' he said. 'I mean the heat? – the air is terribly clear and you don't always realize –'

'I don't feel it,' she said. 'I never feel it.' She touched her hair, running her fingers through it. The paler streak of it, uplifted, exposed the mass of pure black hair below, and he realized how thick and strong and wiry it was. Its heavy sweep, shot with the curious blonde streak, aroused in him the same odd sensation of uneasy intimacy he had experienced in the cabin, smelling the perfume of the handbag, by the disordered bed.

For a moment longer she stood engrossed by the sight of him staring at her hair, and he did not realize how absorbed and uncomfortable it had made him feel until she said:

'Where do we go from here? Where can I get a taxi?'

'I was thinking you could come to the office and leave your things –'

'I'd rather get a hotel,' she said. 'What's the name of yours?'

'Mafalda,' he said. 'It's terribly small and they don't really cater –'

'It doesn't matter if it's reasonable and the beds are clean. Are the beds clean?'

'Quite clean.'

She looked at him without any kind of disturbance, the clear, rather too large blue eyes fixing him with exacting softness and said:

'I think any beds that are clean enough for you ought to be clean enough for me.'

'You can always try it temporarily.'

From the hot taxi she leaned her long body forward and looked at the mounting hillside. Above it successive folds of rock, exposed in crags that seemed sun-blackened, submerged under encrustations of blue-green forests of pine and eucalyptus, fascinated her large blue eyes into a larger stare.

'What's up there?' she said. 'I mean the other side of the mountain?'

'Not much,' he said. 'More rock and forests and so on. Not many people. Over the other side there's a power station. It's lonely. There are places you can't get to.'

She smiled and sat back beside him on the seat, wrapping the surprisingly cool cream gloves deftly one over the other.

'That's where I'd like to go,' she said.

Then, without attaching importance to what she said, without really giving it another thought, he was inspired to remark with sudden cheerfulness that there would probably be, at the hotel, a cup of tea.

3

There were mice in the upper ceilings of the old hotel and he lay listening to them half the night, turning over in his mind what seemed to him the vexing problem of her being there, in that highly unsuitable, dark, cheap hotel where no English visitor ever came except for a temporary night, in sheer high season desperation. He had carefully warned her a number of times that the food would not be English. 'It will be oily and all that,' he said. 'It's something it takes a long time to get used to.' When she reminded him that he at any rate appeared to survive it he did not

dare tell her that it was simply because he could not afford anything else. He had just had to get used to it; and now he did not
ask for anything better and in his limited way he was perfectly
happy. At least he supposed he was.

But something troubled him much more than this. He was
perplexed and worried by a phrase she had used.

'What are you going to do with yourself?' he asked her. 'It
can be terribly exhausting at this time of the year –'

'I'm going to poke about,' she said. 'I want things to do. I want
to see things.'

He grew increasingly uneasy about this as the evening went on.
It was not a good thing to poke your nose into things in Salandar.
It was a place, in the right season, in the delicious winter flower
days, of infinite surface charm. Bougainvilleas covered with steep
massive curtains of purple and sienna-rose all the dry ravines
coming down from the hills; starry scarlet poinsettias lined the
potato patches; a honey odour of incense trees hung over the old
streets at night-time. If underneath all this there were people who
had not enough to eat, who were afraid of something or somebody, who were tubercular or illiterate or superfluous or resentful,
that was no concern of visitors.

'Don't you ever poke about and find out how things really
are?' she said.

'No.'

'Have you been here long?' she said. 'How many years have
you been here?'

'I came here about three and a half years ago. Nearly four.'

It was getting so long ago he could hardly remember exactly.
His time there had gradually become, in the Salandar fashion, a
succession of dull tomorrows.

'How long is it since you went over to the other side of the
island?' she said.

'I'm afraid I've never been over to the other side.'

'By the way you spoke I thought you'd been there often' she,
said.

'No,' he said, 'I've never been there.'

'Haven't you any inclination at all to see what it's like?'

'Not particularly.'

It seemed to him that she did not speak her questions so much as impose them on him with the too large, too brilliant, uneasy eyes.

'What about Santo Carlo?' she said. 'They say that's very interesting. Have you been there?'

No: he had not been to Santo Carlo either.

He found, presently, what seemed to him a happy solution to her restlessness, to the problem of what she should do with herself. It was also a tremendous relief to be able at last to change an uncomfortable subject.

'You could join the club,' he said. 'I don't know why I didn't think of it before.'

'Do you belong?'

'Not now,' he said. 'I gave it up.'

In winter the club was crowded with visitors he did not know; in summer there was no one there. After six months of it he had not considered it worth while to renew the subscription. He decided he would save the money. He had to think of the future.

'What happens there?'

'People play bridge and tennis and that sort of thing and there's a small golf course,' he said. 'It's rather beautiful,' and then added, as if it was an extra thought to impress her: 'You can get tea.'

She did not say anything and he went on:

'You can get a temporary subscription – I think for even a week. I can find out for you – but then if you don't know how long you're going to stay –'

'That was something I was going to talk to you about,' she said.

In speaking of the times of ships he felt more certain of himself. That at least was his job.

'It depends where you want to go from here,' he said. 'If you'll give me some idea of times and places I'll have –'

'When is the next ship in?'

'There'll be nothing in this week. Not until after the week-end,' he said. 'Then the *Alacantara* is due. She's pleasant.'

'It would be nice just to have the sailing times of what's likely to be coming in,' she said. 'Could you? It would be very sweet of you.'

She had asked him so many questions that this final acutely personal one, delivered more softly, in a lowered voice, made him more uneasy than he had been before. He did not grasp even that the conversation had been largely about himself. He felt only another rush of feeling about her: a repetition of the sensation he had had in the cabin, over the handbag and the disorderly bed, and from the way she had run her fingers through her thick black hair.

'You look tired,' she said to him at last. 'It's time you got into that good clean bed.'

In the morning he woke to an air that had in it the breath of ashes. It sprang at his already catarrhal throat with windy choking heat. He grasped then the reason for his lethargy of the previous day, his soporific irritations as he met the boat that he had not expected. The *leste* was blowing: the wind from the northeast that burned with pure incineration off the mainland sand.

This had not prevented Miss Vane from getting up at five o'clock and watching the night-boats, like slowly extinguishing fireflies, bringing in their fish across the bay.

'They looked wonderful,' she said. 'Haven't you ever seen them come in?'

'No.'

'I talked to some of them – the men, I mean. There were two brothers from Santo Carlo –'

'You should be very careful how you talk to these people,' he said.

At breakfast which they had together in the already shuttered little dining-room, in a queer kind of morning twilight through which even her large and exceptionally blue eyes looked almost white in their diffusion, he warned her about the intolerable burning wind.

'It will probably last for two days,' he said. 'Perhaps three. I'm afraid you'll find it very exhausting.'

In a white dress of low cut, with a transparent organdie insertion across the breast, she looked remarkably cool and she said:

'Isn't it a good chance to get up into the hills? Couldn't you take a day off and come with me?'

He rested easily on the firm ground of his local knowledge.

'That's the curious thing about the *leste*,' he said. 'It's even hotter in the hills. You'd hardly believe it, but the coast is going to be the cooler place.'

'I might go myself.'

'Oh! no,' he said. 'Don't think of doing that.'

'Why not?'

'Oh! in the first place – Well, it's hardly the thing. You see you can only drive so far. After that it's a question of mule-track. You need several days –'

'I have plenty of days.'

'Yes, but not while the *leste* is on,' he said. 'Really not. It can be ghastly up there when the *leste* is on.'

'How would you know?' she said. 'You've never been.'

His coffee, which should have been cool after so much conversation, sprang down his already anguished throat like hot acid. He felt unable to speak for some moments and at last she said:

'I think you look awfully tired. Don't you ever want to get away from here?'

'Not particularly. I suppose eventually –'

'Not when the ships come in? Don't you ever suddenly feel hell, for God's sake let me get away – don't you ever feel like that?'

'I can't say I do.'

'I think it might do you good to get away.'

For a second he was touched, and then bewildered, by her concern. He was disturbed too because she had, as he now noticed for the first time, no coffee to drink.

'Didn't you have any coffee?'

'I had orange instead,' she said. 'It's cooler.'

'I suppose I ought to have done that,' he said. 'But I always have coffee. I can't get out of the habit of it somehow –'

'Would you come on this trip to the hills?' she said.

'I honestly don't know.'

'I shall go,' she said. 'I'll fix it up. I like fixing things. Would you come if I fixed it?'

'It's awfully difficult for me to say,' he said. 'You see, everybody's on leave. Charlton, my chief, is on leave. The only really good local clerk has gone to Lisbon for a week. It's very doubtful if I could leave the office in any case –'

'You've got the week-end.'

'I know, but – ' He found himself being hopelessly absorbed, as his breath had been absorbed in the stifling purser's cabin on the ship, by her enlarged diffused eyes, almost pure white, their true colour extinguished until they gave out a curious impression of nakedness in the dark morning shadow. 'And apart from anything else there's the *leste* – '

'If we wait till the *leste* is over?' she said. 'If it blows for two or three days it ought to be over by the week-end, oughtn't it?'

'Well, you can't tell – '

'Shall we chance it?' she said. 'Shall I fix it up?'

'Will it do if I decide this evening?'

'I'm going to fix it during the day,' she said. 'If the *Alacantara* comes next week I haven't much time.'

'All right,' he said. 'I suppose I could come.'

As she got up from the table she smiled and touched his arm, telling him to drink his coffee. Her body was held forward to him, the partially transparent inset of her dress exposing her breast. He was aware of the falling discoloured band of yellow in her intense black hair and it disturbed him again more than anything she had done or said, and as he stared at it she smiled.

'Do I look so awful?' she said. 'I haven't combed my hair since I went down to the harbour. I must go and do it now.'

He called after her to ask her what she was going to do with herself all day. 'You must take it easily. Don't go and exhaust yourself,' he said.

'I'll probably swim,' she called back from the stairs.

'Be careful of the swell,' he said. 'It's terribly deceptive. It can sometimes be twenty or thirty feet even on the calmest days.' After all he had a certain responsibility for her now. 'Don't go out too far.'

4

The road to the central ridge of mountains wound up through gorges of grey volcanic rock, under steep declivities of pine and eucalyptus closely planted as saplings against the erosion of a sparse burnt soil, red and cindrous, veined yellow here and there by courses of long-dried water. The car crept upward very slowly, beetle-wise, on black setts of blistered rock that gave way, beyond the last windowless white houses, to a track of pot-holes sunk in grey and crimson sand.

'It was a stroke of genius to bring the cook,' she said.

He did not feel that this was flattery. It really was, he thought, rather a stroke of genius on his part to think of the cook. The idea of the cook sprang from his recollection that, at the top of the mule-pass, there was also a rest-house. For practically nothing you could put up there, cook meals and so on and do the thing in comfort. He was very pleased about that. It saved a lot of trouble. He didn't think he could have come all the way up that hot dreary track otherwise.

The *leste*, after all, had died. The air in the mountains was still hot, but height began to give it, as the car climbed slowly, a thinness that was fresh and crystalline. Objects began to appear so vivid that they stuck out, projected by strong blue lines that were pulsations rather than shadows. In a curious way everything was enlarged by scintillation.

Perhaps it was this that made Manson, sitting at the back of the car with Miss Vane, fix his eyes hypnotically on the black hair of the cook, sitting in front with the driver.

The head of the cook was like an ebony bowl, polished to a sheen of greasy magnificence by brushings of olive oil. Below it the shoulders were flat and square, the erectness of them giving power to the body that was otherwise quite short and stiff, except when it bent in sudden bows of politeness to Miss Vane.

Sometimes the car jolted violently in and out of potholes and Manson and Miss Vane were pitched helplessly upward and against each other, taken unawares. But the shoulders of Manuel, the cook, were never disturbed by more than a quiver and sometimes it seemed to Manson that they gave a shrug.

This hypnosis about the neck of the cook lasted until the car-road ended and the mule-track began, winding away into a thick scrub of wild bay trees and stunted, blue-needled pines. At the foot of the track the mules were waiting, four flickering skeletons brought up by two bare-foot peasants wearing trousers of striped blue shirt material and black trilby hats.

Manuel loaded two osier baskets of provisions, Manson's ruck-sack and one of Miss Vane's scarlet-labelled too-neat suitcases on to one of the mules, and the peasants began to lead the mules up the hill.

After Manuel had shouted after them the two peasants came back. They both looked down-trodden in protestation and Manuel, standing over them, square and erect, looked more assertive than before.

'What is it, Manuel?' Miss Vane said. 'Is something the matter?'

'No, madame.' He pronounced his English fully and correctly, elongating the final syllable.

'What is it then?'

'They want to go with us, madame.'

'That was the idea, wasn't it?' Manson said.

'It's not necessary, sir. I can manage without them.'

'You know the way?' she said.

'Yes, madame,' he said. 'I've done it before.'

After that the taxi driver drove away and the peasants disappeared up the hill. Manuel took the first and second mules, Miss Vane the third, and Manson the fourth. Manson had never been on a mule before and his legs seemed so much too long that he felt gawkily ridiculous. But looking ahead, beyond Miss Vane and the provision mule to the leading figure of Manuel, he was relieved to see that Manuel looked, as he thought, still more stupid.

His preoccupation with the back of Manuel's neck had been so absorbed that he had not really noticed that Manuel was wearing the black suit of a waiter. And as Manuel turned to look back at the column Manson saw that he was wearing the tie, the shirt front and the collar too.

It took three hours to climb through paths among bay tree and pine and tree-heath and an occasional eucalyptus stunted by height to the size of a currant-bush, as far as the rest-house. As the mules marched slowly upward, jerky and rhythmical, the mountains seemed to march rapidly forward, shutting in the heat and shutting out much of the sky. And as the heat developed oppressively Manson called once to Miss Vane:

'You'd hardly think there would be snow up here, would you?'

'There is no snow up here, sir.'

'I thought there was always snow. After all, it's six thousand –'

'Not on this side, sir. You're thinking of the Santo Carlo side. There is never snow just here.'

Manson did not speak again and it was half an hour before he noticed, glinting in the sun, what he thought were the iron sheds of the power-station framed in a gap ahead.

'I rather think that's the new power-station,' he called to Miss Vane. 'They had great difficulty in getting the pipes up there –'

'That's not the power-station, sir. That's the old pumping station for the *levadas*. They don't use it now.'

'Where is the power-station?' Miss Vane said.

'It's over the other side, madame. You won't be able to see it from this direction.'

'And where is the place you can see the two coasts from?' she said. 'You know – the sea both sides?'

'You will be able to go there from the rest-house, madame,' he said. 'It isn't far. You'll be able to climb up there.'

Manson stretched out his hand and snatched at the leaves of a eucalyptus tree, crushing it sharply with his fingers and then lifting the leaf to his nose. The harsh oily odour of eucalyptus was unpleasant and irritated him. It reminded him of times when, as a child, his chest had been very bad and he had coughed a lot and he had not been able to get his breath.

He unconsciously kept the leaf in his hand until, at the suggestion of Manuel, they stopped to rest. 'We are half way now, madame,' Manuel said.

Manuel poured glasses of export beer for Manson and Miss Vane and served them with stiff politeness and then retired to a respectful distance among the mules. From masses of rock above them, studded with pale flat cacti that were like blown roses of delicate green, water dripped in large slow drips, like summery, thundery rain.

'Well, this is marvellous,' Miss Vane said and lifted her glass to him, smiling with huge blue eyes in which Manson felt he could see all the summery wateriness and the great scintillation of mountain sky.

He lifted his glass to her in return, re-experiencing a sudden rush of the intimacy he had felt over her dishevelled bed and her handbag and that recurred whenever he looked at the yellow streak in her hair. He had a wild idea that presently, at the rest-house, they might be alone together.

'There's an awful smell of eucalyptus,' Miss Vane said.

He flushed, pounding with anger at himself, and said:

'I'm afraid it's me. I crushed a leaf. Don't you like it? – '

'I loathe it,' she said. 'I can't bear it near me. I hate it. You'll have to go and wash your hands.'

He went away in silence and washed his hands among the cacti, under a spilling cleavage of rock. The water was icy in the brilliant, burning air. He washed his hands carefully and then smelled them and it seemed that the smell of eucalyptus remained. Then he washed them again with slow, rejected, clinical care.

It was not until the rest-house came in sight that he emerged from a painful and articulate silence during which he had done nothing but stare at the sweat oozing slowly and darkly down the mule's neck. He was pleasantly startled by hearing Miss Vane call back:

'Hullo there. Asleep?' Her voice was solicitous and friendly once more and was accompanied by a sidelong dazzling smile. 'You can see the rest-house. We're nearly there.'

'I think it was the beer,' he said. 'Made me drowsy – '

'Look at it,' she said. 'It's exciting, isn't it? I'm excited.'

'Oh! yes. It's bigger than I thought – '

'Aren't you excited?' she said. 'This is really something. This is what I wanted.'

The track had widened. She reined the mule and waited for him. Then as she turned the mule half-face to him he noticed the shape of her body, pressed heavily across the dark animal flanks. She had ridden up in a sleeveless thin white dress, the skirt of which was drawn up beyond her knees. He had never been able to make up his mind how old she was and now, in her excitement, her skirt drawn up above bare smooth legs, her eyes enormously shining, he thought she seemed much younger than she had done down in the scorching, withering period of the *leste*, in the town. She seemed to have left her hostile restlessness behind.

'Oh! it's marvellous and it really wasn't far, was it?' she said. 'It didn't seem an hour. It was easy after all.'

He said he didn't think it had been far either and he was aware suddenly that Manuel had gone ahead. The impossible waiter-suit, mule-mounted, was almost at the veranda steps. A hundred yards separated him from Manson and Miss Vane, and again an overpowering sense of intimacy came over Manson, so that he felt tremulously stupid and could not speak to her.

'Now aren't you glad I made you come?' she said.

'Yes,' he said.

'Back there I thought you were mad with me.'

'Oh! no.'

'Not the smallest piece?'

He shook his head. 'Not a little bit,' he said.

The smile went temporarily out of her face. The mule jerked nervously ahead. 'I really thought you were mad,' she said and it did not occur to him until long afterwards that she might have hoped he had been.

5

From Manuel, during the rest of that day and the succeeding day, came an almost constant sound of whistling that jarred and ir-ritated Manson like the scrape of a file. The rest-house, neat and clean, with something not unlike a chapel about its bare white-washed coolness, was divided into three parts. In the large central room Manson and Miss Vane ate at a long mahogany table the meals that Manuel prepared in a kitchen that ran along the north side of a large bird-like cage made of gauze. In this cage Manuel kept up the whistling that continued to infuriate Manson even at night time, as he tried to sleep in the third part, composed of his own bedroom and Miss Vane's on the western side.

Miss Vane was a woman who hated trousers.

'I was born a woman and I'll dress like one,' she said. So she had ridden astride the mule in a loose cool white dress instead of the slacks Manson thought would have been more suitable, even though he disliked them. And all that day and most of the next, Sunday, she lay in front of the rest-house in a sun-suit of vivid green that was boned so tight to the shape of her body that it was like an extra gleaming skin.

As she lay in the sun Manson was aware of two sorts of feeling about her. When she lay on her back he saw the Miss Vane he had met on the ship; the Miss Vane of the hotel and the town, of the advancing, blistering *leste*; the Miss Vane incorrigibly and restlessly prodding him into coming to the mountains. She was the Miss Vane with the startling, discomforting tongue of yellow across her black hair. She was uneasy and he could not get near her.

When she turned over and lay on her face he could not see the yellow streak in her hair. Her head was one gentle mass of pure black, undisrupted by that one peroxide streak that always set him quivering inside. The black-haired Miss Vane did not startle him. She seemed quiet and untroubled. He wanted to thrust his face down into the plain unsullied mass of her thick black hair and let himself speak with tenderness of all sorts of things.

Always, at the point when he felt he could do this, she turned over on her back, lifting the front of her body straight and taut in the sun. The peroxide streak flared up. The eyes, too blue and too brilliant, flashed with exactly the same sort of unreality, as if she had dyed them too.

'Tomorrow we must do something,' she said. 'We can't lie here for ever.'

'It's very pleasant lying here.'

'We must go up to the place where you can see the two coasts. We'll start early and go all day,' she said. 'By the way, I've been meaning to ask you. You must have come out here very young. How old are you?'

'Twenty-seven,' he said.

'I beat you by a year,' she said. 'It's old, isn't it? We're creeping on. Don't you sometimes feel it's old? – all of it slipping away from you? Life and that sort of thing?'

He could hear Manuel whistling in the distance, in the bird cage, and he could see the paler streak in Miss Vane's hair as she turned and stared at the sky.

'I must say I thought you were older,' she said.

He was listening to the inexhaustibly dry, infuriating whistle of Manuel.

'You don't look older,' she said, 'but I think you act older. But then men of your age often do.'

She lifted one hand to shade her eyes from the glare of the sun.

'The sun gets terrific power by midday,' she said. 'I think I ought to have my glasses. Would you fetch them? – do you mind?'

He got up and began to walk away and she called after him:

'In the bedroom. Probably with my dress. I left them there when I changed.'

In the bedroom he remembered the cabin on the ship. He remembered how she liked things to be done for her. But now the bed, neatly made by Manuel, was not dishevelled. It was only her clothes that lay untidily about where she had undressed and thrown them down. He could not find the sun-glasses. They were not with her dress. He picked up her clothes several times and finally laid them on a chair. The glasses were not in her handbag and they were not on the bed.

His inability to find the glasses startled him into nervousness. He approached the bed with trembling hands. He pulled back the coverlet and put his hands under the pillow and let them rest there. He wanted all of a sudden to lie down on the bed. He was caught up in an illusion of lying with her there.

He went quickly out into the sun. From the ledge of short grass, walled by rock, where Miss Vane was lying, he heard voices. And as he came closer he saw that Miss Vane was wearing her sun-glasses.

'It's all right – Manuel found them. I'd left them in the dining-room.'

Manuel, in shirt sleeves, without the black waiter's coat, stood stiffly erect, holding a bunch of two or three roses in his hands.

'Don't you think that's amazing?' Miss Vane said. 'He even finds roses up here.'

'Where on earth do you get roses?' Manson said.

'In the garden, sir. At the back.'

'He says there was a wonderful garden here once. An Englishman made it. He used to come here for the summer. He was a sugar-planter or something. Wasn't that it, Manuel?'

103

Manuel's eyes rested thinly and dryly on some point across the valley.

'Yes, madame. He was sugar. He was sugar, wine, sugar-brandy, coal, sardines, water, everything.' He spoke slowly. 'He took the water from the people and sold it back again.'

'You mean he developed the country,' Manson said.

'That's so, sir.'

Manuel walked away and Manson looked after him. He detected, for the first time, an oddity in Manuel's walk. The right foot, swinging outwardly, stubbed the ground as it came back again. And this weakness, not quite a deformity, suddenly deprived the stocky shoulders of their power.

'Are you looking at his leg?' Miss Vane said. 'He was in an accident or something. With his brother. He was telling me before breakfast. Before you came down. Did he tell you?'

'No.'

'I feel rather sorry for him,' she said.

He sat down in the sun, his mind searching for a change of subject. He stared across the valley, remembering with what thin, dry abstraction Manuel had looked there.

'Oh! I just remembered,' he said. 'After the *Alacantara* on Wednesday there isn't another decent boat for three weeks.'

'No wonder you get a feeling of isolation here.'

'Well, anyway I thought you ought to know. It's a long time.'

'Would you find it long?'

He wanted to say 'It depends'. He wanted to qualify, somehow, the statement he had already made. He knew that what he had to say and feel depended on Miss Vane and whether Miss Vane caught the *Alacantara*. Already he did not want her to catch it. He was afraid of her catching it. But he could not express what he felt and he said:

'That damned man is always whistling. Can you hear it? He's always whistling.'

'I hadn't noticed it.'

When they went in to lunch Manuel stood behind her chair, holding it, pushing it gently forward as she sat down.

As he prepared to serve soup she suddenly waved her hands with impatience at herself and said:

'My bag. Would you think I could be such a dim-wit? I leave it everywhere –'

'I will get it, madame,' Manuel said.

He hurried out of the room with dignified jerky steps.

'I could have got it for you,' Manson said.

'I know you could.' The large flashing blue eyes disarmed him. 'But he likes doing things. He would be hurt if we didn't let him. That's what he's here for.'

Manuel came and put Miss Vane's bag on the lunch-table.

'Thank you, Manuel,' she said.

Manuel served soup from a wicker trolley.

'By the way,' she said, 'we would like to do the climb to the top. How long will it take us?'

'It isn't a climb, madame,' Manuel said. 'It's just a walk. It takes half an hour.'

'You and your inaccessible places,' she said to Manson. 'Everything is too easy for words.'

'What about the Serra?' Manson said. 'That isn't easy, is it?'

'I do not know the Serra, sir.'

'What is the Serra?' she said.

'It's the high plateau,' Manson said. 'The really high one. The really lonely one. Isn't that so, Manuel? – it's lonely. People don't like it, do they?'

'No, sir,' Manuel said. 'People don't like it.'

'Why not?' she said.

'I can't say, madame,' he said. 'I think it's because there's nothing there. People like to have company. They don't like places where there is nothing.'

'I think that's where we should go,' Manson said. 'That would be something worth while.'

'I don't think so, sir.'

'Oh! I most certainly think so,' Manson said. 'After all, that's what we came up here for – the high places and the view and that sort of thing.'

'If the view is no better,' Miss Vane said, 'there's hardly any point in going, is there? Is the view any better?'

'I don't think you can see so far, madame,' Manuel said.

105

'Well, there you are,' she said.

With irritation Manson said: 'I thought you were the adventurous one. I thought you liked it the difficult way.'

'Oh! I do,' she said. 'But if there's no point. I mean if Manuel doesn't think the thing worth while.'

Manson waited for Manuel to clear the soup dishes and take them away through the gauze doors that separated the dining-room from his cage at the back.

'I fail to see what Manuel has to do with it,' he said. 'We can go alone. Manuel isn't obliged to come.'

'What is there about this place?' she said.

'He's afraid of it. They're all afraid of it. They're superstitious about it.'

'Is there anything to be superstitious about?'

'Not a thing.'

'Then why do you suppose they're superstitious?'

'They hate being alone,' he said.

'Don't you?' she said.

'Not a bit,' he said. 'I rather like it – ' Abruptly he realized what he had said and he felt his confidence, which had been mounting and strengthening, suddenly recede. Confusedly he tried to retrieve it and said:

'I didn't mean it like that – I meant I liked being alone in the sense that I wasn't frightened of it – '

'Oh! it doesn't matter,' she said. 'Here comes the food. It looks like a sort of pie – is it, Manuel? Is it pie?'

'Yes, madame,' he said. 'It is steak and kidney pie. Made in the English way.'

After lunch, as they had coffee outside, under a tree he kept telling her was an arbutus, though he was not sure and it was the only way of getting his confidence back, she said:

'About this place. Would you like to go?'

'I'd like to,' he said.

Her eyes, always so large and incorrigibly assertive and apparently forceful, seemed suddenly uncertain. She ran her hand across the streak of paler hair and said:

'It isn't one of those evil places, is it? You know – nothing to do with the dead?'

'It's just high and lonely,' he said. 'It's the crowning point of the island. That's all.'

She stared across the valley, to a far glitter of sun on harsh iron rock, and Manson remembered how Manuel had stared across the valley too.

'You'd really like to go, wouldn't you?' she said. 'We'd have to go alone, I suppose? Manuel wouldn't come.'

He felt an ascendant rush of triumph at the thought of being alone with her.

'I don't think it need bother us,' he said. 'It isn't that far.'

For a moment she did not answer. She had slipped off the dress she had put on to cover her sun-suit during lunch and once again he found himself thinking how taut and mature her body looked, emerging naked and smooth pale brown from the costume of vivid green. If only he could have rubbed out, somehow, the disturbing streak of paler hair.

'You really think it's not one of those evil places?' she said. 'Nothing to do with the dead?'

'No more than anywhere else has.'

'Only I couldn't bear it,' she said, 'if it had anything to do with the dead. And it's been so easy so far.'

6

They arranged to start next morning at nine; but when Manson came out of his bedroom and went out on to the veranda he discovered Miss Vane and Manuel talking at the foot of the steps. Manuel had rigged up a pole on which, at each end, he had hooked a basket for luncheon. As he saw Manson coming he hoisted the pole to his shoulder, balancing the baskets on the curved smooth pole.

With vexation Manson said: 'I thought Manuel wasn't coming.'

'He's coming as far as lunch,' Miss Vane said. 'Then if we want to go on any farther –'

'Of course we want to go farther, don't we?' he said. 'We want to do the whole thing.'

'He says that's up to us.'

'It's amazing how people fold up when it comes to it,' Manson said. 'Good God, you might think it was Everest or something.'

'Well, it's probably as well he is coming,' she said. 'We'd only have to carry the lunch baskets and it's going to be awfully hot.'

Manuel, who had not spoken, began to walk on ahead. Miss Vane followed him and Manson walked some paces behind her. The sunlight behind him was already so crystalline in its subalpine transparence that it shone in Miss Vane's hair with a remarkable effect of edging it with minute thorns of tawny gold.

Presently, across the steep short valley, he could see the high edge of the central plateau. It surprised him, in that first moment, by having something domestic about it. It emerged as a vast and domestic piece of pumice stone abandoned between two vaster shoulders of naked rock. In the strong sunlight he could have sworn that these rocks, perpendicular and iron-grey and treeless to the foot, shot off a spark or two that flashed like signals across the lower valley.

'That's where we're going,' he said to Miss Vane. 'See? – up there.'

'It looks farther off than I thought,' she said.

'We've got all day,' he said. 'After all it's only Monday – you don't have to catch the *Alacantara* today.'

As he spoke of the *Alacantara* he remembered the town: Monday morning, the drawn sun-shutters of the office, the spiritless flat dustiness of rooms shut up for the week-end, the horrible Monday lassitude. A signal from the opposing rocks across the valley shot off with a trick of winking semaphore and expressed his astonished joy at being no longer part of that awful office, watching the cabs on the water-front, the listless boot-blacks rocking on the pavements, the funerals racing away up the hill.

He realized, with a remarkable surge of confidence, that he was free.

'By the way, are you going to catch the *Alacantara*? Have you made up your mind?'

'Not quite.'

'I know her captain,' he said. 'I'd come aboard with you and see that he knew who you were.'

She turned and held out her hand suddenly and said:

'There's room for you to walk on the track with me. Come on. I hate walking alone.'

A fragment of his hesitation came back.

'Come on,' she said. 'Come and walk with me. I hate the feeling of someone being just behind me.'

She reached out and caught his hand and they walked abreast.

'That's better,' she said. 'Now I feel you're with me.'

Sometimes the swaying coolie-like scales of Manuel's baskets disappeared beyond dark shoulders of rock. Manson felt then that Manuel was not part of himself and Miss Vane. He looked up at the enlarging plateau, assuring himself of its unexciting domesticity, feeling contemptuous of people like Manuel who saw it as a formidable and fearsome thing.

At the same time the feeling grew on him also that Miss Vane was slightly afraid. That was why she wanted him to walk with her; that was why she would ask him now and then if he still wanted to go to the top. He had the increasing impression too that she had something on her mind. Perhaps that was why she was continually so forgetful of things like her handbag.

Half way through the morning one of his shoe-laces came undone. He had not brought with him very suitable shoes for walking and the best he could find that day was a pair of old canvas sandals, with rubber soles.

As he stooped to tie the shoe-lace Miss Vane stopped to wait for him. He had some difficulty with the shoe-lace and was afraid of breaking it. When he looked up again Manuel had disappeared and Miss Vane was alone, staring at something far down a long spoon-shaped gorge of rock.

His feelings at seeing her there alone gave him a sort of buoyancy. His shoes were soft on the path. He had nothing to do but creep up to her and put his hands on her hair and turn her face to him and kiss her.

Before he could do anything she turned and pointed down the gorge and said:

'There's something down there. Do you see? Right down. A house or something – two or three houses.'

'Yes. They're houses,' he said.

'I didn't think there were villages up here.'

'It's a longish way away,' he said. 'Probably two or three hours by path.'

'We must ask Manuel about it,' she said.

His feeling of buoyancy died and when they walked on again he automatically fell into the way of walking behind her until she reminded him about it and held out her hand.

Before lunch, which Manuel laid out in a small clearing of pines, in one of those places where water dripped like summery rain from fissures of cacti-studded rock, Manuel asked her stiffly:

'Would you like something to drink before you eat, madame?'

'I would,' she said. 'What is there?'

'There's beer, madame,' he said. 'And gin.'

'What gin is it?' Manson said.

'The best, sir.' Manuel held up the bottle for Manson to see and Manson said:

'Good. We don't want local muck. I'll have gin too.'

He drank the gin rather quickly. Then, looking down over the sliced-out gorges, streamless far below, he used exactly the words Miss Vane had used on the journey up with the mules.

'Well, this is marvellous,' he said. The village of obscure white houses seemed of paltry insignificance, far away. 'It's absolutely marvellous, I think. Don't you?'

'It's lovely.'

'I think it's stunning. How far to the top, Manuel?'

'This is as far as the track goes, sir.'

'I don't get that,' Manson said. 'You can see a path going up there as plain as daylight. I've been watching it. You can see it going most of the way.'

'It's probably made by goats, sir.'

The remark seemed to Manson to have in it the slightest touch of oblique insolence, and he asked abruptly for another gin. He was very glad that Miss Vane decided to have one too.

But the lunch was good. He awarded absolutely top marks to Manuel for the lunch. A slight breeze blew off the upper mountain and cooled the glare of the sun. He took another gin and was aware of the semaphore spark of signals ignited over the black of distant rocks and he remarked several times, munching on big open sandwiches of red beef and peeled eggs and ham, that food always tasted so much better in the open air.

'What is the village, Manuel?' Miss Vane said.

'That's the village of Santa Anna, madame.'

'How far away is it?'

Manuel said: 'Several hours. It would probably take more than half a day to get there. Sometimes there are bad mists too. Then it takes more than a day.'

With another gin, in which he was glad Miss Vane joined him, Manson felt all the flare of antagonism against Manuel come back. The man was a damn know-all. Too smooth by half. Too smooth. Too knowing. Worst of all too damned right.

'Good God, look – there's an eagle,' he said.

A large bird, suspended between the two shoulders of mountain, seemed to hold for a moment the entire sky in its claws.

'That's a buzzard, sir,' Manuel said. 'There are no eagles here.'

Manson stared at the bird that seemed, with motionless deceit, to hold the sky in its claws.

'I'd like another gin,' he said. 'Would you?'

'I will if you will,' she said.

'Good,' he said. 'That'll get us steamed up for the top.'

7

During lunch Miss Vane took off her shoes and for some moments after lunch, when she appeared to have some difficulty in getting them on again, Manson felt impatient and disappointed.

'Oh! it's nothing. It's only that my feet ache a bit.' He saw her look up at the plateau of rock that spanned and blocked, exactly like the barrier of a dam, the entire western reach of valley.

'It looks awfully far,' she said.

'Don't you want to go?'

'It isn't that. I was only wondering about time.'

'I thought you were the one with plenty of time,' he said. 'We ought to have brought the hammock. Then we could have carried you.'

He said the words rather breezily, with a smile.

111

'You think we can make it?' she said. 'I mean in the time? Perhaps we ought to ask Manuel?'

'Oh! damn Manuel,' he said.

Manuel was washing the lunch things under a small fissure of water that broke from perpendicular rock above the path.

'Manuel – how far is it to the top?' she said. 'How long should it take us?'

'You should give two hours, madame.'

'There and back? – or just there?'

'There and back,' he said.

'Oh! that's nothing,' Manson said. 'That's no time.'

The sight of Manuel deferentially wiping a plate with a tea-cloth, in his shirt-sleeves, so like a waiter who had lost his way, made him feel suddenly superior again.

'You're coming, Manuel, aren't you?' she said.

'No, madame, I'm not coming. I shall wait here for you.'

A moment of strained silence seemed to be pinned, suspended, ready to drop, in the immense space of hot noon sky. With irritation Manson heard her break it by saying:

'We've got all afternoon. Won't you change your mind?'

'No thank you, madame.'

'Oh! if the fellow doesn't want to come he doesn't want to come. That's that.'

'I was simply asking,' she said.

A moment later, fired by something between annoyance and exhilaration, he was ready to start.

'If you get tired of waiting,' he said to Manuel, 'you can start back. We know the way.'

The path made a series of regular spiral ascents with growing sharpness, narrowing to a single-line track on which Manson and Miss Vane could well walk together. Disturbed by their feet a rock fell, flattish, skimming like a slate from a house-roof, pitching down, crashing with gunshot echoes into a cauldron of steamy, sunlit haze.

'It's hot, isn't it?' she said. 'You don't really want to go to the top, do you?'

'Of course I do. That's what we came for, didn't we?'

She did not answer and he said:

'I don't wonder the English perfected mountaineering. None of these other chaps seem to have the slightest guts for it.'

The buzzard reappeared in the sky like a growing speck of dust on glass, but this time below and not above him. He stood for a moment in intent exhilaration, watching the descending bird that was really a hundred feet or so below him now. He was amused to think that he had climbed higher than a bird in the sky, higher than Manuel, higher perhaps than anything but a goat or a goat-herd had ever climbed on the island before.

'You know what?' he began to say.

Another rock fell noisily. Its skimming, sliding fall, in clean curvature into hazy space, had the breathless beauty of a ball well thrown. He heard its crash on other rocks below. He listened for some time to its long double-repeated echoes across the valley. Then he realized suddenly that to his half-finished remark there had been no answer.

He turned and saw Miss Vane already forty or fifty feet above him. She was walking steadily. Before he could call she turned and stared back, eyeless in her black sun-glasses, and waved her hand.

'I thought you were the big mountaineer.'

'Oh! wait, wait,' he said. 'We must keep together.'

She seemed to laugh at him before going on. He scrambled after her. And although she was not really hurrying it was several minutes before he reached her. By that time he was glad she was sitting down.

'My God, it's getting hot,' he said.

'You were the one who wanted to do this.'

'I know. I'm all right. We mustn't rush it, that's all. It's like everything else – easy if you keep to a system.'

'My system is to lie down at frequent intervals and stop there,' she said.

As she lay down on the ledge of short dry grass she took off her sun-glasses. The glare of sun, too harsh for her, made her suddenly turn and lie on her face, spreading out her arms. Instantly the sunlight, as it had done earlier in the day, shone on the back of her hair with the brilliant effect of edging it with minute thorns of tawny gold.

113

Suddenly the sensation of uneasy intimacy he had first experienced in the cabin, on the ship, above the dishevelled bed, came rushing back. It became one with the intoxicating experience of having climbed higher than the buzzard on the mountain.

He turned her face and began kissing her. He remembered thinking that that was something he had not bargained for in any system – would not have bargained for it if he had planned it for a thousand years. She moved her lips in a series of small fluttering pulsations that might have been protests or acceptances – he could not tell. The impression was that she was about to let him go and then that she could not bear to let him go. The effect was to rock him gently, in warm blindness, on the edge of the gorge.

He was still in a world of spinning blood and sunlight and tilting rock when he sat up again. Her eyes were intensely blue under lowered lids in the sun. In a flash she shut them against the glare, parting her mouth at the same time.

'That was easy,' she said.

'Easy?'

'I mean I didn't expect you to do it like that,' she said. 'I meant I thought it would be different with you.'

He heard the snapped cry of a bird, like the flap of linen, the only sound in a vast and burning chasm of silence, somewhere above the extreme edge of stunted heath and pine.

'Again,' she said. 'It made me feel better.'

Long before the end of that second kiss he was perfectly sure that she belonged to him. He was so sure that he found himself thinking of the rest-house, the dark cover of evening, the way they would be together long after the infuriating whistling of Manuel had died behind the cage. He felt his pride in his confidence leap up through his body in thrusting, stabbing bursts.

'That made me feel better still,' she said.

'Better?'

'Happier – that's what I mean.'

Suddenly, clearly, and for the first time he found himself wondering why she had bothered to come there at the height of summer.

'Happier? – weren't you before?'

'We ought to have found some shadier spot,' she said. 'I'm melting. Can you see my bag? Where's my bag?'

He did not bother to look for the bag.

'Were you?'

'No: I wasn't,' she said.

'Was that why you came here?'

'Partly.'

Her eyes were shut again. In contrast he felt he saw the shape of her breasts, painfully clear under the thin white dress, stir, wake and look wonderfully up at him.

'Only partly?'

'You remember the day I came and I said there wasn't any colour?'

He remembered that. It seemed a thousand years away.

'It was colour I was looking for,' she said.

A bird-cry, another break of silence, another suspicion of a whispered echo far away between sun-burnt roofs of rock, was enough to make him uneasy again.

'I don't quite understand,' he said. 'Colour?'

'Where's my bag?' she said. 'Can't you see my bag?'

For God's sake, he thought, the bag. Why the bag? Why did she always forget the bag?

'No, it's not here. You can't have brought it,' he said.

'Oh! didn't I?' She sat up, groping in the sun. Her eyes were wide open; he saw them blue and wet, enormous with trouble. Ineffectually he searched for the bag too, knowing it wasn't there. He knew too what she was going to ask and while he was still groping about the grass she said:

'Would you go back and get it? Would you be a dear?'

He knew suddenly that he was a fool. He was a fool and he would go down and get the bag. He was a fool and he would climb up again. In time she would lose the bag again and he would be a fool and find it once more.

'Must you have it? Do you need it to kiss with?'

'Don't talk like that. I'm lost without it, that's all. You can kiss me anyway.'

As she sat upright he kissed her again. He felt her give a great start of excitement, as if all the blood were leaping to the front of her body. Then she broke away and said:

'The bag. Couldn't you get the bag? – would you please?'

'You're not in some kind of trouble, are you?' he said.

'No. No trouble.'

'Tell me what it is.'

'I'm in no trouble – honest to God I'm not in any trouble.'

'What then?'

'I don't know – a sort of hell,' she said. 'Get the bag and I'll tell you about it. You've made me feel better about it already.'

Suddenly where her body had been there was space. Some trick of refraction, a twist in the glare of sun on whiteness, suppressed his power of sight. Instead of her shining body there was a naked gap on the path. As he walked down it to fetch her bag he found he could not see very well. He was aware of groping again, his canvas shoes slithering on scalding dark platters of rock, waking loose stones to curve out on flights of vicious perfection to the steaming haze below.

The infuriating whistle of Manuel brought him back to himself.

'Have you seen Miss Vane's bag?' he shouted.

'Yes, sir. Here it is, sir, with the lunch things.'

Manson grasped the white bag and turned to walk back up the path.

'Aren't you going to the top, sir?'

'Mind your own business!' he said. He stopped. 'Oh! another thing. I think we'll be starting back tomorrow. You'd better get back and start packing.'

'Very well, sir,' Manuel said.

High above the mountainside the sombre hypnotic buzzard had risen again to hold the sky in its claws. It woke in Manson a sudden hatred for the place. The sky of summer seemed to reflect, in a curious harsh and lifeless glare, the depressing slate-like glaze of the high naked edge of plateau. Below, the trees were fired and lost in smouldering ashen dust. From far away a glint of steel in minute winks shot from the mass of pines with the effect of blue glass-paper.

A moment or two later he heard once again that curious sound that was like the dry flap of shaken linen, startling in the thin air.

He heard it at the moment of turning the last of the spirals in the path before reaching Miss Vane. And as he heard it and turned his head he lost his sense of focus again, and a rock fell.

It fell this time from under his feet. It seemed to cross, a second later, a shadow that might have been caused by the buzzard suddenly whipping earthwards to kill. Instead he saw that it was another rock. It fell with bewildering swiftness from under his too-smooth canvas shoes, taking with it a black and slaty shower.

This shower was the entire corner of the path. As it fell it seemed to suck him down. For a second or two he was aware of a conscious effort to save himself. Then, clutching with ferocity at Miss Vane's white bag, he fell too.

8

His impression of coming death was sharp and instantaneous. It was a flame leaping up to meet him like the uprising ball of sun. Its inescapable extinction was like the extinction of Miss Vane's white body on the path. It was there one moment and then, in a final trick of refraction, was black and void.

He half picked himself up in a shower of slate and slate-dust, at the foot of a pine no taller than a man. His left foot was jammed by rock. His fall had ended in a kind of football tackle, not badly aimed at the feet, the roots of the pine. He struggled to free his foot, and the tree-roots, under his weight, cracked under the rock and began to come out like slow-drawn teeth, in gristly pain. He thought he was laughing. Then he knew that he was really sucking air, enormous gasps of it, gorging at it, fighting for it in pure fright with his terrified mouth and tongue.

The last of the tree-roots were sucked out and the tree fell over, letting him down. His foot too was free. He laughed and shouted something. He did not know what it was but the very feeling of coherent air across his tongue gave him enormous hope. He felt suddenly as calm and poised as the buzzard above the valley.

He climbed slowly up on his hands and knees, aware of a slight drag in his left leg. It was not important, he thought, and when he reached the path he sat down with his back against rock and kept saying:

'I'm all right. I'm perfectly all right. I'm absolutely and perfectly all right.'

'Oh! my God. I'm sick,' she said. 'Oh! my God – I'm so sick.'

'I'll hold you. Lie against the rock,' he said.

But he found that he could not hold her. He lay against the rock too, trembling all over. The valley swam below him. Whole waves of dust-bright haze washed over him, drowning him in sweat, leaving him cold.

'I knew I was gone,' he said. 'I know what the end is like now.'

'Let's go down,' she said.

His eyes were shut. His sweating face seemed to be glued against a cool bone of projecting rock.

He thought the rock moved. He discovered then that it was her own face, terribly and dryly cool. His sweat was drying too and he shuddered. Then he felt the sun burning his eyeballs through lids that were like dry thin tissue and he knew that if he did not get up and walk he would slide in weakness, like a dislodged stone, off the edge of the gorge.

They were far down on the path, at the place where they had lunched, before she said:

'I never liked heights. I could never bear them. I hate that awful vertigo.'

He was glad to see that Manuel had taken him at his word and had started back. He was glad too that the path was at last doubly wide, so that the two of them could walk together.

The idea that something was very wrong with his left foot came to him slowly. The drag of it was heavy and finally it woke into pain.

He found himself at last sitting on the path staring into a shoe half full of blood.

'It was all my fault,' she said. 'I wanted to go up there.'

Half-blindly he poured blood on to the dust of the path and struggled to put on his wet, blackening shoe. Somehow he could not get it back.

Nothing of the kind, he thought. He felt tired and sick. Staring at the blood-stained shoe, he remembered clearly how she had not wanted to go. He recalled his own exultation at rising above

Manuel and the bird in the sky. It seemed so ridiculous now that he could only say:

'I didn't want to go either. I hate the damn place.'

He sat there for a long time trying to put on his shoe. He could smell the old corrupt dark smell of blood as it dried. The shoe would not go back and there was something sinister and twisted about the swollen shape of his foot. Long before he gave up trying with the shoe he knew somehow that the foot was not going to take him home.

But now, trying to be bright about things, he said:

'They say it's an ill wind. Now you'll probably get an extra day to catch the *Alacantara*.'

She did not answer.

'You are going to catch it, aren't you?'

'Yes.'

He suddenly wished that something more spectacular had happened back on the path. There was nothing very dramatic after all in cutting a slice or two out of your foot.

'I know her captain,' he said 'I'll see that you get fixed up.'

'I can understand if you're bitter about me,' she said.

'I'm not bitter.'

'You sound bitter.'

'Perhaps because you kissed me up there.'

Strength seemed to drain out of his body and it seemed a long time afterwards before she said:

'Kissing isn't always the start of something. In this case it was the end.'

'The end of what?' he said. 'Probably me.'

'I've been running away from something. That's all. When you kissed me it was the end of running.'

He wanted to say something like 'Glad to have been of service, Miss Vane.' A withering breath of burning rock blew into his face. His foot pained him violently, stabbing in sickening throbs, and he did not answer.

'You've been so sweet to me,' she said. 'Doing what I wanted.'

'Husband,' he said, 'or what?'

'Husband.'

'You must give him the love of a decaying shipping clerk when you get back,' he said. 'Miss Vane.'

'He may not be there when I get back,' she said. 'That's the point. But I've got to try.'

Savagely the heat blew into his face again and the raw weeping soreness of his foot made him sick.

'I'll bet he's a lousy –'

'You might call him that,' she said. 'But then that's sometimes how it is. Some men are lousy and they get under your skin. You know they're lousy and you can't help it. You can't fight them. But thanks to you – thanks to you I've got it worked out now. I can stop running and go back.'

'Good God, don't thank me. That's what I'm for.'

He knew it was no use. It was no good, that way of talking. His foot seemed to enlarge and burst like a bloated blister, bringing his head up with a sharp breath of pain. Above him the sky swung round and quivered. A speck that might have been dust or a buzzard or just the shadow of something fell swiftly from it and cut across his sweat-locked eyes.

She saw his pain and said:

'I'll get Manuel. I'll get you back.'

'Oh! God no. I can make it.'

'I'll get Manuel. It's better.'

He tried to watch her figure going down the path. Weakly he tried to call out to her to come back. Then he was alone and it was no use. He was a darkening, dribbling figure, undramatic and strengthless, slipping down from the rock.

The worst of it, some long time later, was the sight of Manuel, coming to take him away. The correct, oiled, subservient figure. The slight bow. The glance at the foot, the shoe that was black with blood. The cool eyes, the mouth that was so well-shaped, so poised, that it might have ejected at any moment that maddening whistle:

'I told you so.'

9

It was morning, about ten o'clock, when Manuel carried him out to the waiting mules. The crushed arch of his foot might have been made of cactus thorns, each thorn a nerve beating nakedly up and down to the thump of blood. His head, like the foot, seemed to have swollen and he felt the great thudding pulse of it rocking outwards, rolling and striking the sides of the valley.

'I'm going to tie you on to the mule, sir. Just to be safe. In case you feel dizzy.'

'Absolutely all right,' he said. 'Where's madame?'

He could no longer call her Miss Vane. It was madame now.

'She's just getting the last of her things. She's going to ride with you.'

'She's got to catch the *Alacantara*,' he said. 'What about the car?'

'I'm going to telephone for it, sir. Then I'll send the hammock back from the top of the road.'

'Hammock? For Christ's sake what hammock?'

'You'll be better in the hammock, sir.'

He found himself shaking and swaying with sickness, impotent behind the fluttering ears of the mule, the entire valley projected before him in those strong high blue lines that were again pulsations rather than shadow.

'Much better if you let madame push on. I can manage. Let her push on.'

Presently he was aware of a slow transition of scene: rock and pine looming up, starry walls of cactus leaf dripping past, bright under springs, sunlight firing pine-needles to masses of glass-paper, ashy blue under a sickening sky.

Heat lay on the back of his neck, in spite of the towel Manuel had put there, like a burning stone. He wondered why there had been no attempt to escape the heat by starting earlier. Then he remembered not being able to sleep. Great rocks in the valley grating against each other. A far continuous thunder, a power-house noise, from across the plateau. Water, a stream somewhere, drowning him, dragging him under. He remembered falling down.

He had walked out to the veranda, seeing Miss Vane there, in an attempt to show her that there was nothing wrong with his foot. He vividly remembered the band of paler hair across the black front of her head as she turned. He said, 'Hullo' and she screamed and out of the sky at the head of the valley a wing of blackness smothered him.

'The point is that the *Alacantara* is sometimes half a day earlier,' he said. She was riding twenty or thirty paces in front of him. Her hair was a mass of pure black, with no other colour but the outer minute sparkle of tawny fire. It was part of his sickness that his eye saw the fires of each hair with remarkable clearness, so that he felt he could touch them with his hands.

He did in fact lift his hands from the saddle. As he did so the valley swayed. He was no longer part of it. The saddle was not there to grasp, nor the quivering head of the mule, nor her dark brilliant hair.

He was lost in emptiness and found himself crying out like a child. His mouth slobbered as he groped for air. Then the saddle was there, and the mule, and her head far off, black and unaware.

'It's like everything else,' he said. 'Never know where you are. A boat can be two days late. Or half a day early. You never really know.'

If she was listening she showed no sign. For some moments he was under the impression that she had galloped far down the valley and disappeared. He shouted something. Masses of tree-heather, growing taller now as the valley descended, broke apart and revealed her, drawn up and waiting, only a yard or two away.

'Did you say anything?' she said.

'No. All right. Perfectly all right.'

'Say when you don't want to go on.'

He could not check his mule. He seemed to be pitching forward, head first, down the track.

'Did you hear what I said about the *Alacantara*?'

'You mustn't worry about that.'

'She may be early. She goes out on Wednesday. But you never know – she might be in at midnight tonight. She sometimes is.'

'Today is Friday,' she said.

He knew that he could not have heard her correctly. He knew

that it was only yesterday that he had fallen off the track. It was only an hour or two since he had emptied out his shoe, with its old sour smell of blood, like a dirty beaker.

'You probably won't get a passage for two or three weeks,' he said.

She was too far away to answer, a dissolving fragment, under high sun, of pure white and pure black, like a distant road-sign that was the warning of a bend.

'That's the way with this island. It's easy to get here but it's hell's own job to get away.'

Some time later he was aware of the undergrowth of pine giving up a pair of stunted figures in black trilby hats. He saw the canopy of a hammock, red-flowered like an old bed coverlet between the poles. He was saying, 'Let me alone. Let me walk,' and then he was being lifted in. It was rather difficult lifting him in because of his leg and because only one end of the pole could be held up. The other was in the ground, leaving one man free to lift him and set him down.

It was stupid about the leg. As they took him down from the mule he could not feel it at all. Its pain had become self-numbed like the pain of a tooth at a dentist's threshold. All his pain was between his eyes, brightening his vision so that the little flowers of the hammock pattern sprang at him, dancing pink and blue with fire.

'What about you?' he said. 'You push on. You've got to go. Anyway the plane is on Saturdays.'

'That can wait,' she said. 'That isn't important. The important thing is to get you down. We ought to have done it before.'

'You'd got it all so clear,' he said.

The pole straightened. He was lying parallel with the sky. She wiped his face several times with a handkerchief.

'How now?' she said. 'Do you feel fit to go?'

'Fit,' he said. 'Absolutely.' And then in a moment of brightness: 'Don't forget the handbag.'

'I nearly would have done.' His impression was that she was crying. He was not sure. She kissed him gently on the mouth and said: 'Take it easy. Easy does it.'

'Easy,' he said. 'That's what you said before.'

A few moments later the trilby hats began to carry him slowly, in the hammock, down the path. Easy, he thought, that was it. How easy it had been. A ship, a handbag on a bed, a hotel, a *leste* burning through the town, a rest-house, a track to the top of the sky. Easy: that was her word.

'How do you feel?' she said. 'Do you want them to go slower?'

'No,' he said. 'Aren't you really going now?'

'No,' she said. 'Not yet. Not now.'

Delirium exploded a moment later in stars of pain. There was a smell of camphor from the hammock sheet, anaesthetic, making him gasp for breath; and then, unexpectedly, he was aware of a strange impression.

He stared up at the sky. In the centre of it he could have sworn he saw a shadow, huge and descending, in the shape of the buzzard, holding the sky in its claws.

'Easy,' she said, and 'Easy' his mind echoed, remembering the shape of her mouth in the sun.

The next moment he began fighting. 'I won't go!' he shouted. 'I won't go! I won't let it happen to me!' But she did not hear him. The trilby hats did not hear him either, and with calm slowness they carried him forward through the valley, down under the scorning brilliance of noon, towards the sea.

The Queen of Spain Fritillary

I was a dark-haired, pretty and rather tiresome girl of seventeen when my mother and elder sister took me on my first visit to a house called 'Orleans', a short distance above a wide bend of the river and overlooking some miles of meadows, in the valley of the Ouse.

It was one of those rare afternoons in July when the air was drenched in the scent of roses and the fragrance of hay lying thick-cut in field after field along the river as we drove up in the big landaulette taxi we had hired to bring us from the village station. It was very hot that day, in spite of a strong breeze, and with a remarkable shimmering light on all the distances.

This light had one extraordinary effect I shall never forget. As we drove along the road to the house we were, at one point, high above the valley on an open ridge. Below us we could see perhaps a mile of river winding in big curves, under hump-backed bridges of stone, among the rich flat fields of hay.

Suddenly I saw, repeated again and again, all along the stream, what I thought at first were flocks of pure white ducks. They seemed to be floating quite motionless, between dark green banks of reed. Then, as the taxi dropped further and further down the valley, I saw that I was mistaken. What I had thought were ducks were really whole islands, purest white, of water-lilies, in the crown of their bloom.

'I hope you're not going to sulk again, child,' my mother said.

I had not been quite myself that summer; I was probably outgrowing my strength, my mother would tell me. It was true that I was often sulking and I must confess I felt most like sulking when my mother called me child.

It is perhaps a good thing to make it plain, also, that I did not get on at all well with my sister.

Angela was a very determined person of twenty-five, fair-haired, healthy and ambitious, who was going to be married in October. Our visit to this house, with its attractive and un-English name of 'Orleans', was part of a long search for somewhere where she and Ewart Mackeson, her fiancé, a successful junior partner in a leather-tanning company, could live. Mr Ewart Mackeson was a person of ambition too.

It was still fairly easy to get servants in those days and what Mr Mackeson and my sister were looking for was a house of twelve or fifteen rooms, with stables if possible, an orchard or paddock, perhaps a few acres of shooting, a lawn on which to play tennis and an entrance marked 'Tradesmen' at the side.

Neither Angela nor Mr Ewart Mackeson understood architecture, beauty or anything of that sort. What they were looking for was quite simple. It was, as I once told them with what I thought was a flash of enlightened sarcasm, suburbia in tweeds. Mr Ewart Mackeson was in fact an example of a type that has become more and more common with the passing years. He wanted to be an officer in a good suburban regiment, playing the country squire.

You might have thought that that sort of house would not have been difficult to find. The country is after all full of them. It is the sort of house that used so often to be called 'The Grange' or 'The Cedars' or sometimes even 'The Towers'; it almost invariably had virginia creeper covering its red brickwork and well-kept gardens where clipped hedges of box enclosed beds of yellow calceolaria, blue lobelia and scarlet geraniums. It was a type of house – residence is really the right word – built exclusively by and for people like Mr Ewart Mackeson and my sister and in a way it was, I suppose, part of the country's backbone.

There is no doubt that houses have souls, but I suppose they reveal themselves only to certain temperaments to which they are suited. Certainly, that summer, no house revealed its soul to us. We must have looked at twenty or thirty altogether and all of them hopeless. If their views were entrancing their sanitation was primeval; if they possessed stables they were also next to the gas-works; if their gardens were delightful there were odours suspicious of mice in the bedrooms.

Everyone knows, I suppose, about these impossible characteristics of houses for sale and all I really want to make clear is that by that hot afternoon in mid-July I had reached the point when I never wished to see another house. I had in fact made up my mind not to go to see 'Orleans'. I had somehow worked up inside myself such an antipathy towards that house that I spent most of the morning lying at the bottom of the garden, staring into space, sulking.

It is only fair to say that I was very often sulking. One of my most frequent and formidable sulks was in fact about Mr Ewart Mackeson. From the first Mr Mackeson put my back up. It is not possible to explain it easily, but whenever he came into the room I felt myself begin to bristle. In fact there was even more to it than that. One of the first manifestations of my not being well that summer was a tendency to go off to my room and lie down, refusing to eat, when Mr Mackeson came to supper. My blood curdled at the thought of him and his invasion of our three-part feminine privacy.

There was, for example, the instance of the coloured leather. One of Mr Mackeson's more enterprising business experiments was that of tanning leather in exquisite new bright shades. They were really exquisite, some of those chrome yellows, scarlets, royal blues, emeralds, lime greens and even pinks and pigeon greys. The tanning of leather is not, I suppose, a very romantic occupation except to the chemists who conjure up the dyes and it was beyond me to grasp at seventeen that Mr Ewart Mackeson was himself a talented person, something of an artist in his way.

One evening that spring, anyway, he brought along to the house several samples of these bright new leathers to show my sister. He wanted her to choose a colour – if she liked, several colours – so that he could have made for her a pair of shoes and a handbag to match them.

Finally Angela chose a pale green leather, almost the shade of an unripe bean. I did not say anything. A colour can be exquisite in itself and yet be atrocious, pure murder, for a certain type of person. I knew that that pale bean shade would kill my sister's pale hair and features, but I made no comment. And then Mr Mackeson said:

'And what about you, Mrs Burnett? Wouldn't you like to choose something too?'

My mother was a tall pink woman who was sometimes inclined to gush. Alternatively she would simper. She, too, like my sister, was fair and pale. Although her body was angular and thin, she always wore long boned corsets and in summer carried a dark grey parasol to keep the sun from her face, with its unblemished complexion of china-rose. The result was that sometimes she had the appearance of being embalmed.

'Oh! no I couldn't, Ewart, I couldn't. I really couldn't,' she said.

That was, of course, just a pose of hers; it was simply a case of protesting too much. The gush was far too obvious. And presently my mother, after more pressure from Mr Mackeson and more refusal and more protest from her, was choosing her own piece of leather.

'That red, I think. No, the yellow. Shall I? I love the red – I do absolutely love the red. Like a tomato, isn't it? What shall it be, Angela? What do you say?'

Finally, of all things, she chose a yellow. It was a mustard yellow, unfriendly, chemical and hard. It was a hopeless colour for anyone except a dark person like myself, or even a coloured person, to wear.

But I still made no comment. My mother, I remember, made a few more gushing remarks about how heavenly and charming that shade of yellow was and how generous and too nice Mr Ewart Mackeson was, and then he suddenly turned to me and said:

'Now, Laura, what about you? Come on now – what do you fancy?'

I suppose he was simply trying to be ordinarily civil and nice to me; I suppose he could hardly have done less than that. But suddenly I got up, looked witheringly at him and said with sarcasm:

'No thank you. I don't want to look like a mustard plaster. Or something in a pea-green boat for that matter,' and then turned sharply on my heel and went upstairs.

The truth is that I was very fond of my sister. She was already a young woman, wearing woman's clothes, when I was eleven or twelve. I looked up to her with that distant heroine worship that only the very young can give and there was of course nothing at all to affect it or disturb it until Mr Ewart Mackeson appeared. It was very hard for me to accustom myself, though I did not consciously grasp it at the time, that my sister was going to be taken away from me.

From all this it is easy to see why, as I sat in the back of the landaulette taxi that afternoon, staring at the river, the meadows of hay and the water-lilies that looked like crowds of pure white ducks in the simmering light of July, my mother should say:

'I hope you're not going to sulk again, child, I hoped we'd got over that.'

I was in fact not sulking. I was really absorbed in that illusive trick of light that the afternoon had played on me. I was really entranced by the fact that a crowd of ducks had turned themselves into water-lilies and I wanted to be left alone with the idea, entranced, for a little longer.

That was why I said, as the taxi drew up at the iron gates of the house, under a long row of tall, flowering limes:

'I'm not coming in. I'll sit here and wait for you.'

'I shall not argue,' my mother said. She got out of the car and snapped up her dark grey parasol. 'I shall not argue. There's no point in wasting breath. As long as you behave like a child you must be treated as a child.'

I wanted to point out, tensely, that I was not a child. Instead I said:

'I might even start to walk back. You can pick me up on the way.'

'Do entirely as you wish,' my mother said. 'Have it entirely your own way.'

A minute later she disappeared with my sister up the gravel drive, between thick shrubberies of lilac and laurustinus, towards the stone white-windowed house that could be seen, with its high white doorway and its big black iron boot-scraper, at the end.

Presently I heard the door-bell ring. After a few moments I saw an elderly maid in white cap and apron answer the door. Then my mother and sister disappeared into the house and after that I suppose I sat there for four or five minutes before I became aware of an extraordinary thing.

I suddenly experienced an overwhelming curiosity about the house. I felt that I had to see it after all. It was not simply that it was in itself very different from all those virginia-creepered, half-towered desirable residences we had seen all summer. It was not simply because it had no virginia creeper to smother the walls. It was true that it had a big pale yellow rose, with almost plum-coloured foliage, growing above the door, and over one gable one of those huge magnolias, with thick polished leaves, whose flowers are so like large pure cream chalices when they open in late hot summers.

All these things were attractive in themselves but they had nothing to do with what I had started to feel. What I felt had nothing particularly to do with beauty, with the charm of the yellow rose above the doorway, the flowerless magnolia cool in the heat or the drenching fragrance of the long row of limes. It had nothing to do, either, with that curious sensation people so often experience with places, and with houses especially: the sensation, not always pleasant and sometimes uncannily disturbing, that they have been there before.

What I felt was a rather startling sense of communication with that house. Of course the sensory impressions and perception of the very young are often over-acute and perhaps the definition of what I felt may sound absurd. But this is the way youth feels and it did not seem at all absurd to me that afternoon that the house had, as it were, something to say to me. That is perhaps a naïve and clumsy way of putting it and the only other way I can express it is to say that it was rather like your being in a room and hearing urgent whispers of conversation going on in another. In a situation like that you are more than eaten up with overwhelming curiosity. You realize that if you don't listen at that moment, quickly, it will be too late. You will never know what the urgent whispers of conversation are about. It will all be lost and you will regret it for ever.

That was why, a few moments later, I was walking up the drive.

I rang the door-bell twice, but nothing happened. I discovered afterwards that there was only one servant indoors and that she at that moment was showing my mother and my sister through the rooms upstairs.

After another two or three minutes I decided not to ring again and I started to walk back down the drive. And then, for the second time, I experienced that extraordinary feeling of curiosity. And almost at once, not stopping to think, I turned and began to walk round to the side of the house, through a large archway of yew, into the gardens beyond.

The gardens sloped away sharply, in a series of terraces joined by stone steps, to the river. I was surprised to see them, in contrast to the front of the house, running wild. Tall coarse yellow mulleins, with caterpillar-eaten leaves, had sown themselves all through the flower beds, among the roses and even, at one place, in broken cucumber frames. Sunflowers were presently going to obliterate the beds of asparagus. Soon there would be nothing to be seen of a plantation of raspberries, struggling with an invasion of white convolvulus in full trumpet bloom.

I walked slowly through this choking mass of vegetation to the river. A path ran along the bank, heavily shaded by big balsam poplar trees. You could smell the fragrance of balsam leaves in the hot flat air and in the shadow of the trees the river was dark, with deep underskeins of weed.

Halfway along the path was a little wooden landing stage with a seat on it. It was surrounded by a hand-rail and a punt was chained to the end. The punt, the little seat, the landing stage and in fact everything about it were, unlike the garden, surprisingly well kept. The punt had recently been painted a fresh bright green and even the name of the house, 'Orleans', had been picked out in white at the stern end.

I followed the path for forty or fifty yards along the river and began presently to approach the boundaries of the garden on the other side. It was wilder than ever there, with a few straggling pyramid pear-trees growing in long meadow grass as tall as wheat and in full seed.

Beyond all this was another hedge of yew, ten or twelve feet high, with a path cut through the grass beside it. I started to walk up this path. Then, halfway up the slope, I heard a voice. It was a man's voice and it seemed, I thought, to be talking to itself in the hot still air.

And it was talking very remarkably. I am not sure at this distance of time if I can remember word for word exactly what it was

131

saying but presently what I heard was, I think, something like this:

'It forms a ladder of its web so that it can climb up it to any height – even up a pane of glass. They smell awfully disagreeable but apparently the Romans thought them delicious. They were a favourite dish of theirs.'

That was about all I heard before I came upon the man himself, standing by the hedge. He was a man of sixty or so, a little under medium height, rather spruce, with very smooth grey hair. He was wearing a cream shantung summer jacket, grey trousers with a chalk stripe in them and a white panama.

There was nothing in the least remarkable about all this. What was remarkable was that he was holding a branch of about half a dozen leaves in his hand. At first I thought he was talking to these leaves. Then I saw that I was mistaken. Something was crawling up the branch and I concluded, mistakenly as it turned out, that he was talking to that.

It was a thick, pink, naked, quite repulsive caterpillar.

If it is surprising for a girl of seventeen to come upon an elderly gentleman in a strange garden talking to an ugly caterpillar it must be equally surprising for elderly gentlemen to have conferences of this kind interrupted by strange girls of seventeen.

The surprising thing was that he did not show surprise at all. He looked at me, then looked at the caterpillar, which had now reached the tip of the branch, and seemed for a moment undecided which of us to attend to first. Then, very deftly, he turned the branch the other way up, so that the caterpillar could climb up it again, and with the other hand raised his panama.

As he took off his hat I saw that his eyes, remarkably blue in the brilliant sunshine, transfixed me.

'Good afternoon,' he said.

I began to explain how it was I was there, how sorry I was to interrupt him and so on, and he said, 'Yes. Oh! yes. Yes, of course,' several times, watching me with the remarkably blue bright eyes while I in turn stood watching the caterpillar.

'Will this lead me back to the house?' I said.

'One moment. One moment,' he said and then started to address the hedge:

'It seems I have visitors. About the house. You understand,

dear, don't you? I'll show you a figure of the goat later. It's rather a treasure. This one's a bit of a freak of course. He ought not to be out now. He ought to have been out in May, but that's how it is sometimes.'

Of course youth is very quick to spot the ridiculous. And suddenly I thought I'd never seen anything quite as killing as the business of holding this repulsive caterpillar on a stick and carrying on a two-part conversation with it and a hedge. It seemed funnier still when, through a break in the hedge, I saw the flap of a big pink sun-hat on the other side and heard a woman's voice say:

'Of course, dear. That I shall look forward to immensely. Au revoir, Frederick. Good-bye.'

'Au revoir,' he said.

Already by this time the caterpillar had climbed to the top of the branch and now the man in the panama, turning to me, deftly twisted the branch upside down so that the caterpillar could climb up it again.

'Do come this way,' he said.

To my surprise he began to lead me back down the path, towards the river. All the time he held the branch at half-arm's length, rather like a torch, and I didn't think I'd ever see anything quite so fatuous.

As if to make the whole thing more ridiculous he seemed absolutely absorbed in me. He talked very quickly, in rather a flutey sort of voice, asking all sorts of questions. Then, unable to take his eyes off me, he eventually completely forgot the caterpillar, which finally reached the top of the stick and sat there looking most disagreeably naked and slightly bloated.

'So you've come to see this house?' he said. 'Well, well. How nice. Indeed. How nice. These are the only two houses that front on the river here. All the rest of the land, you see, is meadow. With a continual danger of floods, you see, so that you can't build down there. It's only just here, because of this bend and the big bank, that it's been possible to have these houses.'

It was, I still thought, extraordinarily funny: the prattling flutey voice, the enthusiasm, the eagerness, like that of a boy, and always, of course, the caterpillar.

133

And presently the caterpillar itself got funnier still. At the path by the river we stopped for nearly five minutes while he went into a prolonged explanation about the punt and the landing stage. By this time I was not listening very closely and he, more and more absorbed in me, was not looking at the caterpillar.

I saw that it had, in fact, crawled back down the stick and now, slowly and steadily, hunching its back, was crawling up his arm.

'And what is your name? I mean,' he said, 'your Christian name.'

'Laura,' I said.

'How charming,' he said. The little bright blue eyes glittered, dancing with pleasure as the caterpillar crawled up the neat shantung arm. 'And what are you? – I mean how old? Seventeen?'

'Nineteen,' I said.

The whole affair was so ridiculous that the lie about my age was, I thought, not only in keeping with it all but made it, if possible, more fun.

'Still at school?'

'Oh! heavens no,' I said. And this time I didn't lie. 'I haven't been to school all summer.'

'No?' he said. 'Well, you don't look like a schoolgirl. You look too sure of yourself for that.'

I suppose that flattered me: to be told that I looked as old as I had pretended to be. But even the flattery didn't quite cancel out the comic tone of the whole situation. The caterpillar was now, I saw, crawling on his shoulder. I watched it fascinated, ready to shriek if it reached his neck.

He, on the other hand, didn't seem to notice it at all and presently he said, tapping the little seat on the landing stage:

'Come and sit down for a minute and tell me all about yourself.'

'I ought to go,' I said. I began to explain how my mother and my sister would be waiting for me. I said something about their thinking, perhaps, that I might be walking back along the road and he said:

'Who has really come to look at the house? Your mother?'

'Oh! no, my sister. You see, she's to be married soon.'

The caterpillar had reached the lapel of his shantung jacket, just above the buttonhole. It was arching its head this way and that, feeling the air.

'Is your sister like you?'

'She's fair,' I said. 'Like my mother. I am like my father's side.'

The caterpillar decided to start its upward journey towards his neck.

Then I felt I must ask him a question.

'It's such a nice house. Are you going far away?'

'You're almost the first people to have seen it,' he said. 'A man did come down last Sunday. A stockbroker. From Bedford. Do sit down.' He tapped the seat again. 'But I've heard no more. Do you know France?' he said.

He moved along the seat. Skirts were a great deal shorter in those days and I fancied he looked quickly at my legs as I sat down. I thought they were very nice legs and I was glad he seemed to think so too.

'No,' I said. 'I don't know France. I've never been abroad.'

I suppose the fact that I was watching the caterpillar with such unbroken fascination must have misled him into thinking I was staring solely on him. At any rate the bright blue eyes were continually holding mine in a shimmering, captivated smile.

'I used to live a great deal in France,' he said. 'Before the war. Then I came and took this place. But I find the winters very cold in this valley.'

The caterpillar, I noticed, had disappeared.

'Must you go?' he said.

By that time I had really begun to enjoy the whole situation. It appealed enormously to my sense of humour to see that fat bald creature crawling all over him and now disappearing, at last, behind his neck.

'No. I suppose I don't have to,' I said. 'They'll wait for me.'

'Good,' he said. 'Now you can tell me more about yourself.'

It was beautifully dark and cool there on the river bank, under the thick poplars, and when a fish rose, just on the line of shadow, it cut the water with a curved slice of silver before it disappeared.

That was about the only thing that moved in the hot breathless afternoon for the next quarter of an hour, during which he said once:

'Tell me. I've really been most undecided about this house. I'm really very fond of it. But I can't exist in these freezing winters. If this were your house what would you do?'

'Do you live alone?' I said.

I don't know what made me say that. I suppose it's instinctive in any woman, as soon as a man appears on the scene, to try to assess whether he has attachments or not. I don't know of course. It may not have been that. At any rate he said:

'That's another thing. I hardly see a soul from one week's end to another. Except Miss Carfax. She lives in the house next door.'

'Was that Miss Carfax you were talking to?'

'That was Miss Carfax.'

Again I started to search his neck for the caterpillar. It was absolutely fascinating to wonder where it could have got to all that time and I must have been so absorbed that I couldn't have realized fully how much my eyes were fixed on him.

'But let's not talk,' he said, 'about Miss Carfax.'

Suddenly I got the impression that, with the slightest encouragement from me, he would have become emotional. His bright eyes fairly shimmered, like the heat of the afternoon.

A moment later I saw the caterpillar emerge on the other side of his coat collar.

I started laughing at once and he said:

'You're a very gay person, aren't you? Are you always so gay?'

'It doesn't always do to be serious, does it?' I said and because of the caterpillar I was still laughing.

All this, of course, may well have looked like a form of encouragement to him and suddenly he moved along the seat, a little closer to me.

But then, instead of attempting to come any nearer, he merely patted my hand. It was a very brief, avuncular sort of pat, not very serious, but I drew my hand away a little haughtily and with the faintest smile. I was really thinking more of the caterpillar on my own arms and shoulders and I did not grasp, even remotely, that this quick little pat of my hand was really an expression of great shyness on his part.

I suppose youth never thinks of age as being shy. It merely thinks that a person of sixty ought long since to have got over things like that. It is in fact impossible for the young to grasp that the pain of shyness never really leaves some people, however age may seem to give them certainty.

That, anyway, was the one and only attempt he made to pat my hand and presently he said:

'It must be rather interesting to have two fair people and two dark ones in the family. Your mother and sister on the one side and you and your father on the other.'

'My father is dead,' I said.

His comment on that was, as I afterwards discovered, quite typical.

'Do you miss him very much?' he said.

'Very much,' I said. 'Naturally.'

That was another thing I had not, at that time, fully grasped. My father had died the previous summer. Shortly afterwards my sister had got engaged to Ewart Mackeson. It did not occur to me that these two events had anything to do with that sulky adolescent sickness of mine.

'Are you on the telephone?' he suddenly said.

'Yes,' I said. 'Why?'

'If I sell the house I might perhaps give a little farewell party before I go away. If I do I would like to ring you up and invite you. Would you care to come?'

'Thank you,' I said.

In thought he stared at the water, still holding the branch of leaves, and I could not see the caterpillar. I still longed for it to complete the picture of fatuity by crawling up his neck, but a moment later I thought I heard voices from the direction of the mullein-strewn wilderness nearer the house, and soon they were growing louder.

'I think my mother and sister must be coming this way,' I said.

Suddenly I saw that the caterpillar had appeared again. It was sitting on the far lapel of the shantung coat.

'You haven't answered my question,' he said.

That is the sort of opening youth likes and I said at once, with what I thought was splendid sarcasm:

'Since you ask me a new one every five seconds it's rather hard to know which question you mean.'

'About the house.'

Up to that moment I simply couldn't have cared one way or the other whether he sold the house or not. What on earth had I to do with the wretched house? Then from farther up the bank I distinctly heard my sister say:

'I think Ewart will rave about it, don't you? All this bit by the river. I must get him over tomorrow.'

I didn't hesitate a moment longer. I simply turned and smiled at him in a calm off-hand sort of way and said:

'If you mean about selling the house I wouldn't sell it for worlds. Nothing would induce me.'

I thought he seemed relieved at that, almost delighted. He actually gave me a fussy little pat on the shoulder.

'I hope you will come over to tea with me one day,' he said, 'while this beautiful weather lasts. I would love to show you the butterflies.'

I simply couldn't think what on earth he was talking about. He murmured something else about not really wanting, in his heart, to part with the house and how glad he was about my turning up that day and helping him to make up his mind, and then my sister and mother arrived.

He went towards them and, still with the caterpillar sitting on his chest, gave them a little bow, at the same time raising his panama.

'I have been talking to your charming daughter without knowing her name or telling her mine,' he said. 'I'm Frederick Fielding-Brown. Good afternoon.'

'Mrs George Burnett,' my mother said. 'Good afternoon,' and I saw her suddenly look with pale startled eyes at the extraordinary spectacle of the shantung jacket and its naked caterpillar.

'I should like to bring my fiancé over to see the house,' my sister said. 'I love it.'

My sister, seeing the caterpillar too, looked equally startled.

'By all means,' he said, 'though to be perfectly honest I haven't really made up my mind finally whether to sell it or not.'

Back in the car my sister was half-irritated, half-amused.

'Stupid little man,' she said. 'First he wants to sell his house and then he can't make up his mind. And did you ever see any-

thing quite so priceless? That revolting caterpillar on his coat –
did you see that caterpillar?'

I could only stare out of the taxi window and down the valley
to where, on the river, the water-lilies were gleaming as white,
entrancing and duck-like as ever in the sun.

'I didn't see anything,' I said, 'and if it comes to that I don't
think he was stupid. I think he was rather nice. He was very
charming to me.'

Two days later my mother was congratulating me on having at
last had the good sense, as she put it, to shake myself out of
myself.

'A bicycle ride will do you all the good in the world,' she said.
'I can't think why you haven't taken to it before. Would you like
me to pack you some tea?'

'No thank you,' I said. 'I'll stop in a village somewhere and
get some.'

An hour later I was sitting in the drawing room at 'Orleans',
taking tea with Frederick Fielding-Brown. The afternoon was hot
and brilliant. The yellow venetian blinds were drawn half-way
down at the windows. There was a strong scent of lilies in the air.

'I didn't think you would come over so soon after my letter,'
he said.

Youth is not always sarcastic and sharp and quick to see the
comic side of things. Sometimes it is splendidly tactless too.

'I hadn't anything else to do,' I said, 'so I thought I'd just come
over.'

He was very tolerant about that. He smiled and asked me to
help myself to tomato sandwiches. They were, I thought, very
good tomato sandwiches, with rather a special flavour to them. I
remarked on this flavour and felt that I was being clever when I
told him I thought they were piquant.

'That's because I have a tiny touch of mayonnaise and red
pepper put on them,' he said. 'How observant you are.'

He started to pour tea from a conical silver pot, afterwards
filling up the pot with hot water from a little silver spirit kettle.

'I don't suppose you've ever eaten caterpillars of any sort, have
you?' he said.

139

The Grapes of Paradise

Here we were, I thought, back in the madhouse. It was obviously going to be too screamingly funny for words.

Then he began to explain. He started to remind me of the day I had first found him in the garden, talking to the caterpillar, Miss Carfax and the hedge.

'That was a caterpillar of the goat-moth,' he said. 'It seems the Romans ate them. Considered them quite a delicacy. I suppose in the category of frogs and snails. Or grasshoppers perhaps. What they ate them with is another matter.'

'Perhaps mayonnaise,' I said.

There was nothing, I thought, like playing up on these occasions.

'Well, and why not?' he said. 'I suppose if you were brought up on *Cossus ligniperda* and mayonnaise you would think no more of it, in the end, than eating winkles with vinegar and a pin.'

'What is *Cossus ligniperda*?'

'That,' he said, 'is the goat-moth.'

Once or twice before and after this lunatic piece of conversation he remarked on what a charming companion I was and how glad he was that I had been able to come over.

'You are wearing such a pretty dress,' he said. 'It goes well with your dark complexion.'

'Thank you,' I said.

The dress was a bright clear green, lighter and softer than emerald, with short, yellow-trimmed sleeves and a yellow collar. With it I was wearing the yellow shoes that Ewart Mackeson had made for my mother. She didn't like them after all and now, in consequence, I thought they were rather smart on me.

'What material is it?' he said. He fingered one of the sleeves. His hand brushed my bare upper arm and drew away. 'A kind of silk?'

I said I thought it was rayon. By this time, however, he was looking at my shoes. He seemed entranced by them too and he peered at them a long time with absorbed brilliant blue eyes.

'You have wonderful taste,' he said, 'to get shoes to match like that.'

This was, as best as I can give it, the general tone of the afternoon. It was poised somewhere between lunacy and flattery, with a curious overtone of charm. The way he poured tea for me, helped me to sandwiches and finally to dish after dish of large dark ruby strawberries completely immersed in cream – all these things were, I suppose, quite enough to counteract, for a young girl with a fairly high opinion of herself and her beauty, a feeling that she was simply the guest of a hopeless eccentric who didn't know what day it was.

I never intended, of course, to pay another visit. That would have been too much. The idea of striking up a friendship with an elderly man who seriously thought that goat-moths and mayonnaise were a solemn gastronomic possibility was altogether too ludicrous for words.

And it is possible, I think, that I never should have paid another visit if it had not been for an incident that occurred after tea was over and I suddenly got up, now rather bored by that stuffy yellow-shaded drawing-room and its too oppressive fragrance of madonna lilies, and said that I ought to go.

'Oh! no, please. I want you to meet Miss Carfax,' he said. 'Miss Carfax is coming over.'

The life of Frederick Fielding-Brown and that of Miss Carfax were, as I was to discover later, about as ludicrously bound up with each other as he himself was with the business of moths and butterflies.

Every Wednesday afternoon, for example, Frederick Fielding-Brown handed in his card to the house next door and formally went to tea with Miss Carfax; every Sunday afternoon Miss Carfax handed in her card at his house and took tea with him. During the rest of the week they corresponded with each other by a series of daily notes taken to each house by hand, in his case by the garden-boy, in hers by the chauffeur.

These notes pulsated warmly with urgent and stunning discoveries in the world of entomology. Sometimes they were accompanied, in Miss Carfax's case, by little perforated cardboard boxes.

'Is it treasure?' she would write. 'I trust so. I found it in the raspberry canes.'

In a return note he would tell her that her treasure was, after all, no more than a Painted Lady, a Red Admiral, a Tortoiseshell or something of that sort, common to all our counties.

Miss Carfax was, however, never discouraged. Tending her garden, snipping at rambler roses, walking along meadow-paths, by the river, she kept up a great vigilance for things that would interest him, secretly hoping that she would one day come upon something of rare and stupefying importance, such as a Feathered Prominent, a Purple Emperor or a Brixton Beauty.

In turn he wrote notes of discoveries whose detection she apparently found to be nothing short of magical. There would be illuminating occasions like those of the goat-moth, which had made me laugh so much, or the woolly case-bearer, a moth of which, as he explained to me and no doubt also to Miss Carfax, the virgin females sometimes lay fruitful eggs.

The way in which these two elderly people twittered backwards and forwards to each other's houses, taking tea, writing notes, exchanging larvae and so on, prattling passionately through the garden hedge, tremulous with discovery, was of course just the thing that a young girl would find amusing and fatuous. For the life of me I simply couldn't, I'm afraid, see what all the fuss was for.

That was why I thought Miss Carfax looked quite pathetic, almost imbecile with excitement, as she came rushing into the drawing-room that afternoon, carrying with trembling care a little cardboard box, saying:

'I really think I have something, Frederick, I really think I've something for you at last.'

I ought to explain that, just before this happened, he had been trying to persuade me to come to tea another day. We were sitting on a narrow sofa. It was in a kind of French marquetry style and it was too high for comfort. It reminded me very much of the seat by the river and once again he started patting my hands.

'Come again, will you? While this beautiful weather lasts? Do you like raspberries?'

If you can imagine an elderly man shyly patting your hand, looking intensely into your eyes and saying, 'Do you like raspberries?' you will know something of what I felt that afternoon just before Miss Carfax burst in.

Then he said:

'Come early. We'll take the punt on the river. We'll go down to where the water-lilies are.'

Suddenly, at the mention of water-lilies, I felt quite differently about the whole affair. He seemed to me suddenly very sweet, in that avuncular attentive way of his; he was full of eager, tender charm.

'I should love to see the water-lilies,' I said. 'From the road they look like ducks – '

'Then you will?' he said. 'You – '

I hadn't time to answer before the maid was knocking on the door and, a moment later, showing Miss Carfax into the room.

'I really think I have something – '

Her hands fluttered, but I noticed that he did not seem to be looking either at them or at the little box they were holding. Instead he gave me an engaging, pitying little smile – pitying, that is, for Miss Carfax, who was so absorbed in taking the lid off the box that she didn't even know I was there.

'My dear,' he said gently, 'allow me to introduce Miss Burnett. Miss Carfax – Miss Burnett.'

In her fluttering struggle with the box Miss Carfax managed to acknowledge me with a kind of unsmiling grin. I ought to have explained that she was of course old too – that is, fifty-six or fifty-seven I should say – with long angular teeth, straight as piano keys.

'There!' she said. 'There!'

'Miss Burnett and I have had a most delightful tea together,' he said. 'I'm sure we ate more strawberries than were good for us, but some things are irresistible when the season's so short – '

'Look,' she said. 'Look, Frederick. Please look, will you?'

He was, during all this time, looking at me. Now he gave a cursory glance at the box, just in time to see a large brown-pink moth fly upwards, towards the light, and attach itself to one of the venetian blinds.

'Oh! it's gone! – it's out – '

'Why don't you use the cyanide I gave you?' he said sharply. 'Either that or keep the lid on.'

Her eyes seemed to give a pained grey jolt as he said this. Her hands flapped helplessly and she said:

'Can we catch it? What kind is it, Frederick? It's so huge. I thought it might be a Great Brocade –'

He laughed and it seemed to stun her. She stood mute in the middle of the room.

'I'm surprised,' he said. 'I'm really surprised at you, dear. I think even Miss Burnett would know our common Privet Hawk.'

Soon, after all her excitement, she seemed to become slack and baggy. She sat down and we talked a bit. I can't think what about – more moths, I think, and how good the strawberries were. I could see, however, that she was never really listening. Her bemused eyes wandered sometimes to where the moth was folded on the venetian blinds and sometimes she sucked at her big teeth and swallowed hard so that her Adam's apple quivered.

Then, after she had gone, he actually laughed at her.

'A Great Brocade,' he said. 'If she lives to be a hundred she'll never find a Great Brocade.'

Then I said what I suppose was rather a foolish thing.

'That doesn't give her very much time, does it?'

Of course that was clever and quick and I must say he absolutely loved it too. 'Most amusing,' he said. 'But naughty. Very naughty.'

'Well,' I said, 'isn't it nice to be naughty sometimes?'

It was that, I suppose, that set the tone for the rest of the afternoon and the future. We sat on the little sofa again and he squeezed my hand. His fingers were hot and sticky. Then I crossed my legs and pulled my skirt down over my knees and he said:

'What about tea again? Which day? We'll have masses of raspberries and cream and go to see the water-lilies afterwards.'

'Which day would you like me to come?'

'Whichever day you wish,' he said. 'All days are your days. Tomorrow – Friday, Saturday, Sunday – they're all yours. Just say.'

'Sunday,' I said.

So, without thinking, I went over again on Sunday. It was a warm breezy afternoon and we ate many dishes of raspberries for tea – very special, beautiful yellow ones, I remember, as well as the ordinary red kind – and afterwards, as he had promised, we took the punt and paddled slowly down the river to where the water-lilies were.

Perhaps it was the warm sleepy wind, perhaps it was the sight of occasional pairs of lovers lying in the long grasses by the waterside, or it may have been merely that funny, sensuous sort of feeling that floating on water gives you – I don't know, but that afternoon I began to lead him on a little, just for fun.

'You look very hot, paddling all the time,' I said once. 'Why don't we tie up the punt for a while?'

So we tied up the punt and got out and I lay down on the river-bank in the tall whitening August grasses. They were so high, these grasses, as high as oats and almost the same gold-white ripe colour, with bowed feathery heads of seed, that they made a wall round me where I lay on my back, staring at the sky.

Before long, as I lay there, he leaned over and, for the first time, kissed me. I didn't mind very much; nor was I very excited – that, I suppose, describes it fairly accurately. If a man of sixty wanted to kiss me on a hot July afternoon I thought that, on the other hand, it was silly to be prim about it. On the other hand it wasn't an experience that I'd have sought deliberately as a means of pleasure.

At the same time some pretence of approval or disapproval had to be made and I said:

'Naughty. You know that was very naughty, don't you?'

'You're so very lovely,' he said. 'So absolutely lovely.'

'Flatterer.'

He started to try to kiss me again, but this time I bit my lips and made a face at him.

'You're not eating strawberries and raspberries now,' I said, 'and taking second helpings. It's not good for you.'

'But I feel it's rather like that,' he said. 'I feel the season might be so short.'

'Oh!' I said. 'And who said the season might be short?'

Like that I teased and taunted him for the rest of the afternoon. It was great fun altogether. Sometimes I refused to let him kiss me for a quarter of an hour or twenty minutes at a time and then it was marvellous to see how terribly downcast he was. Then I would pretend I wanted to go home and he would start protesting in awful dismay until I teased him another way and laughed in his face and said:

'I might as well go home as lie here and do nothing. I thought you wanted to kiss me so much? – goodness, you don't even try.'

In that way, playing and kissing in the grasses, we spent the rest of the afternoon. By the time we paddled back to the house he was in a sort of daze. He had the air of a man in a mild state of intoxication. I felt a little heady too – warm from lying in the sun in breezy meadows, from the smell of water and meadow-sweet, and with grains of grass seed in my hair.

Probably that was why neither of us saw Miss Carfax until the punt was actually turning round under the balsam poplars, to-wards the landing stage.

'Isn't that Miss Carfax?' I said.

She was standing in the shade of the river path, in a white sun-hat, staring towards us. When she saw us she turned sharply on her heel and fairly bolted away.

'Where?' he said. 'Where?'

'She's gone now,' I said. 'She just opened her gate and dis-appeared.'

'Oh! my God,' he said suddenly. 'I just remembered. She al-ways comes to tea with me on Sundays.'

After that I suppose I went over to the house perhaps another dozen times or more. Twice I went to dinner. The great thing was, of course, that it took me out of myself. It was fun. I wasn't bored or sulky any more.

The second time I went to dinner it was already September. The mild misty evenings were drawing in. The weather was soft and humid. There were mushrooms in the meadows. I mention this because, earlier that evening, we actually went down to the fields and gathered mushrooms which were afterwards served on toast, as a savoury. After that we ate pears for dessert, the lovely Marie Louise variety, peeling the smooth red skin with little pearl-handled silver knives.

'September is a good month for moths,' he said. 'Would you like to go out after dinner and see what we can find?'

So presently we were walking with a torch through the mullein wilderness, past the choked raspberry canes. He stood quite still once or twice, steadily shining the torch into the darkness under fruit boughs. A desultory moth or two began to dance in the light and he said:

'I didn't bring the cyanide bottle. It's hardly worth it. Mostly what you can see are common *Noctuae*.'

Soon I thought he seemed nervous. He kept switching on the torch and then suddenly putting it off again. One moment the air was dancing with a crowd of small light wings and the next I was groping, half-blinded, for the path among the grasses.

Suddenly he put out the light for the sixth or seventh time, stopped abruptly and took me by the shoulders.

'I want to ask you to marry me,' he said. His hands were shaking dreadfully. 'Will you? I know there is a great difference – but would you? Would you consider it please?'

I simply wanted to laugh outright at him.

'Now I see,' I told him, 'what moth it was you hoped to find out here. The rare nocturnal Laura, eh?'

Nervously he started panting, breathing hard.

'No,' he said. 'No. It's simply – well, I've been trying to say this for some time. Would you? – would you marry me?'

'It's very sweet of you, but – '

'Would you think it over? Think it over and give me an answer another day?'

It was quite ludicrous; he was breathing hard on me, as if blowing on a hot potato.

'Oh! no, really,' I started to say. 'Thank you, but – ' After all what sort of encouragement had I given him to get him to the point of asking me this?

'You've kissed me very often. You've given me such a lot of pleasure,' he said. 'It's been six weeks since you kissed me that Sunday afternoon – '

'Yes, but kissing,' I said. 'Kissing is kissing and there's a great deal of difference between kissing and getting married. You're old enough to know that.'

'Yes, but you see I don't know.' He sounded sad and dithering. 'I don't know. I don't know about these things.'

'Then,' I teased him, 'it's time you learned.' Suddenly, in a way, I felt sorry for him. I linked my arm in his and we started to walk back to the house. He did not shine the torch any more. He seemed to have forgotten it. I simply felt him groping forward intensely in the September darkness.

'I'm so fond of you. I love you so much,' he said, 'I can't explain how much I love you.'

'Yes and I'm fond of you,' I said. 'But –'

'I'm old. I know,' he said. 'I'm too old for you. Isn't that it?'

'It isn't that,' I said and suddenly I arrived again at another of youth's splendid moments of tactfulness. 'After all I'm only seventeen and I've got my life to think of –'

'Seventeen?' he said. 'You told me you were nineteen. You see, I was thinking that if you were nineteen it wouldn't be long before you came of age. The difference wouldn't seem so great then –'

'Seventeen,' I said. 'I was just teasing you.'

He was absolutely silent for the rest of the way back to the house. We had hardly arrived there before the maid, Mabel, came in with a note on a silver salver.

'With Miss Carfax's compliments, sir,' she said.

He read the note, crumpled it up and threw it in the fireplace.

'Miss Carfax is going away for a few days,' he said, 'and thinks I ought to know.' He took my hands and held them in his, together. 'Good-bye, my dear. I don't suppose you'll be coming to see me again, will you? After this?'

'Oh! good gracious,' I said, 'why not? Of course I'm coming to see you. That's if you ever ask me.'

'Ask you?' he said. 'Oh! my God, ask you?' and presently in that awfully sweet nervous way of his he was kissing my hands.

Five days later I went over to see him on the last visit I ever made.

It began to rain sharply and heavily that afternoon as I bicycled the last mile or so to the house. By the time I arrived my dress, my stockings, and my hair were soaking.

'You must go up at once and take a bath,' he said, 'and put on a dressing gown. You mustn't catch cold whatever you do. Mabel will dry your things. Come down when you've finished and hot tea and toast will be ready.'

There is a wonderful sensation of luxury about taking a hot bath on a dull afternoon with rain streaming down on the windows outside, but I am not sure it is not equalled by putting on, afterwards, a more luxurious dressing gown than you yourself own. It was probably because of this that I spent a long time over that bath and afterwards drying and brushing and setting my hair. All this time the rain streamed down on the windows and it must have been nearly five o'clock by the time I went downstairs.

I forgot to say, by the way, how full that house was of moths and butterflies. Mostly they were kept in special mahogany cabinets with long sliding drawers. But they were also mounted, separately or in small selected groups, in glass-covered cases that hung about the walls like pictures. I used sometimes to ask if he hadn't every single native species among all the hundreds that lay in the drawers and hung on the walls and up the stairs, but he would say:

'Well, no, not quite every one. You see I make it a point of honour only to mount those I've collected myself. You can buy specimens of the rarest things of course but it really isn't the same. The thrill isn't there.'

As I went downstairs that afternoon, wearing the heavy silk dressing gown he had lent me, I stopped once or twice to look at the cases hanging all down the walls on either side of the stairs. I think they were mostly common species that hung there but even among the commonest there are some of the most beautiful and I was looking at a group of meadow browns I hadn't seen before when, from the drawing-room, I suddenly heard voices.

It was not only because the door was open a little but because the voices had begun slightly to raise their pitch that I heard them more clearly as I came to the foot of the stairs.

'It's merely a point of honour with me, that's all,' I heard him say.

'You mean you won't accept it?' It was Miss Carfax speaking and her voice was sharp and thin. 'Is that it?'

'My dear –'

'Or is it just that you won't accept it from me? Perhaps that's it?'

'Not at all,' he said. 'It's simply that I never mount –'

'You do know what it is, I suppose, don't you?' she said. Her

149

voice was growing tauter. 'You've hardly even looked at it.'

'Of course I know what it is,' he said. 'It's a Queen of Spain Fritillary.'

'Is it rare? I heard you say once –'

'It's rare in this country,' he said, 'but not in France. I had scores of specimens in France but when the war came I left them there.'

'I heard you say once you hadn't got one,' she said. 'I remembered the name so well. I thought the name was so beautiful. Now it seems you had hundreds. Well, scores –'

'But not British,' he said. 'A British specimen –'

'This is British!' she said. 'That is the whole point of it! I understand that!' Her voice was rising towards breaking pitch, thin with anger. 'I took great care about that – that was why I bought it for you. Don't you understand? It was just a little present I thought I should like to bring back for you –'

At that moment she opened the door. I heard him begin to say, 'Look, my dear. I appreciate all that. That I appreciate –' when she turned and saw me standing in the hall-way outside.

For a moment or two she couldn't speak. Her mouth opened itself and stuck there in a stiff long-toothed gap, painfully ludicrous and paralysed.

Behind her Frederick Fielding-Brown appeared and began to say, 'Miss Burnett got caught in the rain –' and then got no further. She suddenly turned and gave a sort of hysterical hiss into his face. It was the sort of sound that cats make when they spit at each other and then she shouted:

'I wonder if you're quite so particular about accepting what she has to give you? Do you make that a point of honour, I wonder?'

The front door slammed. It was all so innocent on my part, my being there in the dressing gown, that I wanted to howl with laughter. How absolutely and madly idiotic the old could make themselves look, I thought, and then I saw that Frederick Fielding-Brown, still clutching the handle of the drawing-room door, was white and shaking.

'Come and sit down,' he said. 'That has upset me.'

His voice was quite sepulchral. 'She came just as tea arrived.

Now we must ring for more toast. Would you ring?' he asked me. 'My hands are shaking. The toast is cold.'

It was nearly a week later when my mother, after supper, sat reading the local evening paper. My sister and Ewart Mackeson had at last found themselves a suitable house in which to live. It was nicely gabled, with much ivy growing on the walls, an important-looking coach-house with a weathercock, an acre or two of rabbit shooting, a tradesman's entrance and a tennis court. My sister was quite crazy about the tennis court and the prospect of giving garden parties there and every evening now she and Ewart Mackeson would be over at the house, measuring it for carpets and curtains.

'Wasn't that house called "Orleans"?' my mother said. 'The one we went to see?'

'Yes,' I said.

'An awful thing has happened,' she said, 'if that's the same house. Was that gentleman's name Carfax? Didn't he live there with his sister?'

'No,' I said. 'His name was Fielding-Brown.'

'That's right. Then it is the same,' she said. 'It's here. Listen. It says that a Miss Gertrude Carfax was found dead by the river there last Sunday and that her body was first discovered by her friend and neighbour from "Orleans", the residence next door.'

Before I could say anything my mother began to read the coroner's report. 'Cyanide,' she said. 'How dreadful. What a dreadful thing. How awful. With cyanide.'

I stayed in my room for several days after that, in what my mother said was one of my old, inexplicable, maddening fits of sulking.

'If you are going to start that again,' she said, 'I warn you that I won't put up with it. You will go and stay with your aunt at Southsea for a week or two. You can get some sea air inside you and plenty of exercise and see what that will do. Once and for all I will not have that sulking.'

One of the parts of the world that has not changed much in over thirty years is that wide stretch of river in the valley of the Ouse. Like much else, of course, it has changed a little. The house called

'Orleans', for example, has a different name. Whoever owns it calls it 'The Prospect' now. They have also pollarded the limes, cut away the old mullein wilderness at the back and laid steep well-mown lawns that run right down to the huge balsam poplars by the riverside.

But on the whole it has not changed much. And in summer, now that I am almost as old as Miss Carfax, which of course is not really old as we think of age today, I like to go and look at it. I like to stand on the high road above the valley and stare down at the water-lilies that are so much like white ducks, the crowds of little blue and amber butterflies that tremble about the grass-seed and the lovers who lie kissing in the meadows, not caring if they are seen, on Sunday afternoons.

And as I do so I remember, always, the Queen of Spain Fritillary.

An Aspidistra in Babylon

Nearly forty years ago, when I was a young girl and my mother, a widow, kept a small boarding-house at one end of the sea-front the houses there ran in a sparkling crescent of white and cream under the massive shoulder of chalk cliff on which the castle and its garrison stands. From a distance the castle still looks like an enormous bastion of pumice-coloured flint. By contrast, in those days, the curving line of houses always looked like a freshly starched collar, intensely stiff and respectable, against the strip of biscuit-coloured shingle and the sea.

A great deal of this, I must point out, has changed now. During the war bombs ripped out the entire centre of the collar and you can still see the dirty scars made by shells on the grassy slopes above the town. But two things remain exactly as they were when I lived with my mother there and, in the long blistering summer of 1921, when I was eighteen, I first met an officer in the Guards, a man of forty, named Captain Archie Blaine.

The first thing that has never changed at all is the castle itself. It has the imperishable and inviolate air that belongs to great churches and high mountains. But sometimes, especially on rainy days, it also looks like a prison. At other times something about the particular arrangement of the battlements gives it the appearance of a great clenched granite fist, fingers perpendicular, threatening the sea. The other thing about the town that remains unchanged is far less spectacular. It is, perhaps, even rather trivial, though it may be its very triviality that makes it stick in my mind.

It is simply that all the chimney pots on the houses remaining in the crescent are a very bright, impossible canary yellow. They are also unusually tall and as they stand there above the roofs in blocks of six, eight or even a dozen they have exactly the appearance of lofty organ pipes. You fully expect them to start playing solemn tunes. Of course nothing of the kind ever happens and the only sound you ever hear from them is the greedy squawks of the many huge hungry sea-gulls that sit on them and, by some curious trick of light, or perhaps because the pots are that quite impossible yellow, often look like gross blue owls.

Speaking of this curious trick of colour, I have now remembered a third thing that never changes. It is the extraordinary light that, whenever the sun shines, hangs above the crescent, the castle, the chalk cliffs, the harbour, the sea-walls and the sea. It is not that it is merely of a strikingly pure candescence. It seems actually to leap in air. In some curious way it is uncannily transcendent. It seems to lift you off the ground.

On very hot days, when the chalk of the cliffs looks more naked than usual and there is the faintest ripple on the sea, it has still another quality. It suddenly robs your eyes of the power of focus.

It was on just such a day of naked, blinding light, in June, that I first met Captain Blaine.

2

Of course in a garrison town the one consistently unsurprising thing is to meet a soldier. They are naturally everywhere. You can't escape them. The rankers come into town to drink beer, eat fish and chips and get off with girls. The officers, less evident simply because there are fewer of them, come in to drink at the better hotels or have occasional dinner parties, mostly on Saturdays. The rankers get very drunk and rowdy and fight among themselves when they can't find marines or sailors to fight with, which isn't very often. The officers also get very drunk and are finally carried home up the hill, in their own exclusive fashion, in taxi-cabs. The fights, especially with marines, are apt to be rather bloody.

Nearly forty years ago there were also, of course, many more pubs to get drunk in than there are now. Soldiers, too, were soldiers, not mere conscripted cyphers serving a couple of reluctant years and wearing luminous socks and drain-pipe trousers in off-duty hours. They were cast in Kipling's belching, bawdy mould. They were what Rupert Brooke calls somewhere 'loud and black of mouth' and their women weren't much better.

Small wonder, I suppose, that my mother had her own special name for that brawling soldiers' town.

'Babylon,' she called it. 'That Babylon. Keep away from that Babylon,' she always said to me. 'Don't ever go near that Babylon.'

When you add to all this the fact that ships from the continent were coming into the harbour every day, regularly bringing French and Belgian sailors ashore or foreign visitors on a ten-hour excursion spree, you would naturally come to the conclusion that the town, whatever else it might be, was never dull. You would naturally think also that in that robust male Babylon a girl of eighteen wouldn't have much difficulty in getting herself noticed, taken out or even made a fuss of by a man.

Both conclusions would be very wrong. To me, at least until that blistering eventful summer of 1921, it was never anything but infinitely and terribly dull. It was so dull that I couldn't even hate it. Today I think it a very pretty, charming town, full of colouring and bristling with a certain character. In those days it was just a smudge on the shore.

As to the men, the soldiers and all the rest, I simply didn't exist for them. This is not entirely surprising, however, since I was clearly infinitely and terribly dull myself. The best description of myself that I can think of is to say that I was as dull as one of the many aspidistras that cluttered up the rooms, the hallway and even the dining tables of our little boarding-house. I was just that – a female aspidistra and nothing more.

For example I had, until my seventeenth year, worn my hair down my back in a long thick plait tied with a large plain black ribbon. It was rather greasy hair, dark and unwaved, of the kind that most women struggle frantically to alter or at all costs to disguise. I just wasn't aware of it. When I looked in the mirror I saw it simply as a frame for a rather narrow paste-coloured face in which the dark brown eyes were too large and consequently much out of proportion. Naturally I wore no make-up either, so that my forehead and my rather high cheekbones always shone very soapily.

The one thing about myself I might have claimed as not being dull was my figure. My body was slender but very smooth and without a single blemish except a perfectly circular brown mole,

155

rather large, between my left breast and my shoulder. But since no one except myself ever saw my body or caught even the faintest glimpse of the mole it really wasn't very important to me. I ought to add here that although my legs were really quite shapely I naturally wore black woollen stockings.

My mother wore black stockings too. In fact she wore nothing but black, continuously. Mourning for my father, who had died ten years before, had become a habit. Widowhood was a cross to be serenely and, when possible, silently borne.

I must refrain from being unjust to my mother, especially as what happened to me that summer was not really of her making, but she was a woman who had life neatly summed up in a series of catch-phrases, all of them fallacies.

Her favourite among these was 'If you trust other people they will trust you.' Second only to this, I fancy, was 'If you don't want people to think ill of you don't begin by thinking ill of them.' Under such fallacious guidance, delivered in her mournful, rather monotonous voice, all individuality in me had died. I was dull only because I was fearful of doing anything opposed to these apparently solemn truths of hers.

Ruby is an illustration of this curious and important business. Ruby was one of our chambermaids, a generously-built, good-looking, juicy girl of twenty-eight or so with reddish hair and half-dissolute grey-green eyes that always looked much older than the rest of her. I liked Ruby and I have good cause to remember, and be grateful for, those half-dissolute, old-looking eyes.

On her days off Ruby was, in fact, part of that Babylon my mother always warned me so much about. She was the good time free-and-easy, the soldiers' friend.

'Over-affectionate, duckie, that's me. Give, give, that's my trouble. Never know when to stop. Ought to think about settling down. Never will, though.'

I very much liked going into the maids' room, behind the kitchen, and talking to Ruby, or even upstairs to her room, where we could be alone. Chambermaids didn't have luxuries like bathrooms in those days and sometimes I went into her bedroom and caught her having what she called a strip-wash, bare to the waist, over her marble wash-stand.

'Come in, duckie. Sit on the bed. Don't mind me. Up as far as possible and down as far as possible. Got to get the muck off today somehow. Only had a cat-lick yesterday.'

Ruby's ripe and infectious laugh always bounced about the bedroom as generously as her big breasts swung above the soapy water as she bent to wash them.

I not only liked Ruby; I was fascinated by her. I was also, I confess, sometimes a little horrified. I was horrified, for instance, when I caught her washing one day and found her back and shoulders scored with a sickly mass of black and yellow bruises.

'Ruby,' I said. 'Your back! Whatever happened? Whatever on earth did you do?'

Ruby, far from being concerned, merely filled the bedroom with her customary ripe and careless laughter.

'Bit of love, duckie, that's all. They get taken a bit fierce like that sometimes.'

'You mean a man did it? You mean you actually –'

Ruby pealed with laughter again.

'Oh! that's all right, duckie,' she said. 'That's a good sign, that is. You know they got it bad then. Know they really feel about you.'

My mother's counsel of putting yourself into other people's places, under other people's skins, didn't work out very well that day. Try as I would I couldn't get under Ruby's handsome, dissolute skin and imagine myself being beaten black and yellow for love and what Elizabeth Barrett Browning called 'for love's sake only'.

Two days after this revealing occurrence it was Ruby's afternoon off. After lunch had been served my mother was taking her usual hour's rest in her bedroom. I was in our private sitting-room, alone, reading verse, which as you've probably gathered I liked to do. Verse, in fact, was the only thing through which, ever so remotely, I came near to finding myself. I had naturally gleaned all I knew of love from what I read in verse.

That afternoon, I remember, was extraordinarily hot and still, without a single breath of breeze across the harbour, and it must have been at its hottest when, about half past three, one of the other maids tapped on the door, came in and said:

'Sorry to disturb you, Miss Christine, but your mother's sound asleep and I don't like to wake her. Can you come a minute? There's an officer here who says he'd like to speak to you. A Captain Blaine.'

When I am reading I have a curious habit of tucking one foot under me and sitting on it. After a time the foot either goes to sleep or gets stiff and twisted so that when I get up I find myself temporarily off balance, walking for the next half minute or so as if I'd sprained my ankle.

This is how I went out to make my first acquaintance with Captain Blaine. I imagine I must have looked pretty silly as I hobbled into the hallway, which incidentally was paved with those cold and slippery Italian mosaic tiles which were so fashionable years ago and the result was that the first thing the Captain did was to take a swift and inquiring look at my legs.

'I'm so sorry. I hope I haven't disturbed you?' he said. 'Have you hurt your foot?'

With a rush of diffidence I blushed and assured him I hadn't. I'd merely sat on it.

He gave a short engaging chuckle.

'Really?' he said. 'I always thought legs were for standing on?'

'Oh! that's just me,' I said. I tried to speak coolly as a means of suppressing my growing shyness. 'I like to be different.'

For the second time he gave that engaging chuckle of his. At the same time he shot another quick and inquiring glance at me. His face was also turned towards the sea, so that for a moment or two the reflected light of it, with that curious blinding power I have already tried to describe, was full in his eyes.

They were eyes of a very remarkable and liquid quality of blueness. If I describe them as being without depth it will perhaps convey the impression that they were shallow. On the contrary they were extraordinarily subtle. They were like the petals of certain sorts of flowers that appear at first glance to be merely of a single, solid colour and then suddenly prove to be excitingly iridescent.

What made them still more arresting was that they were un-

An Aspidistra in Babylon

commonly cool, not to say glacial, in that awfully hot afternoon, and that they were set in a face that in all other respects was very dark – dark brows, dark chin and jowls, dark guardsman's moustache and rather fine dark nostrils.

'Terribly remiss of me,' he said suddenly. 'Didn't introduce myself. Blaine.' His officer's cap was tucked with military correctness under one arm. The uniform was a bluish-grey, a sort of pigeon colour, high in the collar. Magnificently band-box, the whole thing. 'I called to inquire about a room.'

He gave that engaging chuckle again and signalled vivid assurances with iridescent eyes.

'Oh! not for myself. I'm up at the castle. Quarters there. No,' he said, 'it's for an aunt of mine. She's a shade shaky. Asthma – heart gets strained.'

'When would you want the room?' I said. 'For how long?'

'Depends. Might be a long time. Might be very short.' He gave a sort of resigned shrug of the shoulders. 'Never really tell, with this heart thing. It's dry here. She's been living in the West Country – far too damp for her. I thought if I got her here – one never knows. Might hang on for years.'

Was she really an invalid? I asked. My mother didn't like invalids about the place and nor did the maids. In fact they were all rather against the tyranny of long lets.

'Oh! no,' he said. 'Far from it. Very spry. Even gads about a bit.'

I hardly knew what to say. I started to explain to him that I could do nothing without asking my mother but that she was asleep and I didn't want to wake her.

He was at once all charm and solicitude.

'Oh! don't give it a thought. Wouldn't dream of letting you wake her. Certainly not. I can come back. When would it be convenient to see her?'

I suggested that evening, perhaps about six, and he said:

'Admirable. Couldn't be better. I'll trot along then.'

He turned to go and then suddenly paused at the open door of the hallway. The smell of sea and seaweed was very strong in the hot calm air and the brass curb of the doorstep shone like a strip of fire. A channel steamer coming in stern first across the harbour

159

was making smoke and the cloud of it was the only blemish on the blinding purity of the day.

'I do hope we can fix things up,' he said. 'Sort of duty to see that she's all right, if you know what I mean. I'm her only relative. Must do the best for her.'

He flashed another winning blue signal at me with those remarkable eyes of his and then stared at the steamer crossing the harbour, at the same time giving the briefest sigh.

'What a day to be crossing. What a thought, eh? Get the Blue Train from Paris tonight and in Nice tomorrow. What about that?'

The fact that the question was purely rhetorical didn't prevent my saying an abysmally stupid thing.

'I don't know. Where's Nice?' I said.

He was quick to seize on this piece of idiotic innocence of mine and said:

'You've never heard of Nice? Now that I just won't believe.'

'Truly,' I said.

'Just won't, just can't and just don't believe.'

Suddenly, for the second time, I felt myself flushing and once again I was completely hypnotized by the remarkably charming, iridescent stare of his.

'Just isn't possible,' he said. 'You're pulling my leg.'

'Oh! but it is,' I assured him. 'It is. I wouldn't dream of saying something I didn't mean.'

Perhaps it sounds a little exaggerated but that intensely naïve remark of mine was perhaps the most important thing I ever said to Captain Blaine. If I had stripped myself stark naked on the doorstep in the blinding sunshine I could hardly have revealed more of myself to him.

'I suppose you've been there very often?' I said. 'Is it wonderful?'

'Practically lived there before the war. Couldn't tear myself away. Wine three francs a bottle. Wonderful? It's divine. It's celestial. If you can imagine heaven mating with paradise Nice would be their daughter.'

This slightly extravagant turn of phrase both amused and captivated me. I laughed aloud.

'It sounds marvellous,' I said. 'I shall have to start saving all my pennies and get there.'

'Ah! the pennies, the pennies,' he said. He actually gave me a brief, reassuring, friendly pinch on the arm. 'The pennies. You've hit it now, girl. There's the rub. Plenty of pennies, that's the snag. That's the form. That's what you must have.'

He gave an almost sorrowful shake of the head, at the same time chuckling again. A moment later he put on his cap, shook me by the hand and saluted.

'Good-bye. Charmed to meet you. Back at six.'

He crossed the road to where a small dark red coupé was parked in the blazing sun and I stood for a minute longer at the doorway, watching him crank it up, get into it and, after a careless wave of the hand to me, drive it away.

As it disappeared along the promenade that old trick of light played itself on me again. But this time I was more than dazzled by it. For quite some seconds I was almost blind.

Of course it just isn't possible to capture an entire personality in one short meeting, however much you may delude yourself you may have done so, and my experience with Captain Blaine that afternoon was very comparable to what I have at times experienced with certain kinds of flowers.

I am referring more particularly to flowers that are strongly perfumed: carnations, roses, lilies, and so on. My experience has often been that in the first rapturous moment of burying your face in their petals you really seem to drink in perfume in one great exquisite liquid draught. But only a few seconds later, when you seek to repeat the experience, you are doomed to disappointment. For some reason the perfume is no longer there. In that first eager rush of thirst you seem to have drained the petals dry. The flower is temporarily exhausted. The scent is dead.

This was very much my experience with Captain Blaine at our second meeting that day. All that hot afternoon the air was full of Captain Blaine. I suppose I must have sat in the sitting room until nearly six o'clock, trying as I so often did to read verse and yet never managing to focus a single line, and all the time I was as powerfully and keenly aware of his presence as if the room had been full of flowers. In the hot June quietness I kept drinking and drinking him in.

Perhaps I'm not putting all this in the best possible way, but what I am trying to say is that I wanted to repeat that first delicious and exciting experience in exactly its original form when Captain Blaine came back at six o'clock. I wanted, as with a flower, to re-experience that first divine deep drink at the perfume.

And, as with a flower, I was disappointed.

There may have been several reasons for this. In the first place Captain Blaine was very late in arriving. It was in fact nearly eight o'clock before he arrived. This, as I later discovered, was quite typical of him and afterwards it never surprised me.

In the second place he was slightly drunk. This, in my innocence, I didn't appreciate at the time and quite understandably, since when Archie Blaine was drunk it was never in a disgusting, obvious, tedious way but only in an apparent stiffening up of the entire muscular system, so that he looked if anything more correct than ever.

The third reason, I think, was the presence of my mother. As I have tried to indicate she always made me feel not merely something other than myself but something very much less than myself. And that evening I not only felt her influence very strongly. I was effaced; I simply wasn't there. And as a result Captain Blaine hardly took the trouble to look or speak to me.

'My aunt, Miss Charlesworth,' he explained to my mother – it simply didn't occur to him to apologize for being late, for the simple reason that he was one of those people to whom time, especially other people's time, means absolutely nothing – 'is asthmatical. Not chronically bad, you understand. But occasionally it brings on bronchial relapses. It's hard on the ticker.'

Most of the time I kept watching those captivating iridescent eyes of his, waiting for a sign of recognition and all the while totally unaware of the reason for their inability to focus me.

'She needs quiet and a dry climate. That's why I want to get her here. And particularly in your boarding house, because it's at the quiet end of the promenade and she has the lawns and the gardens just opposite. She can be really quiet here.'

Would she need extra attention, any nursing or anything of that kind? my mother asked.

'None whatever. None whatever. Absolutely none. Perfectly capable of looking after herself. It's just the occasional bronchial threat, that's all. Otherwise she'll be perfectly content to do her reading, her bit of crochet and so on. And two or three afternoons a week I'll run her along the coast in the car.'

There was of course nothing very difficult or complicated about all this and soon my mother and Captain Blaine were fixing terms. Miss Charlesworth would arrive during the following week-end. He would meet her at the station. And if all went well she would stay for at least the rest of the summer and perhaps much longer.

'Goodnight, madam, and thank you,' he said to my mother, 'most awfully obliged,' and at last departed with that over-stiff bearing of his that had me utterly and completely fooled.

There was a great sickening stupid lump in my throat when he had gone but somehow I managed to say:

'What did you think of him? Did you like him?'

'He talks too much,' my mother said. That was all. 'He talks too much.'

An awful sort of cold blackness came over me. If my mother had said outright, in the plainest and most unequivocal of terms, that she thought Captain Blaine was nothing more than an evil and corrupting influence I couldn't have been more outraged. I just turned and rushed madly upstairs and lay there for the rest of the evening in the bed, beating my hands in dark hatred on the counterpane.

Women, nevertheless, have strange intuitions about men. They possess an uncanny curious sixth sense about them. They also have, of course, their blindnesses and that day my mother divined something about Captain Blaine that it took me almost the rest of that year to discover.

Where I had detected in the air, in my thirsty adolescent eagerness, only perfumes and charms and iridescence, only the dazzle of summer, my mother had already seen a cloud.

3

Miss Charlesworth duly arrived on the following Saturday afternoon, dutifully fetched from the station by Captain Blaine in the little red coupé.

'Bertie dear,' was Captain Blaine's affectionate way of addressing her. 'Bertie dear.'

She was a tallish, rather angular woman of seventy whose face, under its crimped white hair, had the appearance of being made of pinkish-mauve enamel that had got rather dusty. She was in fact very much over-powdered, just as she was also very much over-dressed, in a very lacy kind of way, and over-jewelled and and over-trunked.

In all I think she brought with her seven or eight large travelling trunks that day. She also had a great deal of subsidiary paraphernalia in the way of parasols, umbrellas, walking sticks, clocks, reticules, sewing-bags, jewel cases and that sort of thing. I fully expected her also to produce either pince-nez or lorgnettes or both, but in fact she did nothing of the kind, and for a very good reason.

Her large grey eyes were as sharp and apparently youthful as my own. She had no need of glasses.

Ruby, who had a quick knack of summing up the foibles, oddities, and shortcomings of guests both male and female, at once called her the Duchess.

'Couldn't have more clothes, anyway, duckie, even if she was,' she said to me. 'Twenty-three dresses I counted in the wardrobe this morning. And four jewel cases. Worth a bob or two I should say.'

It duly became apparent, as Captain Blaine had suggested, that Miss Charlesworth, for all her appearance of excessive fussiness, was going to be, as a guest, of little or no bother to us. She clearly belonged to that race of gentlefolk who, though never having to work, are highly self-sufficient. They are monuments of busyness.

Miss Charlesworth, in fact, read a great deal, crocheted and knitted a great deal, played patience a great deal and wrote, every morning between eleven and one, great quantities of letters.

It was one of these letters that brought me my next meeting with Captain Blaine. One brilliant morning in early July Miss Charlesworth rang the bell in the writing-room and asked the answering parlourmaid if she could see my mother.

'I'm most anxious to get a note to my nephew at the garrison,' she explained, 'and I wondered if one of the maids could take it.'

My mother, apologizing, proceeded to explain that it was exceedingly difficult to spare one of the girls at that time of day and why didn't Miss Charlesworth telephone?

The answer was typical.

'I dislike telephones,' Miss Charlesworth said. 'In fact I distrust them. They lack privacy. What I have to say to Captain Blaine is confidential.'

At this moment I went past the writing-room door on my way to the kitchen and it prompted my mother to say:

'I'm sure Christine would take it, however. Wouldn't you, Christine? A note for Captain Blaine?'

'Deliver it to him personally, child,' Miss Charlesworth said. 'Personally. Remember – I trust you.'

As I walked up the long curving road to the castle just after two o'clock that afternoon it was very hot. The high, white cliffs glared with an almost savage light above the sea and although I had put on the coolest and lightest of dresses, a simple pale cream shantung, I felt awfully nervous and clammy. I was nervous because I could foresee some difficulty in finding Captain Blaine, for the simple reason that although from a distance the castle looks no more than a single solid block of masonry it is in fact almost a little town. It is a positive labyrinth up there of streets, squares, terraces of houses, quarters, stables, armouries, and heaven knows what.

And then, almost at the top of the hill, when I was already within sight of the sentry boxes at the gates, I had a stroke of luck. I heard a car changing gear on the hill behind me and when I turned to look at it I saw that familiar dark red coupé, with the hood down, and in it Captain Blaine.

As it went past me I waved Miss Charlesworth's envelope and shouted. Twenty yards farther on the car stopped and I started running.

Even on the hottest days there is always an uplift of breeze on that hill and as I ran forward a sudden light whirl of wind caught at my big-brimmed white straw hat and lifted the shantung skirt above my knees.

I was still trying to hold down hat and skirt when I reached Captain Blaine, who stared at me with those iridescent eyes dancing with astonishment.

'Good God, girl, I didn't know you.'

'I've got a note for you,' I said, panting slightly, 'from Miss Charlesworth.'

'Awfully, awfully sorry,' he said. 'Really didn't know you. You look different somehow.'

I was foolish enough, believe it or not, to ask 'How?'

'Don't know.' He sat there in the driving seat looking at me quizzically, all charm. 'Must be the dress. No it isn't. I know. It's the hat. I've never seen you in a hat before.'

I flushed. It's always the little things that get women. It's always the stupid little trivialities that trap them.

'Makes you look older. More mature.'

'Oh! really?'

As if he hadn't already said enough to have me in helpless enslavement he suddenly smiled and said, with bland enchantment:

'You suit the day. You look like a bit of sunlight blown up from the sea.'

Could any girl, I ask you, want more than that? I lapped up these blandishments as a kitten laps up warm new milk.

'Oh! the note,' I said, giggling slightly. 'I was forgetting the note. It was a bit of luck seeing you like this. Miss Charlesworth said to be sure to give you the note personally. She trusted me to do that, she said.'

A sharp change came over his face. He even ignored the note in his penetrating eagerness to make quite sure what I had said.

'She said what?'

'She said she trusted me.'

A smile crept back so slowly to his face that its final rest there gave it a look of quite innocent astonishment.

'Do you know you've just said something very remarkable?' he said.

'Me?' I said and I giggled nervously again. 'How?'

'My aunt has never trusted anyone in her life,' he said. 'Not a soul.'

By this time he had put the note in his pocket and I stood there for some seconds with nothing to say, aware only of the sun flashing on the bonnet of the car, his tunic buttons and far below us on the surface of the sea.

'You saw all that paraphernalia she brought?' he said. 'That's an example of how little she trusts people. That's her all, in those damn trunks. Lugs it all from place to place, wherever she goes, like a camel train. She wouldn't trust a fly.'

It is hardly necessary, I imagine, to say how all this affected me. It was like being told that you, in a whole flock of sparrows, have really turned out, after all, to be nothing less than a golden oriole.

'Most remarkable thing I ever heard,' he said. 'You must be an extraordinary person. Can't believe it – Bertie *trusting* you.'

The barely visible line of summer horizon seemed to tilt as another rise of breeze caught my hat and lifted it up, half sideways, from my face.

'Had lunch?' he said.

'Oh! yes,' I said. 'But I suppose you haven't, have you? Please don't let me keep you.'

'Never have any, not when it's so hot,' he said. 'Get a pretty square breakfast and then carry through to dinner. Always got to do the dinner anyway. Can't escape that. Mess tradition, the colonel and that sort of thing.'

He opened the door of the car.

'Hop in. I'll drive you back. Come to that, I'll drive you anywhere.' He smiled in that marvellously iridescent way of his, full into my eyes. 'Game? What say?'

What indeed could I say? My grasp of the next few succeeding moments was so vague that I actually forgot, as we whirled round the high corner beyond the castle, to hold on to my hat. With a whistling explosion it blew off my head and landed in the back seat and my hair started flowing in the wind.

I suppose he must have asked me at least a dozen times where I would like to be driven that afternoon before I really woke up to a clear realization of what was going on.

'Tea somewhere? Along the coast?' He was voluble and gay. 'Where's the nearest lighthouse?'

'Oh! I hate lighthouses. They give me a queer feeling in my legs,' I said, laughing. 'No, no – inland. Let's go inland.'

Suddenly I knew where I wanted to go.

'Do you know the forest?' I said. 'It's about six or seven miles from here. You turn off at a mill. I often go out there, especially in spring. It's full of primroses in spring. They're the nearest primroses to the sea.'

I often think women who wear their hair short never really know that wonderful feeling of liquid exhilaration that comes from having a warm wind blow like water through hair that is really long.

There is no other sensation quite like it in the world and by the time we had reached the outskirts of beech and oak and sweet chestnut that make up the forest I was in a state of breathless, half-orgiastic delight.

'Well, this is my forest,' I said.

When Captain Blaine finally pulled up the car at a point where the trees almost met overhead, we were in a sort of deep green tunnel, wonderfully cool, without sunshine.

'Your forest? Yours?'

'That's how I always think of it,' I said. 'Nobody else ever comes here anyway. Not a soul.'

'Until today.'

I wasn't sure at that moment whether he was teasing me or not. He got out of the car and came round to my side of it, holding the door open for me. In that exhilarating rush across the hills I had quite forgotten all about my appearance and when he opened the door there suddenly was my skirt, blown half-way above my knees, showing an inch or two of bare thigh above the stockings.

But somehow it didn't worry me and with a giggle I jumped down from the car and said:

'Oh! that was the most terrific, terrific drive. Divine. My head's going round and round and round.'

'What shall we do?' he said.

'Let's walk,' I said. 'I'll show you a place where the beech-leaves lie about a yard thick, even in summer. I call it the place of the everlasting leaves.'

If Captain Archie Blaine regarded these outpourings as so much adolescent saccharine he never revealed it by a single word, a smile or the flicker of an eye. In fact he actually seemed to be so much in sympathy with them that he suddenly took my hand. As he did so I felt a cool new thrill go through me from my thighs to my hair and a moment later I started half running through the forest, through shadow hardly ever broken by sunlight, to that secret beech-leaf altar of mine where from time to time I thought nothing of lying and dreaming half a day away.

When we got there I lay down in the deep dry leaves, as I always liked to do, and he took off his tunic and lay there with me.

We talked a bit, I quite forget what about now, but presently the conversation got round, as it was always to do sooner or later to Miss Charlesworth.

'You know I'm really terribly glad about you and Bertie. It's really wonderful that she's at last got somebody she feels she can trust. You'll be a great help to her, I know.'

For the life of me I couldn't imagine how I could be of help to a lady like Miss Charlesworth, and to be perfectly honest I wasn't very interested.

'She's really got nobody in the world except me,' he said. 'And now you come along. Somebody she can really trust. A god-send.'

At this point I did what I thought was a clever thing. I decided to tease him a bit.

'I think,' I said, 'you're trying to flatter me.'

Lying flat on my back I looked up through the masses of gold-green branches, biting my lip, then laughing.

'Nothing farther from my mind.'

'Flatterer, that's what you are.'

'Don't girls like to be flattered?'

'Oh! to a certain extent I suppose,' I said in that airy, part mocking sort of way that adolescence deludes itself sounds like the tried wisdom of experience. 'All depends.'

Naturally he asked on what?

'I suppose,' I said, 'on she who is to be flattered.'

That was a fine self-revelatory remark if you like: not that I knew it at the time.

'Absolutely right,' he said. 'How clever of you.'

I laughed. Quite naturally it was clever of me.

Suddenly he turned his body, half sat up and leaned on one elbow, looking at me.

'May I ask you something?'

'Ask away,' I said. That cool thrill had started to creep up through my body again. 'I like answering questions.'

'Answer this then,' he said. His eyes were shining with excruciating brightness, even in the shade. 'If I say I like you without your hat, is that flattery?'

'No,' I said, laughing. 'That's a lie. Because you said you liked me with it.'

'It's neither,' he said. 'Because I love you with it and I love you without it. Either way.'

A moment later he was kissing me. He had an especially warm, obliterating way of kissing and though I suppose he must have kissed me in that same way hundreds of times afterwards I think I never quite got over that first fine careless bit of rapture. It was like being kissed, I remember thinking, by a man with all summer on his lips.

It might have been an hour or even two hours later that I roused myself from a half-dream and heard him talking yet again of Miss Charlesworth. By this time the top of my dress was all unbuttoned and I might have been lying on cushions of velvet as I lay there drowsily and listened.

'I really can't get over the fact that Bertie trusts you,' he was saying. 'Mind if I ask you something else?'

'Again? You and your questions.'

'Do you trust me?'

Involuntarily I lifted my hands and caught his face.

'Oh! of course,' I said. 'Of course I do. Absolutely. Always. Whatever made you think I mightn't?'

'Nothing. I just wanted to know.'

'Oh! that really hurt,' I said. 'I can't bear to feel that you even thought I didn't trust you.'

I started to look with prolonged earnest tenderness straight into his eyes, but before I could speak again the phantom figure of my mother was on the scene.

'I always trust people,' I said. 'Everybody. If you trust them they trust you. Don't you see?'

Except for that enchanting laugh of his Captain Blaine didn't bother to answer. A moment later he was forcing me gently back into the deep dry bed of leaves, stroking my hair and neck and discovering, for the first but not the last time, that mole on my naked shoulder.

4

I don't know if you've ever had the experience of hearing your soul singing on a dark night full of stars? Yes, I know it sounds ridiculous: too extravagantly silly for words. But that, in fact, is the way your soul is apt to behave on a dark night full of stars when you are only eighteen and a girl at that.

My soul did an awful lot of singing in July, August, and September of that year and not only on dark nights full of stars. It sang with equal rapture on white afternoons along the cliffs, through diamond dancing mornings by the sea and through breathless evenings in the forest or the car. First love, they will tell you, is apt to be a painful process, a complex fusion of heart-ache and joy, but I can only say that for me, during those three hot months, it was quite truthfully all joy, all singing.

Much of the joy arose, also, from the simplest things. Take, for example, our habit of lying on the cliffs and watching the sea. You might think that a man of forty and a good deal of experience, like Captain Blaine, would pretty soon grow tired of that.

Not at all. On the contrary it was he who would suggest, over and over again, that that was the way we should while away an evening or an afternoon. He had rather a pretty and amusing phrase for it, too.

He called it 'spying on our dream'.

I must explain all this with care. It's really of the utmost importance to convey exactly how that dream was conjured.

From the cliffs you can, of course, see miles out to sea. Ships from all over the world are passing and crossing all day and all night and on fine days you can see the cliffs of France with ease. By day they look like a piece of roughly cut cheese lying on the far horizon. By night you can pick out scores of lights from ships and lightships and shore.

It was those lights and those cliffs that formed the gateway to this dream of ours and it was Captain Blaine, lying on his back with those intensely iridescent eyes of his fixed on the sky, perhaps with his head in my lap, who was never tired of explaining it all to me. And naturally it was I, in turn, who was never tired of listening.

'Lovely spring days in Monte. And then over into Italy – Bordighera, San Remo, Lerici. The coast of flowers. Oh! Millions of flowers. Acres of carnations. Endless carnations even in winter. Lemon trees. Roses. Mimosa – it's the scent of mimosa that gets me. I never smell it without feeling I'm back there. Magical, extraordinary, how it takes you back. And there's a little restaurant down the street from the casino where they serve incredible prawns and you have iced Montrachet that's absolute nectar straight from heaven – what's that line? – "as though on manna I had fed and drunk the milk of paradise".'

Oh! yes, I forgot: Captain Blaine knew a little poetry too.

And it was always some remark of mine like 'Oh! darling, I can't wait to get there' that set him laughing in that chuckling way of his and finally brought the conversation round to what he called the wherewithal.

'The pennies, girl, the pennies. There's the rub. Of course I'll get something when Bertie's snuffed it – but when, I ask you, when? Dammit, it's mine by right. I'm her only kith and kin. The sole remaining Blaine. You'd think she might cough up a little allowance for her only nephew, wouldn't you? But not Bertie.

Oh! I love her, I adore the old girl, but I must say I get to thinking it's rather hard cheese sometimes.'

It was true, as my mother said, that he talked too much: but oh! how persuasively.

'I think she's mean,' I would say. 'Downright mean.'

'Oh, no, girl. Oh! no. Not mean. You've got her wrong there. Just careful, that's all. Just plain distrustful. That's what makes her go about in this snail-like fashion – carrying all her riches on her back. But when you think that just one bit of jewellery – and by the way she never wears the important bits, never – would fetch a comfortable fifteen hundred or perhaps even more I must say it tries the old faith a bit hard.'

'Selfish old thing.'

'That bedroom of hers must be just like a vault. An absolute treasure house. You won't believe this, I suppose, will you, girl? But when she lived down in the west country she had the place guarded by six wretched great mastiffs. One at the front gate, one at the back, one at the front door, one at the kitchen, one outside the bedroom door and one actually on the ruddy bed. Fortunately her doctor got wind of it and told her he strongly disapproved. Bad for the asthma and all that.'

'Is she likely to last long with this asthma?'

'Nature's wonderful, girl. Bertie's just a creaking gate. The sort that lasts for ever. No: I'm afraid there's nothing for it but to face things with the same fortitude and resignation the Blaines have allegedly been famous for ever since Colonel James August Blaine amputated his own left leg at Blenheim with nothing but a potato peeler and a quart of brandy.'

Stupid though this no doubt sounds it was heaven to me to hear him talk like that. He really made you think that all that business of not being able to get his hands on Miss Charlesworth's money was nothing but mere lighthearted nonsense after all.

But for me it wasn't a lighthearted joke. More and more, as the summer went on, I found myself looking at the whole thing in that familiar trusting way of mine. I began again that old habit, so firmly instilled into me by my mother, of putting myself into other people's places, into and under other people's skins – in this case, Captain Blaine's.

I even began to talk about it. Not to my mother, naturally. My mother stood remarkably aloof from me in the matter of Captain Blaine. She stood apart like a silent shadow of disapproval – hoping, I suppose, that in the fullness of time I should get over it, as young girls are eternally supposed to get over their first fiery infatuations.

I began to talk, instead, to Ruby. Nothing pleased Ruby more than to talk to me of her newest loves – I really think she attached herself to a new uniform of some sort every time she went down to that beery Babylon of ours – and I must say she made a good listener when I talked to her of mine.

Finally, after one especially ecstatic confessional in her bedroom she said in a casual way that she hoped I hadn't done anything in any way naughty with Captain Blaine?

I wasn't slow to confess that I had in fact been naughty with Captain Blaine, not once but several times, and that I liked it. In fact, though I didn't say so, I was rather proud.

'Hope your mother don't get wind of it,' Ruby said. 'She wouldn't care much for that.'

'Oh! pot to mother.'

'Well, it's too late now, duckie,' Ruby said, 'but take my advice. Be careful.'

I laughed and said she was the one to talk, wasn't she?

'Oh! me, I'm different,' Ruby said. 'You can't count me. I'm past praying for, duckie. I like company, I do, and how many glasses o' stout do you think I can afford out o' the fifteen bob your ma pays me here? A girl's got to have a wet now and then, hasn't she? And if a chap pays for a few he's entitled to a bit of comfort, don't you think?'

After this Ruby gave one of her slow ripe laughs and said that you couldn't expect a man to give something for nothing all the time.

This sounded a good opportunity of saying that, as it happened, Captain Blaine had nothing to give.

'Don't get you, duckie.'

I went on to explain how broke Captain Blaine was and what a mean business it was he wasn't being helped by Miss Charlesworth.

'Officers are always broke, duckie. Live above their income by nature. It's the done thing. Take no notice o' that. Does he drink?'

'Not that I know of.'

'All officers drink, duckie. What about gambling? Cards?'

'I never heard him talk of it.'

'They all gamble, duckie. Second nature.'

I felt a little annoyed with Ruby for not understanding the situation more intelligently and I asked her rather tartly how she would like it if all her family fortune were tied up with one person while other people had to scrape along?

'Don't know about that, duckie, I'm sure. My ma left three pound ten to get herself buried with and fifteen bob still on the slate at the Queen's Head. That's all I know about fortunes.'

'Well, Miss Charlesworth's worth a fortune,' I said, 'and it's plain mean. Plain unfair. Some of her bits of jewellery alone are worth a thousand apiece.'

'Oh?' Ruby said. 'How did you find that out? Ever seen 'em?'

'Of course not,' I said. 'Captain Blaine told me.'

'I see,' Ruby said. 'I see.'

After that, in her casual, free and easy way, looking at me with those too-old, half-dissolute eyes of hers, Ruby used to ask me a great deal about Captain Blaine. But the curious thing was that though I talked on and on about him in that ecstatic confessional way of mine, telling her everything or practically everything, she didn't comment very much, though I didn't notice it very greatly at the time.

All I did notice was that she seemed consistently cool about all the stupendous ardours of my great affair, so much so that I went as far as to tell her one afternoon that I didn't think she had the remotest idea of what love was all about.

'Shouldn't wonder, duckie. Shouldn't wonder.'

In support of my claim, if you can believe it, I even quoted poetry at her. She didn't know, I supposed, a wonderful poem that began *I wonder, by my troth, what thou and I did till we loved*? Whether she did or not, I told her, that was how lovers all through the ages had felt and it included me.

'That's how you feel all right, duckie,' Ruby said. 'Well, once anyway.'

175

A few evenings later I was walking to the town to post some letters when I came upon Ruby and a Sergeant of Marines unsteadily winding sea-wards under the street gas-lights. The sergeant, in Ruby's words, was sloshed. Ruby, who was trying to save him from falling down, wasn't a great deal better. And as I dropped the letters into the box I heard the sergeant being sick in the gutter and Ruby, for some godless reason, laughing aloud.

No, Ruby I said to myself, you just don't know. You never will know. Oh! how could you know?

5

It is always very difficult, I suppose, to say exactly where and how an obsession begins. It is rather like trying to trace the origins of a cold. What started it? Where did you pick up the germ? When did the chill begin?

I find it hard to recall now a single word of Captain Blaine's that might be said to have started my obsession with the key of one of Miss Charlesworth's jewel boxes. In fact I am perfectly sure that he was careful never to utter one. It was really much simpler to take me along the cliffs and hold me in long paradisal embraces and tell me how beautiful I was and invite me, in those extraordinary hypnotic words of his, to spy on our dream.

I forgot to say, by the way, that I often went to Miss Charlesworth's room. Part of her expression of trust in me – I rather think she went further than that, I think she even liked me – was to send for me quite often and ask me to perform various little services. I posted letters, bought stamps, changed books at the local library – nothing very much really, except that it meant that, as the summer went on, I became more and more familiar with the territory of that room.

It was the untidiest room I have ever seen. It was like the crazy repository of an industriously hoarding jackdaw. It was an elegantly shabby ruin of unlocked cabin trunks, travelling-cases, Gladstone bags, straw dress cases, handbags, reticules, sunshades, and umbrellas. And of course jewel cases – altogether five of them.

Looking back now, I feel more than ever certain that it was an afternoon in late September that my obsession with those boxes really started. Miss Charlesworth had asked if I would catch the six o'clock post with her letters and at the same time bring back some stamps for her.

But when I got back with the stamps and took them up to her room and knocked on the door there was a sudden agitated jackdaw screech in answer.

'Yes? Who is it? Who is it? Who is it there now?'

'It's me,' I said. 'I've brought the stamps. It's Christine.'

'Christine, you must wait. Just a minute. Just a minute. Wait there.'

There was a sound of heavy trunks being moved. I heard the clatter of an overturning water jug as something struck the washstand.

After several minutes and more noises the key turned in the lock and the door opened to a gap of eight or nine inches. An agitated Miss Charlesworth appeared in the gap and put out a hand and said she would take the stamps now.

It was quite clear that one of the cabin trunks was wedged up against the door and I wondered why.

'What is it, Miss Charlesworth?' I said. 'Is anything the matter? Is there anything I can do?'

'No, nothing, nothing. Just give me the stamps, that's all.'

As I handed the stamps through the gap in the door I said:

'Are you sure, Miss Charlesworth? You haven't been trying to move those heavy trunks, have you?'

'No, no. I've just lost something. Mislaid something, that's all.'

I suggested that perhaps I might help her find it, whatever it was, but she hesitated before answering. She started licking her lips and swallowing very hard.

'Well, possibly you could. Perhaps you could. Your eyes are younger than mine.'

Though my eyes might have been younger they certainly weren't any keener than Miss Charlesworth's and it was only when I went into the room and found myself in the centre of that shabbily elegant ruin that I realized why it was that even she couldn't find what she was looking for.

Where only one jackdaw had worked before, a whole flock, it seemed to me, had now been madly at work in the bedroom.

Chairs and tables and chests-of-drawers and trunks were piled against each other. The carpet was half-rolled back. The bed was askew across the fireplace. The mattress was propped up at one end with a brass coal-scuttle and over by the window there was even an open pale pink sunshade.

The cause of all this, it seemed to me, was rather trivial. Miss Charlesworth had lost a key.

'Oh! is that all?' I said. 'We'll soon find that once we get things straightened out a bit.'

'I've been looking for over an hour already,' she said. 'Ever since you've been gone. It simply isn't here.'

'When did you last have it?'

'This afternoon. Early this afternoon.'

'Then it must be here,' I said. 'What sort of key is it?'

'It's the key of one of the jewel boxes,' Miss Charlesworth said. 'This one. The tortoiseshell.'

It was really very handsome, that big tortoiseshell box with its silver lock and hinges. There was something very rich about the opulent polish of that deep brown shell. Involuntarily I smoothed my fingers across the lid of it and at the same moment I started thinking of Captain Blaine.

'Did you want something out of the box?' I said. 'Haven't you got another key?'

'I never have duplicate keys,' Miss Charlesworth said. 'I would never entertain the idea.'

'But if you had another key,' I said, 'you could open the box. It's all so simple.'

'I don't want to open the box!' she half-shouted at me. 'I don't want to open the box! I simply want to be sure that no one else has the key. All I want is the key.'

Obsessions, I suppose, often have the effect of clouding the faculties, upsetting the reason and that sort of thing. They are a kind of disease. In my case the effect was entirely opposite. In my first moment of obsession, confronted by a stupidly, agitated old woman fussing over a lost key, I began to feel remarkably logical, extraordinarily cool.

'Then we shall just have to set about finding the key,' I said, 'shan't we?'

It took me the better part of another hour to put some order into that crazy jackdaw chaos and at the end of it Miss Charlesworth was crying gently.

'It just simply isn't here. It just simply isn't here.'

The worst of over-heavy make-up is that it doesn't take very kindly to tears. Miss Charlesworth's face now looked like a rosymauve daub in a child's painting book when the colours have run.

'Please don't agitate yourself, Miss Charlesworth,' I said. 'It's all very simple. You must simply get somebody in the town to cut you another key.'

'Oh! no, oh! no, oh! no.'

In my cool way I took no notice of these protestations.

'In fact if I were you,' I said, 'I should have duplicate keys cut for all your cases at the same time. It's the only sensible, prudent thing to do.'

I think it was that word prudent that got her. She seemed to pull herself momentarily and sharply out of her agitation.

'Prudent? You mean to say you don't think I've been very prudent about matters?'

'No,' I said, 'frankly I don't. If you've got a box of jewellery and you can't open it what on earth's the use of it? It might just as well be full of sea-shells. In fact the really prudent thing would be to deposit the whole lot with a bank and forget it.'

'Oh! no. I hate banks. I distrust banks. I really distrust them.'

At this moment I took her by the hands. They were very skinny hands and they were hot and trembling.

'But you did say once you trusted me, didn't you, Miss Charlesworth?'

'Yes, I did. I did indeed.'

With cool reassurance I patted her hands.

'All right,' I said, 'I'll go down to Carter's the ironmongers in the morning and they'll send a man up.'

By this time she was crying again, though more vigorously than before, rather as if in relief, and at the same time saying between her sobs how greatly indebted she was to me for all my help and comfort and patience and so on. It really seemed an awful fuss to make over that stupid little key.

The following morning I got the man from Carter's to call.

179

Before I left for the town Miss Charlesworth confided in me that she'd hardly slept a wink all night but that things were better now. She had seen the force of my logic suggesting that all four boxes should have new keys. It would be the prudent thing to do.

That, of course, is another curious thing about obsession. It breeds its own logic; everything about it has a way of seeming inevitable, of being right.

That was why, later on that afternoon, when I called at Carter's a second time and told them that Miss Charlesworth had changed her mind and had decided to have duplicate keys cut for all the boxes it seemed a logical rather than merely a clever part of the pattern.

Even Carter's agreed that it was the sensible, prudent thing to do.

6

It took about a week to get the keys made but, like the Frenchman who is warned that alcohol kills slowly, I was in no hurry. The holiday season in a seaside town is inevitably a great time for key-cutting. Hotel guests have a tiresome habit of losing keys or taking them away and forgetting to post them back.

I spent a good deal of that time trying to decide whether or not to tell Captain Blaine. It is of course not obsession that clouds the faculties or bends the reason at all, but pure innocence. And no one in the world could have been more obligingly, sublimely innocent than I was that summer. I have already described how my soul had acquired the habit of singing but you might well think that in three months it would have got over that. Not at all. Even seduction hadn't sullied me.

The rest of the time I spent in going over and over the fabric of my – or rather our – dream. I suppose it's really the oldest and most universal of all the silly dreams that women feed on: the desire to escape familiar drudgery, to exchange the commonplace for the celestial, to put trust in unfamiliar princes and finally be carried splendidly away.

In the same way I saw myself over and over again on the afternoon cross-channel steamer, eating dinner on the Blue Train, waking up to the carnation world of the Mediterranean, opening windows on to the blue heaven of Shelley's Italy. I was about to leave our rather stuffy little boarding-house, the smell of frying fish and bacon, the front drawing-room that still actually had curtains of green chenille, antimacassars, and brass pots of aspidistra. I was going to leave the world of guests who didn't know how to behave at table, who complained of how the soup was cold and the potatoes underdone and bony, who fussed over damp sheets and forgot to tip the maids.

I was going, above all, to leave my mother, with her tedious philosophy of putting herself into other people's places, her infinite timidity and her spurious wisdom about trusting other people in order that they, in turn, could trust you. Weeks of silent disapprobation had turned my mother more and more into a kind of shadowy smudge and I was, thank God, going to escape from that too.

The day I collected the keys from the ironmongers I decided to tell Captain Blaine what I was doing – or rather to tell him half of it and later surprise him with the rest.

'Supposing I told you, darling, that I could get the money to go away,' I said. 'When could we go? Soon?'

'Now steady, girl,' he said. 'I'm a soldier. I just can't walk out like that.'

'You could get leave.'

'I suppose so. But where's this money coming from, girl? Dammit, I'm broke. I tell you I'm solid, stony broke.'

'You won't be tomorrow.'

'She talks to me in riddles,' he said. He laughed, half-mockingly I thought. 'She fills my head with dreams. But the cash, girl, the cash. Show me the tree where grows the cash.'

I loved, as I say, to hear him talk in that extravagant fashion and I said:

'Well, first I've got forty pounds of my own. We could buy the tickets with that.'

'With you now?'

Yes, I told him, I'd got it with me now. That made him laugh again, not mockingly this time, and he said:

'Comic, funny little girl. How long do you suppose we'd last on forty pounds?'

'Forty pounds is only the beginning,' I said. 'Tomorrow you can have a thousand.'

He gave a long sharp whistle of astonishment.

'There must be something wrong with your little head, girl,' he said. 'You must have got in a draught.'

No, I told him, there was nothing wrong with my little head and I hadn't been in a draught and there and then I decided to tell him the rest. When he heard what I had to say he suddenly took my face in his two hands in a rhapsodic gesture of delight.

'Clever little girl,' he said. 'I always knew you were a clever little girl.'

He couldn't have put it more plainly if he'd said outright that I'd done exactly what he hoped and expected I'd do. And in turn I felt supremely flattered because I'd so successfully put myself in his place, into and under his skin.

'Now this, I think,' he said, 'is what we'll do. Tomorrow, when I take Bertie for her drive, I'll invite the old girl out to lunch up in town. I'll lunch her at the Carlton. Oysters, champagne, pheasant, a marvellous soufflé, green Chartreuse. I know she wants to see her lawyers in town and I'll say "Bertie dear, it's exhausting doing that journey back at the end of the day. I'll wire for a room for you for a couple of days. The change will pep you up. You were coughing yesterday." '

'And what then?'

He laughed: again, as I fondly understood it, not mockingly.

'The rest, dear girl,' he said, 'is largely up to you. What you h ve to look for is an emerald and diamond tiara. It's really big. You can't mistake it. No: perhaps not, after all. Too big. A bit too conspicuous. Better concentrate on rings. Bring a sample half dozen. They're mostly emerald and diamond too. That way we can dispose of them one at a time, whenever the champagne runs dry.'

Yes: he talked too much. But I, as I listened to him in brittle excitement, all tension, hardly talked at all. And later that night, in bed, I was vaguely aware that that brittle tension had been responsible already for a great change in me.

My soul had actually, at last, stopped its starry singing.

7

Two days later Miss Charlesworth went to London with Captain Blaine, who had my forty pounds in his pocket and a large companionable smile on his face as he called and drove her to the station. I still felt tense and brittle as I watched them from an upstairs window and I hardly knew how I'd get through the day until seven o'clock, when he'd be coming back again.

That afternoon was Ruby's half day. She generally left the boarding-house about three o'clock but that day I decided to give her until four. But to my utter astonishment I was on my way up the back stairs, with a skeleton house-key to Miss Charlesworth's room in my hand, when Ruby suddenly came tripping down, humming happily to herself, all her war-paint on.

'Hello, duckie. Just off. Bit late today. Wrecked my face first time and had to do it all over again. Bit excited I expect.'

'Excited?'

I was so excited and staggered myself that I hadn't the wit to hide the key. I just stood there twisting it round and round in my fingers.

'Like the hat?' Ruby said. It was a big and floppy yellow straw, with a single magenta rose on it twice as large as a saucer. 'Had it re-trimmed. Excited? – I should say. It's my birthday. Going to lash out tonight and have supper at the Royal Clarence with my sister. You know, the one who works in the café. Been saving up for it. Going to do it big.'

Ruby gave one of her ripe explosive laughs and I, having nothing to say, simply stood there twisting the key.

'You look a bit pale, duckie,' Ruby said when that laugh of hers had finally stopped rudely slitting the air. She peered at me sharply from a face as heavily pink with powder as a marshmallow. She was really very handsome with all her war-paint on and you hardly knew her as the rather blowsy rag doll who, in the mornings, emptied bedroom slops and scrubbed the floors. 'Feeling under par?'

No, I was not, I told her and again I stood witlessly fumbling with the key.

'Well, cheery-bye, then,' Ruby said. My heart was racing frenziedly. 'Expect I'll be late. Going on to the Tennis Club dance afterwards. They'll probably wheel me home about four. Don't tell your Ma.'

I vaguely muttered something about wishing her a good time and then she was away downstairs. At the foot she turned and looked back at me, the heavy dark mascara on the lashes of her eyes making them look bigger and juicier than ever.

'Have a lay down, duckie,' she said. 'Don't like that look you got.'

A moment later the big floppy hat and the equally floppy dress, a bright petunia satin, had disappeared.

I gave her another five minutes and then let myself into Miss Charlesworth's bedroom. If my soul had stopped singing my heart certainly hadn't stopped racing and as I put the key into the tortoiseshell jewel box it felt like a toy windmill whirling madly round and round.

In my witless excitement I hadn't even had the sense to take the key out of the bedroom door and about a minute later the door suddenly opened and there stood Ruby.

There was a curiously impassive look on her juicy red lips and in those old grey eyes that I'd never seen before and she simply stood for a full minute without speaking, quietly staring through me.

When she spoke at last it was in a level whisper. It couldn't have startled me more if it had been a bomb.

'Looking for something, duckie?'

I couldn't speak. My tongue felt frozen. I simply stood there goggling. And then something extraordinary happened. At the very moment when I felt sure she was about to start pleading with me about this and that she simply uttered one more sentence and it hit me like a whip.

'I'll drink your health tonight, duckie,' she said, again in that level whisper, 'I really will.'

That was all. I actually felt my eye-balls jump and a moment later that big floppy hat of hers had disappeared completely for the second time.

I suppose I stood there for fully half a minute before realizing that the only clever thing to do was to try and call her back. I remember actually rushing out on to the landing and calling 'Ruby' several times before realizing with horror that someone else might hear me. It was too late anyway by that time and all I could think of doing next was to rush back into the bedroom, grab up seven or eight rings and then lock the box and the bedroom door before scrambling upstairs to my room.

For the next three hours I couldn't make up my mind who I wanted to see most: Captain Blaine or Ruby. I lay on the bed in unparalleled idiotic confusion, incapable of thinking, my mind a jelly. I hadn't even looked to see what the rings were like but had simply thrown them loose, like so many peppermint lumps, into my bag.

At seven o'clock I went out to meet Captain Blaine. At the eastern end of the front there used to be public gardens with lawns and beds of geraniums and fuchsia in summer-time and it was a good place for meeting. I waited there till eight o'clock. I've explained before, I think, how Captain Blaine often kept me waiting, sometimes for an hour or more. 'Not because I didn't want to come, girl, but because other chaps decreed otherwise,' was how he would charmingly explain it. 'In the army most of the money and the time you have are really someone else's.'

At half past eight I walked to the railway station. There were two more trains from London that night: one at nine and the last at midnight. When Captain Blaine didn't come on the nine o'clock train I walked up the hill to the garrison. Now and then I saw an officer or a group of officers walking towards me down the hill and my heart started racing again. But Captain Blaine was never among them and by ten o'clock I was back in the gardens, staring at the flowers.

I went over the same futile procedure a second time after meeting the train at midnight and it was one o'clock in the morning before I was back outside the rear door of the boarding-house, waiting for Ruby. It was getting cold by that time and now and then I had an intolerable fit of trembling.

Yet the most vivid thing I can remember about that grotesque wandering of mine is not the cold or the trembling or the impossible racing of my heart every time I heard footsteps in the darkness, but the curious sensation that I had no longer any legs. I had somehow been left with two fleshless husks, above which my body simply drifted emptily along.

It was after three o'clock when Ruby finally appeared. I knew it was Ruby some time before she got to me. It was not merely that I recognized that big floppy straw hat and its magenta rose as she swung it under the one remaining street light.

Ruby, unlike me, was in a happy frame of mind. She was singing.

8

'Hullo, duckie,' she said and it was almost as if she knew I'd be waiting there. 'You'll miss your beauty sleep if you're not careful, won't you?'

Without hesitation she threw back her blonde head and laughed in that rich, air-splitting fashion of hers. Then she swung unsteadily on her feet and did a complete turn on her heels, ending up with her back to me.

'Do me up, duckie, will you?' she said. 'I've come unput somehow. I'm blowed if I didn't feel a draught down my back and now I know.'

I didn't speak a word. My hands were cold too and they trembled as I did up four or five buttons at the back of her dress. I couldn't do up the two top buttons because they were missing and in fact the dress was torn for five or six inches at one side of the neck, as if someone had tried to rip it off her.

'Torn a bit, aren't I?' she said. 'Thought so. Comes of struggling.' She laughed in rousing fashion again. She wasn't quite sloshed. She was just gay and happy. 'Never struggle, duckie. Don't know, though. It's more fun. They like it better if you do.'

All this time we were about a hundred yards from the boardinghouse and we hadn't moved an inch nearer since meeting. I didn't want to move either until I'd asked her one question.

'Ruby,' I said. 'I want to ask you something. Are you going to tell anyone you saw me in Miss Charlesworth's bedroom?'

'Me?' Ruby said. She swayed tipsily on her heels, at the same time swinging the big straw hat. 'Duckie, I never tell tales out of school.'

In my distraught and stupid innocence I actually wanted to thank her but before I could find the words she said:

'Drank your health, duckie. Like I said I would. And guess who with?'

The sergeant of marines struck me as the most likely companion for our Ruby at health-drinking time, but the thought of him had hardly crossed my mind before she was laughing again and saying:

'Your friend. You know. Your friend.'

'What friend?'

'Your captain. Miss Charlesworth's nephew. Him.'

The strange sensation of having no legs extended itself suddenly to the rest of my body. I remembered simply floating there like an empty husk, speechless, frozen stiff.

'Me and my sister saw him first at the Royal Clarence. Supper with champagne and oysters. With a friend of his, Lieutenant Pascoe. Know him? Thin fellow, very dark, with a moustache. Started making eyes at my sister while we were eating our peach melba. She's a corker, my sister. She's the pretty one.'

I was still speechless, just a husk.

'Then this Lieutenant Pascoe sends the waiter over and says would we have a glass of the widow? They were celebrating some battle or other. Can't think of the name now. Couldn't understand what he meant by the widow at first and then it turns out it's champagne. Are you listening, duckie?'

I was listening; but not with my ears. That wretched, idiotic soul of mine was the only thing about me capable of that simple act of reception.

'Well, I could see this Lieutenant was plain sunk on my sister. Couldn't blame him, either, could you? She's the glamour kid. Figure like an hour glass. Hardly any waist. Long legs and a bust like Venus. She's a lot younger than me too and she's got the look in her eye.'

As she was saying all this she swung the hat again and did a few staggering whirls on the pavement, half in the act of dancing.

'Then before you know what's happening we're all in Captain

187

Blaine's car and off to the Tennis Dance, with my sister practically
on the lieutenant's lap at the back and me in front with the captain. Am I telling the tale all right, duckie?'

She was telling the tale all right. How much of it was gospel
truth I was too distraught to decide, but I've since often comforted myself with the thought that I suppose you really need to
have lost innocence, as Ruby had, before you really understand it.

'Then the fun started. My sister's the one that always causes it.
She lets the men dance close to her and it drives them up the cliff.
She does it on purpose. She says so. It makes 'em mad. By the
way, I thought you said the Captain didn't drink?'

Ruby laughed again in what I then thought was a horribly raw,
distasteful way.

'Not much, duckie, not much. One of these days they'll float
a cross-channel boat on what he puts away. I'll say this though.
He never gets mardy and moody on it. He knows what to do with
a girl.'

Have you ever seen anyone shocked into speechlessness? Two
or three years ago I saw a young man on a cross-channel steamer,
in a rough passage, who was shocked by fright into a temporary
dumb paralysis. The stewards had to hold him up. Like mine, his
legs might just as well not have been there and his lips and his
tongue were incapable of working.

I was paralysed too as I stood there staring at Ruby. Even my
wretched soul wasn't doing much listening by that time. And
what, after all, can you expect? How much can you ask of your
soul? After weeks of abandoned singing you can't suddenly start
asking it to play at mathematics and work out emotional logar-
ithms, can you? You simply can't ask it that.

I haven't the remotest idea of how much longer Ruby and I
stood there on the pavement together but suddenly that raw laugh
of hers was splitting the air again and she was saying:

'Oh! he knows what a girl wants all right. Not surprised you
let him do what he likes with you. Who wouldn't? He can give
you the lot and well wrapped up too. Needn't have ripped my
dress though. I was all ready to take it off in the car if he'd waited.'

Suddenly everything inside me broke. The use in my legs came
back with such a stunning shock that I started running. I could

really hear again. I caught on the night air the noise of a gull croaking across the harbour, then the sound of my own feet and then the last raw peal of Ruby laughing.

A few minutes later I was dashing up the back stairs of the boarding-house when suddenly I heard my mother hissing at me. I had utterly forgotten my mother and now it was she who shocked me to a standstill.

'Where ever have you been, child? Where on earth have you been? My dear God, where ever have you been?'

I hadn't time to answer this agitated heart-cry before Ruby was there behind her at the foot of the stairs, casually swinging the big yellow straw hat and saying in the sweetest, friendliest, most off-hand way, as if we'd just got back from a picnic:

'Been to the Tennis Dance with me, ma'am. I'm to blame. Should have ought to have told you. It's all right, ma'am. It's done her the world of good to have a bit of dancing.'

9

My mother is dead now. Ruby is dead too. She was having a drink with a Polish sailor one evening in the Prince of Orange, in the middle of the blitz, when a thousand-pounder blew both of them, and the pub, to all eternity. The boarding-house got its own hit a little later and I live now with my husband in a flat at the other end of the promenade. Oh! yes, I'm married, and most respectably.

I still like to walk by the sea. I'm still fond of taking my thoughts for solitary airings along the shore. And sometimes on fine hot summer days I find myself looking at the yellow chimney pots that are so like organ pipes and the gulls that sit on them so like fat blue owls.

And sometimes when I look up at them the brilliance of the light tricks me again. I'm temporarily blinded and the sky is empty. All I am aware of is the raw hungry croak of gulls, which in turn remind me of the voice of Ruby, talking to me in the days when my soul did such a lot of singing.

'Yes, that's how you feel all right, duckie. Well once, anyway.'

And then the trick of light is over. From the far parapets of the castle and the high white cliffs of chalk down to the smallest glistening crests of the sheltered waves in the harbour and the blue plump feathers of the screeching gulls sitting on those impossible yellow chimney pots every detail shows up with unmistakable reality.

For the space of a second or two I can smell once again the breath of corruption. Then I give a long cold shudder of relief and it's all as clear as crystal in the summer air.

A Month by the Lake

Over the lake the weather had settled into such tranquil late magnificence that Miss Bentley had decided to stay another month: the entire month of October.

Already in the distances the morning mountains sometimes revealed the thinnest night-caps of pure fresh snow; but below them, by noon, every fissure in the bare perpendicular falls of rock was distinctly carved, clear dark purple in the sun. Even farther below them the masses of pine and chestnut and beech and walnut caught the smouldering light of afternoon like clusters of solid coral, pale amber, bronze or bright rusty from the harsh heat of summer. Still farther below them the vines on their narrow terraces were hung with palest ripe green grapes, misted with olive bloom. Farthest below of all, below the umbrella pines, the erect black plumes of cypresses and the shining flowerless thickets of camellia, tender torches of oleanders still bloomed along the lakeside: pure white, pale yellow, pink and vermilion, flowering in front of houses that melted into the honied impermanence of soft distances until they were nothing but stumps of burned-down candles melting in pearly air.

One by one Miss Bentley had watched the guests of the white *albergo* depart until now, at last, only herself and Major Wilshaw remained. By noon, now, Major Wilshaw too would be gone: a ghost departed with the family of machine-tool manufacturers from Milan, charmers all, the husband a joker in cool sky-blue suits, the wife a splendid cushion of dark fat velvet, the two little girls like sallow angels for whom Major Wilshaw was fond of doing tricks with handkerchiefs, English pennies and bits of string.

With them had gone the two American ladies, school-teachers from Ohio, who had become ill, as Miss Bentley had firmly predicted they would, from living too much on ice-water, green salad and uncooked pears. And with them all the rest whose time or money or interest was not unlimited: the Swiss honeymooners from Schaffhausen, the German chemist and his wife from Frankfurt, the two couples from Yorkshire whom Miss Bentley had christened the gawpy-talkies, the car dealer and his alleged wife, really mistress, from Brussels – mistress, Miss Bentley was sure, because she always passed him the sugar at breakfast, although he clearly never took sugar in his coffee – and finally the sock-knitting English governess with the silent, fallow-timid boy from Turin, a little wooden human carving snatched from the shadows of some impossible Catholic altar.

Now, when Major Wilshaw had gone, there would be no one left but herself; Maria, who cleaned the bedrooms; Enrico, who waited at table; the two cooks and Signora Fascioli, who owned the hotel.

Alone, she would watch the lamps of summer burn quickly out; she would eat another ton of spaghetti – Bolognese or Milanese on alternate days, except Sundays, when it was tagliatelli – peel with meticulous care the last of the pears and purple figs, manicure her nails every Wednesday and Saturday, wash her hair every Friday, swim when she felt like it and take at least one more excursion by funicular to the Monte and look down for the last time on the lake below – its great pattern of inlets and curves, she always thought, so like some great blue glass lioness, sprawled and glittering between the mountains and the plain.

From her favourite place on the patio, a viewpoint from which she could watch the lake-steamers glide like long white water-birds from the gap between the two islands opposite the hotel, Miss Bentley watched Major Wilshaw come down the hotel steps, folding up, with care, the bill he had just paid.

'Ah! there you are. Thought I should find you here.'

The most remarkable feature of Major Wilshaw was not, in Miss Bentley's eyes, the singularly fine straight nose; or the way the greyish hair crinkled bushily into his neck, or the sharp pale blue eyes; or the fact that he had, with his loose brown trousers, bright blue shirt and chrome yellow tie, a rather gay, gamey appearance, an air of wishing to be something rather dashing.

To Miss Bentley the most remarkable feature about Major Wilshaw was his small flat pink ears. They were not only exceptionally small for a man who was thickish, upright and rather tall. They were very delicately, very intricately fashioned. Nothing in the entire human body, Miss Bentley would tell herself, had quite the same fascinating quality as ears. All the attraction of mood and response and character and emotion lay, of course, in the mouth and eyes: everyone knew that. But ears were, Miss Bentley thought, far more wonderful. Ears were unchanging and undying. They remained, in some strange way, uncoarsened, undepraved, unwrinkled and unaged by time. In the ears of the aged you could see the flesh of youth; in a sense they were immortal and never grew old.

Perhaps it was for this reason that Miss Bentley always greeted Major Wilshaw with oblique, off-the-target glances, never looking him straight in the eyes.

'Well: I'm afraid it's good-bye.'

'Oh! come, surely not good-bye,' Miss Bentley said. 'Say *arrivederci*.'

She smiled, putting her book on the little white wooden table at her side. At forty-seven she could give Major Wilshaw a few years, she thought, though perhaps not very many. His hair was already grey; her own was still a rich honey brown, without a touch of age.

'What time does your train go?' she said. 'I forget.'

The train, she knew quite well, went at half past twelve. She saw it regularly every day, creeping up from Milan along the lakeside.

'Half past twelve.'

'Really! I thought it was earlier.'

'No: half past,' the major said. 'Twelve thirty-one to be exact.'

Something, she suddenly thought, seemed to be troubling him. He took from his pocket his newly paid hotel bill and began to to examine it covertly.

'So you're really going,' she said.

'I'm really going.'

'Which way are you going?' she said. 'You did tell me. I forget.'

She had not forgotten. She knew very well that he was going by way of Domodossola, the Simplon, Brig, Montreux, Lausanne and the spaces of France beyond.

'Via Domodossola, the Simplon, Brig, Montreux and that way,' he began to say and then broke off, looking perplexed. 'I don't think my bill's quite right,' he said, 'it doesn't somehow –'

A little fussily the major began to examine the bill, turning his head sideways towards her, so that once again she could see the fine, small ears. Miss Bentley thought there were many ears, even male ones, that were like sea-shells; but the fascination of Major Wilshaw's ears was much more like that of certain flowers. Perhaps that was ridiculous and which particular flower they most resembled was something that, so far, had persisted in eluding her; but she was perfectly sure that, one day, she would discover which one it was.

'No: it isn't right,' he said. 'They've charged me far too much –'

Folding and re-folding the bill, he looked up at her, helpless and troubled.

'May I look?' she said. 'Perhaps –'

'Please,' he said. 'Please. I always say it pays to check these things –'

Miss Bentley took the bill, read through it once and gave it back to him.

'It adds up all right to me,' she said. 'I think you're adding the one as a one instead of as a seven. See? – it has the little stroke across its middle.'

'Of course, of course, how stupid,' the major said.

Below, across the lake, the peep of a steamer whistle broke the tranquil morning air, echoed across the flat honey-blue water and re-echoed in the scarcely visible mountains.

'That's the twelve o'clock steamer,' Miss Bentley said.

'Already?' the major said. 'I'm afraid I must go if it is. I'm afraid it's good-bye.'

'Are you always nervous when you travel?' Miss Bentley said.

'Well, not exactly nervous. But you know –'

'Just in a state of this and that. I know,' she said. 'You feel you're neither here nor there.'

That, he had noticed, was a favourite phrase of hers: a state of this and that. She was rather given to such odd, half-slangy quips that hit off moments, people and moods with dry and sometimes satirical exactitude.

'That's it, that's it,' he said. 'A state of this and that. Wondering if you've got everything. If there's anything you've forgotten.'

'And have you got everything?'

'I think so, I fancy so.' Uncertainly he fumbled at the pocket of his jacket. 'I checked —'

'Ticket?'

'Yes, yes. Ticket.'

'Passport? You told me you once forgot your passport.'

'In my suitcase.'

'Never keep it in your suitcase,' she said. 'You're done if someone snitches it. Suitcase and passport gone in one. Always keep it on you.'

'Of course, of course,' he said. 'I'll do it. I'll see to that.'

'Well then,' she said, 'if you've got everything.'

She got up and the major extended his hand.

'Well, good-bye, Miss Bentley. It's been absolutely —'

'Oh! not here,' she said. 'I'm coming down the steps.'

'How nice of you, how kind,' he said. 'There's absolutely no need —'

Miss Bentley was suddenly aware, as she descended the white steps of the terrace slightly behind him, of two eventful things. The first was the unexpected elucidation of the private mystery that had troubled her ever since the first evening she had seen the major doing tricks for the amusement of the two sallow little angels from Milan.

It was the sudden revelation that the major's left ear was, more than anything, like a small pink rose. The particular rose she had in mind was flattish, inclined to be oval in shape, and mysteriously crinkling to a soft inner heart.

'So it is,' she said and the major, turning to say 'Pardon?' saw on her face a look of extraordinary revelation.

'Did you say something?'

'No,' she said. 'No. Nothing at all.'

A moment later she was aware of the second event. Voices were suddenly laughing gaily in Italian by the front door of the hotel. Signor Fascioli was rushing down the steps, laughing too. And there, by the door of a cream familiar Fiat, were the two sallow little angels from Milan, dancing up and down, yellow

195

dresses flouncing. The splendid dark fat cushion of a wife was there and Signor Bompiani, gay and immaculate in light blue linen, was waving both hands above his head in the direction of Miss Bentley and Major Wilshaw, giving greeting in the manner of a boxer:

'Major! Miss Bentley! We are here! Back again! Time for a nice cup of tea!'

This was his favourite, much-repeated joke about the English.

'Not to *stay*?'

'To stay. Of course. The weather is so beautiful – *bella, bella bella* – To stay, of course!'

'*Molto bella*,' Miss Bentley said. 'Oh! so beautiful. How nice to see you.'

'Shake hands, Major, shake hands.'

'The major is going,' Miss Bentley said. 'You're just in time to say good-bye.'

'The major is going? No? Where? Why? Away? Not –'

'Away,' the major said. 'England.'

'We arrive. You depart. That's very sad. That's not very well arranged, Major –'

The two sallow little angels began dancing about Major Wilshaw, pleading in Italian, pulling his sleeves and hands.

'They wish a trick!'

'Oh! no. I'm sorry. I must get the train –'

'They wish one trick before you go!'

'It's getting awfully late –'

'In the car they speak of nothing but tricks. Tricks from the major. They wish all the time tricks from the major!'

'Just one then. One quickly –'

The major, stooping down, began to do his little trick with English pennies. It consisted, in essentials, of losing the pennies one by one in the hair of – but suddenly, in surprise, Miss Bentley was not watching.

In the excitement she had not noticed, by the door of the car, a girl with smooth fair hair, wearing a plain black skirt, rather full, and a plain white blouse. Nor had the major seen her either; but now, suddenly, the trick completed, he straightened up, turned and caught sight of her standing there.

Miss Bentley had never seen in the eyes of a girl a look of such open unequivocal indifference, so cool in contemplation, and suddenly Signor Bompiani was saying:

'Ah! badly arranged again, forgive me, badly arranged. I am so sorry – this is Miss Beaumont. She is with us for three months to learn Italian and also to teach the kids a little English, I hope. Miss Beaumont, please to allow me to introduce Miss Bentley and Major Wilshaw.'

'How do you do,' Miss Beaumont said.

On the major's face a stunned, excruciating look of pure shyness developed into one of actual embarrassment. Opening his mouth to speak he succeeded only in giving a brief gape of astonishment. At the same time he averted his face, as if unable suddenly to look at the girl.

'The taxi has been waiting ten minutes, Major Wilshaw,' Signora Fascioli said. 'You will miss the train –'

'Oh! must you go, Major?' Signor Bompiani said. 'No more tricks?'

'I must go, I must really get on. I'll say good-bye –'

'Good-bye then, Major. Good-bye,' Signor Bompiani said.

'You will miss the train, Major!'

'Good-bye! Good-bye!' the angels shouted.

'Not good-bye,' Miss Bentley said. '*Arrivederci!*'

'*Arrivederci!*' everyone shouted. '*Arrivederci!*'

'*Arrivederci*,' the major said. 'Good-bye.'

Framed against the exquisite background of the lake, the major lifted his hand and took off his small green homburg hat in farewell. Behind him the mountains, half-dissolved in dreamy amber haze, threw into sharp relief the yellow tie, the glazed blue eyes and above all the small pink ears for which Miss Bentley felt she had found, at last, the perfect, happy comparison.

She, too, raised her hand, waving it in farewell; and then realized, a moment later, that the eyes of the major were not looking back at her. Nor were they looking at Signora Fascioli, the Bompianis, Maria and Enrico, or the little angels who, no longer dancing, were simply crooking slow, sad fingers.

They were not even looking at Miss Beaumont. With melancholy transparence they appeared to be held in a trance by which it seemed almost certain for a second or two that the major had forgotten who and where he was. He stood for a moment longer in this lost enchantment, eyes blank and almost white in the sun, and then suddenly turned and groped into the taxi.

'Come back next year!' Miss Bentley called and down on the lake the short rude peep of the departing steamer mocked the flawless distances in answer.

Three quarters of an hour later, sitting alone at her table under the arbour of virginia creeper at the end of the patio, Miss Bentley was raising a glass of *valpolicella* to her lips in readiness to wash down the last mouthful of *spaghetti bolognese*. The glass never reached her lips and as she set it slowly down on the table, with a surprise far greater than she had seen on the face of Major Wilshaw when he had first become aware of the cool detached Miss Beaumont, her mouth too fell open, as the major's had done, with a gape of astonishment.

The major himself was just driving up to the hotel in an open taxi, holding his green homburg hat on his knees.

Her first impulse, as the taxi drew up, was to call out to him. Then she checked it. A great air of preoccupation shrouded the major, who was staring down at his feet.

She turned quickly to glance at the Bompianis and Miss Beaumont, lunching at their long table at the farther end of the arbour. The two children were drinking red wine in water and Miss Beaumont, with white meticulous fingers, was washing, peeling and eating a bunch of pale green grapes. Miss Beaumont, she realized for the first time, was, in her thin, measured way, a very pretty creature.

When she looked back at the road through the screen of virginia creeper leaves she saw Maria was helping to unload the major's suitcases but that the major had already disappeared. Instinctively she looked up towards the window of the room he occupied on the second floor of the hotel and then realized how stupid it was to expect to see him there so quickly or even to see him there at all. At the same time she found herself suffering from the temporary illusion that the major had, after all, not appeared on the road from the lake so suddenly.

'It was probably,' she thought, 'that I just wanted him to appear.'

Three or four minutes later Enrico, the thin hollow-eyed waiter, came out of the hotel carrying tablecloth, napkins, cutlery, pepper and salt pots and a small white plate. She watched him lay the table that the major always occupied and then, when he had finished, called him over.

'Is there another visitor?'

'The table,' he said, 'is for Major Wilshaw.'

'The major left this morning for Domodossola.'

'The major is back.'

'Did he miss the train?'

'I think so, madam. I don't know.'

'Bring my fruit,' she said, 'will you please?'

For the next three quarters of an hour she sat washing and peeling the grapes and dark blue figs of which she never tired. She washed the fruit slowly and thoughtfully, watching with fascination the pearls of air gather delicately on the grapeskins under the water, her eyes at the same time ready to lift themselves towards the door of the hotel.

After twenty minutes the Bompianis got up from their table. Mrs Bompiani, who did not speak English, smiled in Miss Bentley's direction as she rose. Mr Bompiani, red-flushed beneath the eyes from wine, smiled at Miss Bentley too and said simply, with satisfied brevity: 'Shut-eye.' The two children waved spidery fingers and Miss Beaumont, who had changed her white blouse for a scarlet sleeveless one, seemed to begin to smile and then decided not to.

After the voices of the children had died away the afternoon became quite silent, wrapped in thin hot haze. The lake took on a golden glassy skin, without a stir of air. Once Enrico appeared at the door of the hotel, looked in Miss Bentley's direction, saw that she was still peeling grapes and then went away.

It was nearly an hour before she saw the major, who had changed now into a light shantung suit slightly creased from packing, with a brown silk shirt and pale green tie, walking towards her under the screen of virginia creeper.

'I suppose you're surprised?'

'Not a bit,' she said. 'I felt all along you'd mistaken the time of the train.'

'I didn't miss the train.'

He glanced round as if, she thought, looking for the Bompianis, and then said:

'May I join you? I'm not eating.'

'No lunch?'

'They're bringing me some coffee.'

She sat for some moments contemplating in silence the small pink ears. She thought there seemed something covert, complicated and sad about Major Wilshaw, more especially about the eyes, which were downcast as he played with a spoon, not often looking up at her.

'So you came back.'

'I came back.'

She decided suddenly, for no reason, not to ask why.

'You should have something to eat,' she said. 'You look tired.'

'Do I? I don't feel it,' he said. 'I'll be all right with just the coffee.'

Flawlessly the lake lay shining in the afternoon sun, the oleanders alight along the shore. She found herself not only extraordinarily glad that he was back but even happier not to be alone. Then when Enrico brought the coffee she found herself instinctively passing the sugar, saying:

'Sugar? You take a lot, I know.'

Thoughtfully unwrapping the sugar cubes, Major Wilshaw stared with light blue eyes at the hazed quiet skin of the lake.

'What do you do when you suddenly have damn funny impulses?' he said.

She found herself laughing.

'Oh! I suppose you don't have such things,' he said.

'Why not? I have wild, unconquerable desires too,' Miss Bentley said, 'if it comes to that.'

She was sorry, a moment later, that she had mocked him. That was rather her way sometimes, she thought, to mock, to be a little trite. It was not really herself who spoke on such occasions. It was really – puzzled, she shied away from a complexity too difficult to explain.

'I'm talking about an impulse that stops you,' the major said. 'Not the other kind.'

'Not the urging, to-hell-with-it-kind?'

'No. The sort with a voice,' he said.

This is too ridiculous, she thought. Men simply don't talk like this. Nor women either.

'No, seriously, seriously,' he said.

'You're going to tell me you were walking across the station, ready to get on the train, when a voice said, "Don't go. Don't do it. Go back to the *Albergo Bianco* and stay a few more days".'

'Something like that.'

'That was simply commonsense speaking. You needn't have gone in the first place. You know that. In this marvellous, wonderful weather.'

'I know it sounds silly –'

'Not a bit. Not silly at all. Commonsense. The sanest, most sensible thing to do. Who'd leave all this if they didn't have to? Look at it!' With rapturous hands she pointed down to the lake laced in its tender honey-skin of autumn light. 'Not me, that's certain. I'm not sure I shan't stay all winter.'

He started to speak, then stopped and poured himself more coffee. She pushed the sugar-bowl across to him a second time and then watched him unwrap two of the papered cubes and drop them in the cup.

'You're walking along a street to go somewhere. You know perfectly well where you're going – what time and so on and all that. And suddenly you don't go. You're turned back by something and the whole day, perhaps a great bit of life, is different. You've done that surely?'

Of course she had done that, she told him. Everybody had done that.

'Do you feel life has a pattern?' he said 'A predetermined one, I mean?'

'Oh! Heaven help us,' she said. 'Don't go into that. If I'd felt my life had had a predetermined pattern I'd probably have cut my throat at the age of six.'

She laughed again, but she noticed that he did not laugh in reply.

'How long are you going to stay?' she said, 'now you're back?'

He simply shrugged his shoulders slightly, an almost imperceptible muscular quiver, and again lifted his coffee cup.

'Stay a whole month,' she said. 'Stay until another impulse strikes you.'

He gave the faintest of smiles and then started biting his lip.

'Well, here we all are again,' she said, 'anyway. You, the Bompianis, those two little angels and me. I think it's absolutely wonderful.'

'Yes.'

'Do you remember that picnic we had in the mountains?' she said. 'Do you suppose we could manage another picnic like that? I'd cheerfully arrange it if the Bompianis would offer the car like they did last time. I'm sure they would, except that this time, of course, there's Miss Beaumont –'

'Oh?' He spoke very abruptly, almost sharply. 'Is that her name?'

'I think that's what they said –'

'I didn't catch it, I didn't catch it,' he said.

'I shall always remember that picnic. That cold spring water the children washed their feet in and the wild raspberries and the little wild cyclamen they were selling along the roadside, at the village down the valley. I'd never seen wild cyclamen before. I didn't even know there were wild cyclamen –'

She broke off and saw, from the far-away look on his face, that the major was not listening. Nor was he looking at her. And then she remembered, suddenly, when she had seen that same look of lost enchantment on his face before.

And getting up from the table, pushing away her glass and picking up her book, she remembered Miss Beaumont. It was Miss Beaumont who had inspired it all.

About four o'clock Major Wilshaw walked down to the town, called at the post office and sent a telegram to the Wilshaw Light Metal Construction Co. Ltd, of which he was managing director, saying 'Delayed for further week possibly more address me as previously case urgency.' Then he bought himself a day-old English newspaper from the kiosk at the steamer landing stage, glanced at the headlines and walked back to the hotel.

He had already changed his clothes a second time. Now he was wearing a soft blue suit in mohair with a deep cream shirt and a pale blue silk tie. His shoes were of light brown turned calf and he was without a hat. His grey hair was well and scrupulously brushed, giving him a certain military appearance, though in fact he was not a military man. During the war he had joined up in his age-group as his turn came and had risen to the rank of major in the Royal Engineers purely because he was an engineer by profession and because establishment happened to call for another major at a certain time. He never stopped to ask why, after the war, he continued to use his rank. A great many majors and quite a few captains did and he never stopped to ask why they did so either. During a war so many people got into the habit of using ranks and after the war it was natural and easy to go on with it as before.

At fifty-one he was unmarried, successful, prodigiously competent, and, as he liked to think, very young in mind. His impression of Miss Bentley was that she was, in spite of her ungreyed brown hair, her liveliness of speech and generally pleasant air, well settled in middle age. He thought that he could give her quite a few years. One of the things that success in business enabled him to do was to expend a good deal of time, care and money on his choice of clothes. He thought a man ought not only to dress well but, rather like an animal adopting protective colouring, to dress according to his immediate surroundings. That was why he wore simple plain blue suits at the office, sober clerical greys when he did business in London and now, on the lake, a variety of light, sunny blues, yellows, browns and greens that matched the burning autumn mountains, the honey expanses of water, the oleanders, the Italianate villas and skies. That, he thought, was the kind of thing that kept him young.

During the three weeks he had been on the lake he had become quite friendly, in an unadventurous detached sort of way, with Miss Bentley. She was what he called a decent old stick. She was not at all bad-looking, he thought, and she dressed herself rather as his secretary in the office did, neatly and freshly, with what he called a slightly starched-and-ironed effect. She used just enough make-up to keep herself from dullness. Her hands and hair were always scrupulous. He was unaware that she found the shape of his ears both baffling and attractive or that she had searched for a long time for a fitting description of their delicacy. She had a certain mustardy sense of humour, a little dry and hot on the tongue as it were, and when she trotted out phrases like 'Oh! I have wild and unconquerable desires if it comes to that' he knew she was merely being funny and that she didn't mean it at all. Or perhaps, he thought, it was a sort of protection against something, though what it was he didn't know.

What Miss Bentley called his rather gay and gamey air rose largely from his choice of clothes; but it sprang also from a conviction that he was attractive to girls. He rather fancied himself in that way. At home, in the town where the Wilshaw Light Metal Construction Company occupied several pleasant acres of ground, he ran about in an open cream sports car, played tennis, belonged to a country club and knew of one or two hotels in the country where the food was good. From time to time he struck up acquaintances with girls who also ran about with him in the sports car, played tennis, belonged to the country club, went to eat with him in country hotels and then, for some reason he could never define, suddenly left him to marry men who toiled in printing works, ran unsuccessful market gardens or were just plain ten-pound-a-week clerks in offices. He could never understand these things; it puzzled him always to wonder why.

At fifty-one his figure was still good, if a little solid, the stomach muscles still hard and taut, and one of the things he did rather well was to play tennis. On holidays he always took a couple of rackets with him, together with a supply of good correct clothes. But people generally, he thought, didn't play tennis quite so much as before and he found it always rather hard to get a partner.

Once he asked Miss Bentley if she played and all he had got was one of her mustardy answers:

'Oh! Love and all that. No. I'm afraid it never attracted me. Oh! except one thing – that business of love meaning nothing. Why does it? Of course one knows it does anyway, but did some cynic start the game?'

As he walked back along the road to the hotel he remembered his tennis. He remembered too his explanation of why he had suddenly changed his mind about the train to Domodossola. It wasn't a specially good explanation. It was true, in a sense, that he had been brought to a sudden standstill by a voice. But the voice was neither that of a mystic warning him to go back nor of a guardian angel seeking to change the course of his destiny. He hadn't on the whole been very explicit about it, but it was the best he could do. The voice was really the voice of Miss Beaumont – not so much her speaking voice, in reality, as the voice communicating itself to him through the cool calm blue eyes – suddenly binding him in a compelling, instantaneous attraction.

When he reached the hotel he saw with considerable pleasure that Miss Beaumont was sitting on the terrace with the Bompiani children. The girl, who had been drinking coffee, looked splendidly fair, cool and bored as she stared at the lake below. The two little girls, who had been drinking orange juice, now greeted him with lips stained with bright yellow moustaches, shouting:

'Tricks! Tricks! Tricks! *Prego, prego*! Tricks!'

'Good afternoon.' He smiled with charm and friendliness at Miss Beaumont, who herself stared in answer. 'May I sit down?'

'Tricks! Tricks!'

'I suppose you wonder why I'm back. Absolutely impossible to resist the lake in this weather, that's all – I just couldn't resist it.' Miss Beaumont neither smiled nor made a comment. 'Don't you think it's beautiful?'

'I like Garda better.'

He started to do his tricks. He was, he thought, rather good with the tricks. Children always liked them. He had first taken up tricks and conjuring generally as a boy, and by now he had forgotten the best of them. But at home he still had the first box he had bought with his pocket money, still neatly packed away in his bedroom, after forty years. Among the tricks was a very good one by which you turned water into wine. There was also another in which you invited several people to write whatever they liked on a paper, seal it in an envelope and hand it to you. Then, one by one, you held the envelopes up to the light, concentrated for a few moments and then, before opening the envelope, told the

audience exactly what they had written. It was always a tremendous, baffling success but of course you needed a collaborator.

On the table were a few wrapped cubes of sugar left over from
Miss Beaumont's coffee. He palmed them, made a few mysterious
dabs at the air and then produced them from the ears of the
Bompiani little girls.

Shrieking with laughter, they broke into brief wild English:

'More! Again! More, more!'

'Ah! and now where? Now?'

Opening his hands, he revealed them both quite empty.

'Gone, you see, gone. Gone! – where?'

Baffled, as they always were, the little Bompiani children
searched his inner sleeves. Deftly, in triumph, he produced the
sugar from the side of Miss Beaumont's hair.

It was clear, in a moment, that Miss Beaumont did not think
the trick either very successful or very amusing, but the little
Bompiani angels danced with delight, half-hysterically.

'Freda! Freda! Freda!' they said.

'Ah! yes, that time it was Freda,' he said. 'Sugar in Freda's hair.
But not now – not this time. This time in – !'

'Rosali! Rosali!'

To shrieking laughter he opened his hands and again they were
empty.

'I'm afraid I've done this trick so many times it's getting stale,'
he said.

'Yes,' Miss Beaumont said. 'I suppose it must be.'

'I'll have to think up new ones. I know several. It just needs
thinking.'

'Yes.'

'Do you play tennis?' he suddenly said.

'Occasionally.'

'Oh! really! oh! fine. They have very good courts at the
Splendide that you can hire. I wonder –'

'I haven't a racket.'

'I always bring two,' the major said. 'It would be awfully nice
if you'd care to – perhaps tomorrow?'

'Tomorrow we go to Orta.'

'Well, there's plenty of time. How long are you here?'

She shrugged her shoulders.

'Three weeks. A month. I wouldn't know.'

'Then there's bags of time,' the major said. 'By the way the swimming is pretty good in the lake. The water's still warm. Do you – '

'Tricks! Tricks!' the children shrieked. 'Tricks!'

The insistent voices pierced the afternoon air wildly, maddening as discharging pop-guns.

'Tricks! Sugar in Freda's hair! Tricks!'

'Oh! my God, these kids,' the girl said. 'Three weeks of this will drive me batty.'

'Let's have a drink this evening somewhere,' the major said. 'We could nip down into the town – '

Before Miss Beaumont could answer, and as if by a process of telepathy, Miss Bentley appeared at the door of the hotel, calling the major by name, waving a handful of letters.

'Anything to post, Major Wilshaw?'

'No, I don't think so. Many thanks.'

'I'm walking to the town before dinner – I just wondered – nothing you want?'

He called no, nothing, thanking her all the same, and Miss Bentley called back:

'Are the children restless? Would they care to come?'

'May they really?' Miss Beaumont said. 'Isn't it an awful trouble?'

'Absolutely not.'

Miss Bentley, calling the little angels, held out both hands. Major Wilshaw called back something about his tricks being exhausted and how he would have to think up new ones and then remembered something else and said:

'Oh! there is just one thing you could do for me, Miss Bentley. That's if it's no trouble. If you haven't too much to do yourself – '

'I'm picking up a couple of dresses, that's all,' Miss Bentley said. 'I must have something new if I'm to stay here another month.'

'Excuse me a moment,' the major said to Miss Beaumont. 'Don't run away.'

Walking across to Miss Bentley he stopped half-way, took from his pocket a fountain pen and notebook and wrote something down, afterwards tearing out the page.

'Just a telegram if you wouldn't mind. I think it'll be five hundred lire. Something like that –'

'Oh! not to worry now,' Miss Bentley said. 'I'll tell you at dinner –'

'Awfully kind of you, Miss Bentley. More than kind.'

'Not a bit,' she said. 'Come along, angels. No, no, no! Take care! Don't run into the road!'

Back at the table, sitting facing Miss Beaumont, looking into the cool prepossessing eyes, wonderfully blue and bored, the major felt run through him the first of a series of exciting, scurrying emotions and tried suddenly to disguise them by an appearance of casualness:

'She's an awfully decent old stick, really. Terribly kind. Quite witty too. Sits hours staring at the lake, dreaming. Quite happy, I suppose, wondering what she might have had –'

'And what might she have had?'

The major, unable to put into words what Miss Bentley might have had, suddenly felt obliged to change the subject and looked up at the hills.

'You can walk quite a way through the vineyards,' he said. 'There's an old back road goes up behind the hotel and you come out above the terraces. It's a magnificent view. Would you care to walk up?'

'Oh! it's awfully hot –'

'Still two hours before dinner,' the major said. 'There's a little *trattoria* up the top where we could get a glass of wine.'

'I don't like wine,' the girl said. 'By golly, the time drags here. I thought it was later.'

By the time the major and Miss Beaumont had reached the upper terraces of vines, from which the view over the descending trellises of misty olive fruit was, as the major had said, so magnificent, Miss Bentley had reached the post office down in the town.

There, for the first time, she looked at the major's telegram.

'Please post soonest box conjuring tricks bottom left hand corner wardrobe dressing-room,' it read, 'regards Wilshaw.'

As the days went past Miss Bentley continued to sit on the terrace, watching the sky, the mountains, the lake and the steamers crossing the lake; watching too the oleanders still opening fresh sprays of white, pink, vermilion and yellow flower.

After a week or so the gathering of grapes began on the terraces above the hotel and all day she could hear the voices of workers calling, chattering and laughing across the vineyards. In mornings of exquisite light she watched the mountains emerge from shrouds of mist, mostly a pure ochreous bloom, occasionally pale rose and more rarely still a tender egg-shell green below which the distant houses looked more than ever like squat white candles gently melting; sometimes making in the mellow air the only visible division between land and water, just as the thin snow caps made the only perceptible division between land and sky.

She also watched Major Wilshaw. For the first few mornings he appeared on the terrace with his customary fresh briskness, immaculate. She saw him look with eagerness from table to table, searching for Miss Beaumont, who was never there. At the fourth morning he inquired for her.

'Miss Beaumont not down?'

'She never eats breakfast.'

'No?' He appeared startled, even shocked. 'Not eat breakfast? How –'

'She told me so.'

After that Major Wilshaw did not appear for breakfast either.

He would appear instead about eleven o'clock, carrying a towel, ready for his swim.

'Miss Beaumont not about?'

'Haven't seen her.'

'She was coming for a swim at eleven o'clock.' He glanced hurriedly at his watch, fretting. 'It's a quarter past already.'

'She hates getting up,' Miss Bentley said. 'There are people who do, you know.'

The major fretted until a quarter to twelve and then said:

'Damn. I hate missing my swim. I hate swimming by myself too.'

Miss Bentley did not answer but found herself looking obliquely, instead, at the small fresh pink ears. This glance seemed to startle the major into new thoughts and he said:

'I suppose you wouldn't care to come? No, I don't suppose – '

She smiled in her quizzical, rather ironic way.

'Are you asking me?'

'Oh yes – I'm sorry, Miss Bentley. Of course I am, of course.'

'Thank you. If you'll wait for me I'll get my costume.'

Ten minutes later they were walking down the steps of the terrace when Miss Beaumont appeared at the foot of them.

'Where on earth have you been?'

'Waiting,' the major said. 'Here on the terrace. Waiting. Have you only just – ?'

'I was here all the time,' Miss Beaumont said. She spoke frigidly. 'In the garden. In the garden was where you said.'

Humbled and confused, the major made groping attempts at apology, almost stuttering. Miss Beaumont, cooler than ever, more aloof and more distant, gazed into air. Miss Bentley said nothing but:

'Well, if we're going, shall we go?'

The figure of Miss Beaumont was virginal, slender and wiry, with small, sharp, up-pointed breasts. As she walked she held her shoulders well back, self-consciously, swinging her hands elaborately. The major, as the three of them walked down the hillside towards the lake, seemed stunned and mesmerized by this, keeping his eyes fixed on her in a stupor of admiration, not once glancing at Miss Bentley.

In the hot brilliant noon unexpected numbers of people were swimming in the lake or lying on concrete, below lines of bathing huts, sunning themselves.

As he saw them the major hurried forward, murmuring something about grabbing a cubicle before it was too late, and then came back, three or four minutes later, dismayed.

'Rather as I suspected,' he said. 'Only two huts left. Do you mind? – you will have to share I'm afraid. I'm awfully sorry – '

'Oh! that's all right,' Miss Beaumont said and stared away, glassily.

Only five minutes later the major saw a white-costumed Miss Bentley emerge first from the cubicle, smiling strangely. Sitting on warm concrete, he was dangling his legs above the lake and turned in time to see the smile break into open laughter.

'What are you laughing at?'

'Oh, nothing.'

'It seems to tickle you tremendously all the same.'

Once again Miss Bentley's strange smile broke into open laughter.

'Not going to share the joke?'

'Oh, it was nothing,' Miss Bentley said. 'It was just that I don't think Miss Beaumont liked sharing the cubicle, that's all. She's rather shy.'

Before the major could make up his mind what to say about this Miss Bentley was lying full length on the concrete. With sensations of surprise and disbelief he found himself staring at her figure, relaxed and brown in its white two-piece suit in the sun. It was a remarkably taut, clean, smooth figure for a woman to whom, as he thought, he could give a few years. The legs were firm, hairless and shapely. The flesh on the rather long sloping shoulders was wonderfully clean and golden and the bust held itself upright, like that of a girl, self-supported.

Miss Bentley, who had closed her eyes for a moment or two against the brilliance of the sun, now opened them suddenly and found the major staring at her body. With warm, unsurprised, unequivocal eyes she looked straight back at him and said:

'By the way, I meant to have asked you. Have your tricks come?'

'No. I can't understand it. It's been nearly two weeks now. It's rather tiresome. The children keep pestering and I promise them every day.'

'Could they be held by the Customs?'

'Good gracious.' The thought had on Major Wilshaw the effect of revelation. 'I never thought of that.'

'I think you'll probably find that that's what happened,' Miss Bentley said.

He was about to say something about what a genius she had for putting her finger on the solution to a problem when he turned and saw that Miss Beaumont had left the cubicle and was walking across to where he and Miss Bentley sat by the lakeside.

Seeing her, he was unaccountably depressed by an effect of flatness about the dark red costume. The legs were extraordinarily thin, like a boy's, and too hollow at the thighs. He experienced the impression that Miss Beaumont, who looked so arrestingly pretty in cool silk frocks, now looked meagre, a mere slice of a girl, skimpy. He was so uneasy that he could not think what had happened to her.

He stood up. At the same moment Miss Bentley stood up too, erect and full, her brown hair remarkably thick and bright against the golden sloping shoulders. Miss Beaumont was tying a red bathing hat on her head and this, as it enclosed her hair, made her look more than ever like a boy. Immature and white, her shoulders were awkwardly twisted, showing salt-cellars.

'Ah! there you are at last,' the major said. 'Ready?'

'There's no great hurry, is there?' she said.

With studied rapture Miss Bentley turned and stared into the tranquil heart of the lake, disturbed here and there only by the faintest silver ruffles, little islands of coat-of-mail that drifted, sparkled, took to air and floated away.

'Heavens, this lake looks as deep as the end of time this morning,' she said. 'Don't you think so? I've noticed it before on these hot, still days.'

She turned to Miss Beaumont, whose toe-nails were painted red, giving her a still more unreal, doll-like appearance.

'I'll give you one guess how deep it is,' Miss Bentley said.

Miss Beaumont too gazed at the lake, silent, evidently not wanting to guess at its depth and giving once more, as a consequence, an impression of compressed virginal aloofness.

'Fourteen hundred feet they tell me,' Miss Bentley said.

A moment later she dived. As she did so Major Wilshaw realized that he had never seen her swim before. He had no idea whether she swam well or badly.

A second later he realized that she had totally disappeared. The great depth of the lake had swallowed her. In a stupefying moment of astonishment, followed by shock, he was pained by an unpleasant sensation. He was unaware of giving a gasp of alarm or of walking several paces towards the edge of the water and, at last, of letting out a half-choked breath, part in relief, part

in sheer admiration, as Miss Bentley surfaced thirty yards away,
turned belly-wise like a clean white fish and floated in the sun.

As his alarm drained away he turned to see Miss Beaumont
sitting down.

'What was all the fuss about?'

'Fuss? Oh, nothing. I just wondered when – Aren't you
coming in?'

'Not yet,' the girl said. 'I'm rather chilly. I'll lie in the sun.'

He turned from the flat figure to face a sun that, even at the
angle of October, sliced at his eyes with clear hot brightness. A
moment later he dived and swam slowly and unhurriedly out to
where Miss Bentley floated, face upwards, perfectly still.

To his fresh surprise she again had on her face the strange
smile that had mystified him a few minutes before.

'No idea you swam so well.'

She did not answer. Instead, for the second or third time, the
smile broke into actual laughter.

'Oh! look, aren't you going to share this joke with me?'

'Some jokes make you laugh more when you don't share them,'
Miss Bentley said. 'They sort of evaporate when you start telling.'

'I've got an idea it's about me,' he said.

'Oh! good lord no.'

'About Miss Beaumont then?'

Again she did not answer and he knew now that the joke,
whatever it was, was about Miss Beaumont.

He paddled water. Small brilliant pearls of water lay in the
hollow above Miss Bentley's breasts. She kept her hands flicking,
fin-like, at full length and the smile on her face did not fade.

'Might just as well tell me.'

'I don't think it would be fair on Miss Beaumont.'

It suddenly amused her to tease the major and with lazy
strokes she started swimming on her back, towards a diving raft
that lay fifteen yards away. He followed at a slow crawl, keeping
some distance behind.

On the raft two muscular, good-looking Italians, about twenty
or so, sleek, with black hair, walnut bodies and brief blue swimming trunks, watched her come in, heave herself to the raft and
sit dripping in the sun. She lifted herself aboard the raft in one

easy swinging movement and the Italians smiled across at each other as the major followed, heaving himself up with difficulty, in several puffing movements, his own weight too much for him, so that in the end Miss Bentley stretched out and gave him a hand.

'Funny how I've never seen you down at the Lido before,' the major said. 'How did you get so brown?'

'You always come in the mornings,' Miss Bentley said. 'I always come in the afternoons, when you're napping. I have lunch earlier than you.'

She turned and lay on her back, wet hair spread outwards, and the two Italians stared at her full, prostrate body as it glittered in the sun.

The major lay down too and after five minutes or so turned his head, saw that her eyes were closed and said:

'Going to swim any more?'

'I think so, yes. And you?'

'I don't think so. I think I'll lie in the sun.'

A moment or two later she dived, came up only a few yards away and started to swim with an easy crawl along the path of the sun. Almost immediately she had dived the taller, older of the two young Italians dived too and swam with long strokes after her.

Miss Bentley, turning some moments later to float on her back, found him smiling brilliantly alongside her.

'Hullo.'

'Hullo,' she said.

'Hot today.' His smile was very white. A crucifix glittered gold on the wet black hairs of his chest. 'Are you thirsty?'

'Not very. Why?'

'I thought if you thirsty you have drink with me?'

Miss Bentley smiled, lapping water with outstretched fingers.

'That sounds nice. Did the other one dare you?'

'Did what? *Prego?*'

'Oh! it doesn't matter. Where do you drink anyway?'

He pointed shorewards with a very brown, very well-manicured hand.

'At the little *caffè* at the end of the Lido. Just there. You take coffee, vermouth, what you like. Oh! him?' he said, pointing back to the raft. 'He's my brother.'

Miss Bentley, not answering at once, turned to see where the major was. She discovered him to be sitting upright on the raft, watching her. The sight of him sitting there gave her so much satisfaction that she smiled again and then turned, still smiling, to the Italian boy.

'I don't think my friend would like it.'

'No? You have to ask him?'

'No, but –'

She gave him the kind of glance that Major Wilshaw often found quizzical, sometimes ironical, but not really coquettish, and the boy seemed to find it so attractive that he swam closer.

'Then will you come?'

'I don't think so. I think my friend would be very jealous. I think he wouldn't like it.'

'Jealous?' the boy said. 'It's very good to be jealous. That's good.'

She felt his hand brush itself quickly across her back.

'He's watching. Another thing – You're much too close to me.'

'Of course,' he said. 'If I didn't want to be close to you I would be sitting on the raft. Like your friend.'

Slowly and boldly his eyes travelled the full length, from hair to toes, of her floating body.

'Will you come now?' he said. 'They have very good *orvieto* at the *caffè*. After the swim it very good –'

'Supposing I preferred coffee?'

'Very well, then. Good. Coffee! –'

He smiled handsomely, brilliantly again, with vanity, pleased with himself. 'I suppose he does it every day,' she told herself and smiled too.

As they swam shorewards together he kept very close to her and once or twice he touched her arm, but she did not protest or move away. Nor did she once look back to where a stunned Major Wilshaw, squatting on the raft with his arms huddled across his knees, was staring at her across the tranquil surface of the lake, solemnly, with disbelieving eyes.

It was after five o'clock when she was sitting on the patio, drinking tea with slices of lemon in it, and Major Wilshaw appeared. It was the first time she had seen him since midday and now he was carrying a parcel in his hands.

'You were quite right about the tricks,' he said. 'There was a mess-up about a customs form. Cost me another five hundred lire but anyway I've got them now.'

'The children will be thrilled.'

The major continued to stand by her table, a little coolly, as if purposely intending not to sit down.

'Won't you have some tea?' Miss Bentley said. 'We could easily ask for another cup.'

'I had a cup in the town.'

He shifted uneasily from one foot to another, at the same time changing the parcel from hand to hand.

'You disappeared rather quickly all of a sudden this morning,' he said.

'Oh! did I?'

'I thought it was rather swift.'

She played with a slice of lemon in her cup, submerging it and poking at it thoughtfully with a spoon.

'I didn't want to play gooseberry,' she said, 'that's all.'

'I don't know about gooseberry.'

She did not answer; she drank tea instead and the major went on:

'After all, the three of us went down together and I naturally thought – You didn't come back to lunch, either, did you?'

'No,' she said. 'I had lunch at the *caffè*.'

'Oh?' he said. 'With the two Italian boys?'

'With one of them.'

She looked up as she said this and she thought the face of the major flushed.

'He's rather nice,' she said. 'And I think rather well off too. His father makes motor tyres.'

The major, lifting his head suddenly, made a quick short noise of expiration, somewhere between a snort and a sigh.

'What was all that in aid of?' Miss Bentley said.

'Nothing. Only I didn't think you were a pick-up.'

'Of course it was a pick-up.' She said this with deliberate emphasis and it amused her to see his face as she teased him.

'Well!' he said. 'Well!'

'What's wrong with a pick-up?' she said. 'After all, thousands of women all over the world are simply longing for a pick-up. It's all they dream about. Every night. Every day.'

'Yes, but really I must say it's rather surprising in *you*, isn't it?' the major said. 'And with – with this boy.'

'Why with me? And why not with a boy? After all,' she said, 'you have your Miss Beaumont.'

'That's rather different.'

'Is it?' she said. 'I don't see how. Miss Beaumont and the Italian boy are about the same age as each other. So are you and I.'

'Yes, but I mean. With an older woman and a young – '

He broke off suddenly, unable to complete the sentence in which he was clearly going to say that he thought that when women of her age chose to consort with young men of twenty it was something rather cheap, unladylike and distasteful. After this he stood stiffly, almost to attention, with an air of offence, not speaking.

'I'm sorry if I made you angry.'

'Oh! you didn't make me angry.' She looked up to see a flush of anger on his face and felt extraordinarily pleased that it was there. 'Not a bit.'

Pleasantly, coolly and without haste, aware of the major's discomfort, she poured herself another cup of tea, put sugar and lemon into it and stirred it delicately with her spoon.

'What about the tricks?' she said. 'Will you do them tonight?'

'That's really what I wanted to see you about,' the major said. He relaxed a little. He even allowed himself the beginnings of a short stiff smile. 'You see it's slightly awkward – '

'In what way?

'Well, in at least one of the tricks, probably two, I need a collaborator and I rather thought – '

'Wouldn't Miss Beaumont do?'

'Oh! no, no, no, no. I don't think so. You see – '

'When is all this going to be?' Miss Bentley said and again

she turned on him her slightly quizzical, slightly ironical smile. 'This trickery and collaboration?'

'I thought if we rehearsed a bit we could do it by tomorrow night.'

She drank the remainder of her tea. And then, wiping her lips and the tips of her fingers with a paper serviette, which she afterwards crumpled up in her hands, she came to a sudden decision which astounded herself.

'I'm afraid I can't tomorrow,' she said. 'I'm driving into Pallanza to have dinner with this young man.'

She looked up suddenly to see the effect of her words on the major and found his face unexpectedly blank and the colour of greyish cardboard.

'I see,' he said and then turned suddenly and walked away across the terrace and into the hotel, leaving her staring at the lake, across the pink-blue surface of which a steamer was cutting, like a white knife, a path against the sun.

Suddenly, as he disappeared, she was aware of feeling uneasy, no longer so confident in herself. The tea and the lemon abruptly started to repeat themselves and she knew that if she were not very careful they would bring on an uncomfortable attack of heartburn.

The following evening, shortly before seven o'clock, she started to walk into the town. As she went down the steps of the hotel Major Wilshaw appeared suddenly from the garden, almost as if he had been waiting in hiding, hoping to catch her.

'I thought you were driving to Pallanza.'

'So I am. But something happened to the boy's car and he said would I walk to meet him.'

The major stood awkwardly, first on one foot, then the other. She thought he combined an appearance of great smartness with considerable uneasiness as he fingered the lapel of his suit of navy blue mohair. A little cream handkerchief showed triangular-wise from the breast pocket. He fingered that too and said:

'Actually Miss Beaumont and I are dining out too. It's nice to have a change sometimes.'

'Oh! Where?'

'At the Splendide. We can dance there.'

She moved to go away.

'Oh! about the tricks,' he said.

'Yes?'

'I've got it all fixed for tomorrow. I want to do it properly. Signora Fascioli says I can use the writing-room. Of course I shall invite her.'

'Naturally.'

He suddenly made such a mess of fingering the handkerchief that he pulled it out in entirety, together with a small silver pencil, which fell on the steps.

'That wasn't very clever,' he said, without laughing. 'I'll have to do better than that.'

She began to feel highly uneasy herself as he stooped to pick up the pencil.

'Well, I'll have to fly now,' she said. 'I'll be late otherwise.'

Fumbling hopelessly with pencil and handkerchief he said:

'What I wanted to say was would you? – you know, just help a bit? – tomorrow?'

'If you think I'd be any good.'

'Of course, of course. Thank you. Well, I mustn't keep you – '

She hurried away, not looking back. She kept up a quick pace for a hundred yards or so and then fell into a slow, dawdling walk. Across the lake, where the sun had already set, an orange-green glow, touched with purple, lay softly on the more distant water. The mountains above it were also purple, except at the tips. There they were pink-amber in the afterglow, and along the shore and in the valleys the lights of towns were coming on.

In the town she bought an English newspaper. Then she went into a small side-street restaurant and ordered an omelette and made it last as long as she could. In the paper she read, as she sipped at a glass of *valpolicella*, that the weather in London was unusually cold for mid-October. Snow had already fallen in the Cairngorm mountains of Scotland. An actress she had once seen in a play had died from an overdose of sleeping tablets. Some shares she held in rubber had fallen six points or so.

After the omelette she ordered cheese and fruit. Then, because there were many grapes on the dish, both green and black ones, she made the cheese and fruit last almost twice as long as the omelette had done. By that time she had read most of the things in the paper.

Afterwards she ordered coffee and sat for some time trying to work out how long it would take anyone to drive to Pallanza, have dinner at leisure and drive back again She supposed that she ought to add to this another half an hour, or even more, for saying good-night to a young, handsome and easy-spoken Italian with plenty of energy, money and time to spare and she decided it would be at least eleven o'clock before she dare be seen walking up the steps of the hotel, where on hot nights guests often sat until midnight, talking.

By this time it was only nine o'clock and she ordered a brandy with fresh coffee and started to do the crossword in the newspaper. The words of the crossword did not come to her very easily. She found herself thinking of Major Wilshaw and Miss Beaumont and what dinner might be like at the Splendide and if the band was good for dancing. She smiled once into space as she remembered the incident in the bathing cubicle when she and Miss Beaumont were undressing together but the waiter misinterpreted the smile as a gesture that she wanted him and came over, bowing, and said:

'Yes, signora? Is something you wanted?'

'Just the bill,' she said and wondered miserably what had made her say so.

As she walked slowly back along the promenade by the lakeside the night was extraordinarily warm and still and she could sometimes catch the faint vanilla-like scent of oleanders blooming under the street-lights, about the path.

Then a hundred yards away from the entrance to the Splendide she saw the unmistakable figure of Major Wilshaw, with Miss Beaumont, leave the hotel, cross the street and come straight towards her.

In panic she turned completely round, walked back several yards and hid behind a clump of oleanders, from which she pretended to be gazing, with her face in her hands, at the lights of Pallanza, several miles away. As the major and Miss Beaumont passed her she heard the major say, without drawing any answer from Miss Beaumont:

'I should like to have had little invitation cards printed. Fun for the children, I thought. But then of course, there isn't time and I'll have to write them.'

As they passed out of hearing Miss Bentley suddenly hated herself for the stupid evening she had spent and then hated Miss Beaumont even more for not responding with a single word to the major's charming thought.

The major walked on with Miss Beaumont until they came to a *caffè* where, between small candle-lit tables, a two-piece orchestra consisting of piano and piano accordion were playing. Dinner at the Splendide had been taken in a large, echoing, chandeliered room in which the seven waiters had outnumbered the guests by two and there had been, because of the lateness of the season, no dancing.

One of the things the major had discovered he disliked most in life was dancing on a floor, between very small tables, measuring perhaps six feet by four, and he began to think with envy of Miss Bentley, dining quietly at Pallanza, perhaps under one of those charming arbours of vines so common to Italy, or under a canopy of trained chestnut branches.

'Oh! this is fun,' Miss Beaumont said. 'I feel like sticking a candle in your hair.'

'Oh, please don't.'

'Oh, come on,' she said. 'Take your back hair down. Have fun. Somebody told me this is the place where they dance on the tables.'

The two-piece band poured music down his throat from a distance of two yards like a blast from a furnace door. The hard thin body of Miss Beaumont flung him from side to side. Her breasts pressed against him with the hardness of two shapely little Easter eggs and now and then she chanted into his ear, in an abrasive voice, the brittle, chirpy words of songs she knew.

'And relax, relax,' she said. 'Let your feet go. Your bones are set. Let your feet go.'

Some time later they were served with a luke-warm soup that looked like porridge and that the major discovered, with violent distaste, was made entirely of garlic, finely shredded. With difficulty and wretchedness he ate several spoonfuls, washing it down with sharp red wine, and wondered miserably how long his breath would smell.

'Glorious fun,' Miss Beaumont said. 'Come on, you old candlestick, dance with me.'

Later, towards eleven o'clock, a young Italian girl danced on a table, to be joined presently by one of the waiters. Miss Beaumont climbed on a table and started dancing too, kicking her thin legs, shouting to the major to join her. The table was not large enough for two and he succeeded in getting up on another, but some moments later the table suddenly collapsed and the major fell heavily, bruising his shin against a chair. When he tried to dance again the garlic, quarrelling already with the wine, started repeating violently, making him belch, and he felt strong waves of hot nausea begin to rise.

When Miss Beaumont came down from the table and danced with him on the floor again she said:

'What on earth are you hobbling for?'

'I barked my shin. It's rather painful.'

'Oh! rub it with brandy!' she said. 'You won't die.'

After that they drank more red wine, followed by a sweet liqueur tasting strangely of perfumed oranges It too quarrelled with the garlic and soon a painful area of burning, deep and formidable, settled about the major's chest.

As he drove Miss Beaumont home in a taxi, soon after one o'clock, he could not decide if she were tipsy, happy or merely excited, but suddenly he decided to interpret her mood as one in which, at all costs, she longed for him to kiss her.

To his surprise, as his hands touched her body, she pushed him away.

'If you're going to kiss me, kiss me,' she said. 'Don't creep all over me.'

The major, who had no intention of creeping all over her and who also flattered himself that he was capable of reasonable be-haviour, did not know what to say. The attempt to kiss her, when he made it at last, was not successful, partly because, perhaps for the twentieth or thirtieth time, the garlic again began to rise.

Up in his room the major discovered, after an hour, that he could not sleep at all. The garlic, the sharp red wine, the strange orange liqueur and a repetitive taste of a portion of scampi he had eaten at dinner quarrelled with continual violence just above his heart.

He got up at last, switched on the light and unpacked the box of tricks that had given him so much pleasure as a boy. He decided to put in some practice on the tricks but after some moments he discovered that he had, over the years, forgotten most of them, particularly the one where he needed the collaboration of Miss Bentley.

Depressed and worn out, he went to the window and stared at the diminishing number of lights on the shores of the lake below. As he stood there a car drew up outside, its door banged, and he looked down to see a woman alighting.

Though the woman was in fact Signora Fascioli coming home late from visiting her eldest sister in Arona he was sure, in the darkness, that it was Miss Bentley, at last returning from Pallanza.

The thought depressed him more than ever. He experienced a pitiful moment of jealousy and then decided he hated himself as much as Miss Bentley. The garlic began to rise again and he drank several glasses of water, together with three aspirins, before going back to bed, to lie there miserably wondering how many coffee beans he would have to chew in the morning before he was again a civilized, presentable man.

The following evening, after dinner, the major put on his little performance of tricks in the writing-room. He had gone to the trouble of writing out little cards of invitation, which the Bompiani children clutched with delight and on which he described himself as *Major Paulo: the Magic Wanderer*. He had remembered in time that he had called himself *the Magic Wanderer* as a boy. It was still rather good, he thought. The *Major Paulo* was an afterthought and because of it Miss Bentley grasped, for the first time, that his name was Paul.

The Bompiani family, with Miss Bentley, Miss Beaumont, Signora Fascioli, Maria, Enrico and the two cooks sat in rows of chairs. The major had the tricks set out on a table covered with a red cloth he had borrowed from Signora Fascioli. He had rehearsed the tricks very hard during the late morning and afternoon and he had let Miss Bentley into the necessary secrets of collaboration. She seemed in some way subdued, her enthusiasm restricted, he thought, but he hoped things would go very well all the same.

When he appeared, bowed and took up his magic wand the Bompiani family led the applause and the children stood up, clapping and dancing.

'Thank you, thank you,' he said. 'Thank you. Now, ladies and gentlemen, *signori e signore*, if you will let me have your kind attention, a few examples of the magic art – '

Miss Beaumont stared with stony eyes. Miss Bentley felt unaccountably nervous, still despising herself. The Bompiani children shrieked far too much, she thought, and the whisperings of Maria and one of the cooks, in local Italian, got on her nerves.

The major first did a trick where he turned water into wine. That always went well. He was pleased that there were many 'Bravos!' mostly led by Signor Bompiani and taken up by the two little angels in a chanting chorus. After this he did a trick in which he made a fool's cap of thick white paper, poured a glass of milk into it and then abruptly screwed up the empty fool's cap and threw it away. That went very well too and again there was much applause, many 'Bravos!' and much admiring laughter. Before, during and after each trick he waved his magic wand.

After several other tricks, including one in which he cut a thick silk rope in half and joined it together again, and then a piece of baffling illusion with a black box, the time came for him to collaborate with Miss Bentley.

'For this trick I also need the collaboration of the audience,' he said, 'Signor Bompiani – perhaps you would be good enough to translate please?'

Signor Bompiani, who had a melodious, easy voice, translated at some length, so that by the time he had finished Miss Bentley felt more unsure of herself than ever. She found herself wanting the trick to succeed even more than the major did and she began to be afraid that the two cooks, who looked dopey as they listened, did not understand.

'It is all very simple,' the major said. 'You will each write whatever you like on a piece of paper, put the paper into an envelope and then seal it down. Please remember what you have written, because I shall then take each envelope *and*, *without opening it*, tell you what it is.'

'We write in Italian or English?' Signora Fascioli said.

'Whichever you like,' the major said. 'But in Italian only the simple words!'

Miss Beaumont, who looked more distant than ever, was seen to dash off a single word. Signor Bompiani wrote three pieces, one each for the little angels. The cooks and Enrico sucked their pencils. Someone was heard distinctively to say *O! Sole Mio* and behind Miss Bentley there were sudden reproving cat-like hissings.

The major collected the envelopes. As he collected them he chattered a good deal, in traditional conjuring fashion, distracting attention and at the same time creating an air of expectancy.

'Now!' he said. 'I am ready to read your minds. Envelope Number One!'

He stared with intensity, for twenty seconds or so, at the first envelope, holding it up to the light of the central chandelier.

'I think,' he said at last, 'yes, I think I penetrate the veil of the first mind. I think I know what words this envelope contains. Yes!' He spoke slowly, passing his hands in mystical, groping fashion in front of his eyes. 'I think – yes, I am sure.' With drama, flourishing the envelope, he proclaimed: 'I think the words this envelope contains are *The Spring in the mountains.*' He paused. 'Did anyone write that?'

The major had arranged with Miss Bentley that at this point there should be a dramatic pause: almost as if the trick, in its first moment, had failed. Miss Bentley, as she heard her own words read out, felt her throat become harsh and dry. She was unable to frame her words. She felt as if years went by before she was able to say, quietly:

'Yes. I wrote *the spring in the mountains.*'

The major made a gesture of modest triumph. There was again much applause. 'Bravo! Bravo!' everyone said and Signor Bompiani exclaimed in round, melodious English: 'Jolly good, major. Jolly good.'

While this was going on the major swiftly tore open the envelope, memorized its contents and picked up the next one. Holding it up to the light he suddenly said:

'Ah! I know what you are saying. You are saying that when I hold the envelope up to the light the envelope becomes transparent. That is not so. Signor Bompiani – would you oblige? Take the envelope please and hold it up to the light. Is the envelope transparent or not?'

Signor Bompiani took the envelope and held it up to the light.

'Thick as London fog,' he said. 'Can't see a blooming thing.'

'Thank you, sir,' the major said. There was some laughter. One of the cooks giggled. The two Bompiani angels started giggling too. 'Yes, this one I think is easy. Did someone write *God Save the Queen*?'

'Guilty,' Signor Bompiani said. 'I wrote it for this one,' and picked up the younger of the two children and put her on his knee.

'Bravo!' everyone said, with applause. 'Bravo!'

The trick, Miss Bentley thought, was going quite well after all. The worst, she felt, was over. She sucked her lips in relief, feeling saliva flow warmly down to her throat, melting the dry harshness there. She had now no more to do except listen and during the next few moments she heard Signora Fascioli confess to have written, in English, *There'll always be an England*, and Signor Bompiani, also in English, to *A nice cup of tea*. It was Enrico who had written *O Sole Mio* after all.

Suddenly it seemed to Miss Bentley that the major grew uneasy. After Enrico's *O Sole Mio* he seemed all at once to lose buoyancy. She thought he looked irritated, flushed and a little under pressure.

'This envelope contains only a single word,' he said in a slow voice, at last. '*Candlestick*. Did someone write that? *Candlestick*?'

'I did,' Miss Beaumont said.

'Thank you,' the major said. His voice carried a thin, restrained note of sarcasm. 'Thank you.'

From that moment the trick began to go wrong. Miss Bentley sat watching the major's small pink ears flush to a dark, bruised red. After the neat envelope he paused, looked very confused, said something about 'it's very hard to concentrate on this one.

I have to confess this one is very difficult', and then looked into
the audience and said:

'Was there someone who didn't write *anything*?'

No one answered.

'Signor Bompiani.'

Signor Bompiani translated. One of the cooks raised her hand
and said something. The Italians laughed and Signor Bompiani
translated what the cook had said.

'She wrote nothing, she says. She says she hadn't time to think.
She requires a lot of time for thinking.'

The major made a regretful gesture of resignation and said
the spell was broken. The children, who had not understood the
trick in the first place, looked more than ever mystified, and the
major consoled them into fresh delight and giggling by producing
round, bright pink sweets from their hair.

'Shame!' Signor Bompiani said. 'Won't you go on? It was
marvellous.'

'It is too difficult now,' the major said. 'The spell is broken.'

'Still, it was marvellous,' Signor Bompiani said. Starting to
applaud, he looked for approval towards his wife, who smiled
also. 'Marvellous!' she said with her handsome, fat, velvety lips
and applauded too.

'I can't think how you do it, Major,' Signor Bompiani said
and then everyone said 'Marvellous!' or 'Bravo!' and clapped
their hands.

Only Miss Beaumont, Miss Bentley noticed, did not clap her
hands. Instead she took out her lipstick and touched up her lips
and while the major did a final trick of pulling unending streams
of coloured paper from his mouth, Miss Bentley, watching her,
wondered what *Candlestick* meant and why it had offended the
major into sarcasm. She supposed Miss Beaumont in turn wondered what *The spring in the mountains* meant and she hardly
knew herself what had made her choose the words. They had
come to her suddenly, in a moment of mysterious enlighten-
ment, in the odd way that things sometimes do, without thought
or premeditation.

She discovered suddenly that she had been lost in a little day-
dream in which her eyes had been fixed once again on Major

227

Wilshaw's ears. Hastily she re-focused her eyes to find that Signor Bompiani was making a little speech, partly of thanks and partly, as it turned out, of invitation.

'On behalf of you all I thank the major most profoundly for a wonderful treat – is that the word? – treat? Yes? A great treat, Major, thank you.' The audience, led by Signor Bompiani, applauded once again. 'And now, something else. The Bompianis, I am sad to say, must go back to Milano the day after tomorrow.'

'Oh, no. No, no,' the major said. 'That's too bad.'

'Work. One must work,' Signor Bompiani said. 'Still, what about a picnic? A farewell, final picnic? Tomorrow?'

While Signor Bompiani was saying this Signora Fascioli slipped out of the room, beckoning Enrico, Maria and the two cooks to go with her.

'What do you say? Where shall we go? Where we went before? – to the place in the mountains?'

'Splendid,' the major said. 'Couldn't be better.'

'Good,' Signor Bompiani said. 'The only trouble is that we are one more this time. That makes it more difficult for the car.'

'It's easy to hire another car,' Miss Bentley said. 'The major and I would stand for that.'

Miss Beaumont suddenly spoke for only the second time.

'Or you could ask your Italian boy-friend along,' she said. 'That would even up the party. He has a car.'

Before Miss Bentley could recover from annoyance and astonishment Signor Bompiani was saying:

'Oh! Oh! Boy-friend? Miss Bentley? – an *Italian* boy-friend?'

'We simply had a swim together.'

'Oh?' Miss Beaumont said. 'I'm sorry. I thought it was lunch. And dinner too.'

Miss Bentley suddenly found herself in a hideous trap, not knowing what to answer. She was saved by Signor Bompiani, who laughed melodiously and said with generosity:

'Well, of course, invite him. The car would be most useful. It would be fun. What is his name? Perhaps we know him? Do you know his name?'

'I think his name is Balzari,' Miss Bentley said. 'His father manufactures motor-car tyres. But we –'

'Of course we know him! Very well. Of course. Balzari. They have a villa here. Which boy is this? – the elder or the younger? There are two brothers.'

'I think his name is Vittorio –'

'Vittorio – the elder one. The other one is named Carlo, of course,' Signor Bompiani said. 'Nice boys. I shall telephone him myself.'

He began to take charge of the party, talking generously of drinks, occasionally saying 'Let's all have a nice cup of tea,' his favourite joke about the English, shepherding everyone forward to the patio, where little green and crimson lights were hung about the arbours of trellis work. Miss Bentley took the opportunity of hurrying ahead, murmuring about the need for her wrap and how she would get it from upstairs. The Bompiani angels clung to the major, one at each hand, with their mother just behind, leaving Signor Bompiani and Miss Beaumont to come from the writing-room last, together.

'Well, Freda, that was nice, eh?' He patted Miss Beaumont in a friendly way on the shoulder. 'Didn't you enjoy that? Didn't you think the trick with the envelopes was a good one? I can't think how the major does it at all.'

'I know how it's done,' Miss Beaumont said. 'It's as old as the hills.'

Upstairs, in her room, where the lights of the lake shining through the slats of the Venetian blinds made cage-like bars on the white ceiling, Miss Bentley sat looking at her quivering, foolish hands.

For the picnic lunch there were large piles of cold pork and salami, pink stacks of ham, two dishes of pâté, a whole *Bel Paese*, large nests of hard-boiled eggs, much bread and two baskets of fruit, mostly green and black grapes, with a few last blue figs and big butter-coloured pears. There were four flasks of *valpolicelli* to drink, with white vermouth for those who preferred it, and mineral water for the angels. Miss Bentley and Signora Bompiani separated the slices of meat and laid them thickly on rounds of buttered bread. Miss Beaumont tied bibs on the children while Signor Bompiani and Vittorio, the Italian boy, who to Miss

Bentley's relief had driven up with the major in his car, opened and poured out the wine. All across the mountains a still sharp light lay wonderfully distilled above the distances, with pure noon transparence, and the lake, more than ever like a pale blue glass lioness, was clearly visible below.

'Shall we drink to our meeting next summer?' Signor Bompiani said. Gaily he raised his glass to everybody; the wine glowed with a brilliant heart of fire in the sun. 'Let's drink to that, shall we?'

'Cheers,' the major said. '*Salut. Santé*. And everything else besides. To next year.'

Everyone drank wine as they sat about on short grass burned to bleached matting by the long summer. From somewhere higher up the slope, among the rocks, the sound of a spring breaking and beginning to run down the mountainside was the only sound in the fresh bright air except the sound of voices.

'Will you come back next year, Major?'

'My goodness I hope so.'

'And what about you, Miss Bentley?'

Miss Bentley, caught unawares by the question, did not know what to say.

'I may do,' she said. 'I shall see – '

'Or perhaps you prefer Pallanza?' Miss Beaumont said.

Looking up suddenly at this remark, Major Wilshaw saw on Miss Bentley's face something he had never seen there before. She had totally lost her look of assurance. Her expression was one of indecisive, rather helpless pain and suddenly it hurt him to see it there.

'Well, Pallanza is very nice,' Signor Bompiani said. 'But not so nice as this. What do you say, Vittorio? You like Pallanza?'

'No. Pallanza's noisy,' the boy said.

In panic Miss Bentley wondered how long the conversation would go on but the major said quickly, changing the subject almost desperately, that he thought the nicest place he had seen in all Italy was a little town in one of the steep river valleys between Bolzano and Venice. Tobacco grew all along the sides of the valley and he thought it was very lovely there.

'Stupid of me, though,' he said. 'I can't even remember the name of it now.'

'Ah, Venice,' Signor Bompiani said. 'Venice.' He turned to the boy. 'Vittorio really comes from Venice, don't you?'

'My family has a house there.'

Part of a slice of ham hung down from the astonished lips of Miss Beaumont as she heard this. Her eyes fixed themselves on Vittorio Balzari with unbelief, fascination and with less coolness than she reserved for Miss Bentley and Major Wilshaw. Then she became aware of the pink trembling piece of ham dangling from her lips and pushed it hastily in and said:

'You have three houses? One in Milan, one in Venice, and one here?'

'Four, really,' he said. 'My mother has a flat in Rome too.'

Miss Beaumont swallowed her ham and tried to look as if, every day of her life, she heard of people who had houses in each of four illustrious and beautiful towns in Italy.

'How nice,' she said. 'Don't you find it hard to get servants for all these places?'

'No,' he said. 'In Italy we have plenty.'

'How many do you need for four houses?' Miss Beaumont said.

'I think we have twenty-seven – no, twenty-eight – waiters,' he said.

Everyone laughed at this, especially the three English, who were delighted at the misuse of the word waiters. Even Miss Bentley laughed. The major was quick to notice on her face a little break in the veil of pained, indecisive tension. He was glad he had been skilful in changing the subject of Pallanza.

Through the rest of the lunch he found himself looking more and more at her face, which from his lower position on the slope appeared to him framed completely against the sky, clear sharp blue above the mountains. And presently he found that he was looking at her, though he did not realize it at first, with tenderness. He felt he suddenly wanted to leave the pleasant arena of the laughing picnic and walk with Miss Bentley somewhere farther up the slopes, among the rocks, in complete solitude, where the spring rose.

Then he remembered the sentence she had written for the trick, *The spring in the mountains*, and he wondered what could have made her write the words. She had been very quiet, almost without a word, throughout the entire picnic. Now a puff of breeze had blown a few strands of her brown hair down across her forehead and eyes and in preoccupation she had not pushed it back again. He watched this brown curl of hair with new fascination and thought it gave her a certain lightness, a prettiness, he had never seen there before.

Then he was aware of Vittorio filling up his glass again and Signor Bompiani, who loved any excuse for drinking and even more for proposing a toast, raised his glass to everyone again and said:

'We have already drunk to next year. Now let's drink to this year. It's been wonderful.'

Everyone drank and agreed it had been wonderful.

'And to our English friends.'

'Thank you. And to our Italian friends.'

'Thank you, Major. Most kind.'

'And to the children. Our little angels,' the major said. 'If only we could all grow up so beautiful.'

Everyone laughed at the ambiguity of this remark, which Signor Bompiani translated for his wife, and Miss Beaumont said, 'Thank you,' with the faintest, most distant touch of sarcasm.

Then the two children suddenly raised their glasses of mineral water and drank too, to the amusement of everybody, and there were fresh shrieks of laughter.

'Any more ham?' Signor Bompiani said. 'No more ham? No more salami? No more cheese? No, no, not for me.' He laughed loudly. 'If I eat more I must take too much shut-eye!'

As the major watched Miss Bentley quietly peeling a ripe fig and then sucking the light pink flesh from the broken purple balloon of skin he made up his mind that he would, somehow, get her to walk with him, after lunch, farther up the mountainside. His only fear was that Vittorio would ask her first and again he felt a stab of jealousy about the boy and the journey to Pallanza, which had ended with the miserable fiasco of Miss Beaumont, the garlic and the incident of the candlestick, that blistering, sarcastic, crushing word.

Then he saw, after a time, that Signor Bompiani and his wife were already asleep among the rocks. The children were resting too, stretched out in the sun. Miss Bentley and Miss Beaumont were packing up the picnic things, disdaining help from men, though Vittorio was hovering near them: waiting, the major hoped, for Miss Beaumont to be free.

For five minutes he wandered away among the rocks, hoping that when he got back again Miss Bentley would be alone. When he did get back she was alone but, like the Bompianis, already lying down among the rocks, in the sun, with eyes closed.

He lay down too, the sun hot on his face, the air powdery dry with a smell of thin autumnal earth long burned by summer. There was not a sound in the air except the sharp falling water of the spring rising invisibly, some distance up the gorge, from the rocks. Vittorio and Miss Beaumont had wandered away too and even the children did not stir.

He found he could not close his eyes at all. For a long time, lying face sideways, he watched Miss Bentley. The strand of hair had fallen down, for a second time, across her face. He wondered again what had happened at Pallanza to make her so unhappy and why she had written the words about the spring.

Suddenly she opened her eyes and lay there looking at him. He stared back at her without a flicker. Her eyes had no movement either. Her stare was profound, enraptured and mute and for a long time the two of them lay there in a trance, looking at each other, never moving, in air so quiet that the major could separate each sound of falling water from the other as clearly as notes on a flute.

It was a spell he never wanted to be broken but the children, leaping up suddenly, broke it with laughter. Hearing them, the Bompianis woke too and Signor Bompiani said:

'Well, did you sleep, Major? I dreamed I was the owner of a banana plantation on some island somewhere. How do you account for that? Too much salami and cheese I suppose.'

A few minutes later Vittorio and Miss Beaumont came back: Miss Beaumont, the major thought, looked thinly haughty;

Vittorio rather baffled. Seeing them, Signor Bompiani said he was glad they were back. The air was far up and so late in the year got cold very quickly. For the children's sake they ought to go.

Two minutes later, although it was only three o'clock, the sun dipped behind a bastion of westerly mountainside, leaving a sheet of cold purple shadow through which the sound of spring water seemed suddenly to fall with iciness.

'Time for a nice cup of tea!' Signor Bompiani said: his favourite joke about England.

He led the way down the mountainside, carrying the younger child. The major carried the other angel and the rest followed, single file, with the picnic baskets.

At the foot of the path, just before they reached the cars, Signor Bompiani turned and called back:

'By the way, Major, when do you leave?'

'Not sure. I've stayed over three weeks longer than I meant already.'

Signor Bompiani turned again and called back.

'What about you, Miss Bentley?'

Miss Bentley seemed to hesitate uncomfortably before answering. With a curiously constricted feeling about his heart the major stared ahead across the lake, waiting for what she had to say.

'Two days after you,' Miss Bentley said. 'Sunday.'

'Well, make the most of them,' Signor Bompiani called.

The major felt himself sharply catch his breath, but whether in relief or astonishment or from the sudden chill of the air he never knew. Half an hour later the two cars, descending rapidly, were down in the warmth, among the still-blooming oleanders, of the lakeside.

Two mornings later Miss Bentley sat on the terrace, staring at a boiled egg. She could not think what had caused her to order a boiled egg for breakfast and she was just thinking that, after all, she did not want it very much when the major appeared.

'Do you mind if I join you?' he said. 'Is that a boiled egg you've got?'

'I thought I'd order one.'

'I think I might order one myself.'

The major rang a bell on one of the trellis posts along the terrace and, when Enrico came, ordered a boiled egg.

'Four minutes,' he said.

It was, it seemed to him, the longest four minutes of his life. Like Miss Bentley he did not know what prompted him to order the boiled egg and he knew, some time before it came, that he did not want it very much either. A recollection of Pallanza, Miss Beaumont's sarcasm about his tricks, the strange moments when he had stared at Miss Bentley at the picnic and above all the fact that Miss Bentley was going away next morning made him something more than tongue-tied and uneasy. He felt a little sick too.

'Do start,' he said. 'Don't wait. Mine is sure to be some time.'

Miss Bentley picked up a knife and prepared to slice the top off her egg. The morning sun drew from the knife blade a flick of silver light as, almost at once, she laid it down again.

The major, not daring to ask her what her plans were for her last day by the lake, raised his face to the sun and said:

'The sun's really quite warm when you think it's nearly November.'

'Yes, it's quite warm.'

'It's really been quite exceptionally warm all the month.'

'Exceptionally warm,' she said. 'Even the Italians say it's been exceptionally warm.'

Presently the egg arrived and the major found himself staring at it, unable to attack it, exactly as Miss Bentley had done.

'It seems awfully quiet without the Bompianis,' he said.

She looked away at the lake. 'Yes,' she said.

'They were so gay.'

'I suppose they were. The children got on your nerves sometimes.'

'Oh! did they? I never noticed that.'

Miss Bentley looked from the lake to her egg and then back to the lake again. As she did so the major remembered the morning, almost a month before, when she had said good-bye to him, checked his hotel bill for him and had talked to him, with such efficient assurance, about the necessity of not packing his passport and ticket with his luggage. Then she had kept her eyes fixed

235

on the side of his face and it was he who was nervous. Now she simply stared at the egg and the lake and could not look at him.

He tapped at the top of his egg with a spoon.

'I thought – '

'What are – '

The major stopped tapping the egg.

'I'm sorry. Please – '

'It's nothing,' Miss Bentley said, 'I was only going to say – I mean you're up rather early. Are you having a swim today?'

'No. As a matter of fact,' the major said, 'I was thinking of going up to the mountains.'

'By funicular?'

'No. You can get a bus to that village – the one where the level crossing is – and then walk from there.'

'It's quicker by funicular.'

A sudden impression that the egg might not be very fresh caused him to feel a wave of nausea. It caught in his throat. He swallowed, pushed the egg away and found himself saying:

'I suppose you wouldn't care to come? We could probably get a bite at the village and a glass of wine.'

'I really ought to do my packing.'

'It really won't take all that long,' the major said. 'I plan to be back by three.'

She made another meaningless gesture with the knife, picking it up as if to attack the egg and then putting it down again.

'I simply must do my packing,' she said.

Another pointless gesture with the knife irritated him.

'You've got hours,' he said. 'What time does your train go tomorrow?'

'That's another thing,' she said. 'I've got to get my sleeper ticket fixed. I've only an open one at the moment. I ought to have done it before – '

'Perhaps you'd rather say good-bye to Pallanza?' he said. 'I'll go to Locarno for the day.'

The jolt of pain across her face was quick and shocked, but it followed him down the hill. Walking quickly towards the lake, angry, almost marching, he suddenly hoped he would never see Miss Bentley again. His embittered remark about Pallanza was a fitting end to something that, even before the pantomime of the eggs, had begun to swell with prickly irritations. That was the way with women. You offered, you cajoled, you were reasonable, you were generous and suddenly for no reason they took flight and hid themselves away.

He decided suddenly he was in time to catch the ten o'clock steamer, make the trip up the lake, spend the day in Locarno and come back late by train. By that time Miss Bentley would have gone to bed. In the morning he would order his breakfast upstairs, read for a couple of hours and not come down till lunch time. By twelve-thirty Miss Bentley would be gone. He would have seen the last of her.

Then suddenly he was thinking 'Why the devil should I? Why, when I don't want to? Why go to Locarno when what you really want to do is to go to the mountains? Why be bludgeoned by Miss Bentley?'

He turned away from the lake and was just in time to catch a bus, in which he got a back window-seat, at the *piazza*. It took him, with many stops, up the long valley where groups of workers, some of them women still in big rice-straw sun-hats, were still gathering grapes among the vines. Over everything hung a light dust-coloured haze. The sun was hot on the windows of the bus and at one of the stops he looked out to see a hatless young Italian girl, arrogant, strong and brown as mahogany, taking off her woollen jumper among the vines. As she crossed her hands and seized the tips of the jumper and pulled it over her head she revealed underneath it the high line of her breasts, updrawn, in a white sleeveless blouse.

She laughed openly as she saw him looking at her. Then she hung the jumper over the vines and, still looking at him and still laughing, made as if to pull off the blouse too. He smiled back at her as the bus drove away and she suddenly plucked a bunch of grapes and pretended to throw it after him, following him with roving, arrogant eyes.

As the bus travelled away from the vineyards he half-wished he had got out, stopped and spent the day there. That would have been a great way to spend a day. He had always wanted to help with the vines. That would have been quite a Bacchanalian revel there, he thought, in the hot sun, in the alley-ways of vines, among the piled skips of grapes, with the brown arrogant girls.

By the time he got off the bus it was twelve o'clock. He was quite hungry and he had forgotten the look, on Miss Bentley's face, of arid, fleeting pain.

At the foot of the narrow road to the mountains stood a *caffè* where, on his first visit with the Bompianis and Miss Bentley, children had arrived, selling flowers. He sat at a table outside and waited. Beyond an open door screened by a curtain of coloured beads he could hear the family having lunch. He listened for some time to the murmur of voices and the sharp sounds of knives and forks and then pressed a bell in the wall.

A girl in a white sleeveless dress came, wiping food from her mouth with the corner of her apron.

'You speak English?'

'Little, little,' she said.

She smiled as she spoke. He noticed her very slim, long fingers, almost as straight as wheat stalks and the same yellowish-tawny colour. Dark hair grew thick in her neck and under her arms and her feet were bare.

'Bring me a half bottle of *orvieto*,' he said. 'And some cheese.'

'Bread with the cheese?'

She smiled again as she spoke. It was a very pleasant smile, he thought, not so bold, ripe and ready as the smile of the girl in the vineyard, but still a wonderfully pleasant, easy smile.

He responded by smiling too. She was eighteen or nineteen, he thought, though you could never tell in the south. Perhaps she was younger. 'Yes, bread, please,' he said and he watched the swing of her bare legs as she moved away.

When she came with the wine she smiled again, staying at the same time to talk a little and not only to uncork the wine but to pour it out for him; and once again he could not help thinking that the smile, like the smile of the girl in the vineyard, was specially, exclusively and solely for him. Wonderful, he thought, to drowse away the whole afternoon there, repeating the wine and the smiles until the bus came back.

'Very beautiful here,' he said. '*Molto bella*. In the mountains.'

'In the town is better.'

'You think it's better in the town? Not in the mountains? Why?'

She shrugged her shoulders slightly and with one long finger drew indeterminate patterns with a drop or two of spilled wine across the table-top.

'In the town more fun.'

'Oh! you know the word fun, do you?' he said.

'Yes, I know it,' she said. The corners of her mouth sprang up, quick and pretty. 'You think I shouldn't know?'

They responded quickly, he thought. Bathed in a glow of pleasure, the wine cold and fresh in his mouth, he sat for an hour alone, gazing at the mountains. Nobody else was eating or drinking and in the house the noises of the family gradually quietened down.

When he finally rang for the bill and the girl came he delayed her by searching in the wrong pocket for his money and then by producing a note for five thousand lire, hoping she had no change. But she had change and he sat in fascination as she counted the notes out for him on the table, his veins racing with pleasure and satisfaction as he followed the line of her bare arms to the shoulders, until finally he ran his fingers down her arm and pressed a note in her hand.

'*Basta! Basta!*' she said. She swung round in a flare of fury, pointing to the mountains. '*Basta!*' He thought she would either strike him or spit at him before she found her English again. 'We sell wine and food here! Not *me!*'

She actually did spit as, a moment later, she turned and swung into the house again. He picked up his change and started away up the road, but a rattle of curtain beads made him turn suddenly and he saw the girl appear again, this time with another, older girl, perhaps her sister, and from the beads they mocked him.

'*Papa!*' the elder one shouted. She stuck out her tongue. '*Papa!*'

He walked frigidly up the mountainside, among the rocks. He suddenly felt completely stripped. He felt he would hear for the rest of his life the jeers of the two girls from behind the curtains.

He climbed up to where the spring broke from the rocks. It was farther up than he thought and the spring itself, bursting from a wall of rock, came out faster than he remembered. Instinctively he held his hand under the descending water and the shock of it, pure ice, fell like a lock on his pulse, making him gasp for breath.

For a long time he sat listening to the water. There was nothing in it now that soothed him. It cut down into the tendons of his pride as harshly as the water itself had locked its ice on his wrist. It seemed to expose skin after skin of folly: his incredible folly about Miss Beaumont, his utter folly about the stupid, pompous tricks.

He remembered Miss Bentley. He had been, above all, an impertinent, impossible fool about Miss Bentley. With ruthlessness he had thrown at her his trite and embittered taunt about Pallanza and had fled the instant she stared at him with pain.

He started to walk back down the slope. It had been more than an hour since he had first walked up. The sun was moving rapidly westward. Already, across the fields of rock, there were big purple flanks of shadow.

Where the picnics had taken place, on a circular ledge of exposed burnt grass, the sun still shone.

He stopped suddenly at the edge of this grass and stared. In the centre of it, more or less exactly where she had lain at the picnic, Miss Bentley lay in the sun, arms outstretched, eyes closed.

He sat down. With compressed astonishment Miss Bentley opened her eyes and looked at him.

'You said you were going to Locarno.'

He searched for something to say in answer. A recollection of the blistering taunt from behind the curtain of the little *caffè* shot through him and kept him silent instead. Then he remembered his own impossible taunt about Pallanza and suddenly, for the first time, he felt he began to understand her pain.

'What made you come up here?' he said.

'I came to listen to the spring.'

A further recollection of the stupid evening of his tricks made him realize, for the first time too, why she had written her words about the spring. Then he was sure, suddenly, and also for the first time, that the complications about her, about himself, about everything, were slipping away.

'I'm glad you came up,' he said.

He thought he saw on her face a look of inexpressible gratitude for this remark and suddenly he bent down and kissed her.

When it was over she lay, with the faintest of smiles, looking up at him.

'That was a nice impulse,' she said. 'Even better than the one you had when you missed the train.'

'You told me to stay until a new one struck me,' he said. 'Do you remember?'

Miss Bentley found herself looking, as she had so often done, at the major's ears, that were so like small tight pink roses. She actually lifted her hand and touched one of them with the tips of her fingers. A moment later she felt an impulse of her own: an impulse to tell the major not only what his ears looked like but to confess that she too had been a fool and had never been to Pallanza.

Instead she checked herself. She was quiet and she stared at the sky. There were many ways of pursuing happiness and perhaps half of them were stupid. Most of the time you were a fool and the rest of it in pain.

The major, she decided, need never know about Pallanza. She merely smiled up at him and said:

'Such a nice impulse that I hope you'll be struck by it again.'

'I might,' he said. 'On condition.'

The major laughed for the first time, looking down into Miss Bentley's clear brown eyes.

'Tell me the joke about Miss Beaumont,' he said. 'That day at the cubicle. You remember.'

Miss Bentley began laughing too.

'It wouldn't be fair on Miss Beaumont.'

'Miss Beaumont has gone,' the major said. 'Damn Miss Beaumont.'

Miss Bentley laughed again, gaily this time, with growing excitement, and then calmed herself.

'All right,' she said. 'Come nearer. How can I possibly tell you if you sit up there?'

Laughing again, she pulled the face of the major down to her, putting her mouth against one of his small pink ears.

'Good God,' he said. 'No.'

'You see how unobservant men really are.'

He drew slightly away from her, looking down at her body, seeing it not only as it lay there in the sunlight of afternoon but also as he had seen it, floating, unexpectedly splendid, in the lake below.

'Much depends,' he said, 'on what there is to observe.'

She laughed again. With rising excitement he felt his hands slip to her breasts. Her thoughts were suddenly a racing jumble of bright impressions that included the sky, the mountains, the oleanders by the lakeside and the lake itself, stretched like a blue glass lioness in the autumn sun.

Suddenly she stopped laughing and was quiet again, holding his hands against her.

'Listen to the water,' she said. 'To the spring. Can you hear it?'

Over the mountainside there was no sound except the sound of falling water. Listening, the major heard it, as he always did, like cold music, with all its sharp and separate flutings descending rapidly and brilliantly, exhilarating in the clear still air.

Miss Bentley listened too. She supposed she had wanted all her life to listen to that sound, but now she did not hear it as the major did.

'It's like eternity, that sound,' she said. With an amazement of joy she heard it pouring through herself. 'The sound of a spring rising in the mountains.'

A Prospect of Orchards

Many years ago I belonged to a young men's club where I used to play chess, read magazines and also box quite frequently, though not very seriously, with a man named Arthur Templeton. We must have been, I think, eighteen or nineteen at the time.

Templeton was a shortish leaden-footed man with weak brown eyes whose responses were those of a duck with its legs tied. His jaw was babyish, smooth and hairless, like a pale pink egg. I had taken up boxing because once, at school, in a playful scuffle, a young ox of a farmer's son had struck me on the chest with a blow of such short-armed ferocity that I was convinced my heart had stopped beating. Soon afterwards I found a friendly ex-policeman who gave me lessons, taught me that the essential art of the game lay in footwork and in a maxim of six short words: hit, stop, jab, and get away. Presently I was practising these principles on Arthur Templeton, to whose pink hairless jaw I sent so many unresisted straight lefts that it became intolerably embarrassing – so embarrassing indeed that I presently became profoundly sorry for him and gave up boxing altogether.

The friendships of youth are so often impermanent that it is perhaps not surprising that Arthur Templeton's pale pink jaw presently faded from my life with no tremor either of interest or regret. There had been no pleasure whatsoever in boxing with Arthur Templeton, exactly as there can be no pleasure in catching over and over again the same gullible gudgeon from a brook. Arthur Templeton was what is known, popularly, as a glutton for punishment and if I had any reason to be glad about anything between us it was solely because I had decided that the punishment was not, if I could help it, coming from me.

Twenty-five years later I was travelling home on a cold April evening in a train that entered a tunnel and then emerged, some minutes later, into a bright stretch of downland dried stark white by the long drought of spring.

A dazzle of sunlight after the murk of the tunnel suddenly woke life into the eyes of the man sitting opposite me. He inclined towards me a head of pinkish baldness, half holding out his hand.

'I rather think we know each other,' he said, 'don't we?'

I hesitated; there was, for me, no hope of any clue of recognition except in the brown retiring eyes and the egg-like shaven jaw.

'Templeton. Arthur,' he said.

'Good heavens, of course,' I said. 'We used to box together.'

It is a curious and not uncommon characteristic of rather short men that they seem, if anything, to grow shorter as time goes on. Arthur Templeton, who had entirely ignored my reference to boxing, seemed not merely to have grown shorter; he had grown baldish and fleshy, with the same superciliousness of lip that frequently goes not only with men of short build but also with very fat girls who desperately attempt to conceal, by an intensely aloof proudness of face, the pain and embarrassment of their unhappy figures.

In a strange way Arthur Templeton was not at all unlike one of those fat girls. In a supercilious, aloof, but indeterminate face the one thing about him that had never changed was the pink, egg-like, ever-inviting jaw.

He seemed, I thought, extraordinarily full of confidence too.

'Never hear anything of you,' he said. 'What are you doing nowadays?'

I told him very briefly what I was doing and I felt it did not impress him. Without comment but with a sharp uppish turn of the head he looked instead at the too-clear sky, greenish now above the setting sun, across the spring-dried hills.

'Looks like another frost.'

'Nearly full moon,' I said. 'What do you do?'

'Fruit,' he said. 'Apples.'

In a fruit-growing district there is hardly anything less exciting than a meeting with yet another man who grows apples. But he went on quickly, a moment later:

'Got them on a new system,' and then added, again with that

supercilious turn of the head, 'or it will be when I'm ready. I'm not ready yet.'

'What sort of system?'

'I'm developing an entirely new kind of apple.'

I did not comment on this. As I grow older I grow more and more convinced that there are two things the world does not need and can long do without. One is a blue rose; the other is an entirely new kind of apple. There are some limits, I feel, to an interference with established nature.

The train, at this moment, rushed past an orchard of apple-trees, the white smoke whirling and ducking among the black, pink-knotted arms of blossom. I stared at the smoke fading against the setting sun, the low clouds almost the colour of the still unshorn sheep grazing under the boughs, and then Arthur Templeton said:

'I don't mean *that* kind of apple.' He pointed with a gesture of contempt at the pink aisles of blossom. He seemed to sense, I thought, something of my distrust, if not my scepticism, about an interference with nature. 'I don't mean that kind of thing. That's muck.'

The apple trees looked, I thought, very beautiful, very delicate in the setting sun, the pink of the half-opened buds strange and sharp against the pale green cooling sky.

'You can produce that stuff by the ton,' he said. 'Anybody can produce that muck. No, what I mean –'

If I was abruptly arrested into looking at him quickly it was mainly because his voice had become raised. It suddenly squeaked at me.

'No, what I mean' – he thrust out his pinkish egg-like jaw and I was startled into a half-remorseful recollection of how easily and how often he had presented it to me in just that same way, many years before – 'is something absolutely new.'

Scepticism, like a troublesome eyelash, is sometimes difficult to remove from the eye in a matter of seconds and his brown eyes became aggressive, quite fork-like, as they tried to remove the doubt from my own.

'You probably don't believe me but I've very nearly got it,' he said. 'An apple that tastes like a pear – in fact has all the characteristics of a pear but remains a true apple just the same.'

Mankind delights in an abundance of useless follies. Not the least of these is the evolution of fruits which take on strange flavours to which they are not entitled, still less suited, and which nobody wants anyway. Perhaps the light of scepticism still glowed in my eye.

'You don't believe it's possible?' he said.

'Oh! anything's possible,' I said. 'After all there's a strawberry grape –'

'Not the same thing,' he snapped. 'Not the same thing at all.'

'And isn't there a pea-bean?'

'Entirely different again. Absolutely different. Not the same at all.'

'I've even heard of mint flavoured with pineapple –'

With eyes shining brown, unsuspicious, resolved and deadly serious, he looked at me with withering calm.

'You probably haven't gone into this sort of thing very much.'

'I can't say I have.'

'Ever hear of a man named Professor Kurt Schumann?'

'No.'

'California,' he said. 'He's been working on the same lines for years. Published several papers. Oh! you can read them. They're interesting. But I believe –'

He broke off the sentence. At this point of the railway line there is a long curve at the end of the gradient where trains begin to brake very hard before running into the next station. As the brakes now went on the train jolted roughly and I thought the jerking movement gave to his apparently confident, supercilious face, taken unawares, a surprising touch of innocence. He looked suddenly insecure.

A moment later, as when he had so often, in the past, offered the pink egg-like jaw for me to hit, I felt intolerably and inexplicably sorry for him.

'Well, this is my stop,' he said. 'Do you often come down by this train?'

'Fairly often.'

'Why don't you hop off and see us some time?' he said. 'You could quite easily catch the next one down. We're five minutes up the road, that's all. You could see the orchards and the whole place and I'd show you a bit of what I'm doing. We've got quite a nice place up there. Still developing of course –'

The train was stopping. He seemed about to give me a limp, podgy hand. Abruptly he changed his mind, putting on his small green homburg hat instead. For some reason the hat made him look shorter than ever. It had a green cord round the brim. It was not unlike the kind of hat you sometimes see men wearing in the Alpine villages of Austria. It had a small pink and blue feather in one side.

'Well, what about it?' he said. 'Any day.'

I have often discovered that people on trains who impulsively invite you to visit their homes next time you are passing are almost always considerably surprised and embarrassed when you take them at their word.

'Well –'

'Give us a tinkle,' he said. 'If I'm not there my wife will be.'

As I murmured the faint whispers of half-promises the train stopped. He got out. From the platform he said 'Good-bye. See you anon, perhaps,' and lifted his still apparently supercilious face towards the smoky head of the train.

A few moments later, as the train drew out, I watched him walking, duck-footed, through the ticket barrier, podgy face thrust forward, the chin round, pink and protuberant, almost as if inviting some kind of punishment from the frosting sky.

2

It is more than likely that Arthur Templeton might have faded with insignificance from my life for a second time if it had not been that, two evenings later, my telephone rang and a woman's voice, piercing as a drill, asked if it could speak to me.

'Speaking,' I said.

'Oh! hullo,' she said. 'It's Valerie.'

I could not recall, at that moment, any woman by the name of Valerie.

'Valerie Templeton. Arthur's wife,' she said. 'Hullo, are you there?'

'Yes, I'm here.'

'Oh! good, I thought you'd gone. Did I surprise you?'

She had surprised me, though I didn't confess it.

'I wondered if I would,' she said. 'Don't you remember me?'
I did not remember her.

'That's partly Arthur's fault for not telling you,' she said.
'But then he wouldn't. Hopeless to expect it. You know Arthur,
don't you?'

The fact that I knew neither Arthur nor his wife kept me locked
in puzzled silence again.

This silence was presently broken by a fluffy giggle, less piercing
but more forbidding than the speaking voice itself, that seemed
to me like a nervous attempt to be something more than friendly.

'I believe you're kidding. You're putting it all on,' she said.
'You mean you don't remember the Pendlebury sisters?'

In a flash, across twenty-five years of time, I remembered the
three Pendlebury sisters. They were fair-haired and very plump.
They had faces like damp white cushions.

'Of course,' I said. 'Of course.'

'Well, I'm Valerie,' she said. 'The musical one. Have you got
me now?'

I had got her now, but the fact did nothing but keep me silent
again.

'Aren't you rather musical too?' she said.

'I'm very fond of music.'

'Well, that's what I really rang about,' she said. 'We know
quite a few musical people here. Quite a circle of us. Not a lot
of course – there aren't a lot, are there? You know what I mean?
Well, not when you're stuck in the country anyway.'

I had not time to think what she meant before she went on:

'Would you like to drop in one evening on your way down
from town? Arthur said you might. We sometimes have concerts.'

'Yes, he asked me,' I said. 'He wanted me to drop in and look
at the experiments.'

'The what?'

The voice pierced my ear-drums so effectively that I was glad
to use it as an excuse that I hadn't heard.

'He wanted me to look at the farm and –'

'What about Tuesday?' she said. 'If you came down on the five-fifteen?'

I said something about not being quite sure about Tuesday.

'Well, try,' she said. 'I'm dying to renew old acquaintance.' The fluffy, intimate giggle tripped about my ear for the second time. 'Any time. Just drop in. It would be awfully nice. No ceremony at all. Open house and that sort of thing.'

The following Tuesday evening, as I left the train and walked along the side of the valley towards Arthur Templeton's house, it seemed that every branch of every orchard was in blossom. It was very warm for April and under a white-blue sky blackbirds were singing with choking, thrilling richness among miles of pink and snowy boughs. There are springs of accidental perfection when, for a few days, all the blossom of all the orchards meets, cherry and apple and plum and pear, like a great lacy gathering of cloud; and this was one of them.

Foolishly I had neglected to ask the name of the Templeton house and when I stopped at the first neat, well-ordered farm standing at the fringe of a wide apron of blossoming cherries a heathery tweed-coated man came out of a barn to tell me, rather testily, I thought:

'Next one up the road. Can't miss it. One with the gas-tarred barn.'

Unlike Housman I am not sure which is the loveliest of trees; and as I walked up the road, between black-boughed cherries on one side and the pink up-curled horns of apple branches on the other, I felt as much impressed by the orderliness in everything, by the strict-pruned sentinels everywhere lined up in the April evening sun, as I did by the clouds of gathered blossom folded into every corner of the little valley.

Then I came, suddenly, on the gas-tarred barn. It had something of the appearance of a battered black saucepan with a makeshift lid of corrugated iron, three parts rusty, that had been tossed on top of it by a fluky throw. Some parts of it hung perilously over the western eave ready to fall. Below it a pile of rock, half-hidden by rising nettles, had wrecked a wooden trailer, turning it upside down, revealing a hole in its belly through which, presently, the nettles too would grow.

Beyond all this was the house. It struck me as being rather like a ship stranded on a muddy shore. Its upper structure, of thin weather-board, was flaky white; the Plimsoll line of red lower brick actually had in it two round portholes of thick green glass on either side of a half-glass door.

Up one wall of the house grew a vast espalier pear-tree that in its pruned stiffness was exactly like some compound arrangement of ladders for scaling the side of a ship. It was the only orderly thing in sight. All along its black, scaly branches there was not a single spray of flower.

When there was no answer to my third ring at the doorbell I started to wander about the farmyard. I had in mind to look for the seat of Arthur Templeton's experiments, for the system, well-ordered but revolutionary, by which apples would be married to pears and in time produce a sweeter, different progeny, but warm odours low on the April air led me to an arrangement of pigsties, hideous as concrete pill-boxes left over from an abandoned war, ranged between a duck pond and a clump of elder trees.

Two pale pink sows stood up to their shoulders in dung-steeped straw and contemplated me. A few white ducks were shovelling about the mud on the banks of the pond. If they inspired in me a thought of Arthur Templeton it was not through motives of vindictiveness. I was simply wondering where he was.

Presently, glancing round at a small orchard of apples, haphazardly filled in with young plums where wind or man had removed an older tree, I caught sight, out of the corner of my eye, of a figure who did not seem to belong to this scene.

It was a big, chunky man with gingerish hair and a red bow tie, hatless, who was carrying a 'cello in a brown canvas case. We exchanged a silent, distant, not unhostile stare before he hurried across the concrete and, without knocking, disappeared through the front door of the house.

His arrival became the signal, two minutes later, for my own moment of recognition. Across the yard, towards the pigsties, came the hurried fluffy giggle I had heard twice or more on the telephone.

'Well, there you are! Haven't changed a bit. I'd have known you anywhere.'

This was more than I could say of Valerie Templeton.

'Didn't you ring?' She was wearing spectacles with rims of exceptionally pale golden tortoiseshell, almost the colour of honey. 'I didn't hear you. I was probably practising.'

I said I had rung; the fluffy giggle was all the answer she gave me for another twenty seconds or so, during which she held out both hands, clasping my right one.

'Nice to see you,' she said. 'Damn nice. Really damn nice. How long has it been?'

If I did not answer this question in terms of specific years it was not only because I could not remember but because I was arrested, indeed astonished, by Valerie Templeton.

With the years Arthur Templeton, who in my youth had been short, weak-eyed and full of hesitancy, had grown fattish, supercilious and seemingly full of confidence. His wife, who like her two sisters had once had a face like a white plush cushion, had lost all trace of that upholstered appearance that was all I could remember of her girlhood except her fair long hair. Now the hair was piled into tiers of little watch-spring curls above a face whose cheek bones were like pared clenched knuckles. The flesh had the shining prettiness of wax, the same unreal, doll-like air, and the blue eyes were hungry.

'I was looking for Arthur,' I said.

'Oh! you know what Arthur is,' he said. 'Vague as they make them. He's gone into the town about some pigs or something. Probably forgotten you were ever coming.'

She turned on me a deliberately fascinating smile, flashing the honey-rimmed spectacles. Her mouth and her teeth, I noticed, were rather large, and perhaps it was this that gave her giggle its fluffy but unsoothing sound.

'More than you can accuse me of,' she said. 'I've been thinking about you all day. You know – wondering.'

If I had known her better I might have thought she was trying to mock me. She lifted her head and threw it slightly backwards and the gesture, like a pulled lever, released the giggle once again.

'Well, come in anyway,' she said. 'Arthur may be years. We're just having a snifter and then we're going to try the Dvorak. You know the one I mean?' With closed mouth she hummed some bars of the piece I did not recognize. 'The Quintet,' she said. 'Tum-ti-tum-ti – you know, and then that typical Dvorak lilt – tah! – you know what I mean? Damn difficult though. Hell to play.'

The interior of the house, first in an entrance hall crowded in every corner with stained mackintoshes, muddy gum-boots, baskets and several sacks that might have held samples of Arthur Templeton's apples, and then in a long sitting room furnished in dusty brown coco-matting, with chairs and settees loose-covered in bright orange linen and piled with many pink and purple velvet cushions, had the same shabby gimcrack air as the yard outside. A big tobacco-brown pseudo baronial sideboard, littered with sheets of music, stood against one wall. A black, oddly compressed baby grand seemed to cower in the opposite corner – cower, I think, is the appropriate word, for the entire bulk of the chunky 'cello-player was sprawled weightily across it, as across a bar.

After the 'cello-player, who was drinking whisky, had been introduced to me as 'Sandy – he's the unlucky one because the 'cello part's absolute murder, but you know it, don't you?' two more people arrived. Both were carrying fiddles.

It would have been hard to detect, at first glance, whether they were men or women except for the fact that one of them sported a tender, light fawn beard. A premature baldness at the temples threw into relief the heavy side curls of his hair. The sunken washed blue eyes gave him an air of sickness over which Valerie Templeton fussed with solicitude, mothering him with giggles as she unravelled the big thick red scarf that had coiled itself about his thin neck like a scarlet python.

'Thought you two were never coming,' she said. 'Bet you dawdled in the bushes on the way, didn't you? Iris Bensted! – come clean.'

If there was the remotest chance of Iris Bensted coming clean I did not detect it. She turned on the rest of us a pair of remote dark eyes as unmoved and glistening as a cow's. Her black hair was cut monkishly, in a low fringe that, trimmed as with the aid of a basin, reached to within an inch of her thick rough brows.

The fact that she was wearing a heavy cable-stitch sweater in bright green and black loose trousers accounted for my not being able to determine, with immediate certainty, what her sex was.

'Well, drinks for everybody, Sandy,' Valerie Templeton said, 'come on. Pour out, sweetheart.'

After laboriously detaching himself from the baby grand the 'cello-player poured, in a muffled, sloppy sort of way, drinks for the rest of us and presently we were standing about the room with glasses in our hands, I in a world that had taken me slightly by surprise and in which I found myself constantly wondering, and with growing depression, where Arthur Templeton could be.

'Well, I suppose we ought to make a bash at it,' Valerie Templeton said once and I assumed this meant the music. 'Sometimes I don't know why we chose the damn Dvorak. It's stinking difficult. Maddening. Absolute hell. Do you think we're bats to take it on?' she said to me, 'do you? Or what?'

No answers, I discovered, were expected to these questions, for the simple reason that Valerie Templeton always provided them, in the shape of her fluffy nervous giggles, herself.

Twilight was almost upon us before the tuning of strings began. Outside, somewhere in the region of the orchard, a blackbird was still singing – heard, I think, by no one but myself as I went to shut a casement window in answer to Valerie Templeton's abrupt demand:

'Somebody shut the window please. It's getting chilly.'

A second or so before shutting the casement I thought I caught sight of a light in the barn across the yard. Falling darkness was shutting out the sprinkled knots of blossom on the rows of ill-pruned apple trees and a few moments later the closing of the window shut out altogether the last, rapturous singing of the blackbird.

Turning back to the room I found Valerie Templeton switching on the light and heard her say, with a sort of half-aggrieved note of apology to me:

'Don't know if you'll be able to bear it. You see we have to play the damn thing as a quartet – haven't got a blasted viola yet. Sandy – did you see that girl? Is she coming, do you know?'

'Sunday,' Sandy said.

If the need had been for a double-bass the lugubrious mutterings of the red-bowed 'cello-player would have provided it as he sat, softly belching whisky, tuning his strings.

253

'Let's hope to God she's good,' Valerie Templeton said.

'Let's hope to God she comes,' the 'cello-player said, 'or else we'll have to get the cat in.'

'*You* don't play the viola, do you?' she said to me. 'Too much to hope, I suppose?'

'Too much,' I said.

I sat listening, for some forty minutes longer, to the rattling of the quintet's partly assembled skeleton. Valerie Templeton played the piano like a hen pecking at a bowl of maize. In all her hungry, crouching, spectacled actions above the cowering little grand piano there was an aggressive sinewy desperation.

At ten o'clock, my mind on the last train home, I rose to go.

'Oh! must you? Was it hell? God, I bet we've bored you.' She started pulling with nervous brittleness at the joints of her fingers, as if chastising them for being responsible for the noises I had heard. 'Pity Arthur wasn't here. You could have nattered with Arthur.'

'Where is Arthur?' I said.

'Search me,' she said. 'You know what Arthur is.'

'Perhaps experimenting,' I said.

'This is the second time I've heard about these experiments,' she said. 'What's it all about?'

'Search me,' I said.

She laughed at that, rather sharply I thought, and then, in spite of my protests, she came to the door to say good night to me. In the hall she turned on me the glittering, honey rims of her spectacles and said:

'Too much to hope you'll drop in again, I suppose? You've had a bore of an evening – honest, haven't you?'

'Not a bit,' I said. 'Fascinating.'

'Well, drop in whenever you like,' she said. 'You will, won't you?' She raised her hands in the beginnings of a flutter of invitation, smiling open-mouthed, so that for a moment I was almost sure she was about to flirt with me. I was mistaken. 'After all one's got to meet somebody now and then besides *that* crowd.' She made a gesture back towards the sitting room where all was silent now. 'One's got to *live*, hasn't one? – if you know what I mean.'

Outside, in the April darkness, the blackbird had stopped its singing. The apple boughs were invisible beyond the pond. Across the yard the only glimmer of light came in a few yellow perpendicular pencil cracks through the timbers of the gas-tarred barn.

I crossed the yard, pushed open the half-fastened door of the barn and looked inside.

Sitting on a box, in the light of a hurricane lamp, crouching over a bed of straw on which stretched a shadowy figure I found for a moment or two difficult to identify, sat Arthur Templeton.

'There you are,' I said. 'Just going. Sorry I missed you.'

'Caught me at a bad time,' he said. 'Been running all over the place for a vet and couldn't find one.'

From among the straw came a grunt or two that reminded me for a moment of the mutterings of the 'cello-player. A ripple of pink-white legs against a barrel of ruckled teats solved for me, a moment later, the brief mystery of Arthur Templeton's vigil and he said:

'Have to watch her. Not sure there isn't another one.'

At the same time he turned towards me the unresisting weak brown eyes, no longer supercilious but remarkably placid now in the lamplight, into which I had so often looked when we had boxed together and which had made me so intolerably embarrassed and often so intolerably sad for him.

'Don't suppose you'll drop in again?' he said. 'Like to show you –'

'Perhaps next week,' I said.

He was still smiling as I crept out. Outside not a whisper of a sound broke the April night silence above the orchards, the boughs of which grew whiter and whiter as my eyes became accustomed to a darkness in which I walked slowly, brooding more and more on Arthur Templeton, crouched in the lamplight, bringing pigs into the world.

3

When I next called at the Templetons' house, about a week later, it was raining hard. Everywhere blossom was falling from the apple trees. The valley that with its many orchards had looked so like a delicate encampment of cloud had now begun to look soiled and ragged under drenching evening rain.

There is something intangibly melancholy in the first vanishing of spring blossom and perhaps it was this, combined with the dry scratching of strings from the house, that made me wish I hadn't called. In vain I looked into the gas-tarred barn across the farm yard, hoping to see Arthur Templeton inside it, mothering his little pigs or perhaps – an even vainer hope – engaged in marrying the apple to the pear. All the sounds and movements I found there came solely from the flood of water pouring down from a roof hole on to the wheel of an ancient haycutter and dripping from there to a rusty hip-bath half full of sprouting swedes.

I need not have worried, as it happened, about the intangible melancholy of the April evening permeating the heart of anyone but myself. I am perhaps oversensitive to the moods of earth and rain. I ought to have been prepared for the fact that there are people who eagerly grasp at the enclosing shrouds of sodden English evenings as heaven-sent excuses for romping jollity.

In the house, in fact, the Templetons were holding a party – or at least Mrs Templeton was. The sound of strings came from Iris Bensted's fiddle. She was being helped by the bearded fellow fiddle-player, now vamping at the piano. On the floor, from which the dusty coco-matting had been dragged back, several couples including the 'cello-player and Valerie Templeton, in a brilliant emerald dress, were dancing.

'Ah! there you are!' Seeing me, she disengaged herself from the embraces of the 'cello-player and came tripping across the floor, locking and unlocking nervous welcoming fingers. 'You see, I told you it was a surprise, didn't I?'

This remark referred to a telephone conversation of the previous day in which she had urged on me the necessity of being an absolute dear and dropping in on them – 'because it's going to be a surprise, dear, and I think you'll like it.'

'It's my birthday!' she now said to me. 'And there's me and my candles!'

With gay imprecision she flung her arms about the air, directing my glance to the baronial sideboard, on which stood an iced birthday cake of astounding appearance which I thought for a moment had actually been made of painted cardboard.

'Do you like it? or do you think it's *terrible*?'

Gazing at this strange object, the cake, I did not know what to say. The icing had been coloured a livid vitriolic blue. Round it were set, in a double arc, numbers of bright magenta candles.

I was saved from making any comment on this by Valerie Templeton's hand suddenly clutching at my sleeve.

'You're wringing wet!' she said. 'You walked up in the rain. Where was your overcoat?'

'It was fine when I left for town this morning –'

'You'd better come upstairs and dry off or you'll catch your death or something. Your hair's all wet too. Silly man. Look at your hair.'

I started to say something about the difficulties of looking at your own hair but in her adamant, challenging, desperate fashion she seized my arm and led me away.

Upstairs we spent ten ruffled, uncomfortable, conflicting minutes in the bathroom.

'Rub your hair hard with this warm towel. I'll dry your jacket. It's not through to your shoulders, is it?'

I begged her several times not to fuss with me but she took no notice and presently she insisted I took my jacket off. After this she ran her hands over the shoulders of my shirt, then over the cuffs and the collar.

Presently, still towelling my hair, I stood facing her.

'You look funny with your hair all ruffled,' she said.

'Naturally.'

I was annoyed; I spoke acidly and she smiled at me.

'I mean funny nice.'

'Whatever that may mean.'

She laughed again, not quite so fluffily as she did sometimes, but in a lower voice, more smoothly.

'I hoped it might mean you'd give me a birthday kiss.'

'What gave you that idea?'

'You're funny. You're awfully nice,' she said. 'You always were.'

The retreat from kisses he does not want is one of the unpleasantest things that can happen to a man. I began to be angry.

'Do your eyes always go that bright blue colour when you're angry?' she said.

'I'm not angry,' I said. 'Nor is my head quite so wet as you think it is.'

'That was good. You were always quick-witted.'

I started savagely to comb my hair. She laughed and tried to take the comb away.

'Kiss me,' she said. 'Come on, kiss me.'

'Now look, let's get downstairs –'

'Kiss me,' she said and it was hard to tell whether her voice was wild or miserable, or, like her eyes, simply desperate with hunger. 'Come on, be a sport. Kiss me. Just once. Be a sport. Show me how you –'

What followed was so impossibly absurd that I can only describe it, if the simile is not too ridiculous, as trying to avoid being caressed by a mule that is at the same time frantically struggling to kick over the traces. We rocked, stupid and dishevelled, about the bathroom. She aimed a whole volley of vindictively amorous kisses at my face and laughed unflinchingly, showing a quivering crimson tongue.

'Be a sport. My God,' she kept saying, 'you and me could have fun.'

'Have fun with Arthur!' I said.

It was suddenly as if I had translated into action precisely what I had in mind to do to her. If I had suddenly held her silly face under the cold bath-tap I could not have shocked her more completely to her senses.

'My God, my God, Arthur,' she said. 'Arthur! – Arthur!'

She stood looking at me with a mixture of pity, contempt, misery – all sorts of things. She even laughed again. The vindictively amorous hunger faded in a second, completely.

'Better get back to the party,' she said.

She picked up my jacket from the floor and gave it back to me.

I put it on. 'Now you're talking sense,' I said. 'Why didn't you say that before?'

She didn't answer. I brushed my hand across the damp lapels of my jacket and buttoned it up.

'Damn it,' I said. 'Arthur's a good sort.'

From behind the honey rims of the spectacles she stood looking at me in a final moment of supremely miserable, withering calm.

'Good sort?' she said. 'Good sort? – that's what the road to hell's paved with! – good sorts.'

We had scarcely been downstairs for a quarter of a minute before we were confronted by a dutiful Arthur Templeton, the good sort, holding an empty tray.

'Drink?'

Before I could answer his question she was rasping at him:

'Of course he wants a drink! Don't be woolly. What the hell do you think he wants? – the evening paper or something? What's the use of prancing about with an empty tray?'

He took this searing punishment like a lamb.

'Gin, whisky or a glass of red wine?'

'Glass of wine, Arthur, thanks,' I said.

To my surprise, as Arthur retreated, she became her old giggling self again.

'I *knew* you were a red wine man,' she said. 'You can see it in your eye.'

A minute later, Arthur Templeton came back, bearing a glass of cold red wine in his hand.

'Oh! grip, Arthur, grip!' she said. 'First the tray without the glass. Now the glass without the tray!'

'Sorry,' Arthur said to me and held out not only the glass but that smooth inviting jaw, supercilious no longer, which I had struck so often many years before.

'I wanted something different,' she said. It was lost on me for a moment, as I watched Arthur Templeton retreating, duck-footed, among the dancers, that she was referring yet again to the cake on the sideboard. 'I get so tired of white, don't you? Everybody gets so stuck in awful ruts, don't they? Don't you always think it looks like a starched shirt front, that white icing – so terribly chapel-and-church?'

I was about to admit that there was some truth in this when she waved her indecisive hands again, giggling with a voice that flapped featherily, and said:

'You know a few people, don't you? You don't want to be

introduced all over the place, do you? We don't want to be formal, do we? If you get stuck with anybody ghastly make signals and I'll come and rescue.'

'I'll probably talk to Arthur,' I said.

'God, that's a prospect,' she said. From behind her honey rims she darted arrowing glances about the room and its crowd of dancers, as if seeking someone who would save me from this fate. 'Oh! I know – you haven't met the kid yet. The viola player. That's her – over there, talking to Sandy.'

A girl of perhaps nineteen or twenty, pretty, fair-haired, with a golden plum-like skin, looking not at all unlike the Valerie Templeton I remembered from the years when I boxed with Arthur, stood leaning against the far wall, talking to the 'cello-player.

'She isn't bad,' Valerie Templeton said. 'She's a pupil of Sandy's – of course he couldn't teach pussy, but the poor devil's got to live, I suppose. Come on, let's drag him away – he's breathing all over her.'

She needed no assistance, I noticed, in dragging the 'cello-player away.

'Come on, you coarse brute,' she said playfully. 'Come and dance with me.'

In an atmosphere of stringy pandemonium I talked, for the next fifteen or twenty minutes, to the girl who played the viola. Anthea Barlow was her name. I had not been mistaken in thinking that on her fair soft skin there was downy plum-like bloom. Her eyes too had a surface of tenderest limpidity through which the pupils shone with disarming brilliance – innocent as forget-me-nots, or so it seemed to me.

As I struggled to make small conversation about music she turned these eyes on me with continually mounting surprise.

'Oh! really,' she would say. 'Do you think so? I never thought of that. Isn't that interesting?'

I had just begun to think of making the necessary signals to Valerie Templeton when Arthur arrived.

'Gin, whisky or red wine?'

His simple catechism having been repeated, he stood back, staring at the girl, his hands twisting at his empty tray.

'Well, I don't really know,' the girl began to say and then hesitated, turning on him the eyes of forget-me-not innocence, as if in appeal.

'Do you think I might have orange?'

'Orange,' he said, 'of course. At least I think so.'

'Is it an awful trouble?'

'Oh! no,' he said. 'Oh! no. Fresh orange or bottle? No trouble.'

'Would there be fresh?' she said.

'Oh! I'm sure there is,' he said. 'I'm sure – certain there must be.'

He retreated, face still towards us for some paces, as I remembered him so often retreating across the canvas of the boxing ring many years before.

'Are you sure it isn't an awful bother?' she called after him.

He simply went, not answering. It could not conceivably have been his first meeting with her or his first glance into those almost too blue, too innocent eyes of disarming tenderness, but I thought I caught in his retreating, suddenly suffocated eyes a look of stupefaction.

He was back in five minutes, eager as a lackey expecting a tip, bearing a long glass of crushed fresh orange juice, a basin of sugar and several straws on a tray.

'Hope I haven't been too long,' he said.

There was no suggestion of pity in her long, smiling glance at him. Nor did her eyes turn on him with that wide and mounting surprise she had exercised on me. I could see, instead, that she was greatly flattered by what she saw.

'Something else I can get you?' he said. 'There are some quite decent sandwiches. *Foie gras*, I think. Shall I go and see? Or would you rather have ham?'

'Would it be an awful –'

He went like a shot, not waiting for an answer. With blue eyes downcast and seemingly more than ever innocent, she sucked at orange juice through a pair of straws. An uncomfortable suspicion that she did not know what *foie gras* was entered my mind and leapt out again, still more uncomfortably, an instant later. And it was like a mere mocking echo of it when I heard him say:

'Terribly sorry. They weren't *foie gras*. They're smoked trout *pâté*. I brought some along –'

'Oh! Do you mind after all?' she said, 'I'd really rather have ham.'

He had hardly finished the third of these dutiful errands for her when the shrill voice of Valerie Templeton began urgently calling him, piercing as a drill above the dance music, to attend to one of her own. He obeyed that call too with his strange, unhesitant, duck-footed alacrity.

When he had retreated again the forget-me-not eyes turned themselves on me as transparent as beads of glass.

'He's a lamb.'

It might have been not inappropriate, I thought, if she'd called him a dog.

'Have you known him long?'

'No,' I said.

'I had an idea you knew him quite well.'

'Hardly at all,' I said.

'Oh! really,' she said. 'How interesting.'

The evening offered no opportunity to know him better – except for one swift and tiny incident the significance of which, an hour later, very nearly escaped me.

'Cake being cut! Cake being cut!' I heard several voices call. 'Matches, somebody! Candles!'

This time, oppressed by the growing warmth of a room stuffy with dancers, I had gone to open a window, not to close one. To my surprise the rain had stopped. In a calm, cuckoo-less April darkness only the last drippings of a leaking gutter and the running of a ditch somewhere over against the pond broke the silence below a sky pricked with almost frosty stars.

I turned from this scene of fresh and scintillating air to see a handful of flame rising like the burners of a blue gas-ring in the middle of the baronial sideboard. Somebody had switched the electric lights out and Valerie Templeton's birthday candles were all the illumination – their flames pretty as crocuses on slender magenta stems – that now broke the darkness of the room.

'One good puff!' somebody was shouting. 'Deep breath! Now! –'

A fluffy hurricane, part giggle, part expiration, swept about the candle flames, making them flutter sideways like golden flags. About half of Valerie Templeton's forty-five years were extinguished in a single second. The rest rallied, uprighted themselves and burned unquenchably on.

The beginning of a witty quip about a woman's age was drowned in sudden laughter. The lights went up. A few moments later Valerie Templeton, over-flushed, her indecisive hands held steady by the hairy paw of the 'cello-player, was cutting into the blue crust of the birthday cake, among the ring of half-black, half-flaming candles.

'Happy birthday!' several people shouted. There were waves of laughter. 'Jolly good luck! – '

The knife made a sudden slip against the side of the cake's blue and brittle decorations and in laughing disgust Valerie Templeton threw it on the sideboard, uplifting at the same time a pair of tipsy arms that the 'cello-player a moment later folded to his shoulders, on which she in turn laid a head of golden watch-spring curls, slightly ruffled, to be borne away to dancing.

Among all these incidents not one surprised me. It was only some ten or fifteen minutes later, when every guest had toyed or was toying with a segment of blue-edged birthday cake, that I looked across the room to see Arthur Templeton engaged on yet another errand of mercy, carrying a plate of cake to Anthea Barlow, the viola-player, still standing apart in the corner of the room.

I was too far away, in that moment, to hear what comment she offered as Arthur Templeton stood before her, like a servant placing a long-awaited offering under a pair of too bright eyes, but I could see that she hesitated.

He greeted this hesitation with an eager outward thrust of the jaw. I saw her mouth move in return, first with words, then with the fraction of a smile, and a moment later he was on the run again, bearing the plate away.

Half a minute later I pressed my way among the dancers and past the sideboard. With bent head Arthur Templeton was engaged in an absorbed meticulous task there, a knife in his hand.

In the light of two or three of Valerie Templeton's still remaining, still burning candles he was engaged in paring from a wedge of birthday cake, as from a piece of cheese, every vestige of blue icing.

And as I turned away I saw in the corner the waiting figure of Anthea Barlow, both hands slightly upraised in front of her body – for all the world as if she was about to clap them and bring him running.

4

I suppose I went to that house again three or four times, perhaps even five or six, before I finally grasped about Arthur Templeton a conclusion I ought to have reached not less than twenty years before. It was not until a burning, breathless evening in August – there had been no drop of rain since June and now in the farmyard the dregs of the never handsome duck-pond had dried to a black-green crust that sprouted a crop of skeleton elder-boughs and rusted tins – that I realized how abysmally, intolerably lonely he was. I had really been very obtuse; even the little pigs should have made it clear to me.

When I arrived that evening he was standing, shirt-sleeved, against the door post of the barn, gazing out across the yard. At the sound of my footsteps across the sun-baked track that led in from the road he jerked his body off the post and abruptly started forward – eager, as I thought, to greet me.

As soon as he saw who it was, however, he relaxed – no, relaxed is altogether too mild and indefinite a word. He flopped – exactly as if winded, punctured or worn out by heat or something – against the open door.

'Thought for a minute it was Miss Barlow,' he said. I fastened on the formal prefix to Anthea Barlow's name with a glance of inquiry at him that gave me nothing at all in answer. He was simply staring at the road. 'Her bus only gets as far as the station. She has to walk up the hill.'

Suddenly in that airless blistering evening I found myself facing the stifling prospect of Valerie Templeton's quintet, sawing its way through an August heat-wave. I half-heard, I thought, a warning echo of screaming strings on the breathless air and said quickly, a second later:

'I didn't really mean to stay. I just dropped in for a minute. If there's a rehearsal I'll just say "Hullo" to Valerie and then –'

'Oh! there's no practice,' he said. 'Valerie's taken the car down to the sea. She's rented a bungalow there. She'll be gone a night or two –'

His face became a mask, offering me no help at all. Behind and beyond him the face of the land, its light soil burnt out by weeks of sun, had become a mask too, with hardly a trace of the green that had graced it in early spring, at the time of apple bloom. A kind of brown crust, in reality the shrivelled leaves of long un-watered trees, had spread about the branches of the orchard. On the house the pear-tree was a mere trellis of blistered timber. Even elderberries were withering and falling, like shrivelled pepper-corns, from their branches above the dried-up pond. Over the western crest of the hill the sun was dropping into a shimmering sky of smoky-purple haze, burning like a deep flame above an altar.

'God, it's hot,' he said. A glaze had spread across his eyes. 'I'll get you a drink –'

'No, no,' I said. 'Don't bother –'

Almost before I had finished speaking he threw out an extra-ordinary remark.

'Reminds me of once when we were boxing,' he said. 'We started in September that year – the club opened about the third week – and all of a sudden we had a heat-wave.'

Not once, all that summer, had he ever mentioned the pain-ful, long-buried episode of our boxing.

'Can't say I remember that,' I began to say.

'Oh! I do, I do,' he said. 'Perfectly. You were pretty accurate that night. I just couldn't get the measure of you –'

Here I found myself thirsting to ask him something that had perplexed me for a long long time.

'You never hit me back enough,' I said. 'You never covered up. If you'd covered up more you could have hit me more.'

'That's where I went wrong?'

265

'Mostly,' I said. 'You didn't hit me back enough, man. Why on earth didn't you?'

Gropingly the brown eyes searched the road beyond me.

'I suppose because I rather liked you.'

It was a remark that I found so astonishing that I could give it no answer at all. In the following silence he became jumpy again, eyes again searching the road, and he finally looked at his watch.

'Anthea must have missed her bus,' he said in a dry voice. 'I think I'll walk down to meet her. Will you wait? The house is open. Help yourself to a drink – everything's on the sideboard.'

He started to duck-paddle across the yard and then stopped so suddenly that he actually raised a skid of dust with his feet as he turned.

'I suppose you know all about us?' he said. 'I mean, Miss Barlow and me? I suppose everybody knows.'

I did not know; I was happily free of any tongues that must have been whispering among the orchards.

'I thought everybody probably knew – you know, with Valerie going away and all that. She's got this bungalow by the sea. Shares it with Sandy. You remember Sandy? It's all –'

Every trace of that protective supercilious glaze I had noted on that first sharp spring evening in the train, together with its puffed air of confidence, had left him now.

'You'll wait, won't you?' he said. 'Do wait. Don't go till I come back. Help yourself to a drink. Hang on, old man, won't you –'

With such jittery affectionate terms he crossed the yard, half-running, and went down the hill beyond.

When he had gone at last I went into the house and poured myself a long drink from the sideboard on which Valerie Templeton had extinguished some of the burning candles of her years and where Arthur had so carefully pared away for Anthea Barlow the unwanted rind of the birthday cake's harsh blue icing.

Even then it still didn't occur to me how deeply, how intolerably lonely he was.

'He's just a stupid coward,' I kept telling myself. 'That's all. A plain stupid coward. That's why he didn't hit me. That's why –'

'Anybody at home?'

My thoughts on cowardice, themselves more than a little stupid, were suddenly brought to an end by the voice of Anthea Barlow, calling through the open front door of the house from the farmyard.

'Oh! it's you,' she said when I went to the door, 'isn't Arthur? –'

'He went down the road to meet you,' I said, 'only five minutes ago.'

'I got off the bus at the other stop,' she said, 'and walked up by the foot-path. It was cooler that way – well, anyway not quite so hot.'

In the heat of the evening she looked flushed and exhausted. She received with a panting smile my suggestion that I should get her a drink and then, as I poured it out at the baronial sideboard, made one of her own.

'Let's sit outside,' she said. 'I can't bear this room. I hate that awful sideboard.'

On what ought to have been a lawn but that was now a ruckled brown mattress of untrimmed grass scorched yellow-brown by summer we sat in discoloured canvas deck-chairs, sipping drinks and gazing through the hot evening to the orchard beyond.

This was the orchard where, as I had once so fondly imagined, those great experiments of Arthur Templeton's would find their genesis and their final fruit and perhaps she read my thoughts as we sat staring at the summer-blistered boughs, under the farthest of which I could just make out the growing litter of piglets and their sow, rooting dustily.

'Arthur's going to do a lot of new grafting in the orchard next winter,' she said.

'Oh?'

'You know the way I mean?' she said. 'You cut down the old branches and graft on different varieties.'

'Yes.'

'You know he's got this wonderful idea of a new kind of apple?' she said, 'don't you?'

There is some virtue in lying on certain occasions and I felt this was one of them.

'No,' I said.

'It's this marvellous idea of an entirely different kind of fruit,' she said, 'a cross between an apple and a pear. He's been working on it for years. There's a professor in – ' She went on with Arthur's story, in Arthur's words, and I listened, musing and dazed. The sow and her litter had been turned into the orchard, I now realized, in order to scavenge on the little prematurely ripened fruit that drought had brought down from the boughs, and they wandered gruntingly under the trees, picking up a yellow scrap or two here and there.

'Of course it'll take years,' she said. 'There's a tremendous lot of work – research and all that. But wouldn't it be marvellous?'

'Marvellous.'

'I can't help thinking of the first time you would offer a fruit like that to someone,' she said. ' "Have an apple," you'd say, and then you'd wait to see the look on their faces.'

'What look?'

'Oh! you know, the look of – the great surprise. The apple wouldn't have the taste they thought it would. You'd really catch them, wouldn't you?'

I was saved from any answer to this by the sudden voice of Arthur Templeton, whistling from the yard. It was a peculiar whistle, low, bird-like, on three abbreviated notes, and suddenly I realized it was his secret, personal call.

'That's Arthur,' she said. 'That's his whistle now.'

She jumped up from the deck chair and started running round the side of the house to the farmyard beyond. I ought to have stayed where I was, but curiosity impelled me, with my drink still in my hand, to the edge of the lawn, where a gap in a trellis-work of withered rambler roses gave me a view of the dusty square of yard.

It was then that I witnessed, at last, the exposure of his loneliness. The girl was standing with her back to me and she looked, I thought, for all the world as I remembered Valerie Templeton looking, fair, plump and soft, more than twenty years before. And suddenly I realized that he was not really looking at her. Hungrily and helplessly he stood staring at her with an adoration that was not meant for her at all.

A Prospect of Orchards

'Because I rather liked you,' I could hear him saying to me
again. 'I suppose because I rather liked you.'

A moment later I went to replace my empty glass on the
baronial sideboard that Anthea Barlow hated so much. And
soon I came out of the house to find her talking to Arthur at the
gate of the orchard – and, to my surprise, arguing with him
slightly.

'I'll say good-bye,' I said.

'Oh! before you go,' she said, 'you can settle something.
Arthur and I are going for a walk. Arthur says it'll be much hotter
that way – up the hill – and I say it'll be much hotter *that* way –
down the hill. What do you think?'

'Oh! I didn't really say that,' he started to say. 'I wanted to
go which way was best, that's all. Whichever way you want.'

His voice was like a broken echo. His jaw was smoothly held
out, unprotected, ever-inviting.

'There's probably more breeze on the hill,' I managed to say.

'Well, of course,' she said. 'Come on, you silly man.' She
turned to me with a look of triumph that was neither warm nor
radiant. 'Isn't that just like him?' she said and it might have been
the voice of Valerie Templeton.

I watched them walk up the slope of the hill, between the
apple trees. With intensely focused light the sun was burning
every moment with deeper, fiercer orange beyond the scrubby
blackened apple boughs, under which the pigs were still rootling.
At the crest of the slope Arthur Templeton and the girl stopped
for a moment and she stooped and picked up a yellow apple and
held it in her hands: an apple that might well, I thought, have
been a pear.

A second later she threw it away. It needed only a call from her
to set him running after it, like a dog running for a ball or like
one of the pigs searching for the dropped fruits of summer; but
it never came.

They disappeared at last into the sun. Above where it blazed
there was not a single sacrificial fleece of cloud and there was not
a breath of air to break the evening silence of all the miles of
orchards about the valley until, some moments later, I heard a
sound.

It was the sound of Anthea Barlow laughing. But what she was laughing at – whether it was Arthur Templeton or the little pigs or the apple that would taste like a pear or simply at some other prospect of orchards in the future – it was quite impossible to say.

The Grapes of Paradise

I first caught sight of him about three o'clock in the afternoon, at the start of a humid and torrential squall of rain on the water-front of Papeete. He was tall, lean and English to the bone, with eyes of transparent whitish blue and receding fair hair that made him look much older than he really was. The hair badly needed trimming at the neck. His shirt of pale lavender, sun-faded and worn outside his crumpled brown trousers and with a small design of darting indigo fish across it, was remarkably subdued for those parts and had not been washed for some time. It was too early to tell whether he was ill, drunk or troubled, or perhaps all three, but he was completely oblivious of the rain.

He was in fact not drunk. He had not been drunk for some considerable time. All he was doing was to watch the passage of a little motor-schooner beating shorewards through the gap of coral reef a mile or two out to sea. The flow of ocean in and out of the gap was very fast there and he kept beating his hands together like a man watching a horse-race in which he is afraid his favourite cannot win.

I watched all this through the open door of a barber's saloon. He stood quite alone on the waterfront in the rain, staring at the schooner, the breadth of the street away. Inside the reef the squall of rain became sometimes so dark that beyond it there appeared to be continuous plumes of dirty smoke where normally the vast breaking crests of spray on the collar of rocks would have shown like the rearing waves of pure white horses.

Somewhere between plumes of smoke and rain the schooner, rolling like a squat white drum, occasionally disappeared. All the time, far beyond her and the smoking reef, the Pacific flared in sunlight, a harsh clear glitter outside the storm, and beyond it all the fantastic mountains of another island glowed like half-melted pale green candles in the sky.

When the rain suddenly stopped he stood watching for nearly

another ten minutes until the schooner drifted in at last and tied up below him, fifty yards away. As soon as she tied up he started to walk towards her. Then he suddenly stopped, seemed to change his mind completely and turned on his heel.

That was the first time I ever saw his face. My impression had been that he was about to meet someone off the schooner, that they hadn't arrived and that he was disappointed. Instead I saw that his eyes were extraordinarily savage: not savage with anger or the intensity of disappointment but inwardly savage, with pure blind melancholy, perhaps against himself.

That was the second impression I got: that, when he came and sat in the barber's chair next to me, hair and face and the balding reaches about his temples still streaming with rain, he was living in a state of emotional sightlessness. He picked up a towel from a wash-basin and started to rub his face and hair. His shirt was open down the front, showing a chest of pale amber hair, and he dried that too. When he had finished he lay back in the chair, shut his eyes and stretched out his arms to the wet knees of his trousers. The hands went limp, turning downwards, loosely, as if he were very tired, and as they did so I saw a scar, ten or twelve inches long, a raw brown-pink slash running from above one wrist to the muscle of the upper arm.

The barber began to comb and cut his hair without a word. Soon after he had started a girl came along the pavement outside, wheeling a bicycle. She stopped, leaned one foot against the bicycle and stared at the four men in the saloon.

'Hullo, Harry,' she said.

She spoke in good English, but he made no effort to open his eyes or answer. She was not wearing the customary *pereu* of Tahitian girls, but a sleeveless dress of pale green, with no design at all. Her hair was not plaited but was brushed in two dry black bunches, like combed rope, over her bare shoulders. She was pretty in the pert and delicate way, light and bird-like, that comes when Chinese blood is mixed with Polynesian, and her waist and legs were wonderfully fine and slender.

For another ten minutes or so, leaning on the bicycle at the open door of the saloon, she went on talking to him, saying that she hadn't seen him lately, asking if he'd seen this person or that and why did he never come dancing at the New Pacific now? All the time he neither opened his eyes nor answered.

'They tell me you're off on the next flying-boat,' she said, but even that had no effect on him.

By this time the sun was shining again and the air, delicious after the rain, was steaming hotly. The handles of the girl's bicycle glittered as she twisted them. Her hair had steel blue lights in it as she flicked it back over her shoulders and she said, for the last time:

'Well, tell me if you do, Harry. I'll come and see you off. I'll come and say good-bye.'

Impassively he ordered a massage. He seemed to know instinctively, without turning his head, that she had left. A few moments later he actually opened his eyes. All the keener edge of their savagery had now become blurred and their queer white blueness was merely glassy as he turned to me.

'English paper you're reading?'

'Yes,' I said. 'Have it if you like. You're welcome.'

'No thanks.'

'Absolutely the latest,' I said. 'Only two weeks old.'

Jokes that fail with strangers in strange places are colder than icebergs. He did not answer.

Outside the saloon the street had already steamed to concrete dryness. At the extreme end of the reef the rearing lines of seafoam pranced with splendour in the sun. Beyond it the distant island slopes glowed with deeper, clearer green, the candle fissures almost purple in the far brilliant air.

'They tell me the other island is very beautiful,' I said.

'Not been there yet?'

'Not yet.'

'Schooner twice a week,' he said.

His voice was unexpectedly soft. The short cryptic words that ought to have made it sharp had in fact the opposite effect. He gave an impression of talking quietly to himself, meditating.

'Anywhere to stay when you get there?' I said.

'Rest-house.'

'Any good?'

273

'Don't know,' he said. 'Haven't seen it for a month or two. Dare say it's good. Dare say they'd fit you up.'

This, the longest piece of conversation he had offered so far, was also remarkable because during the final part of it he actually turned and gave me a glance that had in it the beginnings of a smile.

'What are you here for?' he said. 'Usual thing? Looking for the lost Loti Lotus Land or the Gauguin ghosts?'

These sentences were neither cryptic nor bitter. Nor were they exactly sarcastic or sad. The odd thing about them was their emptiness. They might have been a few spiritless puffs of air let out of a paper bag.

'I'm not sure what I've come for,' I said. 'It's like eating mangoes for the first time. You know they won't taste like oranges but what else do you expect? You don't know.'

He may have thought that this showed, perhaps, a slightly higher degree of intelligence than anything I had said before because he then said:

'That'll save you a load of disappointment. Oh! the girls are beautiful – some of them. Oh! They'll give you what you ask for.'

The barber, who had finished my hair, now gave me the towel. For a few minutes I sat reflectively rubbing my neck and face and ears. It was so hot already after the rain that my eyes were damp with sweat and my throat was parched.

'Like to join me in a drink?' I said. 'When you've finished? It's pretty hot in here.'

'I don't,' he said. 'Don't drink, I mean.'

'We could get a taxi and drive back to the hotel,' I said. 'It's cooler there.'

'I'll be ten minutes yet,' he said.

I couldn't make up my mind whether this meant he was coming or not until he said, 'I'm afraid I'm only an orange-juicer. Or passion-fruit.' He actually gave a laugh in that dry puffed way of his and again nothing, I thought, could have been more passionless.

Twenty minutes later we were driving along the waterfront, past the Postes et Télégraphe building, the last shops and the thick bright hedges of hibiscus and bignonia that flank the gardens along the black sand shore. Heat beat up in slaty glittering waves from the tarmac, sprang from waste stretches of dust under thin high palms and turned the yellow bells of creepers on fences to fleshy shimmering gold.

At the hotel he ordered, as he had promised, an orange juice. The handsomest of Tahitian girls brought it, with a glass bowl of ice and a soda siphon, on a bamboo tray.

'Nice to see you up here again, Mr Rockley,' she said. 'Soda? Have you enough ice in there?'

He made no answer. Instead he sat looking beyond the low tidal stretches of water inside the reef and then far beyond the rearing crests of the reef to where, more fantastic than ever in the more westerly angle of sun, the mountains rose like pale green candles melting but never lessening in the harsh fine air.

'Cheers,' I said.

'Good luck,' he said.

He lay back in his chair, white-blue eyes empty again and almost completely transparent, his arms flat out, the palms turned down, the fingers twitching. The scar was like a jagged brown boot-lace. And suddenly I realized that his habit of sitting with his palms downward, twitching his fingers, must have grown unconsciously out of pain.

Then he saw me looking at it. He looked surprisingly neat and respectable now, with his fresh-trimmed, fresh-massaged hair, but the barber had not been able to trim his voice or change its tone at all. It was still remarkably soft, passionless and unabrupt as he ran one finger down the scar, stared at it in silence for a moment and then said:

'Take good care nobody does that to you.'

2

He was single, unassuming, friendly and about thirty-five. He had come down to Tahiti from Vancouver, crossing the Pacific by way of Fiji, Samoa and the Cook Islands, three months before, full of conventional thoughts about romantic places.

He had in fact been overworking and had been given three months leave by the firm of industrial bankers for which he

worked in Vancouver and when I talked to him that first afternoon, over his modest orange-juice, with his eyes almost always
fixed on the mountains, he had already taken a month more than
his time.

At first there was nothing at all unconventional in what he
had to say. There is a common expression about Tahiti which is,
I suppose, often made about other places but is made with more
truth about this island that everyone so much expects to be a
paradise. Two weeks there are too long, it says, and a year not
long enough.

He had not been on the island more than a day or two before
he felt convinced of the truth of the first part of the expression.
When he arrived by flying boat, in the cool of a tropical evening,
an hour before dusk, the waterfront was gay with a great crowd
of girls in brilliant crimson *pereus*, women in pretty summer
dresses, men in bright-patterned shirts, almost all of them carrying *leis* or *couronnes* of orchid, gardenia, hibiscus, jasmine and
tiare flower. Most of them were shouting, laughing, throwing
kisses and waving their hands; a few were weeping with joy.
There were so many flowers that he felt that every garden had
been stripped. The air was sweet and sickly with the scent of them.

Out of all this, as he stepped ashore, a plump Tahitian girl
came forward, put her gold-brown arms on his shoulders,
laughed softly and kissed him splendidly on the lips. After that
she put a *lei* of frangipani round his neck and then suddenly
went away to do the same service for another visitor. Then
another girl put another *lei* round his neck, this time of small
cherry-coloured hibiscus and jasmine, and then another girl a
third. He felt slightly embarrassed by this excess of flowers, which
were by now piled like Elizabethan ruffles up to his ears, but he
laughed too when he saw that all of his fellow passengers were
also hidden under flowers, some of them under six or seven *leis*
of purple, white, orange and vermilion, some of the women
wearing enchanting *couronnes*, gay little hats of purple orchid
bloom.

That night at the hotel, on the edge of the lagoon, under
electrically lighted coconut palms that sometimes fluttered in a
wave of cool wind coming off the sea, where until long past

midnight fishing boats with flares were floating about the black water, he drank champagne and did a little dancing to the three-piece orchestra of two men and a girl, who played mostly Tahitian tunes. The girl also sang songs and as time went on he thought all the songs had in them the same indescribable sadness. Two other girls, one of them not more than twelve, both bare to the navel except for a strip of covering across their breasts, did several native dances, swinging and rolling their hips, making gestures of voluptuous and graceful supplication with their light-brown hands, swishing their light skirts of hibiscus bark – not grass, as he had always imagined – dryly in the night air.

He had several dances with one or two of the women passengers from the plane and one each, out of courtesy, with the two air hostesses, pleasant girls from Adelaide. He bought a drink or two at the bar. The atmosphere had in it a great sense of careless easiness. Frenchmen danced with Tahitian girls; French women with Tahitian men.

'It was all very nice and free and easy and fresh to me,' he said, 'except that I might just as well have been in Nice or San Francisco or Paris or Sydney, though I didn't know it at the time.'

In the morning he took a taxi, drove into the town, cashed a cheque at the Bank of Indo-China and looked at the shops. The cashing of the cheque took him the better part of an hour and a half and in less than half that time he had looked at all the shops. The town had something of the air of a dusty and fly-blown French provincial town crossed with a mid-western shack-town populated mostly by Chinese. A few ancient white-painted schooners were being loaded with crates and barrels and bicycles and all manner of goods on the waterfront, where loafers sat about drinking milk out of green coconuts or bottles of fruit juice out of straws, spitting at the dust.

'It all looked so bloody fly-blown and so tatty,' he said, 'I could have vomited.'

That very morning, in fact, he went into the offices of the Pacific Navigation Company, cancelled his passage of three months hence and took a ticket on the next plane outward.

'It was as bad as that,' he said, 'and what made it worse was that nobody seemed to care a damn whether I went or stayed.'

Then he went back to the hotel, stripped off, put on his swimming trunks and went down to the sea. The beach of black sand, such as there was of it, looked like a foundry yard. The lagoon of black water illuminated by the flares of mysterious midnight fishing-boats had become a stretch of tidal junk-yard, one foot deep, filled with countless black clusters of sea-birds and lengths of what looked like yellow intestine.

At the end of fifty yards of jetty sprouted a lump of coral rock. On the rock a French girl with a figure as flat as a boy's and legs like white peeled sticks sat staring down into forty feet of dark blue water from which rose shadowy mountains of rust-brown coral, murderous as steel.

'I'm glad you came,' she said. 'If there's someone watching, the sharks don't follow me.'

He decided not to swim. Instead he went back to the bar, sat on a high bamboo stool just as he was in his swimming trunks, and dejectedly ordered himself a whisky. He sat drinking till three o'clock.

He was still drinking, but still more dejectedly, three weeks later. By that time he had toured the island twice, had eaten sucking pig several times and had not taken a single swim in the repulsive, sea-edged lagoon. The dazzling beaches of white coral of which he had heard so much and of which he had actually seen pictures on posters simply did not exist. In the shops he bought as presents a few shells of polished mother-of-pearl, a boar's tusk and a piece of native wood carving in the form of a pineapple cut in half. He sat in bars and watched dust blow out of pot-holes in the road outside and then blow back again. He drank with all sorts of people in all sorts of places and tried to laugh, above the sound of loudspeakers that might have been blaring out of any street between Sydney and Southend, at the jokes they made.

'Better take a *vahini*,' someone said, 'and settle down and get it out of your system.'

He agreed that the girls were beautiful. Their willingness in the realms of cohabitation was not simply legendary. He was fascinated with the splendid handsome readiness of their laughter. He liked above all a certain air of surface shyness in them, the grace of their walk on flat feet and the black strength of their waist-long hair.

'Anyway that's neither here nor there,' he said. 'I never saw one I really wanted. The point is that I suddenly realized that what they say is true. Two weeks are too long and a year isn't long enough. Just before the plane was due out I cancelled my ticket and booked myself on the next one. Then I did the same with that one. And at the end of the month I was – '

He stopped speaking. Since he had hardly given up, for a single second, looking at the fantastic molten candles of the island across the lagoon, it cannot be correct to say that he suddenly looked across at the mountains. It is truer to say, perhaps, that he woke up. The remarkable air of sightlessness in the very pale blue eyes was dispersed for a moment or two, enabling him to focus properly on something that it was now obvious he had not been seeing before.

He also pointed – with, I noticed, his scarless arm.

'At the end of the month I was over there.' He turned to me now, as he had done in the barber's shop, with the beginnings of a smile. 'I don't suppose you saw the schooner come in this afternoon? The one in the squall?'

'I did,' I said.

'That's the one,' he said. 'Takes four hours. That's the way you get there.'

3

The schooner, throbbing and rolling like a butter churn, loaded with everything from cows and bicycles to barrels of *vin ordinaire*, took him over to the island almost exactly a month after he had first arrived in Tahiti. By that time he had drifted into a habit of getting mildly drunk every night and sometimes also at the lunch hour: not because he particularly wanted to get drunk but because of all the pleasant pointless things there were to do this required least energy and passed most time.

As the schooner drew nearer to the island he gradually realized that the mountains he had previously seen only from a distance were really less like candles than gigantic chimneys, massed to the very ridges with vegetation. Their outline made a strange green graph, rising and falling violently, against the sky. Along the coast and a mile or two out from shore the reef was locked like a stupendous jagged collar on which the sea rode with unremitting roar, magnificently springing with high snow-white arches of spray.

After two or three stops at little village landing-places where boys sold him slices of frost-fleshed water melon on the quayside the schooner finally ran, about mid afternoon, into a long still lagoon. He had already noted with some pleasure that the sand about the villages was white. Now the schooner began to run so near to the coast that he could have leaned out and thrown a stone on to the strips of pure white coral beach that ran everywhere out from thickets of bread-fruit, wild plantains, palms and the tall yellow-flowered hibiscus from whose bark the so-called grass for skirts was made.

The water in this land-locked lagoon was so still and undistorted that it made him feel extraordinarily peaceful. In occasional shallow bays it was pure yellow in colour, turning to greenish blue, then pure bold indigo as the water deepened. The only disturbance on it was the wash of the schooner and occasionally, far off on the flat sun-white surface, a flight of little fish, pure frantic silver, scared from the water by some predatory chaser like a flight of birds.

His destination was the last stopping place but one along the lagoon, a wooden landing stage behind which was a solitary palm-thatched house and at the side of which stood, on stilts, in shallow yellow-blue water, what he took to be the rest-house. Like a fairly large square bamboo band-stand, it rose from the strip of pure white shore.

A boy of twelve came down from the house to greet him, to smile enormously and to take his bag. He stood for a moment in the glare of sunshine, waving his hand to the departing schooner. As it throbbed down the lagoon, farther into the intensely green shadow of the mountains, the sound of its engines dying away, he was aware of his sense of tranquillity deepening. This is it, he started thinking, this is what I came to see.

Then, as he turned to go up to the house, an extraordinary thing occurred. Perhaps it was merely extraordinary, he explained to me, because he hadn't expected it. He had told no one he was coming there but now, as he turned, someone was waiting there to greet him.

It was a girl, holding an enormous crimson *lei* in her hands. He supposed, he said, it was the largest *lei* he had ever seen, a great flowery boa of petals minutely crinkled, so that they looked like feathers packed together.

But it was not this in itself that was remarkable. What immediately struck him as so extraordinary was that the girl, though quite young, eighteen or nineteen, was the ugliest he had ever seen. It was difficult to convey the peculiar quality of her ugliness but it was, he explained to me after several attempts, exactly that of a primitive idol hacked out of a golden-coloured wood, and not very well hacked at that.

She was so ugly, in fact, that she was, in a peculiar way, quite handsome. Her frame was tall and massive. Her bare feet were immensely broad and flat, with gripping toes. Her hands, which would have made a lesser *lei* look no longer than one of the necklaces of pink coral he had often seen in the shops, were like great golden-brown crabs with extended claws. Her legs, he said, were like those of a billiard table built in smooth shining mahogany and her arms, no less powerful, were as broad as hams where they joined the wide naked shoulders.

These were his own descriptions and he apologized for mixing them up a little but he went on to say that all the skin of her body was very fine, with a look of being oiled and polished. It was her face that had the rough-hewn look. The big dark brown eyes seemed not quite squarely fixed and the mouth seemed to have been plucked severely sideways and upward out of shape, curling the inner edge of the upper lip so that it looked like a half-healed scar. Later he saw in fact that it was a scar, as if at some time she had been violently struck across the face by a blow that had also flattened and broadened the square snout-like nose.

Crowning all this was a mass of overpowering jet-black hair that she wore unplaited. It was like a gigantic wiry horse tail that reached to her massive buttocks. Later she was actually to put on lipstick and an occasional bangle and sometimes a pair of earrings but that day the only decoration she was wearing was a large pure yellow hibiscus over her right ear. That too was an outsize flower, with a big stiff central pistil that stuck out at him like a darting tongue.

Her only garment was the *pereu* in the usual pattern of crimson and white, in this case of leaves and flowers, and it had been wound so tightly across her enormous breasts that she actually seemed to have outgrown it. It left all the upper part of her chest, her arms and her shoulders naked.

When she smiled at him the scarred lip seemed to give a raw flare and he saw that she had one tooth missing just underneath the twist of it, exactly as if knocked out by the blow that had caused the scar.

She placed the *lei* round his neck and greeted him, at first, in French.

'You don't speak English?' he said.

'A little.'

'And the boy?'

'My brother? Just little words of French.'

She led him up to the house. To one side of it, the shady side, a sort of bamboo and palm thatch lean-to hut had been built and there she showed him into a simple room where later he used to lie in bed and stare at the whole tranquil seaward stretch of lagoon.

He continued to speak in English, asking her one or two questions, such as her name and where he would be able to eat and so on, and every time she attempted to answer in English she gave a great crackling laugh, throwing back her head and opening her mouth to its widest, revealing her thick animal tongue stiff and quivering.

He could not quite grasp her Tahitian name. He thought it sounded, at first, like Tavae. He was not sure and tried to repeat it and she laughed again.

'They call me Thérèse too sometimes,' she said. 'Thérèse I like better.'

From that moment onwards he called her Thérèse. 'My name is Rockley,' he said. At first she pronounced it in the French way, as if it had an accent at the end, but later, as time went on, she simply called him Rock.

'Will you have something to drink now?' she said. 'Tea or coffee? Wine or coconut juice or orange?'

He thanked her, said he would have orange but that what he wanted to do most of all was swim.

'Good. You swim,' she said. 'I'll make orange and bring it down to you.'

'Good swimming?' he said. 'No sharks?'

'No. No sharks,' she said and she laughed, raucous, showing her tongue again. 'If sharks come I frighten them.'

He started to unpack his bag. She stood watching for a second or two, then said 'Please: excuse,' and started to go to the door. For so large a girl she moved with remarkable silence and it was several minutes later that he looked up, thinking she had gone altogether, and saw her still standing at the open door.

Then, for the first but not the last time, he got a totally different impression of her. The hut had only one small window so that it was fairly dark inside, and in the strong outside light she stood partly framed in shadow. He could not see the details of her face. She stood with one arm brushing back her hair, looking back at him, one leg crooked in an attitude of being arrested in a turn.

For a moment you could forget then, he said, how ugly she was. You could see how superbly and splendidly she was built. She made on him for a moment the same impression as an inanimate object, something magnificently executed: a well-made boat, an idol, a piece of sculpture, even a mountain.

'If you want something,' she said, 'you must ask me. Or Timi, my brother. Or my mother. How long will you stay here now?' He hesitated, more than anything because he was fascinated by the way she stood there, to all appearances ugly no longer, and she said: 'Oh! well, you tell me later. Doesn't matter. You stay one week – one year – two years!' and then she turned on her heel and went away with a curious massive gracefulness, laughing with throaty splendour.

There was just one more incident that stuck in his mind that afternoon before darkness fell. After he had been swimming for a good hour or more he came out and sat on the landing stage, deliciously wet and refreshed after the first swim he had taken.

Evidently she had been watching for this moment from the house, because a second later she was coming down to the landing stage with a pitcher of orange juice and a glass on a tray.

'You swim long time,' she said. 'You must be thirsty now.'

She sat beside him on the landing stage and poured his drink. She sat with legs curled under her, watching him, pushing back her hair.

'You swim good,' she said. 'I swim every day too. Could you swim to the other side?'

He was still panting from exertion and was able, for a few seconds longer, only to shake his head.

'Sometimes I swim there and back,' she said.

'Oh! not me, not me,' he said. 'Too far. Out of practice.'

'Not so far.'

She laughed, enlarging her scar, and he sat drinking his orange juice, staring across the lagoon. Across the skin-smooth shadows, far off, a shoal of tiny fish burst from the water, as in the earlier afternoon, like fragments of silver. The crests of the mountains, far up, smouldered in sun. The deep far shadows under the thicket of the opposite shore grew greener and greener every moment, solid and glassy and finally untranslucent in the changing air.

He looked along the shore, tired but not too tired, blissfully and completely entranced by the tranquillity, the rapid embalmment of air and water and sky under approaching twilight and by everything he saw from the flaring tips of the mountains to the flick of a canoe paddle far down, seaward, towards the end of the lagoon.

Then he became aware, as he watched, of an unusual thing. In the afternoon, coming along by schooner, he had noticed the flowers of the tall grey-green hibiscus trees, those from the bark of which the so-called grass was made. Like soft pollen-dusty yellow cups they covered the boughs, the sand below the boughs and floated where they fell in water.

Now, to his surprise, the same flowers were red in colour. Both where they grew and where they fell they glowed in a shade of cinnamon, warm and deepening.

His surprise, when he spoke of it, made her laugh again.

'Every day they change,' she said. 'In the morning they begin one colour and as they die they become another colour. In the morning yellow. In the evening red. And then in the morning the new ones yellow again.'

And that, as he said to me, was how he felt about himself. Between morning and evening he had become a different person. It was unquestionable, he thought, that he had found there what he had come to see. And as he looked along the shore, where little fiery jungle cocks, quite tame, strutted scarlet and green about strips of well-watered grass, under palms and among crimson clumps of ginger-lily, he felt that everything was in perfect, ordered pattern, absolutely ordained and right from the changing colours of the hibiscus flowers to the crow of jungle cocks still giving to their hens among the tree-ferns fierce territorial warnings that hawks still hovered somewhere above the steely leaves of palm.

He was ready, he felt, to stay a million years. The pure absolute tranquillity had already started to hold him like a drug. He felt glad already of every breath of it. He was even glad of the big, overpowering, ugly girl who sat with him for nearly an hour longer, telling how she swam the lagoon, how she speared shrimps in fresh-water streams at night-time by shining a lamp into their eyes, and about the changing colours of hibiscus flowers: the soles of her big feet dark and horny like the feet of a bear.

4

He lived, for the next month, the happiest days of his life. The girl, the boy and her mother, a blousy, prematurely paunched woman who spent most of her time in the open kitchen-shed at the back of the house, looked after all his wants with tireless attention and yet left him free.

At the hotel he had eaten mainly European food, more French than anything in character, the sort of food he would have eaten anywhere, and he had liked it very well. Now he learned to eat, and also to like very much, mostly native food: dried raw fish, hot crabs, breadfruit, fried plantains, sweets of guava and coconut cream and curries of various kinds, including the delicate fresh-water shrimps found in the mountain streams. In a sort of dug-out at the back of the house stood a great barrel of *vin ordinaire* from which they drew him wine by the jug. He found it made him sweat a great deal but he drank it constantly.

Every day he swam, before and after breakfast, and then again in the afternoon and evening, half a dozen times between dawn and sunset. When he was tired of swimming he slept; when he was tired of sleeping he walked along the lagoon, either towards its land-locked end where a cluster of fifty or so dwellings lined the road, or seawards, where he could swim again or watch the Pacific hurling itself with its towering white horse waves against the reef, on one part of which, by the gap, the iron skeleton of a wreck stuck up as a mass of twisted junk, rust-orange through the glittering mist of ocean spray.

Occasionally he walked inland, climbing to the lower part of the foothills. In parts old plantations of guava trees had been felled to give more grazing for cattle; the grass was green and fertile. Great jungles of banana flapped overpoweringly above groves of orange and *pamplemousse*, the big pinkish grapefruit of which he never tired at breakfast. Narrow rapid streams watered pleasant little valleys of breadfruit, wild lime and avocado pear, and jungle cocks kept up their ceaseless crows of warning, invisible about the thickets, proud against hovering hawks.

Sometimes, this being the rainier season, it rained torrentially as he walked. He started by running for shelter. In a few days he was walking on through hot quick squalls, his shorts and shirt soaked, taking a bath as he walked. Sometimes, after these storms, he stripped out, hung his clothes on a rock in the sunshine, and swam naked while they dried.

Occasionally the girl came with him. Once as they walked together a sudden squall obliterated half the lagoon, flooding the sandy path under the palms to a depth of six inches. The faces, bodies and clothes of himself and the girl were sluiced as if under warm fire-hoses, so that when it was over she looked like some enormous water-animal that had just dragged itself, blubbering and dripping, from the sea. Then, her hair matted and drenched, the lines of her body more gross than ever under the soaked *pereu*, she looked even uglier than before.

There were two things, all this time, that he liked about her. He was fascinated, first, by her great strength; it impressed him enormously. And the other was, as he put it, that she didn't care a damn.

By that I thought he meant, at first, that she was very free, generous or in some way promiscuous. On the contrary, he said, the very opposite was true. She had a strange, proud, almost virginal sort of dignity.

What he meant, I gathered, was that she was a sort of tomboy. Perhaps, with her great strength, she would naturally have done nothing but heave boats about, swim the breadth of the lagoon, spear fish, roll barrels of *vin ordinaire* up from the schooner, and slog through the thickets with cordwood on her shoulders. His impression was also, since any girl looking into a mirror could hardly have failed to have grasped the ugliness of that kind of face, that she might have given up, as fairly hopeless, the idea that any man, drunk or sober, would find her attractive. Free of feminine obligations, as he saw it, she could behave before him with the physical ease, lack of embarrassment and sheer strength of another male.

She too swam a great deal. In the water, as in every other way, she was massive and powerful in all her movements. At the same time water gave her gracefulness. Wearing an ordinary two-piece swimming costume of black material she swam with superb and easy power, her long black hair trailing out like water-weeds.

One morning she challenged him to swim the breadth of the lagoon with her. He knew that his powers as a swimmer were really not up to this but she said:

'Swim slowly. You can do it. We can rest for an hour on the other side.'

To his surprise he made the opposite shore without much difficulty. He found that he was, in fact, in better physical condition than he had ever been. He felt taut, springy and in splendid shape all over. The wide Pacific air had given him an incredible feeling of buoyancy.

Then, as they swam back, he caught sight of a large indefinable underwater object rolling straight before him in the lagoon. Like a grey sloppy shadow, it made a huge rippling wave as it swam. He took one swift look at it, yelled, 'Sharks! My God, sharks!' and started to lash out in panic in the opposite direction.

He had no sooner turned than he heard her laughing. He turned back to see her waving a knife above her head.

'Ray! That's all!' she was shouting. 'A big ray. That's no harm. That won't hurt you.'

The giant ray, looking as he described it like some sort of indiarubber submarine, rolled ponderously off as he turned and swam back to her. The look of fright on his face must still have been remarkably vivid by the time he reached her because she burst out laughing a second time and said:

'Now you really look like a white man. Very white – *so* funny.'

He did not, he confessed, feel funny at all. He felt more than a little sick. His buoyancy had gone and his legs felt queer and shaky.

'You're not afraid, are you?' she shouted. She held up the knife above her head, cutting at the air with a slash. 'Shall I kill him? I can go after and kill him if you like. Shall I go?'

'Good God, no,' he said. 'Leave the damn thing and let's get out of here.'

'Funny! So funny,' she said.

Then as they swam back, he taking continually involuntary glances over his back to make sure the ray had gone, he said:

'I didn't know you carried a knife. I didn't notice that before.'

She turned in the water, swimming on her back.

'I keep it inside here,' she said. She tapped the folds of her costume about her enormous hips. 'I make a pocket inside.'

He knew that meant there must be sharks and he felt a little sick again.

'You never know,' she said. 'Shall I make a pocket for you? It's easy to sew one in.'

'So is sitting on dry land,' he said and at that she started laughing again.

It was his first and only swim across the breadth of the lagoon and he had to confess he hadn't liked it very much.

'At the same time, when I looked back on it,' he said, 'I got an odd comforting sort of feeling about it. There was nothing to account for it then, but I somehow got the feeling that if there had been trouble she'd have gone through hell to get me out of it.'

After that he kept his swimming to within short distances of the shore. When he wanted to cross the lagoon or change the monotony of swimming he took the outrigger canoe and paddled about instead.

Besides the little outrigger the family had a large craft that carried a single sail. Most of their fishing was done with long five-pronged spears, sometimes at night, by the light of torches of palm-frond, or communal fashion, whenever a shoal moved up the lagoon. Sometimes these shoals took several days, perhaps nearly a week, to move the full length from the reef-gap to the last upper finger of shore. Then the great communal net was thrown out, to be drawn gradually about the shoal, in the upper narrowing reach of water, until the fish could finally be pursed and drawn ashore.

On the last day and during the last hours of this netting every villager, except perhaps a few Chinese share-cropping vanilla up the valleys, came down to help with the great task of pulling in the net. Men, women and children sat on the sand beneath the palms, chattering excitedly until the final hour when every hand was needed for the pulling. After that the catch was distributed communal fashion, according to degrees of labour, and men who had handled the net for days would find themselves with so much fish to spare that they could make it up for market in long strings, sending it over by the next schooner to Papeete.

About a month after Rockley's arrival on the island a shoal of great size, moving very slowly, came up the lagoon. It took several days to travel the three and a half miles of water. It was often difficult, Thérèse said, to gauge the rate at which a shoal could travel, especially a large shoal. There would often be days of tedium, false alarm, rising excitement and much tension before the net could finally be closed.

Rockley had greatly looked forward to helping at one of these catches but the shoal was so slow that on the fifth day he found himself, at midday, rather bored with waiting.

'It's always the same,' the girl said. 'It may be this afternoon. May be tonight. We have to have patience. We can never tell.'

Then he asked her if she would be going to the net that afternoon.

'I must go to the net,' she said. 'It may happen suddenly. If I don't help with the net I get no fish.'

Some time later, after she had served his lunch, he watched her going away to join the boy and her mother at the net. As she walked down the path she turned, waved to him and said:

'You sleep. When it's time I'll send Timi with a message. Then you can come down and you will have fish too.'

'How many do you suppose they'll give me?'

'Oh! plenty. Plenty for strong men. You must pull hard. I'll show you how to pull.'

He slept for a couple of hours, woke suddenly and went down to the landing stage. Across the lagoon the boy was paddling shorewards in the outrigger. Rockley was sure the time had come for closing the net and that the boy had come to fetch him.

'Not yet,' the boy said. 'Long time yet. Perhaps tonight. Hours.'

Rockley sat down on the landing stage and watched the boy beach the outrigger. Then the boy climbed up on the landing stage too and they sat for a few minutes talking.

The afternoon, Rockley said, was very beautiful, with great clusters of sea-packed cloud on the mountains and a light of sheer purity, miraculously soft and limpid, across the glassy water. It was very hot and the fronds of the palms were so still in the heat that they looked as if scissored out of stiff green metal. The only sounds were the crowing of jungle fowl and, from so far off that they seemed strangely small and toy-like, the voices of villagers waiting at the net.

Suddenly he realized that for the first time, in the middle of this exquisite stillness, he was really bored. He had had his fill of swimming; he was tired of waiting for the shoal.

'I felt,' he said, 'as if I'd like a damn good talk to somebody. You know, a good yarn. In fact, to be honest, I was a bit lonely. I suddenly felt a hell of a long way from anywhere.'

Then he made, he said, the first of three serious mistakes. It was a very simple thing and at the time it seemed quite impossible that it could have, as casual things sometimes do, significant consequences.

Without thinking, he asked the boy if he would take him down the lagoon for an hour, in the outrigger, as far as the gap. The boy hesitated. He even looked, Rockley realized afterwards, a little uneasy, almost scared. Then he made various excuses, including the main one that the shoal might be landed at any moment, and Rockley said:

'Oh! Just half an hour then. After that I'll come back with you to the net.'

Distances by water are always deceptive and he had never really had to calculate how long it would take to paddle to the seaward end of the lagoon. It took, in fact, an hour; and then not quite an hour, because of a strong incoming drift, to paddle back again.

It was all so pleasant, unspectacular and dreamy between the walls of palm and the higher jungle thickets that he did not realize that the flowers of the big hibiscus were already turning from yellow to red by the time he and the boy were again opposite the landing stage.

Then he saw the boy suddenly lift his head, brown eyes sharp and startled. From the upper end of the lagoon there was a deep murmur of voices. The boy started paddling furiously, quite agitated now, and Rockley knew that the final netting had begun.

By the time they reached the net, ten minutes later, the water at the end of the lagoon was like a white living cauldron of struggling fish. The boy was so quick to beach the outrigger and run along the shore that he actually tripped, fell and then rushed on, wiping his sandy hands on his bare thighs, quickly spitting on them afterwards.

Perhaps seventy or eighty people, Rockley said, were pulling at the net, and presently he found the boy, the mother and the girl among them. With her colossal mahogany legs locked in the coral sand the girl was not only pulling with all her enormous strength but with a remarkable expression on her face. Her dark eyes were large and blazing, with a peculiar fanatical light in them.

As he took up his place beside her, taking hold of the net, he had no idea that this in fact was anger.

'You said you would show me how to pull!' he said.

She did not speak. She neither turned nor looked at him. She simply stared at the net, the water and the leaping fish and lugged with all her astonishing strength at the net, her expression never altering.

He supposed, he said, that he must have spoken to her a dozen times or more that afternoon as they pulled together at the net, but each time she gave him no hint of a word or look in answer. It was pretty hot and strenuous work and he was glad when it was over. By that time darkness was falling and there were still some hours of work to do with the sorting, sharing and stringing of the fish. He knew that the stringing would in fact go on all night, so that the strings of fish would be ready for the incoming schooner on the following day.

Soon after half past six he started to walk back to the rest-house alone. As he was leaving the net he passed the girl, stopped for a moment and said:

'I am going back to the house. Will you be coming back?'

Again she made no answer.

'No need to come back for me,' he said. 'I can find a little fruit and eat that. Fruit and a little wine – that's enough for me.'

She had not even paused to listen and now by the time he had finished speaking she was already some yards away, striding strongly out of reach of him.

He went back to the rest-house, sat on the little veranda, too tired even to wash, and then drew himself a pitcher of wine. Then he sat on the veranda again, watched the stars in the lagoon and above the fantastic graph-like ridges of the opposite mountains and also the flares burning in a great cluster at the end of the lagoon.

Normally the wine, the evening, the stars and the mysterious waving half-drowned lights of the flares would have soothed him deeply. That evening, instead, he felt bothered – not worried, as he was careful to explain, but bothered – bothered, mystified and slightly irritated. He couldn't think what on earth he had done. The incident of the boy and himself going down the lagoon never occurred to him as the remotest possible cause of anger in anyone. He couldn't explain it at all.

Then, much later that night, he thought he caught a glimpse of what the causes might be. He woke about midnight to the sound of quarrelling. In the house the girl was reviling someone, with great fury, in words he didn't understand. He heard the boy's voice in answer. He got out of bed, went to the door of his room and listened. He thought he heard the sound of beating. After that he went back to bed, listened for a time and thought he heard an even odder sound – that of somebody weeping. But whether it was the boy or his sister crying somewhere outside in the darkness he never knew.

'Before I came down here I read somewhere,' he said, 'that these people were light-hearted, frivolous, courteous, generous but deceitful and cruel.'

He paused and before going on he gave one of those odd smiles of his.

'But that night,' he said, 'I started to find out they could be something else besides.'

5

Next morning, he said, it was impossible to recognize, or even believe in the existence of, the girl of the evening before. If the flowers of the hibiscus trees had been purple that morning instead of yellow the change could not, he said, have surprised him more.

She was smiling broadly as she brought him his breakfast of *pamplemousse*, coffee, fresh-baked Chinese bread and butter, boiled eggs and a basket of oranges, papayas, limes and avocado pears. She actually prepared the *pamplemousse* in front of him. Then she poured his coffee. Then while he was eating the *pamplemousse* she cut a large papaya in half and began to prepare it too, knowing he liked to finish his meal with that. In the bright orange cradles of flesh the black-grey papaya seeds glistened like fat beads of caviare.

All day she remained smiling, attentive, rather talkative and extremely sweet to him. There was no mention either of the incident at the net or of the boy. In the late morning she rolled up the skirt of her *pereu* above her knees, stood in a shallow part of the lagoon and washed her hair. Fresh-fallen hibiscus flowers floated on the water and under and about the landing stage small fish of brilliant blue, with stripes of bright ochre, swam tamely in and out of the sunshine.

One of the pleasantest things about life there, he said, was to watch the Polynesian girls wash their hair. Its great length, its strong blue blackness and the way it glistened as it dried quickly in the sun were all beautiful things to see.

'I watched her half the morning,' he said. 'And she chattered as if she hadn't seen me for years.'

Soon it occurred to him that she was spending more time than usual on her hair, combing it and recombing it, shaking it out and spreading it over her shoulders to dry. At last he spoke about this, teasing her very slightly, and she said:

'Tomorrow night there will be dancing. Had you forgotten?'

Occasionally on Saturday nights young men and girls came up from the village, sometimes bringing a drum, a banjo and a guitar. There would be a good deal of wine-drinking, singing of songs, dancing, noisy frivolity and provocative laughter. A lot of flirting went on and the girls swung taut rubbery hips, their tight skin golden in the lamplight, and curled their fingers in subtle invitation, making the men excited. Most of them wore lipstick, generally of much the same carmine shade as the big hibiscus flowers in their hair.

The following night she too wore lipstick. It was, he said, the first time he had ever seen her wear it and it made a difference to her face that was sharp, uneasy and startling. He was not sure, at first, that it did not make her uglier than ever. The big mouth became more than ever like a scar. But the chief difference, he said, was that it gave her a sort of defiance, a certain touch of savagery that made her look out of place among the smaller, prettier girls.

That evening he danced with her several times and once or twice the banjo played European or American tunes. He drank a fair amount of wine, thought the stars of the southern hemisphere had never looked so huge, soft and flower-like above the lagoon and in general enjoyed himself greatly. She too seemed very happy. The most remarkable thing about her, he said, the thing that never failed to surprise him each time he held her in his arms for the dances, was the lightness of her enormous body. It was quite unbelievably perfect, he said, in its sheer balance and poise.

About midnight he walked outside to light a cigarette, relax a bit and get a breath of air. An exquisite little wind, heavy with warmth and tree perfume, blew for a moment or two across the lagoon, died suddenly and then sprang up again, stirring the fronds of the palms. He stood for a time under a palm tree and watched the stars.

He had drunk, he thought, quite enough wine, though not too much to prevent his remembering, after a few minutes, that he had been told not to stand, sit or lie under palms. Coconuts falling from a great height are projectiles of considerable nuisance and he laughed to himself as he remembered it and moved away.

Then the wind sprang up again across the lagoon, giving quite a gusty shudder in the fronds of palm, almost as if a storm were blowing up. He heard it stir the water, creating a sudden short rush of waves that lapped against the outrigger and rattled the boat chain.

A moment later he saw her come out of the house and down to the landing stage. The fact that she went straight to the boats made him think that possibly she too had heard the stir of wind and had come down, as she sometimes did at night, to see that the canoes were safely moored.

She stood for some minutes on the landing stage. In the rest-house the banjo and the drum were thumping with low regular rhythm, softly, and a long bar of light came from the open walls and across to the landing stage.

She stood just beyond the edge of this light, hands on her hips, looking at the water, and for some time he stood some distance away, uncertain whether to speak or not, watching her.

'Then I made another mistake,' he said. 'Another damn *faux pas*.'

It was four or five days after our first meeting that he got as far as telling me this and up to that time I hadn't attributed to him any great sense of humour at all, but now across his face there went, I thought, the flicker of a grin. A moment later I realized it wasn't a grin. It was a deadly stab of pain.

He walked over to where she was standing on the landing stage. As she heard him coming she turned, moved a step or two and lifted her head. The light from the rest-house was shining behind her now and suddenly he saw her like a big muscular idol, all black except for pure edges of light glimmering along the massive curves of her shoulders, her thick upper arms and the fringes of her hair.

She looked exceptionally dark, powerful and magnificent. The individual features of her face were lost in shadow. All he could see was a great carved head, sharply poised, well up, with its flowing mass of hair. Then she moved again, her eyes glinted quickly in the house lights and he saw her shake back, with a splendid roll of her neck, one side of her hair, showing suddenly the bright yellow saucers of flower above her ear. He saw the sumptuous heave of her breasts and then suddenly, more than a little drunk, he forgot for the first time how ugly she was.

A moment later he was kissing her. Or rather, after the first impact of his lips, she was kissing him. As with everything else she did it was powerful and massive. It was an affair of overwhelming physical splendour. She gripped him with great strength, locking him against her passionately, and in a queer melancholy fashion repeating his name.

6

He realized, next morning, what a stupid mistake he had made. He only hoped she would forget it as soon as he wanted to do.

'The confounded trouble was,' he said, 'that I couldn't forget it. I'd really got quite fond of her – not in love or anything like that, but just fond, in exactly the same way as you get fond of a great big ugly dog. Except for her face there was nothing you couldn't admire and like about her. She was very, very likeable.'

And not only, as he explained, the girl. All of them were very likeable. The mother was eternally pleasant, smiling and soft-eyed. The boy was quick, good-looking, light in frame and sur-

prisingly energetic. He was always fishing, making or mending
the long elliptical baskets of bamboo for keeping fish alive and
fresh under water, doing jobs on the boat or the outrigger.
Occasionally Rockley helped him with these things.

After the incident of kissing the girl he began to welcome
more and more the chance of slipping away to swim or fish with
the boy. He welcomed a chance of mere companionship. That
was one of the ways in which he hoped the girl would see that the
affair of the kiss and what followed it was merely an episode
he didn't want repeated. He was desperately anxious not to
become involved in anything deeper.

'It had just the opposite effect,' he said.

Whatever he did with the boy aroused her to terrible silences:
moods that lasted, sometimes, the greater part of a day. Two
or three times the boy and himself took the outrigger as far as
the seaward end of the lagoon but on the third of these trips she
was so inexplicably sullen, black and mute against him that he
was determined never to make one again.

Another day he and the boy walked up the mountainside, a
distance of four or five miles, to where, on the edge of the thicket,
eight or ten men were felling a tree for a dug-out canoe. He had
very much wanted to see how these canoes were made and he
spent a very pleasant day. After the tree had been felled and
trimmed the men began the preliminary work of hollowing out
the trunk with axes. After they had roughly shaped it, lightening
it a good deal in the process, they would steer it, on rollers, down
the mountainside. The whole business would take a week, perhaps ten days, according to the size of the tree.

It was very pleasant there in the brisker upper air of the
mountainside, sitting under the shade of a big breadfruit tree,
watching the men, quenching his thirst by sucking sweet oranges
gathered from neighbouring trees and listening to the sound of a
stream running down somewhere under a jungle of glinting
elephantine banana leaves. Then as he watched the fresh golden
bodies of the men sweating while they worked on the tree he
remembered how he had once read, probably as a boy, how the
North American had shaped his canoe by filling the hollow with
water, throwing red hot rocks in it and thus giving it curvature.

It was all so interesting that he was glad he had taken his camera with him. It was the kind with the view-finder at the top. He took about a dozen pictures, first of the men working on the hibiscus trunk, then of various groups of them standing on or about the tree, then one or two of the boy, either alone or with the men.

Finally he decided he would like a couple of pictures of himself with the men. He had never let the boy use the camera before but the view-finder was so simple that it took less than a minute to show him how it was used. The boy was not merely delighted about this; he was innocently, worshipfully overjoyed. He fairly danced with the camera, Rockley said, so much so that finally Rockley had to leave the group and demonstrate how the boy must press the camera against his chest in order to prevent it shaking. He found then that the boy's hands were actually quivering, almost shuddering, with excitement.

There was a great deal of jollying, golden-bellied laughter about this and the boy responded by behaving, in a charming way, as if he were a person of singular privilege, almost a hero.

'It did your heart good to see him,' Rockley said.

Later in the afternoon, as he and the boy came down the mountainside, a single cloud on the upper crest of mountain enlarged itself, descended suddenly and broke in a storm. They ran for shelter in a shack owned by a toothless Chinaman who share-cropped vanilla farther up the hill. The rain, warm, steamy and torrential, beat into the great leaves of surrounding forest like a sluice while thunder walked up and down the dark precipitate valleys between strange fires of sun and lightning.

In the middle of all this the Chinaman hobbled out, bandy-legged, into lakes of rain, coming back some minutes later with half a dozen oranges and a spray of vanilla orchid and two vanilla beans. Rockley sat under the wide eaves of the shack and sucked oranges and watched the Chinaman explain, with neither French nor English but only little gestures of a pair of yellow dirty hands and a matchstick, how the cream lips of the little delicate self-sterile ghost-orchid had to be fertilized.

Presently the rain stopped as suddenly as it had begun and there was more laughter, very high-pitched and tinny, from the little Chinaman, as Rockley allowed the boy to take another picture of himself and the Chinaman standing by the door of the shack. All about them the forest sparkled and dripped with water. On Rockley's hands was a strange combined fragrance of oranges and vanilla, at once fresh and exotic, and he felt it had been an enchanted, exhilarating day.

'But that was only half what the boy felt,' he said. 'He was still so excited when we left the Chinaman that I hadn't the heart to take the camera away from him. I let him keep it slung round his neck and he went down the rest of the mountainside like a king.'

Then, as the two of them reached the rest-house, the boy started to run forward. He was twenty yards or so from the house when Thérèse came out of it. As soon as she saw him she stopped. He was still very excited, waving his hands about, making demonstrations with the camera and calling her name.

Then, four or five yards away from her, the boy stopped too. He flicked open the view-finder of the camera and started to look into it, laughing, as if about to take her picture.

'The next thing I knew,' Rockley said, 'was that she had snatched the camera from his neck and was swinging it wildly round her head, like a prehistoric sling or something, as if she was going to bash his brains out.'

The boy ducked in terror, put his hands up to his head to protect himself and then ran to the house. She took a dozen or fifteen furious bare-footed strides after him, screeching madly and still swinging the camera about her head.

It wasn't until the boy disappeared into the house that she seemed to come to her senses. Then her arms suddenly dropped. She stared in a stupefied sort of way at the camera, as if not sure now whether it was a camera or a sling-bag or something else and then came slowly back to Rockley.

'She just stood there, gave me the camera and stared,' Rockley said. 'No recognition in the stare. No contrition. No apology. Nothing like that. Just a long, empty, sightless stare.'

This episode perturbed him so much that he could not sleep that night. After some hours he got up, put on a pair of straw slippers and walked down to the landing stage. He started to smoke a cigarette and think things over. In the pure dark sky the stars seemed more brilliant, more beautiful and more voluminous than ever. He stared at them and their reflection across the lagoon for a long time and then, in spite of them and the pleasure everything about the place had given him, he came to a decision.

'I decided,' he said, 'to get out. The schooner would be arriving in a couple of days. I could catch it and go back to Papeete.'

There wasn't, he said, much reasoning about the decision. He still had several weeks of his leave to go. He disliked Papeete. The trouble was that he had begun to be much more than disturbed. He did not know why, but for some reason he had a queer, fatalistic feeling of impending disaster.

He had already started to walk back to the house when he saw her coming down the stone steps to the landing stage. She suddenly halted half-way up them. This time there was no light from the house behind her. She was simply a shape of vague patterns, her *pereu* hastily wrapped round her, under the brilliant stars.

He was determined that, this time, there should be no nonsense: no more kissing. He was perfectly sober this time, with no fancy illusions about anything, and he walked straight past her, not stopping or turning until he reached the top of the steps.

Then he spoke to her. 'Thérèse,' he said.

She neither turned nor spoke to him.

'Thérèse,' he said, 'I'm going away. By the next schooner.'

There was no sort of movement from her. She was simply an enormous shape carved out of the darkness.

'Good night,' he said. He had already turned on his heel and was walking away. 'I'll be going the day after tomorrow.'

'The schooner doesn't come until the day after that,' she said.

'All right. Good enough,' he said. 'The day after that.'

He walked on. She didn't speak again. He went on and into the house with a feeling of relief mingled with sudden wretched twinges of regret. There was absolutely no reasoning in his going; he did not want to go. But he was convinced, absolutely certain now, that it was the thing he must do.

But before the schooner arrived, three days later, something else happened. He made, he said, the third of his stupid mistakes about her.

7

He was determined to leave in the friendliest possible fashion. He even started to plan little gifts for everybody and for the first of the three days he behaved with polite neutrality. He began by avoiding the boy. He deliberately swam, fished, walked and idled about the place alone. Whenever the boy approached him he made an excuse about a book, a towel, a letter or something and went away.

The immediate result was, as he said, that she couldn't have been sweeter. She was her old friendly, laughing, almost frivolous self again. She prepared his fruit at table, made jokes as she watched him eat and threw back her head in gusts of superb sumptuous laughter.

It was only when the boy came into sight that her attitude and her expression changed. Then she seemed to go blank before him. A sort of blight came over her. Every vestige of light and friendliness was suddenly extinguished. He began to understand then what was the matter with her. For the first time, fully, he realized how jealous she was.

'That was the Polynesian virtue the guide-books had left out,' he said. 'So jealous she couldn't bear to share me with the kid, her own brother. So possessive that she was frantic about a boy, another male.'

The second day, having put his finger on the cause of everything, he decided to keep himself more to himself than ever. As a result, after breakfast, he walked the entire distance to the point at the end of the lagoon. A white sandy track wound pleasantly under high palms past occasional abandoned gardens of half-wild gardenias, croton and tiare trees. A few wooden shacks, some empty, some with a few cockerels crowing about them, were dotted about the thickets. From far off came the inexhaustible thunder of the reef and then, at the very tip of the land, in from the open ocean, the great blown cloud of spume, white and glittering and sometimes rainbow-shot, in the brilliant air.

He was half-way back from the point when a voice hailed him unexpectedly from one of the houses in the thickets on the shoreward side of the track. He turned, stopped and saw a girl waving her hand.

'Hullo there,' she said in English. 'Good morning.' She was walking across the garden towards the thin cane fence that flanked the track. 'I thought it was you.'

He said good morning, staring blankly and did not know what to do.

'You're staying at the rest-house, aren't you?' she said. 'Don't you remember me?'

He said he was sorry: he didn't remember.

'I saw you quite a few times at the New Pacific Hotel,' she said. 'Dancing. Over at Papeete.'

'Oh! yes,' he said.

'I really come from here,' she said. 'I go over for a few weeks sometimes.'

She smiled: uncommonly small, pale and compact, with a delicate upward cast in her eyes that he afterwards knew came from the mingling of Polynesian blood and Chinese. She moved with grace. Her voice was soft and rather high. To look at her after looking at Thérèse was, he said, like looking at a little yellow parakeet after a buzzard, or at one of the little angel-finned blue-and-ochre fish after the giant sloppy ray that had scared him in the lagoon.

'Like it here?' she said. 'I saw you go past once before, but you were with Timi that time and I didn't like to call.'

'I like it very much.'

'How long do you think you'll stay?'

'As a matter of fact,' he said, 'I'm off tomorrow. Catching the schooner.'

'If you like it so much why are you off tomorrow?'

It was altogether too complicated to explain and he said he didn't know.

'Catching the next plane?'

'No,' he said. 'The one after.'

'You look hot,' she said. 'Wouldn't you like to sit down on the veranda a minute and I'll get you something to drink? Some lime or orange – whichever you prefer.'

A few moments later he was sitting down on the veranda of

the little house. Going in and out of the house, getting his drink of orange, she moved with pert grace, not wearing the ordinary *pereu* but a simple waistless dress of yellow with several circles of emerald at the edge of the skirt, her dark hair plaited.

'Pretty as hell,' he said. 'But then, no point in describing her. You've seen her already. That was her outside the barber's shop, that time you first met me.'

He stayed for another hour. She lived with a mother, three elder sisters and an aunt, but that morning they were up at the plantations of vanilla, some way in the hills, fertilizing flowers. It was a job, she explained, for which the big Polynesian girls were far too clumsy but which the delicate fingers of Chinese or part-Chinese did rapidly, skilfully and with perfection.

He could not help being fascinated by her own thin delicate hands as she sat there telling him these things.

'Don't you work in the plantations too?' he asked her.

'Not often,' she said. 'I look after the house mostly and do the cooking. I have a little trouble with my heart sometimes. Nothing much, but the hills are too far for me.'

She put her left hand on her chest, just above her heart, and held it there. She was wearing in her hair not the big customary hibiscus flower but a little cluster of *tiare*, not more than six or seven blooms of small wax-white stars. Her breasts were sharp and upstanding, her arms were almost pure ivory, the nails shapely on the fragile little fingers, and he could smell the fragrance of *tiare* in the air.

The following day the schooner sailed without him.

8

Thérèse was delighted by his sudden change of plans. During the next few days, as she sat about the place at the various tasks of grating coconut, crushing herbs, preparing breadfruit, topping and tailing shrimps, washing and drying her hair, he knew that she was very happy. He heard her singing a good deal. He would not have been surprised if her voice had emerged as a baritone but it was in fact a rather thin soprano, high and pure.

The songs she sang were repetitive, a little melancholy and mostly fairly slow and dreamy, like lullabies. A few weeks before he would have asked about these songs and perhaps have got her to tell him the meaning of the words; but now he was wary of doing anything, even in the most casual way, that she might interpret as affection.

For this reason he made a series of excuses for getting out of various things she wanted him to do. He had, for instance, asked several times about fresh-water shrimps and how she caught them at night, in the little streams, by the light of flares. For some time he had wanted to go on one of these shrimping expeditions but now he made excuses of some sort whenever she mentioned it.

Soon she began to grow more and more persistent about this. In fact, as he said, she started pestering.

'Why don't you come with me? You say you want to come. All the time you say you want to come with me and now you don't come. Why won't you come?'

He would make some excuse about being too tired at night or the wine making him sleepy; or he would change the subject completely.

'I'd rather go fishing for tuna,' he would say. 'Out in the open ocean. They fight so much better than shrimps do.'

This, though it made her laugh, did nothing to stop her persistence.

'We can do both,' she said. 'Tonight we can catch the shrimps. Tomorrow we can take the boat and catch tuna.'

He wanted, in fact, to do neither. What he chiefly wanted to do now, and he found it more attractive every day, was to walk along the lagoon to the house among the thickets and play, as he put it, with the little parakeet there. The little parakeet was, it seemed, amusing in many ways. Her heart, not quite strong enough to stand work in the vanilla plantations or the gradients up into the forests, exercised itself freely in other directions. On hot still afternoons he lay for hours on the beach with her or on a cool truckle bed inside. Parakeets, as he explained, are extremely affectionate creatures. They are also very teachable and quick to learn. And sometimes darkness was already falling when he walked back to the rest-house along the lagoon.

Then, when he got back, Thérèse would say:

'You walk a long time, don't you? How far do you walk every day?'

'I like to look at the wreck,' he would say, 'and wonder how it got there. I like to watch for tuna. I thought I saw tuna leaping yesterday.'

All this time he was afraid she would be suspicious. To his relief and surprise she was not suspicious: not, at any rate, at first. She seemed absolutely content, perfectly happy, simply to have him there. It was enough, it seemed, that he hadn't gone away.

Then, after about a week, she said:

'Don't you get tired of watching the wreck? Soon I shall begin to think you go there to look at something else besides.'

'Such as what?' he said. 'It's beautiful. I like looking at the ocean. I saw a little plane yesterday.'

'Such as the little Chinese girls in the house along there,' she said. 'They're very beautiful too, the little Chinese girls.'

For the moment it was on the tip of his tongue to say that the house was always empty when he passed it, but he saved himself in time.

Even then there was no sign of her suspicion. There was not the faintest hint of jealously. At the same time he felt disturbed. Women, as he remarked, are not compared with cats for nothing. They have infinite capacities for awaiting their time to strike. Gossip, moreover, is the fastest traveller in the world.

He decided, as a result, to go with her on the night-shrimping. That, he thought, would be the clever thing. That would appease her.

They set off the following evening at nine o'clock. The nights were always infinitely beautiful, full of a humid and fragrant softness, under enormous stars. But that night, under dense thickets of hibiscus and breadfruit that overhung the bed of the little stream, the boughs touching overhead in the narrow valley, most of the stars were hidden. He had always thought of the sky, especially that brilliant southern sky, as a companionable place, and that night, under the thick forest leaves, he missed its brightness. As a result he got an increasing sense of uneasiness. There was something uncanny about it all.

Most of the time she walked in her bare feet on the stones of the stream. In her left hand she carried a torch, an ordinary electric battery one, and in her right a thin two-pronged spear. Soon he was watching her shine the torch into little beds of shrimp eyes: the eyes, he thought, like imploring guileless little beads, full of wide and dark surprise, as they looked up to their death-blow.

For about an hour he and the girl walked up the narrow valley. During this time he carried the basket and sometimes he could hear the faintest rustle, a mere papery whisper, as the still-alive shrimps stirred among each other in the darkness.

Finally they came out into a break in the thickets. It was a grassy place, with a number of rocks strewn about it, and he sat down on one of the rocks, putting the basket at his side.

A moment later, in a sudden turn, she shone the torch into his face. 'Oh! accidentally, of course,' he said, 'but for a moment I was half blinded and I couldn't see. You know how it is – your eyes feel stabbed and they start throbbing up and down.'

Then, as his eyes cleared, he saw her standing above him. Whether it was quite accidental again he never quite knew, but he could have sworn the spear was poised. She stood there exactly as if preparing to strike him, just as she struck the shrimps, between his dazzled eyes.

He supposed it must have been accidental, a mere slip of her hand, because a second later she put out the torch and dropped the spear on the ground. She was kneeling in front of him, grasping his hands.

'Please,' she started saying. 'Please, Rock, don't go away. Please.' Her voice had a desperate unnerving break in it. 'You won't go, will you? When you said you would go I thought I would go mad. Quite mad. I couldn't speak about it before, but don't go, Rock, will you? Please don't go.'

As she spoke she drew herself up on her knees, until her face was level with his. Her voice was so uncertain that he actually thought she was sobbing. Even in the brilliance of starlight he was not sure whether her enormous eyes were dry or not. He only remembered with a sudden stab of panic, the night when he had kissed her and had forgotten for a moment how ugly she was.

'Thérèse,' he started saying. 'Look –'

'You could like here. I can build a house. I will build a house and live like your *vahine*. It cost nothing. I'll be your *vahine* and work for you. I'll work for you and you can love me –'

He listened, amazed and at first absolutely speechless. Embarrassed too, he actually managed to stand up without seeming to push her away. A moment later she stood up too, suddenly pressing her body against him, her great arms seizing and holding him in a vice.

'Listen to me,' he started saying again. 'Listen –'

Before he could go on she started kissing him. There was no escaping the big scarred mouth and she was so violent he could not resist her.

'I might just as well have resisted a buffalo,' he said. 'And I believe she might have killed me if I had.'

He admitted, in fact, an extraordinary thing. He was afraid of her, he said, really quite afraid. He feared her physically.

Then, a moment or so later, a curious change came over her. She seemed to go suddenly limp. She let her hands fall loosely at her sides and she sat down on one of the rocks, quietly.

This quietness of hers was so sudden and so complete that it unnerved him as much as her violence had done. She sat staring heavily into the darkness and for about five minutes he stood there watching her. All he could hear was the noise of the stream falling away over its stones among the thickets and the small whisper of shrimps as they rustled in the basket.

Then she started speaking.

'Rock –'

That was as far as she got. Her voice was constricted. The one word was almost a cough.

Then after several more minutes she tried speaking again. By this time her hair had partly fallen over her face and she did not brush it away.

'Rock,' she said, 'I –'

For the second time she couldn't go on. She put her hands on her knees, gripping them, and her hair fell still further forward over her face, almost hiding it completely.

'What were you going to say?' he said.

She gave a great sigh, more like a sudden gasp for breath, and then violently locked her hands together.

'Nothing,' she said. 'Nothing, I –'

'What was it?' he said.

'Nothing,' she said. 'I was thinking –'

She suddenly leapt to her feet, stumbled forward and started clumsily to walk down the mountainside.

'What were you thinking?' he said. He picked up the basket and started after her. 'What was it?'

She didn't answer. It was some moments before he caught up with her, crashing heavily down the mountain path.

'Thérèse,' he said. 'What was it? What were you thinking?'

She crashed on through the thickets, making no attempt to stop or look at him. She blundered forward like an animal that had lost its way. But what really disturbed him was not that, he said. What affected him so much was the enormous and helpless sorrow in her voice when she spoke again.

'Thank God,' she said, 'my thoughts are my own.'

9

He had already made, by that time, the third of his mistakes. He determined not to make another.

'I got the thing taped up,' he said. 'I found you could pick up the schooner at a village on the other side of the island. In fact on schooner days and on Saturdays there was a bus that would take you there. The bus actually came by the rest-house, used the track along the lagoon and went round the island by way of the point.'

Two or three days before the schooner was due he started to get a few of his things together. He would pack them up a few at a time and then, when the girl was down by the landing stage, gutting fish or getting water or washing her hair, walk along the track to the house in the thicket and leave them there. Fortunately he had only one bag and after two or three journeys most of his things were with the parakeet, under the truckle bed.

'I know it probably sounds pretty ungrateful and all that. I wanted to do the decent thing but I could see trouble everywhere,' he said, 'if I didn't get out. Besides, what do you say? If you're going to live with one of these girls you might as well pick a good looking one. A parakeet. Not that I wanted to. One way and another I felt I'd had about enough and a bit over.'

As he said this he gave me another of those dispirited, rather twisted smiles of his.

'And I was just about as wrong about *that*,' he said, 'as I could be.'

Then, on the morning of the day before the schooner was due to arrive, he began to have something approaching misgivings. He felt very sad. He had not only loved it all. It was, as he was never tired of saying, the most beautiful place on earth. The lagoon alone, sheltered and guarded by these fantastic palm-fledged mountains behind which every evening the sunset opened up like a blast furnace, flaring with every colour of flame, was paradise itself.

'They say that the original Garden of Eden was here somewhere in these islands,' he said, 'and my guess is this was it.'

All this, together with his thoughts of how nice the people had been, how tranquil and serenely restful it all was, were enough to explain his sadness.

'I could have wept,' he said. 'In fact I was so damned miserable that when she suggested, that morning, having a trip for a few hours to look for tuna I jumped at it like a shot.'

Then, at the last moment, when the boat was ready, he remembered being alone with her twice before, once on the landing stage and once on the mountain, and he didn't fancy it a third time.

'Let the boy come, won't you?' he said. 'He loves the boat. He handles it well too. Go on – let the boy come.'

The boy was standing on the landing stage, watching his sister and Rockley prepare the boat. He gave an eager glance at her as Rockley spoke. For a moment she hesitated. Then she

309

gave one of those strong sudden twists of her neck, threw her long hair back from her shoulder and said an odd thing.

'If he likes to take the risk,' she said.

At once the boy clambered down into the boat and in five minutes they were sailing seawards down the lagoon on a light warm breeze. Rockley steered, the boy handled the sail and Thérèse squatted in the bows, busying herself with lines and the long white-feathered spinners they were going to use for lures. Rockley noticed that she didn't speak much, though once, when they were almost level with the house where the parakeet lived, she turned full round, faced him and said:

'Wouldn't you rather be walking instead?'

He didn't pay much attention at the time. No one was moving outside the house. He couldn't help wondering what might have happened if the parakeet had suddenly come out, recognized him and waved her hand but nothing happened and the boat sailed tranquilly past the house and the thicket of breadfruit and hibiscus with their pretty scatterings of fallen flowers.

After a time he became more and more aware of the growing thunder of the reef. At the mouth of the lagoon, still a mile or more from the gap, it was already like the battering surge of an enormous waterfall. He was surprised, even at that distance, by the height of the breaking spray and the strength of the tow pouring in through the gap. Beyond it the Pacific looked calm enough, a brilliant slaty blue without so much as a single white crest across it, but he was to discover only a few minutes later that it was really corrugated by deep, long and powerful swells.

Meanwhile the boy took in the sail and Thérèse started to steer, calling to Rockley at the same time to take a paddle. For another twenty minutes he and the boy paddled towards and finally through the gap. It was hard going and once or twice they seemed, he thought, to be making no headway at all against the power of the tow. On both sides the reef rose like rough brown jaws, the coral clear of water, the rust on the wreck glinting scabbily with the colour of old dried blood, in the iridescent sunshine.

By now he was paddling so hard that he had no time even to brush the sweat from his face. He simply let it pour down over his eyes and lips and into his open mouth, the rivulets of it gathering on his neck and chest and pouring down his body. Then his legs began to feel soggy. He was sucking his breath in short desperate gasps. Then he felt the boat give a sudden twist, almost a whip to starboard, and he saw the boy ease his rate of paddling.

Less than a minute later the sail was up again and they were well clear of the reef, out in the open sea.

After the exertion of paddling he felt considerably exhausted: so much so that for a time he paid very little attention to either the girl, who was steering now, or her brother, who once again was handling the sail. He thought he heard her occasionally giving directions to the boy about a change in course but now she spoke in Tahitian and he was not quite sure. He actually shut his eyes for a moment or two. Then he was sharply woken out of himself by a sudden brittleness in her voice, a hard rasping shout, and he opened his eyes to see her hauling on the thick stumpy rod from the bows, her enormous forearms locked stiff with the pull of the line.

A few moments later the first tuna was thrashing about in the well of the boat. It wasn't very large and the girl, as if angry or disappointed about its size, suddenly picked up a short stump of wood and started clubbing it to death. She hit it so severely that it actually gave a shocked sort of leap a foot or two in the air and blood spurted everywhere, spattering her bare feet and shins and over her forearms and hair.

Then she whipped out a knife. It was the same knife she had brandished above the giant ray in the lagoon. It was short, thick and slightly curved.

She bent, a moment later, over the dying fish. She lifted the knife quickly as if she were going to plunge it into the short, iron-smooth body. The boy was at the sail, his back turned.

Rockley waited for the downward cut of the knife. Instead he saw her stand up to her full height. She stood there for a second or two before he realized that her face suddenly looked uglier than ever. He didn't quite grasp it at first. It was evil and dark and the lip was grossly twisted.

Then she gave a grotesque short yell.

'You go to that house!' she yelled. 'You go to that girl. You're going away with her. I saw you take your things. You go to that house, don't you?'

She made a powerful lunge at his face with the knife. He instinctively put up a hand to protect himself and he felt the knife run in a hot sharp line down his outer forearm. He staggered for a moment and the boat started rocking. He was aware of her making a second lunge. She looked queerly unkempt and wild now, her face frighteningly ugly, her black hair sweeping about her hips and blood spattering her legs and arms, and she started yelling again, the words incoherent this time.

The boy too stood up, relinquishing his hold on the sail. He shouted something too, at the same time trying to grab at her arm. She moved so quickly, stabbing air, that he missed her completely, overbalanced and himself made a grab at air.

A moment later the spar, swinging round, struck the boy full across the mouth. He fell like a boxer, backwards, eyes wide and cast upward, stunned before hitting the water.

10

In a flash the girl stooped, picked up the bloody slithering fish in her arms and hurled it over the stern. A moment later she was swimming.

The boy had already disappeared. And for the space of what seemed to be several minutes, though it could not have been more than a moment or two after she dived, Rockley was alone on the sea.

In the confusion he had fallen on his knees. Now he tried for several seconds to get up again.

His arm was drenched in blood. He tried to clutch the side of the boat with his good arm and then, already fainting, with the other. Then his head fell on his arms and blood started spewing over his face and shirt and body.

He came round to find himself hanging over the side of the boat, down which blood was flowing into the sea. He was too weak to do anything for a moment or two but presently he managed to heave his legs upward until he was half on his knees again. Then with his good arm he staggered struggling to drag his shirt over his head.

The shirt was half-way off when he heard the girl shouting. His head was trapped, as it were, in a crazy sort of bag. From a distance her voice sounded unreal and hoarsely muffled. After a second or so he managed to drag the shirt free of his head and then, his eyes woken suddenly by the dazzle of sunlight, he saw the girl.

She was already hanging on to the side of the boat, holding the boy. She was thrashing water violently with her legs and trying at the same time to heave the boy with her enormous arms and shoulders out of the water. It was as much as Rockley could do to crook his good arm over the side and shout for the boy to clutch it. He was relieved then to see the boy shake his head, quickly shut his eyes and then as quickly open them again.

A second or two later the girl gave a tremendous heave and the boy fell face forwards into the boat. As he fell over the side he knocked Rockley, too weak even to kneel now, on to his back. Rockley groped there for a moment, blood pouring down his arms and mingling with tuna blood, and then managed to raise himself on one hand, partly supporting himself on one of the paddles.

He was still struggling up when the girl started screaming. The boy yelled, whipped the paddle suddenly from under Rockley's knees and started madly thrashing water. All the time the girl continued screaming, trying at the same time to heave herself into the boat by her hands.

It was not more than five minutes, Rockley said, at most ten, before he and the boy somehow pulled her aboard. It seemed, he said, like a day. After a time she stopped screaming. Her great scarred mouth folded itself down until the lower lip was invisible and her teeth, clenched far below it, were actually drawing blood.

She still had so much strength that, even then, at the very last moment, she made the final effort of pulling herself aboard. Her entire body seemed to retch itself into the boat with a terrible groan.

She lay there for a minute, perhaps longer, face downwards,

313

before Rockley realized that what he thought was merely the tangled mass of her water-soaked *pereu* folded like a twisted red sheet about the right side of her body was really all that was left, on that side, of her thigh. The teeth of the shark had scoured deep into flesh, so that the bone stared blue.

She somehow turned herself over on her back, still conscious. Rockley picked up his shirt, throwing it over her thigh. Faintness started a second wave of blackness across his eyes and by the time he had defeated it he was aware of the boy using his own shirt to bandage his arm.

Some time later the boy had the sail up again and the breeze, blowing crossways towards the reef, began to take them back to shore. All the time the girl lay starkly conscious, her big hands gripping the sides of the boat in stiff agony, her teeth biting lower and lower into the jaw.

For most of the journey back he was simply unaware of the sea. Once or twice he fainted off again and then he was aware, presently, of kneeling beside her, smoothing her hair with his good hand. There was nothing else he could possibly do for her and it was some time before there was even a hint of conscious recognition in the enormous eyes. Then quite quietly, and with a strength of tone that almost fooled him for a moment into thinking that he was, after all, merely on the fringes of a dream of pure ghastliness, she said:

'I'm glad you're with me.'

He could find nothing to say in answer. It was actually the first time her mouth had relaxed, allowing the teeth to give up the cruel biting of her jaw. Almost at the same time, as if she had suddenly defeated all pain, her hands relaxed too, unlocked themselves from the side of the boat and folded themselves weakly across the front of her body.

'Rock,' she said, 'let me hold your hand.'

For a long time she held his hand while keeping her eyes fixed on his face. 'I'm sorry about the other hand,' she said once and again he could find nothing to say in answer except, so long afterwards that it was merely like an echo that had lost itself across the space of sea and had in some uncanny way floated back again:

'I'm sorry too.'

Half an hour later they were running through the gap. All this time he had been so unaware of both time and distance that he actually saw the reef before being aware of the thunder of its roar about him. In the same way he had forgotten the boy, sitting all the time like a strangely aged little statue, all splashed with blood, never speaking, in the stern.

As they drew into the calmness of the lagoon she actually smiled up at him, held his hand a fraction closer and spoke for the first and only time of the parakeet, the other girl.

'I found out last night,' she said. 'I saw you go there. Then I knew you had been there before.'

It would have been better, he said, if she had stuck the knife into him after all.

'I couldn't sleep last night. Then I came and looked at you while you were asleep,' she said. Her voice was proud and without scorn. 'And I knew you were going away from me.'

Now they were running quite fast into the lagoon. He stared away from her towards the thickets beyond the white strips of beach, hot in the sunshine, and to the rising tiers of palm.

'I said I wouldn't let you go away from me,' she said.

He looked back at her face. Its sudden relaxation after pain into calmness made it appear, quite suddenly, not so large as before. The lips were more compact. Even the big snout-like nostrils seemed to have contracted.

'Now when you go away from me it won't matter.'

He could find nothing to say.

'I told you my thoughts were my own,' she said. 'Do you remember?'

Her voice was very low. He still could not speak or look at her and all his pain and fondness for her dissolved into sudden desolation. He was aware of nothing except a long, profound, tormenting anguish before, for the fifth or sixth time, he fainted away.

When he looked at her again her eyes were staring straight up into glaring sunshine. Her face was no longer placid. In its final moments, no longer ugly, it seemed to have expanded again with remarkable strength, defiantly. With pride she seemed to be

315

glaring back at the flaming sky, handsome and almost contemptuous as she lay there.

A moment later he covered her face. The boat ran past the
house in the thickets, where the little parakeet lived, and all
across the lagoon the crowing of jungle cocks was proud and clear.

More About Penguins and Pelicans

Penguinews, which appears every month, contains details of all the new books issued by Penguins as they are published. It is supplemented by the *Penguin Stock List* which includes around 5,000 titles.

A specimen copy of *Penguinews* will be sent to you free on request. Please write to Dept EP, Penguin Books Ltd, Harmondsworth, Middlesex, for your copy.

In the U.S.A.: For a complete list of books available from Penguins in the United States write to Dept CS, Penguin Books, 625 Madison Avenue, New York, New York 10022.

In Canada: For a complete list of books available from Penguins in Canada write to Penguin Books Canada Ltd, 2801 John Street, Markham, Ontario L3R 1B4.

H. E. Bates's Best-Selling 'Larkin' Books

The Darling Buds of May

Introducing the Larkins, a family with a place in popular mythology.

Here they come, in the first of their hilarious rural adventures, crashing their way through the English countryside in the wake of Pa, the quick-eyed golden-hearted junk-dealer, and Ma, with a mouthful of crisps and a laugh like a jelly.

A Breath of French Air

They're here again – the indestructible Larkins; this time, with Baby Oscar, the Rolls, and Ma's unmarried passport, they're off to France. And with H. E. Bates, you may be sure, there's no French without tears of laughter.

When the Green Woods Laugh

In the third of the Larkin novels H. E. Bates makes the Dragon's Blood and the double scotches hit with no less impact than they did in *The Darling Buds of May*. For the full Larkin orchestra is back on the rural fiddle, and (with Angela Snow around) the Brigadier may be too old to ride but he's young enough to fall.

Oh! To Be in England

Are you taking life too seriously?

What you need is a dose of *Oh! To Be in England* – another splendid thighs-breasts-and-buttercups frolic through the Merrie England of the sixties with the thirsty, happy, lusty, quite uninhibited and now rightly famous junk-dealing family of Larkins.

and

A Little of What You Fancy

H. E. Bates

The Wild Cherry Tree

In each of these ten stories H. E. Bates evokes places and
defines a life you could never before have imagined. A pig
farmer's wife secretly builds up a 'rich, expensive, dazzling'
wardrobe to escape the filthy squalor of her life; a hypo-
critical do-gooder is driven to more than distraction by
two Jaguar-belt sirens; a woman wearing odd stockings
gets involved with a man who reads his newspaper upside
down . . .

The Wild Cherry Tree shows Bates at his most tense and
immediate; observing with baleful accuracy just what
happens when people are 'thrown suddenly with neither
direction nor compass into territory utterly strange or
unexplored'.

and

The Four Beauties
The Triple Echo
Seven by Five
Dulcima
The Song of The Wren
Fair Stood the Wind for France
Love for Lydia
The Scarlet Sword
The Purple Plain
The Jacaranda Tree